COUNTER BALANCE

Also by Jerry May:

The Blackthorn Conspiracy, as written, compiled, and created by Jerry May, Gary L. Hollen, and Dr. John W. Wood, under the pseudonym T.T. Brothers

A Cause Worth Fighting For by Colonel Charles H. Stephens, USA (retired), as compiled, researched, written, and prepared by Colonel Gerald (Jerry) M. May, USAF (retired)

COUNTER BALANCE

PHANTOM FORCE

Jerry May

BRYCE CULLEN PUBLISHING

Copyright © 2015 by Jerry May
All rights reserved.

This book may not be reproduced, in whole or in part, stored in a retrieval system, or transmitted in any form or by any means — electronic, mechanical, or other — without written permission from the publisher, except by a reviewer, who may quote brief passages in a review.

BRYCE CULLEN PUBLISHING

PO Box 731
Alpine, NJ 07620
brycecullen.com

Cover design by Tracey Polson

ISBN 978-1-935752-61-5

Library of Congress Control Number: 2015959308

10 9 8 7 6 5 4 3 2 1

Acknowledgments

Mrs. B. Joyce May—My wife and longtime best friend, who also edits and interprets my thoughts and words for the reading public. When she says it doesn't make sense, I listen.

Teresa A. M. Polson—My most favorite older daughter, whom I love and who is an exceptional and gifted graphic artist. She has taken precious hours out of the limited free time in her private life to make me and my book covers stand out.

Tricia L. May—My most favorite younger daughter, whom I also love and who is a professional logistician and business strategist. She has patiently tutored Dad on certain modern military tactics and equipment that work, and those that don't.

John W. Wood, MD—My friend of six decades, fraternity brother, air force flight surgeon, skilled doctor of ophthalmology, and meticulous editor, who has given me political and military ideas and has remained loyal through more than this book.

Mrs. Rosemary D. Wood—John's wife and best friend to us both. She edits, too. She is a skilled and precise grammarian who can find both unintended and needed punctuation and grammar. Her years as a legislative director for a Congressman provided me invaluable insight.

Colonel J.W. "Bud" Patty III, USA (retired)—A longtime friend and fellow warrior who lived some of these events. He is one of two close friends who served as my model for the lead character in this story. I am sworn to protect his exploits and heroism with anonymity.

Colonel Edward Chandler, USA (retired)—A friend and fellow warrior who also lived some of these events. He and his experiences also served as a model for the lead character in this story. I am also sworn to protect his exploits and heroism with anonymity.

The Reverend Father Norman Desrosiers—An unequivocal and loyal friend and Episcopal priest who began his military service as a covert operations GI and is now a retired air force chaplain and colonel. He understands the human heart and soul, as well as the stress of covert combat operations.

Mr. Gary L. Hollen—A friend of six decades who allows me to use his name, his experience, his humor, his political insights, and his ideas. His imagination and perseverance in writing has been an inspiration to me.

Staff Sergeant Brandon Forshaw, USAF—An Air Force Reserve PJ, a modern day warrior, and a selfless hero who knows how to save lives in time away from his technical aerospace profession. His knowledge of tactics and proficiency with mission capabilities is unparalleled.

John C. "Duke" Westcott—A steadfast friend, fraternity brother, and government and industry intelligence systems professional who has made a decided improvement to the U.S. Intelligence Community.

Contents

Prologue		x
1	A New Beginning—I	1
2	The Plan Unfolds	8
3	An Opposing View	15
4	The Emerging Threat	18
5	Tyrants from the Shadows	25
6	The Grooming of a Tyrant	30
7	Finding a Cause	33
8	Ambition and Revenge	39
9	A Turning Point	43
10	The Precedent	49
11	Ghosts	55
12	Stand By to Jump	61
13	On the Ground	68
14	Strategic Imbalance	71
15	Agree to Disagree	76
16	New Conquests	80
17	After Action Report	83
18	Mission Assessment	89
19	The Aftermath	98
20	New Challenges	101
21	Pushback	107
22	Developments	115

23	A Eulogy for the West	123
24	The Education Continues	127
25	Global Unrest	134
26	Recruiting Report	141
27	Changing Events	143
28	The Next Mission	152
29	Almost a Security Breach	158
30	Deploy—Again	165
31	The Sniper's Girl	169
32	Consensus	174
33	Hostile Operations	183
34	A World Far Away	191
35	In Transit	197
36	Tyrants Galore	202
37	Good Intel	210
38	Restless Constituents	214
39	The Pre-Brief	218
40	Forward Motion	227
41	Possible Bugs and Gas	235
42	Stand By to Launch	244
43	BOOM!	250
44	GO! GO! GO!	255
45	Dead Captives	263
46	The Escape	268
47	Now What?	271
48	R&R	280
49	Where Did That Come From?	288
50	New Information	297
51	Unhappy Trails	304
52	A Startling Revelation	310
53	Closing in on the Targets	315
54	Sealing the Mole Hole	320
55	Cameroonian Unrest	328
56	Something Is Up	334
57	Corruption and War	337
58	The Unveiled Threat	344
59	Summit Results	353

60	Comply or Resist	358
61	A New Terrorist Threat	364
62	Congressional Support	372
63	Get Ready	375
64	Lobbying Pressures	380
65	Moving to Be in Place	384
66	On Board	389
67	Boko Haram Surprise	395
68	North Korean Surprise	399
69	De La Plane Surprise	404
70	The Wrap-Up	410
Epilogue	*A New Beginning—II*	*418*

Prologue

In the last decade of the twentieth century, world governments became increasingly more unstable, uncertain about policies to govern their people, pessimistic about global peace, and fearful of the dangerous course of conquest that radical Islamic extremists and terrorists were pursuing. Those concerns, combined with ineffective and ambivalent foreign policies demonstrated by the nations of the world, made exploitation of small nations by larger countries a new, more insidious threat. Many governments in the Middle East and middle Africa were attacked and weakened by their own citizens. They had all fallen and then been restored, and in most cases, they were no better off afterward. Other nations had begun to financially fail. Some had suffered devalued currency rates, economic recession, and the collapse of socialist policies. In the time during which this story takes place, the United States was not far behind.

By the year 2012 and the years just before this story, the government of the United States had continued unsuccessfully to grapple with poor fiscal practices, out-of-control domestic spending, and a bloated and quasi-functioning financial structure. More and more people found it easier to take from the government than to give to it. At the center of the imploding U.S. dysfunction was a president who kept trying the same failed policies and practices with the expectation of a different outcome. A dysfunctional, gridlocked Congress was no better.

In this story, the United States, as well as other large countries, found that the policies and practices of their administrations represented primarily only the views of elite groups of politicians and ideologues. The goal of the United States became wealth redistribution. Political action in the United States was driven by progressive political thought and practice. But it didn't work between 1913 and 1920 and was discarded. In spite of renewed interest in adopting progressivism, it was still not working for the country.

A clandestine cruise missile attack on Tehran in mid-2017 resulted in the exposure of the Blackthorn Conspiracy, and much of the world took on a cynical, suspicious, and even abusive attitude toward the United States. These same nations were no longer interested in the plights of their neighbors.

The world had thought China, North Korea, Pakistan, Venezuela, Russia, and some countries in middle Africa might become temporary beacons of hope, change, and deliverance for the struggling nations of the Middle East. They didn't. Instead, they became a source of money and influence, and conduits for weaponry. The struggling nations became targets for exploitation.

For its part, the United States, beginning in mid-2013, started taking a deliberate hands-off approach in assisting nations in their internal and external affairs. Instead, the president and his administration chose to focus on domestic priorities, striving to change the construct of democracy in the United States by moving the nation toward socialism. The president's actions and policies weakened the nation and made it vulnerable to attack from both radicals within, and from radical Islamists abroad.

By mid-2017, in this story, the United States appears outwardly and openly ambivalent to saber-rattling. The United States chose to watch international events from afar while minimizing its investment of treasure and manpower outside the United States. It became reluctant to use its influence and power to intercede in activities between belligerents. Even with the inauguration of a new president of the United States in 2017, the United States was regarded as disinterested in world events, considered by international neighbors as being fearful and indecisive, like her previous president had been.

In the time frame of this story, a new principle of diplomacy was adopted: *acquaintance alliance*. In lieu of formal treaties and agreements, nations entered into simple trade and assistance Memoranda of Understanding, with those countries with whom they were acquainted, and who had certain goods, services, and products that their citizens wanted and could afford. This passivity, conservatism, and hesitancy to engage were interpreted by certain tyrants as an invitation to be conquered, then pillaged, then annexed.

But as the world would soon discover, they had underestimated the new president of the United States. She had secretly set a new course for the United States and quietly altered its national defense strategy and its tactical military employment doctrine. The president had known for two years before her election that it was both politically and financially impossible for America to fund and to defend the meek and distraught nations of the world. The United States could no longer be the receiver of 911 calls from nations in trouble, and then stay for many years to rebuild those countries. It was therefore necessary for the United States to find a way to reinsert itself into the community of nations and, at the same time, stop tyranny from consuming continent after continent.

This story is about what *could* be.

1

A New Beginning—I

Washington, D.C., 8:00 a.m., September 2017

She sat behind the massive wooden desk, looking at the mounds of paper strewn across the top. They appeared to be simply thrown around the desk in what an unknowing observer would believe was a random and careless manner. On closer examination, the papers appeared to be in untidy stacks, but each stack was placed on a manila folder with a large black numeral hand-printed on its cover. There were a total of twelve folders on the desk, numbered one through twelve. The stacks of papers either on or in each folder were at least two inches thick. Some of the papers were reports, others were PowerPoint briefings, some were letters and photographs, and still others were an expert's or special appointee's assessment of events. They contained requests for official action or recommendations for no action but needed study. All the papers had official U.S. government logos on them from a variety of departments, agencies, independent counsels, and congressional committees.

She appeared exasperated with the sheer volume of material scattered about the desk, but the exasperation was not so much with the amount of paper, but was more with the large range of topical material that was included. She uttered out loud, "How could he leave here with so many problems pending and no apparent direction for corrective action?"

She reached for the papers in folder number one. In fine print under the numeral were the printed words, *National Security Issues.* Similar titles included: *Foreign Intelligence, International Relations,* the *U.S. Economy,* etc.

It sure looks to me like he was simply overwhelmed with the demands of the job, she thought. She continued muttering to herself, "It looks like the prophecy of H.L. Mencken came to pass." In the 1920s Mencken was quoted as saying, "As the democracy is perfected, the office of the president of the United States will more closely represent the inner soul of the people. On some day in the future the plain folks of the land will at last reach their heart's desire and the White House will be occupied by a downright fool and completely narcissistic moron."

"No, that's very elitist," she muttered again. "That whole thought can't be right. He didn't represent the inner soul of the nation's plain folk. No, inside he had to be a good man."

There was a soft buzz on the intercommunications system. Sally Marie Chenoa, the forty-sixth president of the United States, former two-term governor of the state of Idaho and a Native American with roots that went back to the Black Foot Indian tribes of the early 1780s, is an honored member of the Siksika Nation. Her tribe and the other three tribes fought together, lived together, and shared the same language and the same religion. Unity and national loyalty were ingrained in her culture. They never backed down from a fight.

She depressed the transmit lever and said, "Yes?"

"Madame President, they are here," the president's secretary replied from the outer office.

"Good, send them in," she said. She had a demeanor that was direct and thoughtful, but polite. She was practiced at this management style, and had used it successfully and effectively in her terms as the governor of the state of Idaho. Her lifelong Native American roots had honed her insight to a razor-sharp edge. As a hunter with her father and brothers in the Teton Mountains of her state, her gaze seldom drifted from the target. She didn't suffer fools, and instinctively knew when she was being played and slow-rolled, which now was seldom.

Her handling of the president of the People's Republic of China, or PRC, at the culmination of the Blackthorn Conspiracy in July

2017, after having been inaugurated only seven months earlier, was exemplary. She showed courage, determination, resolve, and political precision in correcting a terrible wrong. Even though the rest of the world had never been informed of how the United States was exonerated from the massive raid on Tehran, they were aware of the new respect and cooperative relationship that had suddenly emerged between the People's Republic of China, their allies, and the United States of America. President Chenoa was politically astute enough to know that, as is often said in the high plains of America, she needed to *"make hay while the sun shines."*

She had already spent the better part of 2017, her first year in office, resolving international and national security issues that needed urgent attention before domestic problems could be addressed and resolved. Now that the Blackthorn Conspiracy was finally behind her, she could focus on courses of action that would lead to permanent domestic and foreign policy actions. She meant to stabilize a chaotic agenda of topics that had been ignored long before she took the oath of office.

She knew that in a time span as short as one week, some international event could suddenly go sour, the political winds could shift, and she could again be the recipient of disdain around the world. Even now, she had discerned that the PRC was gradually moving away from opportunities to curry favor with the United States. She knew the Chinese would never have the relationship with the States that Great Britain and Australia had had. If any relationship was to develop between China and the United States, she subconsciously believed they would be publically cozy for a while, then begin to drift apart as suited the Chinese. That seemed to be what was now happening.

President Chenoa rose from behind the desk as the door opened and a woman and a man entered the office. "Congresswoman Doolin and Senator Smith, thank you both for coming on such short notice. It's good to see you again," she greeted them.

The congresswoman responded by saying, "The pleasure is mine, Madame President. I must say, I'm pleased and flattered you called. Thank you for allowing me to assist in preparing the issues during the debates. You know I will do anything to put this country back on a new and improved road to respectability."

Congresswoman Rosemary Doolin had represented the Seventeenth Florida District in the House of Representatives since 2002. Her constituents loved her because she was honest; she carefully analyze all the issues surrounding an impending vote; and she carefully discriminated between pork and need whenever she voted. There were military bases, headquarters, and aerospace contractors who supported the military in her district, and her colleagues from both sides of the aisle knew she was trustworthy and dependable. Most of all, they knew she was predictable, which was a positive and rare asset in Washington, D.C.

She was effervescent, and there were auras of absolute loyalty about her. Her eyes sparkled with enthusiasm, and she tended to be supportive but also carefully discriminating when asking for comments. She cast discerning votes on the House Appropriations Committee, the Commerce and Justice Committee, the Veterans Affairs Committee, and the prestigious House Select Committee on Intelligence. She was reliable, well connected, and continuously strived to do the right thing in her work. She held a PhD from Harvard University in business management. The nearly 700,000 constituents in her 6,300-square-mile district wouldn't let her retire.

She was married to a prominent, well-respected medical doctor of ophthalmology, and they had raised two grown children; a third had been killed in the line of duty with the United States Navy.

Senator Dennis Randolph Smith, the junior senator from Oregon, stepped forward, extended his hand, and said, "I, too, Madame President, am pleased to be here. It was a great pleasure to have helped to prepare you for the debates last fall. I have been given a classified hint of the purpose of this meeting, and you have my promise that I will give you my best judgment and support for any task entrusted to me."

Senator Smith had been elected to the Senate representing the state of Oregon in 2008. He had been a captain in the United States Air Force. He flew F-15s and F-16s as well as being selected for transition into the new F-22, when he decided he had a different calling. He flew missions over Bosnia Herzegovina, Iraq, and Rwanda, and flew top-cover for covert operations in locations too numerous to identify. He grew up and was educated in Oregon, and he owed his success to his home-grown liberal arts bachelor's and two master's degrees. He also held a law degree in three different in-state universities. He seemed taller than his six feet when he was before groups of friends, admirers, and supporters. His light brown hair was slightly streaked with strands of gray that represented the stress of overseas wars, conflict at home, and controversy in Congress. Acting in Congress seemed somehow to translate its stress to the physical appearance of men and women over the years. Denny's stress was also reflective of the recent death of his wife to whom he had been totally devoted. He walked with the smooth agility of a highly trained athlete and the stealth of an Oregon bobcat seeking an unobstructed path in his search for prey.

In the eight years of his service in the Senate of the United States, he not only commanded the respect of his constituents in all corners of his more than ninety-five-thousand-square-mile, 3.8-million population state, but he was looked to in Washington, D.C., for his leadership in the committees of the Senate on which he served, especially the Senate Armed Services Committee and the Senate Select Committee on Intelligence. He was not liked by some of his senatorial colleagues because of his pragmatic and analytical manner in dealing with issues. But it was safe to say he was respected by the entire Senate. He was regarded by his constituents as deeply committed, discriminating when the chips were down, fair, and always reliable. He quietly supported the candidacy of then Governor Chenoa during her campaign for president, and he acted as an advisor to her campaign staff.

He had three grown children and, since the death of his wife, had dedicated his energies to his work in the United States Senate and the initiatives of the Senate Armed Services Committee.

Denny's demeanor had always been one of conservatism, avoidance of drama, and sidestepping flamboyance. He strived to cut to the chase in congressional and public discussions, and he focused on the mission and the outcome, not the stepping-stones along the route. His air force career had taught him that. He, like President Chenoa, didn't suffer fools easily. On many occasions, his private thoughts about pompous , bloviating government or industry speakers was one of, "*you idiot!*" but he chose to say, "That's an interesting perspective!" He avoided public confrontation and believed that crowds chose sides based on emotion, not logic. He had always believed he could catch more flies with honey than vinegar.

"Please be seated," President Chenoa said. "We may be here for a couple of hours." Denny and Rosemary quickly stole glances at one another, as if to say, *This is unexpected and may be a bigger deal than we anticipated.* That *big deal* would indeed materialize, and unbeknownst to them, they would be the principal architects and orchestrators.

While the president was speaking, as if by practiced scenario, both Denny and Rosemary took out small notepads and pens. They would have questions, but they understood that they might not have another easy chance to ask the chief executive of the United States any follow-up queries. President Chenoa, watching them as she spoke, instinctively nodded her approval.

"I and my closest advisors have been quietly doing research into the membership of both bodies of Congress, seeking the most qualified members with whom we could entrust a mission of a national strategy change that, in the 241-year history of this country, is unparalleled and unprecedented. There is a small amount of risk to all our political careers, but certainly no danger to life and limb. On the other hand, as Winston Churchill once said, 'In a war you can only be killed once. In politics, many times.'"

"I know from past experience that you both are primary players and clear thinkers in key committees. You have come to me again as highly recommended to handle this task. You also have come here with personal success records in winning debates on your respective sides of the Hill, and in your committees. Moreover, you come recommended because of your personal loyalty and sacrifice to this country.

"Rosemary, I know you lost the pride of your life in the death of your daughter, Lieutenant Senior Grade Rose Doolin, on the decks of the USS *Salem* in the Pacific. I am sincerely sorry for your loss. One day, I hope I can convince you that she did not die in vain and her loss has been avenged.

"Denny, your service and the risks you took while on active duty in the air force before your election to the Senate have validated you as one who accepts responsibility, who regards himself as accountable for the plans, execution, and finalization of all missions given. You are known in the military services, and in the Senate, as one who fights to win for this country."

"Madame President, I'm both flattered and honored to hear those types of reports from my colleagues and constituents, but my mantra is simply to do what's right," Denny said while blushing slightly.

"I have to echo Denny's sentiments, Madame President," Rosemary said. "Those are very complimentary reports in today's domestic and international vitriolic atmosphere. It's very difficult to recognize one's allies from one's detractors."

"Well, fortunately, you two are the chosen ones for the task I have in front of me. Be assured that you have me to run interference for you in the future. I have your backs."

2

The Plan Unfolds

Washington, D.C., 9:00 a.m., September 2017

Rosemary and Denny sat side by side on a sofa in the Oval Office waiting intently for the next chapter in this vision for the future to unfold. The president then said, "As we talk further, I think you'll see you will have more allies than you know. So let me give you my perspective of today's environment and what I want to do about it.

"Unemployment rates in the United States vacillate from moderate to high, and business opportunities come and go. Most in the United States continue to be reliant on Middle-Eastern petroleum supplies even though restrictions on drilling and extracting oil from U.S. resources have eased a bit and are not yet maximally producing and distributing. Ideas for wealth redistribution and tax increases continue to be major government discussions. Seasonal opportunities continue to be exploited, which keeps the general economy buoyant. Mercifully, federal government–sponsored bailouts of large private enterprises and the insurance industries have stopped with my election to this office. The people have told my administration that companies and their high-tech advancements must find ways to stay afloat with their own developmental phases or terminate operation. The government can no longer bail them out if the American public has no need for their products."

President Chenoa continued to provide Rosemary and Denny with the full and complete story of the state of the world, and how others saw the United States fitting into the international scheme of things.

"Inordinately high executive bonuses for CEOs are using the taxpayers' money for bailouts and free rides in all social support systems for illegal and undocumented aliens. An increasing dependency on government-funded support in all sectors of the U.S. lifestyle has grown dramatically. The United States continues to move into the status of a bureaucratic, entitlement- oriented "nanny" state, with only fifty percent of the wage-earning population continuing to pay taxes and support our domestic status, while the other fifty percent pay nothing. I plan to stop that.

"In spite of the dire nature of the American economy, the morale of the American people has remained high and engaged. More and more people have become politically active in an effort to turn the U.S. political behemoth in a new direction. In spite of disappointments, my advisors inform me that pride still remains high in several American traditions: our military forces, religious faith, eternal optimism, and unique American ingenuity and innovation. My intelligence reports from embassies around the world and from the intelligence community confirm that other parts of the world have not fared so well."

Denny and Rosemary sat still in their seats, mesmerized at receiving this personal State of the Union message. They disagreed with very little of what the president was saying. If anything, they each believed the countries of the world were worse off and the tyrants who roamed the jungles and deserts of the globe were self-serving despots, downright sons of bitches who took personal pleasure from torturing and murdering their own people.

"Other nations, and especially elite families in those nations, have become resentful that so much attention has been placed on restoring Iran and what was left of the Old Persian Empire after the conspiratorial Blackthorn cruise missile attack earlier this year. Leaders and rulers in other countries, who have always held disdain for the United States and have never liked what we stood for, like us even less now that they believe we are disengaged from the world, and that we have been indecisive and evasive in reaction to crises and scandals at home and abroad.

"Government regimes and elite families among the ruling classes of tyrannical regimes have become outwardly ambivalent about world events. The underprivileged and downtrodden have seen world events as a signal to again become vocal about the repression of their intellectual and political freedoms. They have become emboldened in their public disapproval of governing methods, taxation, shortages of selected necessities of life, and limitations being placed on them that seem intended to suppress motivation and upward mobility. In short, the ruling families from French Guiana, Peru, Bolivia, Yemen, Somalia, Mali, Kenya, Nigeria, Libya, and many other countries have decided they want some of the treasure that is being given so freely by the United States, France, Germany, and China. What we didn't anticipate or plan for was that in this 2017 decade of Middle-Eastern recovery and rejuvenated thought, an aggressive theocratic Islamic jihadist enthusiasm would emerge. Worldwide circumstances were ripe for the rise of local and regional radical Muslim terrorist influences, with jihadist mind-sets reinforced with suicide vests, beheadings, and power bases that continue to cater to public discontent. It is akin to the Arab Spring and Wall Street Occupation demonstrations of the mid- to latter part of 2011, but it is much more insidious, vicious, and violent.

"In short, governments in some nations are able to quell regional and popular supported uprisings, while others can't or won't. Some tolerate the discontent until it becomes too popular and too unwieldy to control, or more powerful and fearsome than the current government power bases. As has been the case over the last century, those movements have spawned many folk heroes and martyrs among the dissidents who grew in stature.

"No internal or even global power structure will choose to confront these movements, and no nation outside of each country's boundaries will choose to send armies or occupying forces to fight them because of the financial burden of maintaining long logistic lines.

"Other global diplomatic communities are quick to publically criticize such rescue antics as knee-jerk reactions resulting from Blackthorn actions. Any nation that is found to be amassing any kinds of forces, or even stockpiling humanitarian materiel resources for the apparent use by an underprivileged nation, have become the focus of global suspicion. Therefore, nations, even those who are the parents of the protectorates, territories, and overseas states, have assumed indecisive 'wait and see' attitudes with these restless countries."

As President Chenoa continued, Denny and Rosemary sensed that the chronology was winding down.

"At this time," the president said, "because of the uncertainty of global events, it has become apparent that most nations want to avoid all-out confrontation, but many are willing to tolerate a certain amount of open dissent—within limits. They tend to look the other way except when rumors of undercurrents and potential violent uprisings are too obvious to be ignored. In today's world, they then begin to openly and verbally wring their hands and ask the United States what it is going to do about the situation.

"The explanation of what the United States does next is long and torturous. We have set precedents that are now expected of us, and relationships and alliances with countries that we have honored for many years. These arrangements have been costly in terms of blood and treasure. We have foreign aid programs that are bleeding us dry. We have internal domestic problems that we can no longer turn a blind eye toward. That does not even address the liberal agenda and ACLU initiatives that accuse the administration of violating untold laws and executive orders against perceived assassinations or atrocities in other countries. There needs to be a drastic change in the way we help our friends, punish our enemies, and at the same time preserve the Union.

"Islamic terrorist groups with jihadist intent in the Middle East are the most predictable. Their religious fervor, however, makes it difficult to maintain an open dialogue because sects within Islam harbor strong disrespect and downright hatred of Western ways. British poet and author Rudyard Kipling made our differences most clear: 'Middle Easterners think in terms of the eventual victory of Islam over their adversaries in hundreds of years, not next year, in thirty years, or even a hundred years. They are so steeped in their religious views that they never forget that on occasion they can be friends with Westerners. We can never be brothers or sisters because we are Christian, they are Muslim. We will always be infidels to them. And you know what they think of, and do to infidels.'

"This is a complicated problem to which there are several answers that, in my mind, we must pursue in parallel. One of the answers is military. I have grappled with this for months, and I continue to reach the same conclusion. I believe we must support the strategic national security concept of the TRIAD: bombers, missiles, and submarines. As long as other large nations have the capability to do us harm, I will continue to believe we need a counterbalance. Some nations feel comforted in attacking other nations because they are weak. No nation ever attacked the United States or any other country because they were too strong.

"My view is that if, and when, we have no choice but to strike with our military, we do so with overwhelming lethal power; we strike in a time of our choosing with overkill, and we abstain from nation-building afterward. Remaining behind without a clear exit strategy portends a long foreign occupation with large ground forces, with no exit in sight.

"I will also continue to interject myself in the decision process to use conventional munitions rather than nuclear. We need to prepare for the worst and hope for the best. I believe that once we release the nuclear genie from the bottle, a holocaust will result. We can't do that frivolously. So, what is the answer?

"The military answer to our dilemma is that we need a highly mobile, versatile, rapid deployment, quick strike, covert operations force to quickly stop problems before they start. We need a phantom force that quietly goes in, fixes the problem, and then quietly gets out. That force must plan, brief, rehearse, and then act. We need a counterbalance. We need to tip the balance of peace in our favor. We need to rid ourselves and the world of this radical Islamic jihadist cancer before it metastasizes."

As if she already knew the question forming in their minds, the president injected a dramatic, knowing pause. "Yes, we could use Reaper III and Vengeance I drones to do this task. But our technology community has developed laser surveillance radar profiling to such an amazing degree and unfortunately has shared it with the world, so that U.S. drone recognition imagers see us coming before we can position them in the target country. We need to get into and out of a nation's ground and air space before they ever know we are there. We need to do it the old-fashioned way, by deception and secrecy.

"Along with the military solution, a diplomatic one must be applied as well. We can't just neutralize the threat, tiptoe out, and leave havoc and chaos in our wake. The process I am advocating requires planning and preparation. We need some time before we decide to take decisive military action, and we should first make moves in diplomacy to find the natural successor to a tyrant who has a more balanced approach to the country's domestic and international problems than does the tyrant. We need some time to find a leader in those countries who will listen—a legitimate state or a non-state actor, someone who is a natural successor who can objectively weigh the pros and cons. That person must be acceptable to our allies, one or two of whom will agree to mentor that individual or group and help them develop a pathway to a peaceful coexistence, health, and regional balance. Notice I did not say someone or an ally to do it our way. No, it must be someone or some international mentor who can lay out the pros and cons of a domestic roadmap that suits the tyrant's nation.

"I have asked the Department of State to give you both free rein to discuss actions with them. Their nominee is the third-ranking person in the department: Deputy Assistant Secretary for Foreign Affairs Marcia F. Vargas. She is fully cleared, can be trusted to protect national security, and will not forward your activity reports unless you ask her to.

"Over the last year, since I have taken office, a few in Congress whom I have queried about such a phantom concept believe such a force is unaffordable, difficult to manage, lacking command and control, and tantamount to using a five-hundred-pound bomb to kill flies. They have prejudged how to employ such a force. They see it as an encroachment into the constituencies that support their reelections, and they believe they each need to be in on the planning and deployment loops of such a concept. I disagree. I have learned over the years that if we want a task to be handled with precision and efficiency, it should be turned over to a U.S. military service. They always know just how much pressure and lethality to apply. They all know we are the good guys. This is the right thing to do. But it will come at a sacrifice of treasure and blood. Thomas Jefferson said before he became the third president of these United States, 'The tree of liberty must be refreshed from time to time with the blood of patriots and tyrants.'

"I have deliberately avoided sharing details of my concept with many in our congressional, military, and industrial communities. There are, however, some in each sector with whom I have shared these thoughts. I value the counsel of those few, and will share their identities with you as time goes on. Meanwhile, I am aware that to change the nation's military force structure to a newer, smaller, swifter, more agile, stealthier, and more lethal multi-service strike force requires a major overhaul of U.S. resources. It will require the concurrence of selected parts of the military-industrial complex. It will require new secrecy regulations, the consent of selected international coalition forces, the U.S. military command structure, and the consent and advocacy of the Congress of the United States. Rest assured, I have not adopted thoughts of how to unfold this concept lightly. That's where you two come in. The chairman of the Joint Chiefs and the Chiefs of Staff of each of the services are already on board."

Denny and Rosemary sat in thoughtful contemplation. They had a thousand questions. But they both knew that it boiled down to one process. The president of the United States knew that Denny and Rosemary were on board. She was asking them to convince a majority of the other 99 members of the Senate and the other 434 members of the House of Representatives to approve of the concept of a counterbalance using a coherent, integrated phantom military force. It was obvious the president would take care of selling it to her cabinet and to the American people and she would keep the Supreme Court busy with other tasks.

Denny and Rosemary glanced at one another, recognizing their task was more daunting than even that of the president's.

3

An Opposing View

Beijing, China, and Pyongyang, North Korea, September 2017

"Mister Minister," said People's Republic of China's Foreign Minister Xi Plon Duk into his encrypted phone. On the other end of the phone was Ming Un Se Tung, foreign minister of the Democratic People's Republic of Korea, or the DPRK. It was no coincidence that his name was similar to that of the premiere of China in the 1950s. Mr. Ming Un Se Tung was a distant relative to the infamous Mao Se Tung. Ming's appointment to the foreign ministry of the DPRK was also no accident. He was North Korean, alright, but his name and bloodline bore a legacy for both the PRC and the DPRK that he would not dare to defame.

"Ah, Mister Minister," replied Ming, knowing full well who was on the other end of the line. "It is an honor to again be speaking with you. It has been more than six months since we have compared notes. To what do I owe the honor of this call?"

Xi responded with a smooth tone in his voice, partly because it was his manner to speak in a quick but mellow voice, but also to ensure that his listener was attentive and attuned to the message he was about to receive.

"Minister Ming, I hope all is well with you in Pyongyang and that the beloved leader is enjoying good health and prosperity."

"He is, indeed, Mister Minister Xi. I will give him your respectful regards."

Minister Xi continued in a more businesslike manner, as he approached the real point of the call. "Minister Ming, when we last spoke of national security matters in South America, the Middle East, and Southeast Asia and in the Pacific region, I committed the People's Republic to provide, ah, certain resources to struggling economies in various parts of the world. I am calling to reiterate our continued interest in doing so but with, of course, a degree of invisibility by my country."

"Ah yes, Minister Xi. And at that same time I committed the Democratic People's Republic to distribute those resources in exchange for your country's continued economic support to the DPRK and for the latitude to negotiate with these emerging nations, certain economic, military, and diplomatic benefits. Those benefits, of course, would include the desires of the PRC to also enjoy the profits of our negotiations as a full partner but with an invisible role as a partner and benefactor of course."

"Well, Minister Ming, I have dispatched a courier to you this evening from Beijing with a diplomatic pouch in which I have outlined a plan to assist a certain individual in South America, and one in the Middle East, who show promise of acceding to our offers of money and weapons to further their aims and goals. I also have it on reasonably good authority that the United States civilian and military communities are in such disarray that they are being governed by strongly diverse political opinions. The American reaction to Blackthorn several months ago was a fluke, based upon a miniscule release of information that spurred them to react in such a way as to only hope all would turn out for the best. I have it on good authority that they were bluffing at the time, and they had little or no proof of ours or anyone else's involvement in the attack on Teheran.

"I have had a lengthy and private conversation with Defense Minister Colonel General Androvich Vukovich of Russia, with the approval of President Pushkin. They are in total accord with our activities, and want to remain an active participant in any and all agreements that will result in acquiring footholds in the Western world. They, like us, believe the apples are ripe for picking, if you understand what I'm saying," he continued.

"I understand completely, Comrade Minister Xi," said Minister Ming.

"But back to the pouch," said Minister Xi. "It contains a list of the amounts of money and certain weapons from the vast arsenal of weaponry from the People's Republic of China, with varying levels of lethality, and it also offers detailed numbers of our military personnel who can provide technical assistance. As you know, we can train people in the application of powerful weaponry. But we must also keep watch over our, ah, investments to ensure they do as instructed and predicted. I am hoping, as we agreed some months ago, that you will intercede for both of us, and achieve the diplomatic and international territorial breakthroughs that will ultimately achieve our long-range strategic goals."

"Of course, Minister Xi, as soon as the courier arrives," said Minister Ming, "I will engage the right representatives in the Democratic People's Republic of Korea's diplomatic and military staffs to pursue the goals of your plan. I might add that I agree with your assessment of the United States and their Canadian, British, and Australian allies. This seems like a particularly propitious time for us to engage new allies in various parts of the world, since the influence of the United States and its European puppets seems to be waning. They are collectively showing signs of weakness, indecision, as well as reluctance to follow through on support of their treaties.

"Rest assured, Minister Xi, I will follow through with appropriate measures, and will apprise you of our progress," replied Comrade Minister Ming.

4

The Emerging Threat

The Pentagon, Washington, D.C., October 2017

Colonel Keith Powers, USAF, was pouring over the minutes-old documents and near-real-time intelligence reports in front of him. He had been a military intelligence officer for twenty-three years. It can be said he knew his profession extremely well. In recent years he served in Iraq, Afghanistan, and Israel on the Syrian border, South Korea on the DMZ, and in the Caribbean area, tracking drug lords from the Key West, Florida, command post. He had come a long way since his childhood in Henderson, North Carolina, just across the southern Virginia state line. He grew up and went to college with every intention of going back to North Carolina to become a tycoon of sorts in the then-booming industrial sector of the state. But as time and events would have it, intriguing activities around the world beckoned him to follow his flag and his country. The air force held out the most intellectually challenging of all the services to him. So here he was, in the center of the most secret of all intelligence correlation centers in the U.S. government.

Only an hour and a half earlier, this same large conference table had been surrounded with Special Operations tacticians, intelligence community analysts, CIA operatives, and military intelligence staff specialists representing each branch of the services. They were not there by happenstance. They were there because within twelve months of her inauguration, President of the United States Sally Marie Chenoa had directed, in a highly classified memo, that a covert operations strike force be assembled for specially designated and general-nature clandestine missions. That was bureaucratese for secretly stopping aggression before it started.

The office in which Powers' activities were conducted was located in the bowels of the Pentagon, in an office called the JCS J-3 Special Operations Division, or SOD. The SOD was commanded by USMC Brigadier General Sandra Hill. Her order to the division was, "Don't let the bureaucratic process slow down subjects that need an immediate decision. If and when necessary, go directly to the next decision level. Then brief me later."

This office had been created years earlier to evaluate, assess, and react to what was then called Low Intensity Conflict, or LIC. It kept track of and reviewed the actions and results of brushfire confrontations between factions within a country or between small nations who exchanged gunfire and artillery rounds. For those purposes, it had established connections with U.S. military commands, foreign military command elements, intelligence sources, and even commercial news broadcasting outlets. The office worked more as an all-source reporting agent and less as an enforcer of international law. In years gone by, this office had a direct line to the assistant secretary of defense for special operations–low intensity conflicts, or ASD/SO-LIC, Mr. Jim Mullaney. It also had a direct hotline to the secretary of defense, Mr. Arnold P. Stoddard, and the national security advisor, retired General Thomas M. Mossman, USAF, in the White House.

In this administration the J-3 SOD office had been given the additional but separate functions of reporting and enforcement, in equal status to its earlier responsibilities. Because the president wished to keep her concept low-key, classified, and maximally effective, she asked for modification of mechanisms, organizations, and processes that already existed. She and her closest advisors agreed that the concept would get less visibility if an existing function simply underwent a charter modification. She was right.

Today the SOD and the SO-LIC offices still gathered global conflict data. But they also hosted and oversaw the meetings of the Strategic Planning Group, or SPG. This group reviewed threats and their immediacy, which was more bureaucratese for "how much time do we have to respond with lethal corrective forces?" After a review of all relevant and available information, they would recommend how to neutralize adverse effects and people. To do so the office was staffed with experts and personnel with unquestioned credentials, broad and deep military tactical experience, familiarity with in-country influences, high degrees of credibility, and direct access to the office of the secretary of defense to facilitate the movement of recommendations and decisions. This meant Powers, ASD/SO-LIC Mullaney, and Secretary Stoddard had direct access to the national security advisor in the West Wing of the White House, day or night. The reporting chain for these types of events had been tested, and it had worked well for over eight months.

The creation of this group, this process, and its subsequent operations was the president's brainchild. The service representatives and various department and agency attendees were there to combine their collective wisdom about international situations that could consume untold resources of the United States. These nations, the situations in them, and events that were unfolding in those countries were assessed. Then, if not dissuaded from their course of action through the use of extraordinary diplomatic persuasive actions, they must somehow be convinced that they could suffer serious setbacks.

This strategy would have to apply to not only aggressive individuals in large countries, but also to tyrants in small nations. This then was the charter of the SPG. Like most specially convened government task groups, they were expected to address real-world events and devise real-world solutions. The mission of this group was not a "what if" or "fictitious scenario" review committee. They would propose real-world answers to real-world problems.

Having met on three previous occasions, no retaliatory recourse had been recommended by any of them, since the errant dictator in the foreign nation being considered either didn't survive internal pressures or the ruler in question had been duly appointed or elected and U.S. policy against assassinations applied.

In this late afternoon meeting, the group was sharing alarming near-real-time data and information derived from on-the-scene observers, military attaches stationed in the country, and paid undercover operatives. These informants were asked to call a nondescript, non-traceable local telephone number with whatever extraneous bits and pieces of information they had. In actuality, the phone number culminated in the Pentagon office via circuitous international routing, which protected both the caller and recipient and also connected to the speakerphone on the conference table.

Each foreign contributor of information believed his or her data was the tidbit that would tip the balance between doing nothing and starting an all-out invasion to stop a murderous maniac from annihilating a town, city, or even a whole country. That was the way tipoff's worked. The tipster didn't know it, but the SPG accessed a wide variety of information and knew how to put the pieces of the puzzle together. This group functioned as a top secret team and had done so for nearly one year with increasing efficiency. It now worked just the way President Chenoa envisioned it.

As the Defense Department budget, personnel, and hardware force structure had shrunk through sequestration and government agency shutdowns, worldwide crises had increased. President Chenoa's SPG concept continued to grow in acceptance and apparent effectiveness against an expanded list of global crises. In scenario after scenario, the group applied the abilities of a phantom force to effect application of covert operations tactics to achieve a successful outcome. It repeatedly worked.

The deliberately small cadre of inter-agency advisors included selected members of the Congress, the departments, the intelligence community, and the joint chiefs of staff. They all repeatedly agreed, "We can't continue the way we have in the past; we need this new strategy to deal with the serious problems that face us and our allies." They all came to the meeting of the SPG with their own agency's agendas, which didn't always coincide with the crises at hand. But rules of engagement and boundaries had to be established.

The group agreed to acknowledge the problem at hand, but it would not disapprove of any agency's individual crisis item. In true U.S. government fashion, it was agreed that individual items would be forwarded to an upper-level group who would be provided recommendations and a prioritization of topics. Then those topics would then be forwarded to parallel groups for managerial decisions and action. Time for deliberation was closely monitored and scrupulously limited. This process gave every agency their "day in court," with a time limit, and at the same time it allowed the SPG to focus on a specific threat without bureaucratic micromanagement from above.

Force and budgetary reductions, imposed by the previous administration, had also dramatically increased and magnified American diplomatic and sovereignty vulnerabilities. It was just a matter of time before some small, medium, or God forbid, large foreign power would come to believe a major strike on the American homeland was essential to make their point. President Chenoa has believed that for more than two years and now believed she was in a position to keep such a debacle from occurring.

Tonight, after the group adjourned and left their analysis and recommendations behind, Powers, with the assistance of an army captain and a navy lieutenant, again reviewed the troop strengths of the aggressor. They evaluated the number of forces owned by the neighboring countries, looked at combat readiness ratings provided by the attaches, and at the hardware possessed by each country, as well as the logistics tails to support hardware use. They finally assessed what they believed to be the country's political will to use it all. Powers even factored in the time of the year, climatologic conditions, foreign travelers in and out of the country, political events, holidays, ongoing religious influences, and details down to each nation's leader's family habits and personal transgressions. He and the two junior officers had pulled conclusions and recommendations from the group, but the final recommendation to go forward or to table follow-on action belonged to Powers. If he believed moving forward up the chain was warranted, he would call the ASD/SO-LIC. The final decision to go further would then be made by Assistant Secretary Mullaney.

In this case, the telltale evidence told Powers that something was about to pop, such as increased troop deployments by the aggressor, atrocities he or his deputies had already committed to cover his tracks, and actions taken by the aggressor-tyrant to guarantee obedience. The final clue Powers looked at was the firepower the aggressor-tyrant had accumulated, especially nuclear, chemical, and biological weapons and what it looked like he was about to do with them.

To the point, Powers was looking at the capabilities amassed by General/President Francois Ricardo De La Plane of French Guiana and his subordinates, and the encouragement he was clandestinely receiving from both North Korean and Chinese operatives. There were other antagonists, probably Middle Eastern, Russian, and Pakistani, but their nationalities were yet to be confirmed. De La Plane had short-range nuclear missiles and some limited chemical or biological weapons of mass destruction, or WMD, and he appeared to have no idea what sort of holocaust he was about to unleash on the Western hemisphere. He did, however, know that he had sufficient weaponry to bring any neighboring country to capitulation.

The time was 1935 hours, and Keith Powers uttered out loud, "Holy crap, this dumb shit is going to move on Surinam and Brazil with nukes and maybe some gas and bugs within six months. We're going to have to take him out." He made a couple of notes on three-by-five cards, then pushed the hotline button to ASD/SO-LIC Mullaney's office.

Mullaney always came to work late in midmorning, and stayed until nearly 10 p.m. each night. In between those hours he was always available on his secure cell phone. His wife was nearly always nipping at his heels about his clandestine activities and his non-availability for prestigious Washington social events. But in fact, she'd known what this job required before he ever accepted the president's personal request to fill the post.

His office hours were synchronized with the time zones in the crises areas of the world. But his availability in the office, in transit to, or from, the office, or anywhere in the Washington, D.C., area was keyed to budding crises; Keith Powers saw to it that his boss was never very far away. In this case, since major crises had only been non-descript glowing embers for the week, Mullaney thought just maybe he might sneak out early to have a martini with his wife, Lisa, and see how her day had gone. But it was not to be. Mullaney had just put his initials on the coordination page of a routine administrative document when the phone buzzed and the button from JCS J-3 Special Ops Division illuminated. He knew right away it was either General Sandra Hill or Colonel Keith Powers. Either one demanded an immediate answer. He picked up the receiver and said, "Mullaney! Right! I'll see you in five minutes."

5

Tyrants from the Shadows

Global Tyranny Begins to Congeal, October 2017

Global tyrannical plans had been swirling since 2011 but are now beginning to congeal with one another; they are seeking unity. They see and have heard what happened to Teheran in June, and they feel inspired to unite and rebel, even though they do not have all the facts. In spite of their ignorance, they were starting to emerge in various parts of the world in an attempt to connect emboldened dictators and tyrants in the weaker parts of the world. Their purpose was to establish a loosely connected relationship with other movements having similar goals and objectives. Some called themselves Sunnis, or Shiias, or Al Shebbab, or Al Quaida, or Al Nusra. They went by any number of names and claimed they were different from each other, but all had much in common. They were all radical Islamists, and on a jihad of one form or another. They claimed to follow the teachings of Mohammed and the Koran and were seeking a union with other radical Islamic jihadists. Above all other visions, motivations, and intentions, they shared one common goal and mission in their lives: They wanted to hate and destroy the Great Satan—the United States and all the Christian infidels who resided therein.

Their intent was to recruit the underprivileged and downtrodden within Middle-Eastern and north and central African countries. They were seeking countries with unhappy and unsatisfied Islamic dissidents. They were looking for populations who had not had the opportunity to complete a university education nor benefited from freedom of choice in their lifestyles. In addition, they had never been allowed to dissent or confront their governing officials and freely question the course of their countries. Indeed, the Islamic terrorist element in each country was looking for young men who were dissatisfied with their way of life, had seen poverty and hopelessness up close and personal, and who had never had enough money, food, hope, or help to better themselves. They sought young men who had strong Islamic loyalties, who felt so devoted to Islam that they could easily begin to cut throats and dismember people out of anger with the international circumstances of the world.

Budding self-appointed leaders had a sixth sense, albeit usually false, that the world was vulnerable to a takeover. They seemed to be salivating to strike terror and fear into the hearts of as many common folk as possible. They focused on nations whose agreements with one another seemed fragile, non-binding, and even fragmented. Unquestioned international leadership was rapidly becoming tentative, even indecisive. International allegiance and respect formerly given to those nations who had earned it, was being withheld. Nations who had been looked to and eagerly given leadership had abrogated it. They did so out fear of international criticism, and because they strongly wished to avoid requests for billions of dollars or Euros to bail out faltering economies, when they themselves are struggling for balanced budgets.

Would-be masochists, tribal chiefs, dictators, gang chieftains, and tyrants had begun to slowly move from obscurity to visibility and recognition. They were doing so with different timetables, tactics, and methods of interpersonal persuasion to reach their goals. They were also doing so initially in disassociation from one another. The common denominator among them all was that there was a tyrant leading each country's errant behavior, and they were each doing so with varying levels of ferocity, barbarism, and malice: first against their own people, then against their closest neighbors. In time, if left unchecked, it would spread far beyond many borders.

Tyrants the world over have unique characteristics and idiosyncrasies. They are all egomaniacal. They have similar upbringings, and the cultural mannerisms and lifetime relationships that motivate them are similar. They also command a certain fascination. They seem to inspire mass movements of their people, and they strike their opposition with fierce destructive force. The goals in their minds are what they think the people want, when in fact the goals and desires of the people are entirely irrelevant to them. All tyrants seem to share a similar vision of how dreams can become reality. Information about who they are, how they were brought up, what they eat, drink, who they see, where they go, their education, and their beliefs all quickly become a matter of their personal dossier.

Most are educated in the Western world. This point is a mystery to most Westerners. The young tyrant–heir apparent is presumably sent to a Western university in a Western nation to find out what the world thinks and why they think it. Once he has learned about Westerners, he appears tolerant and outwardly understanding. But when the heir returns to his nation, he suddenly develops amnesia about the outside world and sees it in terms of its greed, its perceived goals of supremacy, and what he can extort from those nations that educated him.

Tyrants seem to share the same aspirations that translate as a means to an end. They hide large sums of money. They seek nations and the people in those nations who can best help them fulfill their anticipated destiny. They believe that the foreigner who shows up at the doorstep with money and goods is really only there because the foreigner likes him and sympathizes with his and his nation's plight.

Leaders of democratic nations have a certain perverse envy of tyrants and dictators, because tyrants can get things done by just a wave of the hand. They don't have to negotiate compromise and make deals unless it suits them; they don't have to run for election every two, four, or six years; and they can cause their opposition and adversaries to simply disappear if the occasion warrants.

Tyrants have an affinity for gathering intellectuals and many of the brightest minds of their generation into their fold. If the tyrant doesn't like the original thoughts of the intellectual, he can ignore or discredit him as an "idiot." Either way, the intellectual winds up on the scrap heap of unemployed smart persons, and is regarded as not in tune with advanced thinking. If the tyrant simply tires of the opinions of the intellectual or is amazed at the insight of the individual but at the same time is intimidated by his brilliance, the intellectual disappears.

In the waning months of 2014, the world looked on in horror at the brutality and savagery of the Islamic State of Iraq and the Levant, or ISIL. At the same time certain critics who were either trying to curry favor with ISIL or were trying intellectually to separate ISIL's barbarism from its supposed pragmatism, often commented on ISIL's clean, efficient, and streamlined means of solving problems, avoiding political correctness, meeting the needs of poor people, and plowing under pompous democratic administrations who professed to legitimately represent the majority. It is difficult for an educated society to find a balance between beheading and rewarding lazy, unproductive citizens with unlimited food stamps, free cell phones, and unemployment money. History will decide if ISIL was good or bad for humanity.

The tyrants found in the following pages in the years between 2010 and 2020 utilize few new methods and goals from tyrants past. So we can easily generalize that tyrants the world over conform to this description. That which is different, in this decade, however, is that the tyrants export their knowledge and experience to another hemisphere. They also seek to gain theocratic support for their aims and become a component of the movement that seeks to overwhelm and consume regions and nations who base their existence on Judeo-Christian principles. And then there is the "lone wolf" tyrant. He is considered a believer in the radical Islamic theocracy, but he needs no group or deliberative body to give him guidance. He simply hates certain people and societies or nations with such passion, that he knows he must annihilate as many of them as he can, without regard for his own safety or life. He is encouraged and emboldened by YouTube videos and other inflammatory literature.

The United States, for its part, in this first half of the decade was uninvolved, lacking in international prestige, stymied by the alarming rise of radical Islamic groups and fearful of confronting certain domestic and international crises that would result in immersion and involvement. There is also the issue of being labeled politically incorrect or misunderstood. The U.S. government and its administration was tied up with presidential-congressional gridlock, domestic scandals involving the IRS, the NSA, the VA, distribution of welfare and unemployment benefits, and the war in Afghanistan. Issues such as the closure of the Guantanamo Bay prison facilities, concern over criminal activities in the Middle East, Central Africa, the wanton barbarism of ISIL, the expansion of China into the South China Sea, the Russian invasion of Ukraine, and nuclear arms negotiations with Iran, hogged the U.S. political agenda. These activities were considered important, but they were distractions that took time away from domestic political party fund-raising and efforts to elect another Democrat administration to the White House. Tyrannical activities were therefore allowed to run rampant with no American efforts to deter them. But now, in late 2017, there was a change afoot.

Little did any of these maniacal dictatorial creatures know that on a dark night in September 2017, positive, decisive action would begin that would cause them to abandon their verve to stand by the political, military, and religious principles that took them to an exalted position in their countries, albeit primarily by fear, intimidation, and threat of death. Their faith, believed omnipotence, and even the people of their respective realms would eventually abandon them. It would be then that the tyrants would rationalize that they were either destined to be martyrs or they might be immortalized as men who meant well. Once they began to grapple with the category into which they might fall, that is when they decided to flee to survive and fight another day… somewhere else, sometime else, and with unidentified allies whom they believed still had faith in their causes.

6

The Grooming of a Tyrant

Isnard et Priane, French Guiana, May 1995

The dossier of Francois Ricardo De La Plane, of a prominent French Guiana family, is a textbook case of an elitist tyrant. He is a fourth-generation French Guainían who inherited the wealth of his great-grandfather and grandfather. They had mined gold and other minerals, and they struck oil while excavating for precious metals. Francois's whole family spoke fluent French, French with a Cajun influence, Spanish, German, and English. His ancestors did moderately well in their searches for wealth, but they were plagued and hampered by limitations in transportation and access to a sufficient workforce.

Growing up, Francois De La Plane was not always congenial or even-tempered. In his teen years he had a violent, undisciplined temper and would rather fight than calmly discuss differences. This might have been an outgrowth of working in the mines, the petroleum fields, and the banana plantations, with equally aggressive teens from the working class, who were jealous of his status as the son of the owner of the corporation. George Antoine De La Plane, his father, for his part, wanted his son to learn the business from the ground up, much as he and his father had learned it before him.

For his daughter, Joan, named for Joan of Arc, George wanted her life to be different, more aristocratic, better educated, better connected and higher in status than the agrarian life of an Guainía farmer, oil speculator, and miner. No, for his daughter, Joan Ann-Marie De La Plane, George wanted an existence separate and disconnected from what he foresaw as a life of poverty before wealth and a life of chaos before stability. George Antoine De La Plane believed his daughter needed to have strong family ties maintain anonymity and independence, be respected as a special individual, and have a sterling reputation, academic credentials, and peer recognition as a caring, sympathetic entrepreneur. So she was sent away early in her teens, despite her crying protests, to the best schools in America, including the Wakefield School in the Plains, Virginia, and Vassar College in Poughkeepsie, New York. She studied abroad in Paris for two semesters of her junior year at Vassar, and after graduation she attended the Columbia University School of Business, finishing at Yale Law School. She then became consumed with the business regimen of American law, international business, and politics, which led her to a six-figure salary in international business with a renowned corporation.

At the age of thirty, the position as the senior counsel of the corporation gave Joanie the very status in life her father had wanted for her. What her father did not tell her was *why* he wanted these things. It was because he foresaw that times in French Guiana—and throughout the hemisphere and the Old World—might become difficult and aligned with either politically strong nations or politically unsettled nations.

For young Francois, his father set a more aggressive, proactive educational path. Francois's father also knew that his son was willing to pay a higher personal price to succeed. He knew Francois would have difficulty adjusting to a laborer status with his teenage peers and would at first lose many fights over frivolous disagreements. His many losses, when he thought he was right, made a lasting impact on his vision of what actually was right, and how to fix what he believed to be wrong.

On several occasions, when things did not turn out well, Francois would go to a secluded spot and talk to himself. Out loud he would ask, "What went wrong here? What would my father say and do? What should I have done differently? What do I now do?" Then he would sit and think. He would roll over all the pros and cons. He was striving to be objective, discerning, and most importantly, correct.

This ability to rapidly recalibrate and make quick course adjustments in his demeanor and reactions would reappear in later life to bolster him and serve as his motivation to get what he wanted.

On occasions when Francois came home bloodied and beaten from one or two skirmishes, his father would say, "Francois, come, sit, let us talk for a few moments."

Even though he dearly loved and respected his father, he would say, "Father, while I respect your opinions, I'm in no mood for a lecture." But he did listen and learn, and through the years he always remembered and cherished those times with his father and kept them close in his heart and mind.

"I have no intention to lecture you, my son. Let me see if I can dress your wounds. Your cheek is cut and bleeding, and you have a swollen bump on your forehead. Come, sit."

George De La Plane went to a cabinet across the room and selected a bottle of sixty-year-old Remy Martin Napoleon cognac. It was very fine, very old, and very rare. George poured two small glasses, gave one to Francois, and set his own aside. He said, "Here, sip this. Don't gulp it. Sip it. Savor its soothing and refreshing effects, and believe in the clarity of thought it gives you."

He reached for some gauze and some soothing injury cream. "Francois," George continued, "many days in a man's life are not fair. Whether we like what has happened to us in the last twelve hours or not, we leave those unsavory or happy events with mixed feelings, some good, some bad. But we do not dismiss them as irrelevant. Each event is a lesson to be learned. You must decide the lesson and heed it in the future." Then he continued, "If things don't turn out the way we want, we need to bring the memories back to our consciousness, no matter how painful. We need to think of what we did, what we could have done, and what we should do if there is a next time."

Francois took another sip of the cognac. It had a bite to it. But it also warmed his throat and the inside of his chest. It seemed to clear his head for a moment, and it did indeed give him clarity about what had happened to him that day, and to what his father was saying. It stimulated his thoughts. He received the message.

7

Finding a Cause

Isnard et Priane, French Guiana, October 2003

Over the years Francois's father continuously tried various methods to move minerals, precious metals, and petroleum resources out of the country, but access to french transportation systems and taxation began to become more of a burden than an asset. He was an innovative and shrewd businessman and had no patience or tolerance for bureaucratic oversight, taxation, inspection, and price setting. He accumulated wealth, but it was not easy. The French government wanted him to absorb the costs of export and transportation, which he was not willing to do. So he sought and found other markets, mostly legitimate of course, but a few were somewhat nefarious and always well-funded—no questions asked.

He struck a variety of agreements with anonymous groups, neighboring governments, and other industries for his gold, minerals, and petroleum. He diversified his business by investing some of his five thousand acres of land into agricultural products to include coffee, corn, bananas, fruits, vegetables, and rice, because there was an immediate domestic market just down the road or across the next border.

In the late 1990s, Francois was sent abroad to obtain an education and learn how to manage, lead, and negotiate the principles of sound and profitable business. He attended the Columbia University School of Business in New York City, in the United States, where he achieved a respectable grade point average. In his undergraduate years, his undisciplined and often violent temper arose. On several occasions he was embroiled in fighting with other male students over some frivolous incidents, and some not so frivolous. He lost most of these confrontations, primarily because he was confronted by adversaries larger than himself, and because his transgression was based on an affront to his own poor judgment.

Late one night, he returned to his room to hide his humiliation. He didn't want to talk to or see anyone. He just wanted to retreat into his shame and disappointment. He needed encouragement, support, a kind but not solicitous word. He stretched out on his bed and wiped a drop of dried blood from the corner of his mouth. His gaze fell on the textbooks on the shelf at the end of his bed, and the bottle of sixty-year-old Remy Martin Napoleon cognac behind the books. The words of his father ran through his head: *I understand, my son. I sensed you didn't need a reprimand, but instead, encouragement.* The small sip of very old, very rare cognac slid down the back of his throat easily, and suddenly heightened his awareness of what had transpired that day, and what should be different tomorrow. In time, his flashpoint anger would be slower to rise.

He later joined the rugby and boxing teams, which served to help him gain newfound control over his temper, as well as confidence.

After graduating from Columbia, he entered the School of Business Law at Harvard University in Cambridge, Massachusetts. While at Columbia and Harvard, he joined and participated in student activist groups that interpreted most socialist and democratic governments as overly intrusive, dictatorial, and oppressive. He met and got to know people from all walks of life and all forms of government. He came to know they each had a point of view and a philosophy that had redeeming features.

His father communicated to him that the French and neighboring governments of Brazil and Surinam were pressuring him to pay even higher import taxes, and to abide by changing Guianese labor union practices, which were becoming increasingly more oppressive. These highhanded tactics of government and his own admiration for, and respect of, the principles that formed the foundation of Marxism, caused Francois to believe even more in his own dictatorial abilities than those of any government, local or international. Capitalism might have had some redeeming features, but Marxism was more intriguing.

Francois offered to return home to work and fight for the rights of farmers and miners, but his father asked him to complete his education first, and then work to discover how to take back family and worker independence. De La Plane then went to Zurich, Switzerland, to earn a second graduate degree from the University of Zurich in political science. While there, his roommate, Muhammad Al Yamani, a Muslim citizen of Yemen, introduced Francois to the Koran and Sharia law.

Al Yamani invited Francois to visit him in his home on the west coast of Yemen at Al Hudaydah on the Red Sea, near the Gulf of Aden. He explained that his country had been divided into two sections for decades: the Yemen Arab Republic in the north and the People's Democratic Republic of Yemen in the south.

Most recently, with the rise of the Arab Spring in 2010 and 2012, protests in Yemen became widespread and then went underground. The wounds of the preceding conflict in the late 1990s, the bombing of the U.S. Navy USS *Cole* in 2000, the bombing of the American-owned Hilton and Sheraton hotels in downtown Aden in 2002, and the murderous Al Qaida attacks on the French and British embassies in the capital of Saana in 2006, all led to continued unrest in Yemen.

For its part, the United States acceded to the requests from the Yemeni government to send money for "social improvements." Subtly and without fanfare. expensive Russian and Chinese automatic weapons began to be distributed to tribes, groups, sects, and dissidents among the Yemeni population. The country became ripe for foment. Francois could see the anger in the eyes of the friends of Al Yamani. He could feel the sense of frustration they radiated, and he could sense the rising tide of discontent that would someday soon explode like a volcano.

"Francois, my friend," said Al Yamani one day in early 2006. "Come join me in this coming revolution in democracy. You are smart, well-educated in the ways of the world. You are a tactician par excellence. You can help me create order out of this chaos. I see myself as a liberator, a Muslim chieftain, an Imam, a soldier of Allah who will rid the world of Jews and Christians. My nation is not ready yet for me, but my time is coming soon. They know my name. They know and trust my family. You must consent to join me in taking my country back from the infidels, barbarians, and especially the Americans."

Francois replied, "My brother in conflict, Al Yamani, you are as of my own blood, we believe in the same principles, and Allah guides both our spirits and our thoughts. I want to unite with you in this conflict. But the time is not yet right. I have unfinished issues at home that I must deal with. I fear I would be of only limited value to you now while preoccupied with my own family and native country problems. I will, however, plan to join you sometime in the near future in your struggle against imperialists, demagogues, infidels, and foreign forces. Please let me deal with my own difficulties first, so that I can then focus on how best to assist you in this jihad. For now, I need your pledge that you will also assist me in my coming hour of need. I know not when. But when our worlds blend in the glow of supreme unity granted by Allah, we will know."

"You are right, my friend, Francois. You would not be useful to me if you were half here and half in Guiana. In return, I pledge you my support, a position of authority in my eventual regime, and safe haven when you need it," said Al Yamani. The two agreed, and two days later they returned to the university in Zurich, Switzerland.

They continued to be close, to kneel on their individual prayer rugs, facing to the east and praying to Allah together. They also spent hours together laying plans for their separate but converging futures. At the same time, they met and became friends with a young Somali student, Dense Sal Khandar. His family owned a small but prosperous shipping business on the coast of Somalia in the city of Mogadishu. He, too, was a devout Muslim, but he belonged to a cult called the Muslim Brotherhood, which was being quietly infiltrated and re-indoctrinated by an Al Qaida splinter group called Al Shabaab. They claimed they supported those whom they said were people in need. Sal Khandar folded into the friendship of De La Plane and Al Yamani as smoothly as cream blends into coffee.

Another friend of the three was Benjo Ahmadou Adama, from the Cameroons. He was more guarded initially, when the three tried to befriend him. He had been sent to Zurich to get a university graduate degree that would eventually give him legitimacy to be a future leader in his country. The same rationale applied to most middle African and Middle-Eastern students in the university at that time. That legitimacy was never intended to make them learned or better able to understand the world. Rather, it was intended to teach them how the Western world practiced what these countries believed was deceit, subterfuge, and various means of trickery to exploit smaller countries. At least, that is what families and leaders in those countries thought when they allowed their children and young adults to study abroad. And that is what the parents of Al Yamani, Sal Khandar, and Adama believed. Needless to say, they didn't tell their sons those things before seeing them off to Switzerland. Instead, they gave their sons hints of what the future would hold. The parents would leave the final indoctrination to await the return of the sons to their respective countries, and then prepare them there for their greater responsibilities.

Of the four friends, perhaps Benjo Adama had more insight about what his destiny held for him. He was bitter about what he saw as the exploitation of his country by the British, the French, the Portuguese, the Germans, and hordes of Christian missionaries. He was equally dispirited by the repeated jihad of disgruntled Muslim tribes, Al Shabaab, and Boko Haram, which would hit and run, leaving carnage, death, thievery, and devastation in their wakes. No nation, groups of nations, or religious armies seemed to have any goals for this part of new Africa except theft, taxation, and conquest. He wondered when it would end.

Adama was descended from a nineteenth-century family of native settlers who had tried repeatedly to overcome cultural changes that were thrust upon them by foreigners. When the foreigners failed to subdue the populace, local leaders were replaced with indigenous Western descendants from Chad, Nigeria, the Central African Republic, Gabon, and the Republic of the Congo, along with vicious members of the Bornu Empire. They were all internal zealots who represented nondescript tribal interests and offshoots of Islam with Sunni, Sharia, ISIL, and Al Shabaab leanings. None were successful in converting the populace to their way of thinking. They did, however, rape and pillage the land and rob it of all its treasures. Then came

Boko Haram. They roamed the hills and valleys of Nigeria and Cameroon as savages, preying animals, thugs, and criminals who opposed any government by a nation's people and took whatever they wanted using beheading, maiming, and barbaric force. They were still unopposed.

What they and all the totalitarian regimes that preceded them in the Cameroons, along with all totalitarian criminals who have taken over countries in the last one hundred years around the world, have done, is to loot those countries and spill over into neighboring nations, who then themselves begin to live in fear.

As time moved forward, Benjo Adama became more open and bonded with the personalities, thoughts, and philosophies of his three classmates. But he retained a scintilla of doubt, a small germ of curiosity. Were they actually trying to make the region better for Allah, or were they using Islam as a façade for pillaging the region?

The friends vowed to remain tied in praise of Allah and in their mission to rid the world of exploiters and arrogant nations. They also vowed to remain friends and keep in touch in the future. They each extended an open invitation to visit one another's countries at any time, to stay as long as possible, and to help develop each of their nations in a direction that would achieve autonomy, power, and independence.

From this friendship, Francois was convinced the mental discipline of Allah, Islam, and Muslim principles was what was needed in Guiana, led by a benevolent dictator—himself.

8

Ambition and Revenge

Isnard et Priane, French Guiana, August 2006

Francois De La Plane returned home to French Guiana. He was a different man in thought, spirit, and faith. He resented what he took to be Catholic oppression and legal thievery. He fervently but privately believed Allah would show him the pathway ahead. There were also, he believed, issues of oppression in the world he felt strongly about, and he desired to do something about them. He was a man fiercely torn between what he needed and wanted to do, and what he should do. He decided he would confront these demons one at a time.

In spite of the inner peace he claimed he had found, he became incensed and was alarmed to find that his father and mother had been financially beaten into submission, forced to sell much of the fruits of their efforts at ridiculously low prices and dispose of their many holdings to nondescript and anonymous Guianese government entities. Francois was furious with the Guianese government specifically, and all governments in general. He was in awe of Fidel Castro and his family's rise to power in Cuba in the last half of the twentieth century. He knew he had to act, and he liked portions of the Yemeni, Somali, Cuban, Russian, and Chinese models of "structured" governing. He also liked that portion of the American model of freedom to decide issues for himself. But he became more intent on regaining what his family had personally lost. So he reached out to certain foreign entities with whom he had become acquainted. His educated and finely honed demeanor was smoothly persuasive. He continued to read the Koran and to privately pray to Allah for wisdom and strength. It gave him a modicum of solace and perspective.

With unannounced broad countryside support, Francois began to make contact with the governors of commerce, taxation, health services, and defenses. These supposedly untouchable government officials, their families, and business leaders were quietly made offers that they believed they could not refuse. Francois knew he could not have done this without the support of the people and special financial, material support and backing from anonymous international sources.

He had become what he most admired in others around the world in the same station in life—a businessman whose techniques to get what he wanted were based on an implied threat to the domains of those who had what he wanted. His tactics and powers of persuasion attracted the attention of the president of Venezuela, the Dear Leader in the Democratic People's Republic of Korea and others in the Middle East, Somalia, and the Yemeni Leadership Council. His constituent-based popularity became solidified, and he became increasingly politically stronger. In short, he had secretly received money from Venezuela and China, weaponry and missiles from North Korea, and training and advice from the Russian, Syrian, Yemeni, and Somali governments with the proviso that his benefactors would remain anonymous.

In the spring of 2011, Francois hosted a very private dinner and invited guests from those nations who were empowered to grant his requests. A few declined because of schedule conflicts. But De La Plane knew it was more because they desired to keep a low profile in this hemisphere, until they saw whether he would actually succeed. Key supporters sent emissaries to represent their interests. After dinner the guests retired for brandy and cigars to the great room overlooking the lush valleys in French Guiana. He poured himself a small glass of cognac from a special decanter beside a window overlooking an orchard to the west. Francois thought to himself, *This is a special occasion deserving a special drink.* It was very old and very rare. "Yes, Father," he whispered out loud to himself. "I need encouragement."

Francois made cordials available to his guests and then made it clear what he wanted. He knew his foreign guests were empowered to agree to his requests, within reason. After an hour of respectful but frank discussions, De La Plane got what he wanted, which was weapons and money. In exchange, he agreed to coastal access shipping and naval port rights, exchange of military force bases, establishment of diplomatic counsels, possible embassy office locations, and of course mineral rights to the gold in the hills and petroleum in the lowlands of the country. Of course, this was all predicated on him becoming the new unquestioned leader of his nation.

The North Korean envoy was particularly strident in his demands for access to and oversight of the space and missile launch facilities at Kourou on the north coast of French Guiana. He claimed the Dear Leader in the DPRK had only scientific interest in the facilities and wanted to explore the possibility of advancing science in manned space flights from the facility. The envoy proclaimed it would be a great day in the world if a Korean, a Guinean, and other astronauts could be launched from Kourou to explore the frontier of space. Sensing that the money and weapons promises from North Korea were being held in the balance, Francois acceded to those wishes. He did so being fully aware that the distance from Kourou to Washington, D.C., was easily within the range of a nuclear-tipped No Dong intermediate-range ballistic missile, or IRBM. He said, "My friend and comrade, Kim Jo Lin, if this is to be our destiny together, then what is mine, is yours."

After discussions with all his guests about his plans and timelines, all the visitors were assured they had a deal they secretly understood would eventually be better for them than for Francois. With a sufficient fill of excellent French brandy and superlative Cuban cigars, Francois's local guests departed for their residences in town. The foreign visitors, musing happily about their support of the joint political agreement, departed to their individual suites with the very shapely and attractive hostesses who were serving them that night.

By the end of July 2011, De La Plane and his small but growing army of surprisingly, mysteriously well-funded, and equipped followers were emboldened. They forcefully took control of twelve villages along Highway N-1 toward Cayenne, the capital. The villagers along the route became enchanted with this Robin Hood who left money, farming utensils, medical assistance, and promises of better times ahead. He became a folk hero who offered something different from that which the government had provided and then unceremoniously taken away.

After capturing the commitments of all the major government officials and that of the people of French Guiana, Francois made more assertive approaches to the current president, Anton Charles Buttoine, who could see his authority and relevance in French Guiana eroding daily. He, too, was made an offer he could not refuse. He could stay on as the titular head of government and stall and placate the government of France and the European Union, or be shot by a firing squad in the city center as a traitor to the people. He accepted Francois's offer to stay on for an undefined period, but he said he really wanted to soon resign so he could spend more time with his family in Brazil. But first, Francois told him the president had certain "diversionary" duties to perform.

By mid-September 2011, on an admittedly ambitious schedule, Francois Ricardo De La Plane had been dubbed *Il Generale* by some citizens and *Il Presidente* by others as he rapidly gained in popularity among the populace. He captured the imaginations and, more importantly, the loyalty of the citizenry. He also quietly and secretly moved large amounts of American dollars and European Euros to a numbered Swiss bank account. Like all tyrants, he convinced himself that he could never know what the future held.

9

A Turning Point

Cayenne, French Guiana, April 2012

Twelve months after the turning-point dinner in Isnard Et Priane in, De La Plane and French Guiana's financial state had taken a significant turn for the better. A French deputy assistant ministerial secretary for foreign department affairs was dispatched to French Guiana on a fact-finding and investigatory mission. He was arrogant, possessing an air of superiority and a brusque panache. He was immediately disliked by everyone in Guiana with whom he came into contact. When he landed via a commercial flight in the nation's capital, he was met by a low-ranking secretarial assistant to President Buttione and a military reservist lieutenant in the national army. His advertised purpose was to determine why French Guiana was prospering but was not yet paying its taxes to France.

After three days of non-substantive meetings that produced promises of further evaluation, more data-gathering and potential meetings with other government agencies and low-ranking officials, the deputy assistant ministerial secretary met an untimely death. He was found in the bed of a rather attractive woman, the wife of a successful Guiana industrialist who, morally justifiably as well as legally, did not take kindly to interrupting the circumstances in which he abruptly found the panting couple. The industrialist shot the deputy in the forehead with his pistol. When he was interrogated by the police he reportedly said, "I guess this is a fitting death for a Frenchman. I will deal with my wife later."

French Guiana continued to prosper into the new year, and imports of food, oil, and minerals increased. The De La Plane dynasty continued to grow in wealth but also became very confident about its status in the world, and it grew in belligerence. In September 2013, French Brigadier Anton Chevalier, three aides, and two enlisted female administrative specialists were dispatched to consult with the chief of the French Guiana military security forces. His publicized mission was to perform a five-day force assessment review to determine what the Guianian military services required to make them combat-ready to augment French National Forces deployed on NATO missions in Libya, Croatia, Kenya, and Liberia. However, De La Plane and his loyal ministers and department secretaries all knew the general and his staff were really there on an intelligence-gathering mission to find out what De La Plane had planned for the immediate future.

The president and government of France had both privately and publicly expressed their dissatisfaction with De La Plane's activities. But geographical distance, European priorities, and French national financial setbacks had precluded them from interceding with a large presence in the region. Besides, France believed this was a Western hemispheric problem that the United States should solve. President Obama was aware of the French attitude on this issue, and he continued to sympathize with the president of France. He deliberately but diplomatically sidestepped any talk of U.S. action. De La Plane was informed of this political two-step and the low-key U.S. State Department snub of the French national irritation toward French Guiana, which only served to embolden him.

When the general and his staff had completed their report, they were given a modest but appropriate ceremonial departure, and they were airborne from Cayenne International Airport bound for Paris. One hour later, over the Caribbean, the aircraft suddenly disappeared from air traffic control radars and all communication was mysteriously lost. The French Guiana government reported the loss to be the result of a severe mechanical failure aboard the aircraft, and they sent one helicopter out for two hours to conduct search operations.

They found no survivors and minimal aircraft debris. One week later, De La Plane's staff sent a full two-page written report to Paris citing their search-and-rescue actions on behalf of the French government. The issue was then closed by both governments. The French president fumed with exasperation but chose not to physically retaliate against the country and its people. Instead, he imposed an increased tax on the importation of French Beaujolais wine to De La Plane's import-export company in French Guiana.

In late November 2013, after the earlier resignation of President Buttoine and a bland and disappointing six months of governing by the vice president, De La Plane orchestrated months of quiet insurrections and subtle takeovers. These actions barely created ripples in the United States because of its own internal political strife and the administration's own declaration that JV teams were causing temporary disturbances in the Southern Hemisphere and the Middle-Eastern region.

However, in another three months of blatant counterinsurgency and many not-so-subtle aggressive persuasions, in early June 2014, Francois Ricardo De La Plane declared himself a general in the Free Guiana Army. At first it was a laughable freedom force that declared it represented the sovereign nation of French Guiana. As time moved forward two more months, "General De La Plane" began to gain the accolades of the Guianese people as well as notorious international recognition. He also garnered even more military and financial backing from anonymous sources and felt emboldened to announce that when he was inaugurated as commander in chief and then president in January 2015, things would change for the better. He quietly revealed that his country would soon be renamed the Free Caliphate of Guiana.

Having a radical Islamist jihadist caliph suddenly appear in the Western hemisphere with potential devastating military power became a concept that the nations of North America, Central America, and certain countries in South America were extremely and vocally uncomfortable with.

As General De La Plane's death squads and scurrilous bands of thieves and bandits were butchering French, Dutch, Brazilian, and British citizens, taking many of the more well-heeled and politically significant hostage, he began bold cross-border skirmishes into Brazil, Surinam, and even as far away as Colombia. No organized army or nation put up more than mild resistance to his dictatorial military actions, executive decrees, and tax assessments.

Confirmation of his terrorist activities reached the United States, Canada, Britain, France, and the European Union. They were outraged and issued repeated communiqués warning De La Plane of a significant reprisal to his naked aggression. It never came. Even the United Nations Security Council issued a resolution to him to cease and desist his aggressive activities or he would face sanctions. They never came. Soon thereafter it become known that De La Plane's forces had taken the U.S. Air Attaché, the British Naval Attaché, and the French Army Attaché and their families hostage—fifteen foreign nationals in all. It was rumored that there might have been more.

De La Plane warned that any ships, armies, or aircraft that attempted to counter or interfere with his national actions to establish a new government in the new Free Caliphate of Guiana would be met with maximum force. He quietly circulated the rumor that he possessed a nuclear device and a delivery system, and he would retaliate with unmerciful force.

Everyone in the region knew De La Plane's headquarters were located in a hilly area in underground bunkers near the small town of Isnard et Priane, where he had grown up. But under a threat of immediate death, all the people of the town and surrounding villages were sworn to secrecy concerning his exact whereabouts. They were also paid well each month for their silence. He traveled back and forth between his headquarters and Cayenne to shield his exact location.

French Guiana is a nation of only 350,000 people of farm family origins; for the most part, it is a peace-loving and congenial nation. But Francois De La Plane had struck a sensitive economic nerve. People across the nation became excited about the future and the prospect of newfound wealth, curious about the apparent protectivism of Islam, and fearful of the cost of resistance. Nevertheless, De La Plane's army swelled to a force of over 3,700 volunteers and a few selected conscripts. He claimed his officers were trained and experienced warriors from Middle-Eastern campaigns, some were Venezuelan expatriates, some were Middle-Eastern jihadist Muslims, and still others were

African Watusi tribesmen who were considered the most ferocious killers on that continent. Francois moved swiftly and decisively to ensure no other nations had time to muster enough organized resistance to deter him.

Evidence was confirmed by U.S. intelligence sources that De La Plane was indeed supported by Venezuela, North Korea, Somalia, and at least three other unknown nations; Syria, Yemen, Russia, and China were suspected, but were at this time unconfirmed as third parties. By October 2015, Francois Ricardo De La Plane was firmly in control of the Free Caliphate of Guiana, and those independent nations around him feared that they would soon be consumed into De La Plane's sphere of influence.

The United States and the rest of the civilized world were focused on more pressing confrontations in the Middle East. So the activities in French Guiana and the Southern Hemisphere were back-page news.

In early January 2016, eleven months after De La Plane had declared the existence of the Caliphate, the United States intelligence community saw what was coming and quietly scheduled unmanned Global Hawk RQ-4B drones to be flown over the country on randomly scheduled dawn, dusk, and midnight infra-red sorties to gather data that could only be retrieved by overhead assets. These UAVs were joined later by a stealth RQ-170 Sentinel unmanned photo and signals collection flight once a week. It gathered advanced infrared, optical, and communications intelligence.

While the collection assets were operational over Guiana, reports revealed a 250-mile-range air surveillance and warning radar installation was operational near Et Priane, and a small blockhouse was activated under the villa that appeared to be a warning and control center for possible military operations. There was also a concentration of heavily armed troops near the blockhouse: at least two dozen armored personnel carriers; three AT-37, late 1950s vintage, twin-jet tactical support fighter aircraft equipped with rockets, high-caliber, high-rate Gatling-style machine guns, and four 200-pound anti-personnel bombs on alert at Cayenne International Airport; up to six HU-1E tactical support helicopters; and three Transporter Erector Launchers, or TELs, each uploaded with 300-mile travel capability, heat-seeking, quick-targetable, reprogrammable, short-range ballistic missiles.

By July 2016 it was clear; something had to be done quickly to prevent this situation from getting out of hand. A neutralization plan to make De La Plane's offensive force ineffective became clear. The outgoing president was briefed, and he ordered U.S. forces to develop plans and prepare forces for military activities, whatever that meant. The newly formed special operations forces were tasked to rehearse tactical maneuvers. They knew something was going to be directed from the National Command Authorities, but they didn't yet know what it would be. They were, however, committed to the motto of a covert operating force, "Make the enemy sorry he got up that morning." These U.S. forces believed this motto in their hearts, in their minds, and in their trigger fingers.

10

The Precedent

Ad Dawhah, Qatar, July 2017

Events around the world began to take on an ominous hue. Events in French Guiana at this time were still at the wait-and-see stage. The U.S. Secretary of State, The Honorable Jane O'Donnell, was attending a small international gathering in Qatar sponsored by the UN on the need to improve energy production capabilities in the Nubian Desert region and beyond. The United States was still under suspicion by the world because of the Blackthorn catastrophe in Teheran the previous month. The members of the U.S. delegation were cautiously and somewhat coldly received and were treated with a degree of disdain.

Discussions quickly became heated when an Israeli report was issued that said nuclear weapons–grade fissile materiel was being transported between the Suez Canal, Egypt, the Sudan, and Ethiopia on its way to Somalia. The Israeli government and the U.S. Secretary of State provided incontrovertible imagery and e-mail intercept evidence that this had indeed taken place. This evidence was so pertinent that it made the Egyptians, Saudis, and Sudanese embarrassed, and it caused verbal outbursts accusing the U.S. and Israel relationship as being too partisan and in collusion to discredit certain nations in the Gulf. The nuclear materiel was evaluated, measured, and determined by Russian and Chinese independent United Nations representatives as only useful for power-generating plants. The United States, followed by the Israeli delegation, vehemently denied any collusion and apologized if the presentation of factual material was embarrassing to certain conference attendees. But the U.S. delegation said it could not argue with the facts.

Then there was a verbal objection by Secretary O'Donnell, along with evidence, that 950 million U.S. dollars' worth of gold bullion had been recently transported to or through Somalia for "social improvements," but was actually spent on weapons and nuclear hardening of facilities. This left many in the room seriously embarrassed, and a rapid temporary recess was declared by the Yemeni chairman of the meeting. During the recess, Secretary O'Donnell was asked to withdraw her comments and make no further allegations of misuse of money and materiel. She refused and so was asked to excuse herself from the remaining meetings of the group. The Israeli delegation was also asked to leave. At that request, the U.S.-educated Israeli ambassador, Benjamin Goldberg, loudly responded with an American-style retort that is reported to have sounded like, "Thanks, I'm leaving and I'm taking my money and weapons down the road. I've been thrown out of better joints than this."

A relatively toned-down, more objective assessment of the meeting results was dispatched to Washington to President Chenoa for her review. Her response was, "It sounds like we struck a nerve. Maybe we should pursue that to see if there's really anything there." A summary comment by the U.S. Secretary of State at the end of the cable stated that the veracity of the report was irrefutable and that sensitive U.S. tracking sensors had identified the material aboard a vessel as nuclear and it was en route from Port Sudan on the Red Sea to Djibouti in northern Somalia. After that, who knew where it was bound.

According to intelligence sources, the manifest for the vessel classified the cargo as "highly flammable paint products," and a platoon of heavily armed U.S.-trained Somalia Rangers were aboard to protect the cargo, just for safety purposes, of course. The secretary added to her report, "There were eyewitness accounts that a large amount of gold bullion was also stowed aboard the vessel." She also reported that the vessel was moored in Somalia for the time being, but that its final destination was "ill-defined and seemed intentionally made vague and nondescript to disguise its intended final port."

The U.S. president replied, saying, "We'll investigate further with our own methods."

On October 30, 2016, just before the U.S. general elections, it was publicly recalled that Republican Party nominee, presidential hopeful, and probable presidential winner, Governor Chenoa had received a courtesy worldwide intelligence update in September. She remembered the administration at that time was aware of events around the world but either knowingly and negligently, or benignly obliviously, believed global events were mostly unremarkable, more theatrical than threatening. Even the radical Islamic terrorism going on in the Middle East and Africa, and the failure of the legitimate governments in Iraq, Libya, Yemen, and Afghanistan, were regarded as minor setbacks in governing practices. Nevertheless, the administration then reluctantly agreed to stage a closed-door, unclassified, but sensitive "Global Events" presentation for Governor Chenoa and her national security staff, to reinforce an attitude of complete transparency in federal management. Governor Chenoa took a permanent mental note of all the data points and thought at the time, *If I am elected and receive information like this, the country can bet I will not shrug it off until all the facts are clear to me.*

Also at that time, Governor Chenoa was being coached by Senator Denny Smith and Congresswoman Rosemary Doolin, or members of their staff. The governor remembered that the administration had been advised of a classified report about the gold and the alleged nuclear signatures. She recalled that the subject was sloughed off as inconsequential, like so many others within the previous presidential term, such as investments in the solar energy industry that failed; closure of domestic and foreign U.S. facilities due to sequestration; the U.S. marine who was falsely jailed in Mexico; the release of Taliban prisoners from Guantanamo; the Benghazi attack and the Russian invasion of Ukraine; to mention only a few. Administration reports on those actions were, for the most part, presented as "throwaway" comments to the American people and U.S. media sources.

In those days before becoming elected president, she was able to in her best lawyerly and innocent interrogative manner, and she was able to discover facts that never made it to the American people through open news reports. In this instance, she discovered the fissile materiel related to the nuclear signatures aboard the ship came from defunct Russian nuclear missile warheads that had been dismantled in silos. The gold came from the World Bank in Geneva, the release of which had been approved and endorsed by lower-ranking Saudis, Egyptians, and Afghanis assigned to the World Bank's administrative staff.

Her findings and conclusions were back-channeled to Denny and Rosemary through the coaching staff. She now remembers thinking at the time, *I need to file these events away to be sure that it doesn't happen without the United States making some nation accountable for any deleterious actions that occur in later months. The United States will undoubtedly come out on the short end of any political or military reactions to these events. This may not cause serious difficulties this year, or even in two years, but certainly within three years there will be a significant confrontation unless the United States does something about it.*

Little did she know that the timeline was shorter than she could ever imagine.

In mid-November 2016, right after the elections, Denny and Rosemary had a quiet meeting over a bowl of famous Senate bean soup and corn bread. At the end of the lunch, Denny revealed that a few months earlier he had received an unconfirmed rumor from U.S. industry about the gold and the nuclear materiel, but the release of the report had been stonewalled by the White House, which had received his inquiry but had not answered it. He revealed that he knew something was happening in the Middle East; it was not only being glossed over by the administration, but it bode ill for the United States. It appeared as though the president didn't know what to do with the information and wanted to pass it on to the next administration to handle so that he could say, "It didn't happen on my watch!"

They both agreed to broach the subject of the nuclear materiel and the $950 million in gold bullion before their respective armed services and intelligence committees. There was a definite strategic imbalance occurring in the Middle East. The United States was demonstrating timidity to inquiring further, and the other lawmakers needed to be made aware of the implications and U.S. passivity on the issue. They also congratulated themselves on Governor Chenoa's landslide victory in the elections and they both felt some sense of personal victory. A small wave of cautious optimism had been sweeping over Washington in the last few weeks that a welcome change was looming on the horizon. It had nothing to do with elation of a perceived third term of President Obama, nor nothing to do with the election of the first woman Republican elected to the presidency. It had to do with a feeling of national pride that finally someone was going to do something about all the U.S. domestic and international problems.

The feeling was justified. After all, the events in 2014, 2015, and 2016 were overshadowed by political election rhetoric and months of seesaw political activities interspersed with the usual catastrophic weather events that are seldom predictable. Consequently the gold and the nuclear materiel were forgotten by most politicians and the public. Global political events came and went on a weekly basis in all of the military hotspots, and some not-so-hot locations around the world. The transfer of the gold, the nuclear components, the surreptitious sale of large amounts of military hardware to South American, Middle-Eastern, and central African countries were resurrected by investigative media reporters, concerned military forces friendly to the United States and a few honest politicians. Facts were never reported or questioned by more discerning American and foreign analysts. When they were brought before the public, they were dismissed by the outgoing U.S. administration as unconfirmed reports.

The reports that did pique the interest of the liberal American and Middle-Eastern press were the domestic American problems with failed solar energy initiatives, as well as the appointment of so-called czars who were friends of the president and who managed a vast range of governmental issues versus using the established and accepted constitutional structures.

As time went on in those years, additional issues and even scandals began to permeate a government that seemed unable or unwilling to manage the affairs of the nation. The country's Internal Revenue Service became embroiled in issues related to investigating conservative business entities, tax-exempt organizations, suppression of politically oriented investigative practices, inability of the Veterans Administration Hospital services to care for war veterans, closure of government facilities due to tax sequestration legal disagreements, congressional gridlock among themselves, and reports of malfeasance within U.S. intelligence agencies.

In the international arena, there was territorial expansion by Russia into neighboring nations, American weapons and ammunition being secretly sold to foreign drug cartels; U.S. relations with Cuba being normalized without a quid pro quo; Syria using chemical weapons on its own people; millions of U.S. dollars given to the Muslim Brotherhood for their personal use; dangerous war criminals from the Middle East released from Guantanamo Bay facilities; and the United States leading a team of negotiators who agreed to allow Iran to acquire a nuclear weapon, which they said they would use on Israel.

Political, economic, and military security activities in the United States and around the world were in a state of chaotic disarray because of no coherent attention to leadership. But political storm clouds were gathering on the global horizon that many more astute political observers did not avoid seeing.

11

Ghosts

Pensacola Naval Air Station, Florida, September 1, 2017

It was 2315 hours, U.S. Central Standard Time, and Colonel J. W. "Bud" Patrick III, United States Army, and commander of the First Squadron, Special Joint Strike Force, sat strapped in his seat at the front of the cargo bay of the long-range MC-130J, Commando II, Super Hercules four-engine turbo prop. His six foot, two inch 195-pound frame made the bucket seat almost uncomfortable. This special operations cadre was called the Phantom Force because of the manner in which they trained and practiced, and the procedures they used to operate. Their practices and procedures were seldom observed. They got into a target in a stealthy manner and got out the same way. The speed and manner in which they did their jobs was phantom-like and almost ghostly. So they chose their name themselves—the Phantom Force. Their adversaries called them Ghosts.

Tonight the Ghosts aboard the Super Herc were headed south out of Pensacola Naval Air Station, Florida, to an unpublicized South American operating point that was not expecting a visit. Bud Patrick and his Phantoms, however, knew their destination. The mission was classified TOP SECRET, code word Project TEMPEST.

The "Super Herc" just had wheels-up after lifting off runway 19 and was climbing to an altitude of 26,000 feet out over the Gulf. After clearing the end of the runway still under full military power, it passed over Sherman Cove, past Fort McRae on the left and Fort San Carlos on the right. At a point six miles south of Pensacola at an altitude of 12,000 feet, the Herc turned right to a heading of 230. Patrick and his squadron of thirty military specialists included three augmented squads formed around three eight-man teams of multi-service covert operations specialists, plus a command element. Their mission was to silently penetrate and quietly take their target with the fewest shots fired as possible, and then just as quietly and invisibly disappear from the scene. For this mission the teams were code-named Trigger 1, 2, and 3. Patrick's command element was code-named Trigger Lead. Only a few highly placed military leaders and political officials, including the president, knew Colonel Bud Patrick's battalion as the Phantom Force; for this reason of anonymity, those in the chain of command also called them Ghosts.

The Super Herc was abeam of New Orleans at an altitude of 26,000 feet when it took an easy left turn to a heading of 190 degrees toward Brownsville, Texas, at a speed of 285 knots toward the Bay of Campeche, off the coast of Mexico. Before the aircraft would reach its final destination, it would make several course, altitude, and speed changes, appearing to be just one of the many commercial airline island hoppers and Gulf city commuter flights that circumnavigated the cities around the perimeter of the Gulf of Mexico.

Bud Patrick was a twenty-one-year veteran of many joint force and coalition force missions over the years, and he had both the ribbons and the scars to prove it. He was forty-five years old, in excellent physical and mental condition, which is essential in this kind of work. The only scar of battle visible was a two-inch diagonal facial scar on his right cheek. The others were on his back, chest, and arms, long since healed from the global skirmishes he had suffered.

He had a distinguished career as a battle-hardened commander in Iraq, Afghanistan, Mali, Colombia, and Uganda, and the highest of all security clearances. Because of the secrecy of his missions and the places where his squadron trained, his chain of command was short. His regimental commander was a U.S. Navy one-star rear admiral. That admiral and two other regimental flag rank general officers, one an army brigadier and one a marine corps brigadier, reported directly to the chairman of the Joint Chiefs of Staff, a U.S. Navy four-star admiral. The chairman worked for the secretary of defense in concert with the director of national intelligence, the DNI, and the president.

Bud Patrick unbuckled his lap belt and stood in the dim cabin lighting in the dead of night, looking at the forty-seven clandestine covert operations combat force. The force included the best U.S. Navy Seals, U.S. Army Rangers, and Delta Force Green Beret soldiers, U.S. Marines snipers, U.S. Air Force Covert Operations Para-Rescue Jumpers, or PJs, technical specialists, and the most lethal of all the covert operations and clandestine operatives in the CIA. Two Canadian special operations Black Force officers were also attached for collaborative coalition force purposes. Both spoke French and were prepared to act as interpreters. Two U.S. Army interpreters who spoke Cajun French were also assigned. There were also two sniffer dogs and their handlers aboard. The dogs were wrapped in canine armor and chute harnesses for the jump. All three augmented squads were the best trained and able men in the entire United States Armed Forces, coalition forces, and intelligence community.

Patrick's special Joint Strike Force operators were seated down the sides of the aircraft and in the center row of canvas seats, dressed in combat-ready full interceptor Kevlar body armor vests and pants, helmets with night-vision thermal goggles, black, non-reflective, and buoyant fabric protective suits. Bud Patrick was dressed and equipped exactly like his men except for two six-inch-long flexible satellite antennas that protruded from his helmet and were wired to a power pack in his backpack. The two radios and two miniature helmet-mounted video cameras allowed him to communicate via satellite and ground net circuits to both his operators and with the admiral, the chairman at the National Military Command Center, the NMCC, in the bowels of the Pentagon and with his command center-afloat in the Caribbean.

Normally, an operation like this would not be led by the commander and his exec. But this mission was so sensitive, for political, military, and technological reasons, that his orders read "direct hands-on leadership for this mission is mandatory." Patrick's second-in-command, Lieutenant Colonel John "Duke" Westcott, United States Marine Corps, and senior non-commissioned officer Master Chief Petty

Officer Reed Barrett, USN, were each equipped identically to ensure continuity of command in the event the unexpected occurred. Westcott was perfect for this job. He was tall, wily, had a penetrating stare, was physically muscular, and moved like a leopard. Since he had a walking swagger like John Wayne, he was jokingly nicknamed "Duke" in college. It stuck.

The master chief was also lithe, quick, and athletic. Patrick, Westcott, and Barrett appeared so much alike they looked like they might be related. They also all commanded respect and loyalty from each member of the Phantoms. They and each of the men carried lightweight cartridge and utility packet belts and a miniature, lightweight backpack filled with the special lethal tools of each of their individual specialties. All carried a Glock laser-sighted Model 19 pistol each with a 17-round clip plus five clips of extra ammunition. Some of the men were armed with the M249 light machine guns, and some were also armed with M-16A2 rifles with extra clips of ammunition. Others were equipped with the M2A1 .50-caliber machine gun; four were armed with the MK19 grenade machine gun and had four dozen anti-personnel Spider land mines in their ammo belts. The rest were equipped with a variety of anti-personnel mines, flares, point-to-point land and satellite communications gear, the joint tactical radio systems nicknamed JTRS or "jitters," joint warning and reporting sensors, laser designated–range finder fire support devices, and several portable deployable moving target systems sensors.

Collectively, the three enhanced squads of Ghost troops had nearly 75 percent more firepower and lethality than did the ground force they were to intercept and deflect. It was planned that way. Over all the packets of technical tools, they each also wore a simplified parachute harness onto which a specially designed maneuverable, heavy-load black night attack 375-square-foot rectangular parachute would soon be attached, and an oxygen mask and faceplate attached to a small oxygen bottle with a fifteen-minute supply of air in it. The oxygen wasn't normally used at this low altitude, but it was a precaution to ensure their minds and reactions remained alert.

They would exit the MC-130J using the aft cargo ramp in a tailgate maneuver from 15,000 feet above the hilly coastal terrain below. This would be a High Altitude, Low Opening, or HALO, jump. Two Navy

SEALS, two Army Green Beret Ranger Pathfinders, and two Air Force combat control team members were already in place on the ground to laser-mark the landing zones and provide pre-jump intelligence. This autumn mission was expected to be 100 percent successful because of the element of surprise.

Ten miles off the coast, almost directly abeam of the coastal town of Malmaison, French Guiana, the United States aircraft carrier USS *Harry S. Truman*, CVN-75, code named HAMMER, was cruising a lazy back-and-forth course at ten knots. It was capable of much more, but for combat patrol it was not needed. On board were the usual Air Wing of FA-35C stealth, vertical short take-off and landing, called VSTOL, air superiority and tactical ground support fighter aircraft, three EA-6B Prowler and two EA-18 Growler electronic jamming aircraft, several Sea Hawk search-and-rescue helicopters, two of which were currently airborne and circling at 100 feet altitude north of the carrier and the French Guiana coastline. Air Force Special Operations Command from Eglin Air Force Base, Florida, had an AC-130J Ghostrider Gunship orbiting twenty miles off-shore varying his altitudes so as to appear as a spurious radar contact to any land- or sea-based radar that might paint him.

There were also three S-3 Viking twin engine tanker aircraft in stand-by, cockpit alert and launch status to refuel any airborne assets that might need added fuel. There were other surveillance, recovery, and Med-Evac choppers with chemical-biological and radiation treatment packs on-board standing by for launch in the event they were needed. But on this mission the *Truman* also carried six MH-60 C stealth Ghosthawk helicopters each capable of carrying 4,000 pounds of troops and cargo at 100-foot altitudes, at speeds up to 225 miles per hour in nighttime and low-visibility weather with minimal engine and rotor noise that allowed them to operate in "whisper" mode. Three more eight-man squads of multi-service Ghost forces were at ready, awaiting orders to mount up aboard the stealth choppers to augment the three squads already en route to the drop zones when and if required. One Air Force B-2 Spirit and one B-3 Eagle stealth long-range strike bomber were already airborne over the Caribbean along with a KC-10 tanker to augment if needed. Both bomber aircraft were equipped with a payload of two one-thousand-pound air-burst concussion bombs to confuse hostile ground forces and disrupt hostile ground and air communications. They were also equipped with a newly operational version of four long-duration orbiting Collapsible surveillance cruise-Pack Powered Ultralight, or CPPU gliders that are dispensed from high altitude and parachute down to a preset elevation. Once slowed to the proper altitude, they unfold and a small propeller-driven motor activates and all sensors are turned on. They immediately begin to send intelligence, surveillance, and reconnaissance, or ISR, information to the bombers, orbiting command and control aircraft and to ground and sea-based centers. They fly circular orbits overhead at 8,000 feet for up to six hours that could relay communications, video, and disgorge emergency mini-medical and weapons reinforcement assets if required. At the end of six hours they self-destruct so that no evidence of their presence remains behind. The mission planners were confident this mission would not fail.

To the untrained eye of the casual observer, Project TEMPEST could appear as overpreparation for such a small mission objective in a small, rarely heard of South American nation. But if a trigger-happy farmer-soldier became startled and unwittingly or unexpectedly launched a nuclear missile against a neighboring country or released highly toxic VX or ancient mustard gas, everyone in the region for two hundred miles around would have a very bad day. So no, this was not excess mission capability. It was indeed in conformity with the president's request for overwhelming military power, striking in time with essential overkill and absent of any civil engineers to do nation-building after the attack.

A back channel message to the President of France from President Chenoa had alerted them to standby to move into French Guiana to perform peaceful governmental reconstitution. The French president was reported to have given an enthusiastic but barely visible sigh of relief. All cautionary resources had been deployed.

12

Stand By to Jump

Gulf of Mexico, September 2017

The mission for the three streamlined squad-teams of strike "Ghosts" was to infiltrate the enemy territory without detection. They were to para-drop within two hundred meters of the hostile's headquarters, neutralize as many of the terrorist troops as possible, and make the drop zone safe for pickup of friendly hostages. They also needed to kill or capture the enemy commanding general and his deputy, and exit with zero casualties. No friendlies, dead or alive, were to be left behind. The stealth choppers aboard the *Truman* were poised to make the extraction from a nearby landing zone sufficiently large enough for three of the Ghost Hawks to maneuver in and out.

Aboard the MC-130J Super Hercules, Bud Patrick was reviewing their infiltration plan with Lieutenant Colonel "Duke" Westcott, Senior Master Chief Barrett, the three squad-team leaders, their senior non-commissioned officers, NCOs, and the communications support team. They all had trained together for eight weeks at a mock-up enemy command post near MacDill Air Force Base outside Tampa, Florida. They practiced the para-drop, the battle skirmishes, and securing the friendly hostages, the anarchist leader, and his henchmen. They also practiced the neutralization of the combatant hostiles and the exfiltraration maneuvers. When they volunteered for this duty from their respective services, they received basic and advanced infantry tactics and survival training. Because of this training they already knew how to deploy in hostile areas, use combat hand signals, and more importantly, to function as a team. They practiced contingencies, medical emergencies, and radio communications with the simulated USS *Truman* command post. Everything was in readiness. This strike force was set up not to fail.

Bud Patrick began his instructions over the intercommunications systems aboard the aircraft.

"Gentlemen, we have practiced this mission many times, and we have all actions and contingencies memorized."

His words were being broadcast to all team members. They had receivers and headphones built into their helmets, and all could receive but not transmit. This general broadcast technology assured that everyone got the word firsthand. All twenty-nine covert force operators listened intently to what Number 30 was saying.

The commander continued his pre-jump briefing. "This will be a HALO drop. Chutes are set to open when the personal automatic activation device senses fifteen hundred feet above the terrain. Be sure to check your Cyprus II automatic chute-opening devices to assure they are set appropriately. Night vision and infra-red glasses are to be activated not only to guide you to the landing zone, but also to ground landing spots, which are laser-illuminated by the spotters. Make sure your M14 rifles are secured to your left shoulder harness and your assault kit bags are secured by the lanyard attached to your chest pack. This enables it to swing free beneath you as you descend. We will be approaching the Drop Zone, or DZ, at an altitude of nineteen thousand feet, a speed of one hundred seventy knots, and on a heading of one hundred degrees. We will be on altitude, heading, and airspeed of the Caribbean Airways flight that usually flies this course each night. That commercial flight has been unexpectedly cancelled because of a maintenance problem. There is hostile ground-based surveillance radar active in the DZ that the enemy force uses for early warning and detection. Since we will produce a radar cross-section that looks like the Caribbean Airways flight and all jumpers are stealth-equipped, we fully expect that our penetration will be undetected. I will be the first jumper, and the Trigger Lead support members will be followed by the three teams. Use two tandem sticks and maintain normal intervals. All operators will have their night vision goggles and infra-red detection sensors activated in order to see the landing zone perimeter. The descent and touchdown will be silent and each team must maneuver to land within ten yards of their night vision–illuminated team members."

He continued, "Our target has not changed. It is still the large house that looks like a villa with scattered trees and shrubbery. It is well manicured for camouflage purposes. The bunker that houses the enemy command and control is where the hostages are being held in the basement. There are, as you recall, from our intel and practices, two entrances. Team One will position on the small hill fifty meters to the north of the villa entrance number one. Team Two will position approximately seventy-five meters to the east of the villa, between the villa and the transporter-erector-launchers, or TELs, and the nuke missiles. Team Three will locate on the road to the west of the villa and fifty meters away. When we are on ground in position, all operations will simultaneously commence only on my mark."

"Team One will make the initial penetration into the villa via entrance number one. They will capture and hold the enemy general, who, thirty minutes ago, was reported to be in the bunker by IMINT and COMINT sources. We'll get an update on his whereabouts two minutes before entering. Two members of the team will move to the cells down hallway two of the bunker and liberate the hostages. Take them into protective custody and protect them at all costs until they are aboard the choppers. Remember, we want all hostages and prisoners alive. If any of the hostiles resist surrender and positively, absolutely want to die, accommodate them. All of us on this mission, just like all missions, share one common strong desire; we all want to go safely home to our families. You are thoroughly trained to be alert and extra cautious.

"Team Three will deploy five meters apart across the road from the house on the west side. You will be prepared with grenade launchers, suppressive fire, electronic jamming disruption, and proximity flare illumination over the enemy, in order to deter, confuse, and destroy attempts by the platoon of enemy infantry to rush to the bunker of the house. Remember, there are fifteen friendly hostages being held by the enemy. They are military attachés and their families. One family is U.S. Air Force, one is U.K. Navy, and the third is French Army. There are rumored to be Dutch civilians there also. They all know there are risks in this kind of assignment, but they usually have diplomatic immunity; unless their host nation's leaders are crazy. Sinc—the hostages don't know we're coming, they may be initially afraid and confused. If you can manage to keep them calm, they will be more cooperative.

"Once the hostages are liberated and the prisoners are secured, all team members, hostages, and prisoners will move to the stealth chopper landing zone on the north side of the villa for a sequential extraction.

"Team Two will destroy the three TEL vehicles and blow the liquid fuel tanks near those sites to preclude uploading fuel and launch of the missiles. Our explosive ordnance strike technicians will destroy the guidance avionics on the nine missiles in the crates. If we have the 'general,' his deputy, and the Somali colonel advisor in custody, or have confirmed they are dead, no one will remain behind with the launch codes.

"Remember, execute this mission just as we practiced. Two minutes before we jump, we will receive an Execute Plan A–GO code, which translates to everything being on-plan and as practiced." Patrick asked, "Questions?" All team members shook their heads.

Patrick then concluded, "Okay, then, and make sure your squad-teams have no questions. Chute-up in twenty minutes. As jump master, I'll start jump commands at three minutes out. I'll pass a READY code to the *Truman*."

Bud knew that as soon as the first Phantom boots hit the ground someone would inform the tyrant and he would know his minutes were numbered and his atrocities would be ended. But then, Bud also knew that even the most perfect plan could encounter a small, unexpected incident. It had always been that way, and it would always be that way. So he knew some degree of flexibility on missions like these was always necessary.

Two minutes later the *Truman* passed a code of "This is Hammer; this is Hammer; Execute Plan B–GO; Execute Plan B-GO." The six MH-60 Ghost Hawk choppers were lifting off the flight deck of the *Truman* at ten-second intervals, just as planned and practiced. The

Plan B-GO message went to all Trigger Team Lead members over the intercom frequency at the same time Bud received it. As if by command, all heads turned to look at Bud Patrick.

Bud turned to Duke Westcott and Reed Barrett and said, "Damn, things are changing. The tyrant is on the move to points unknown. All else is status quo. We go in and execute the extraction as planned. Stay tuned for what else may change in the next fifteen minutes." Bud then quietly mumbled to himself, *"What was I just saying to myself about being flexible?"*

He and his team knew with this B-GO code that they were to move out to capture the remaining leaders and liberate the fifteen friendly hostages who were incarcerated. He ensured the new B-GO code was received by all Trigger team members simultaneously. All members looked to Bud Patrick and gave the thumbs-up signal. They knew what to expect once on the ground.

At nine minutes before the JUMP signal, Patrick gave the command for all to stand in single file and check the gear and equipment of the team member in front of them. Bud said, "Activate the chest and center back position lights and your helmet strobe lights. We each need to see one another laterally and vertically as we descend. This would be an inappropriate time to have a mid-air fender-bender."

They checked for loose straps, open buttons and buckles, unsecured weapons scabbards, or anything else that could fly away in mid-air. All positioned the O2 masks over their noses and mouths and made checks on oxygen masks, night vision power packs, laser detection operation, and other technical gear operations.

On the ground, General Francois Ricardo De La Plane, the self-proclaimed president and commander-in-chief of the Free Caliphate of French Guiana strode into his underground bunker command post beneath the villa. He appeared self-assured, confident, and arrogant. His army of conscripts, decrepit field hands, and volunteers were poised to move west. Their plan was to move and attack the neighboring country of Surinam and to press on to the capital at Paramaribo. Like all tyrants, he planned to plunder and pillage the countryside as he moved west toward the capital. Francois had become a villainous and vicious self-proclaimed conqueror. Any answer short of *"Oui, Mon Generale"* meant instant death. He, however, issued orders not to hurt innocent bystanders, children, the elderly, or anyone compliant with orders.

His cell phone rang. He took it from his pocket, looked at the video display identifying the caller, and put it up to his ear. "*Oui?...Oui!... Okay!*" He motioned to his second-in-command to follow and walked across the low-lit room to a small cabinet and bookcase located against the wall with a special key-lock on its front. He took out a key from his pocket, opened a lower door, removed a small old bottle from a shelf, and set it on top of the cabinet surface. He and his assistant then turned and walked to a steel door on their left. The obscure door was behind two desks that had four computer screens, three telephones, and a small console box bristling with switches and lights. Four non-commissioned officers sat in front of the computer screens displaying a split-screen video of equipment and entrance accesses around the villa. It was obviously a security system control panel, video security camera–monitoring sensors, and a weapons situation–monitoring capability. Francois opened the steel door. He and his number two stepped through, turned and bolted it from the inside, and hurriedly walked along the dimly lit underground corridor.

Aboard the MC-130J Super Herc, three minutes before the JUMP signal, a voice message crackled over each man's earset from the *Truman*. "This is Hammer, this is Hammer. This is confirmation; this is confirmation; Execute Plan Bravo, Execute Plan Bravo. It is a GO; it is a GO."

At the same time the aircraft load master was lowering the aft platform into the air stream and the inside lighting dimmed so as not to illuminate the sky around the MC-130J. There was the subtle sound of whining hydraulic motors. Then there was a rush of cool air in the fuselage of the Super Herc. Bud Patrick turned from his position at the edge of the platform door. He gave the thumbs-up signal and looked to see that all members responded with the same signal, indicating they understood. Bud looked to his right just inside the hatch opening at the jump signal lights. The yellow light was illuminated. Five seconds later the green light was on. Bud looked to his right, then left, and knew that all five lined up on the door edge were looking to him to leap. He did.

In two-second increments a group of five team members jumped until all were hurtling toward the earth at better than 120 miles per hour.

It was 0112 hours, September 2, 2017.

13

On the Ground

French Guiana, September 2017

In twelve minutes all thirty Phantoms were safely in their appointed locations without incident. Each man quickly disposed of their chutes and expendable descent gear. The sniffer dogs looked to their masters for command. The snipers had quickly moved to their rendezvous point. U.S. Marine Lance Corporal Darrin Hall instructed the other two snipers and their spotters to move silently to their shooter spots.

At 0135 hours all Phantom Force members were in position waiting for the next command. Colonel Bud Patrick whispered over the secure discreet intercom channel to all Force members, "Stand by to move out; on the mark."

Two minutes later all Force members heard over their intercoms, "This is Trigger Lead. Move on my mark in ten seconds." There was a short pause, then all members heard, "…five, four, three, two, one, MARK." Then all hell broke loose.

Sergeant Hall quickly put one thirty-millimeter bullet through each of the foreheads of three TEL guards in a matter of four seconds. All the enemy perimeter guards around the three TELs were neutralized. The three TELs blew up, and vehicle and missile parts went every direction. The missiles in the crates blew and sent a shower of explosive sparks and fire a hundred and fifty feet into the air.

The villa bunker was quietly but forcefully stormed. Once inside, the Phantoms neutralized the guards, doors were blown open, and ornamental brick barriers were blown apart. Team 2 members stormed into the underground bunker command post to the sudden surprise of the ten armed guards and soldiers posted around the area. The Somali colonel and two Somali enlisted guards immediately put their hands in the air, realizing that to do anything threatening meant instant death. The Team 2 Lead quickly surveyed the bunker for any sign of the general or anyone else in authority. He walked briskly over to a steel door in one wall and found it secured from the other side. He shot four rounds through the locking mechanism and pulled the door open. There was a tunnel on the other side but no sounds of running or activity. He quickly made an intercom call to the Trigger Lead to come survey the room. He then directed the Team 2 members to gather up cell phones, computer hard drives, papers, logbooks, and any other pertinent-looking information. The Team 2 Lead then made a circular motion in the air with his right hand and pointed to the entrance door through which they had entered. It meant, *Let's round up the friendlies and get the hell out of here.*

Three Phantoms rushed down the hallway to the cells where the hostages were kept. They cut the padlocks off the cell doors with bolt cutters and quickly stepped into the rooms to find the American, British, French, and Dutch hostages frightened and alarmed, but unharmed. The Phantoms immediately showed the hostages the American flag patches on their uniforms and asked if all were able to move. The hostages mumbled, "Oh, thank God!" and "God bless the USA" with many visible reactions of relief and grateful smiles. The Phantoms gently motioned the hostages to quickly come along to the evacuation point.

Team 3 set up a barrier perimeter fifty yards from the villa and began destroying trucks, Jeeps, armored personnel carriers, and two small Korean-manufactured tactical tanks. There were stacks of armament crates containing small arms, ammunition, and several different types of explosive munitions. It all blew up in a horrendous ball. The team returned suppressive fire from the few troops who recognized they were shooting at a superior force of professional soldiers and stayed mostly hunkered down in trenches and behind protective cover. The Phantoms neutralized more than two hundred enemy troops. The remainder either hid in trenches and holes in the ground or turned to run away from the firepower. The havoc the Phantoms created was so chaotic that the Guianese troops thought it was the end of their world, along with that of everyone on the South American continent.

There was the soft sound of stealth helicopter rotors overhead. The *wup-wup-wup* was not as pronounced as many would have expected it to be. These were the Ghost Hawks arriving to perform the exfiltration.

At the same time, all Phantom Force members heard over their intercommunication units, the command from Bud Patrick, "This is Trigger Lead, this is Trigger Lead; join up, join up, now." That was the practiced command to all troops that the mission was wrapping up, the objective had been taken, and they were to vanish as quietly as they had arrived.

The time was 0246 hours, September 2, 2017.

14

Strategic Imbalance

Washington, D.C., February 2018

Denny Smith was the fourth-ranking Republican on the Senate Armed Services Committee, but he was perhaps the smartest and best-connected on the SASC. He sat three chairs to the left of the chairman of the committee.

On this day in Washington, D.C., the personal cell phone of Denny rang. He was on First Street on Capitol Hill, on his way to a six-person social but business-oriented luncheon at the Monocle Restaurant. He was a bit surprised because he recognized the company of origin in the caller ID window of the phone. He was a bit perturbed because he could not recall anyone to whom he had given this number. If it was a spurious marketing call or a request for a favor, he would change the number within six hours so no one could reach him on that number again. There were many reasons he didn't want just anyone to have this number. With a hint of reluctance in his voice, he spoke, "Hello?"

"Senator, this is Joanie, the general counsel of Systems Analysis Enterprise, SAE Corporation. We met at the Air Force Association Symposium at the Potomac Harbor Gaylord Hotel in Washington in September of last year."

"Oh, yes. I remember," he said somewhat guardedly as he tried to piece together the company, the woman, the conversation, and the context of their talk.

Sensing some guarded tones in the senator's voice, she prompted, "We had a short but intriguing conversation about the costs of government versus the costs of freedom. I remember that we seemed to agree that the effort of managing the balance between peace and war is a difficult and delicate process. I also recall you saying you had added views on the subject. I hope you meant that. I would like to personally and privately discuss them with you. The topic is important to both of us, for more than fiscal reasons."

"Yes, I clearly remember our conversation now. I was sincere in my statement, and I'm always open to hearing supporting and dissenting views. I'm not one to demagogue my thoughts, but as you said, personally and privately, I'm not interested in discussing those subjects in a public forum at this time. As you know, I have some personal observations on those subjects, but I very much like a balanced point of view on items that face my committee."

"Thank you, Senator. I appreciate your honesty and candor. In that vein, I'm following up with you regarding some interesting recent international developments. I am not placed well enough to do a credible true-or-false validation, a risk-benefit analysis, or a balance-of-power evaluation, so I can't tell you what the event that I'm about to pass on means. I can, however, tell you the information is based on irrefutable fact and verification from highly credible sources. You can then discern whether it's of significance. Before I tell you, I hasten to add that I don't expect any insights or promises in return. I know if I give you anything relevant to worldwide circumstances, you may think the points useful or unimportant at this time. I would never expect anything in return for such observations. There is no quid-pro-quo for any information I give you or any individual, country, or special envoy with which my company has contact. That is the way we do business."

Denny raised his eyebrows at this candor, especially from a contractor who relied on her political contacts for survival.

In response, he said, "That's interesting. I appreciate the disclaimer up front. To what, then, do I owe the privilege of this phone call?"

Joanie responded by saying, "Thank you. I'm glad we understand one another." She then continued, "SAE Corporation provides political, financial, social, and military counsel to many nations around the world. We advise them about investments, the prudence of involvement in international affairs, advancements in technology of the international scientific community, and the public happenings of nations that have thoughts of expansion. I'm calling you to tell you that we have observed two unusual events that could portend a major tip in the strategic balance of power in a region around the south of the Mediterranean.

"First, there has been a transfer of a large amount of gold bullion, equivalent to nine hundred fifty million American dollars to an unidentified Middle-Eastern nation."

This caused Denny's brows to rise since he had almost forgotten the gold transfer he'd been told of in 2016. He quickly thought, *What happened to it? Where did it go? Is this a new shipment?* He, of course, said nothing of these thoughts to Joanie, but decided he needed to revisit this subject.

She went on to say, "The exact donor of the gold is nondescript at this time. In addition, the exact recipient of the wealth is unknown, as well. But that nation surely resides somewhere around the Gulf of Hormuz. The routing through the various banks that handle these kinds of transactions is not only mysteriously cumbersome, but it is a bit melodramatic based on the new technologies available to track business messages on the Internet. Given more time and incentive, we could probably put together a plausible, if not precise, routing scenario. But SAE does business with many countries, and becoming too curious about the internal politics of any single nation would leave our clearly identifiable electronic fingerprints on any search we would undertake. Such a search could void or jeopardize our vow of secrecy and independence and immediately terminate agreements with many nations with whom we have close personal business relations. I know you understand."

Since this information was sensitive, if not classified, two years earlier, Denny was curious to see if she would reveal how the information got into the public domain and whether it differed significantly from what he had been told in the fall of 2016. It didn't. If he were to say that it was old news, it would only corroborate that it was true, and he didn't want to validate her report on this open line. And she didn't reveal her source for this information. He listened intently to ensure he heard all the details correctly. He wanted to remember all the nuances and did not want to write down any of the data.

Conversely, he also didn't want to leave the impression that he doubted the veracity of the information, but he did know he needed to verify that the transfer did indeed occur. He was glad this was not a face-to-face meeting where he would be at odds with his own visual expressions by reflecting either a *so what* or a *holy shit* reaction. Instead, he calmly responded by saying, "Yes, you are correct that this action, if and when confirmed, could have an interesting influence on the balance of power in that region of the world. But, depending on the recipient of this newfound wealth and their political leanings, the results could vary dramatically.

"You said you had two events. What is the second piece of information?" Denny asked. He wanted to sound appreciative for the information but at the same time cautious about how relevant he thought the data was. He didn't want to telegraph to Joanie his next move inside his own circle of verification mechanisms. He wanted to be assured he didn't leave her with the notion that she could relay to others among her acquaintances that she knew what Senator Smith was going to do about the tips. He could either be tactical and charge off after verification to seek an impact analysis, or he could be strategic and decide how to determine the veracity of the information and then take a few hours to weigh the impacts and pros and cons if the data were true. In his own mind, he had already decided the latter.

Then Joanie said, "The other data point, Senator, seems to me to be a bit more ominous if true. I don't have a feel for the relevance or the meaning. But there is an unconfirmed report that an unidentified amount of nuclear materiel that may be weapons-grade is also in transit to the same area as the gold. I don't have anything more on that. But I'm sure you have sources that can validate or dismiss that report."

Now he thought, *Damn, this is too coincidental to be new information. There must be a tie to the rumors of 2016. I wonder where this gold and fissile materiel has been.*

Joanie then said, "As I noted earlier, Senator, I would never attempt to compromise your status or future intentions by asking for something in return. Let it suffice to say that any observations I give you now or in the future that allow the United States to assure the peace and security of the world would be payment enough."

"Hmm, thank you, Joanie. Please, let's stay in touch. I'm not certain at this time I will be able to give you any feedback on these items. If it's possible and if it's relevant, I will certainly do so. Call anytime, and I look forward to talking to you again."

"Thank you, Senator. I will indeed call again."

Denny sat down on a streetside bench with his cell phone in his hand and thought for a moment. *Whom should I call next? What should I say or ask?*

15

Agree to Disagree

Washington, D.C., February 2018

It was a crisp, cool, clear winter day at the White House in Washington. The new administration was still hard at work after having only been inaugurated thirteen months earlier. International events related to Blackthorn in Iran in June of 2017, and the French Guiana conflict in September a few months later, had taken over the new president's domestic and foreign relations agendas. As a result, almost everything except the most urgent national initiatives had been put on hold.

President Chenoa's proactive stance of being involved in getting her administration up and operating gave new and unprecedented meaning to the term "hit the ground running." All of the agency and departmental secretarial positions in the new government had nominees confirmed. But the ship of state was still listing badly. President Chenoa had been facing constant requests for assistance to address widespread assaults and attacks on the Constitution of the United States. Likewise, she had an even larger barrage of requests for meetings with politically liberal groups, progressive thinking organizations, and representatives of millions of illegal aliens, anti–law enforcement advocates, as well as leaders of black, Asian, Islamic, and American Indian activist groups. There were also the labor unions who wanted continuation or activation of executive orders granting them immunity from a large variety of wage, price, and tax regulations. As governor of the State of Idaho, she believed, at the time, that requests and pleas for assistance by special interest groups were overwhelming. But at the federal level, the requests had increased fivefold.

The new president found that she now needed to get her arms around as many of the domestic issues that plagued the nation as possible. She knew she could not address national security and foreign relations issues with permanent solutions until she had her domestic house under control. She was also aware that her future national security ideas had to be put on hold temporarily. But the time was rapidly approaching when she could wait no longer.

It was now only two months after Christmas 2017; most of the city was again spinning up to normal operating speed. It had been politically shut down for the holidays, lasting almost four weeks.

At this breakfast hour, there was little activity around the entrance to the Russell Senate Office Building facing Constitution Avenue, but traffic was certainly no less than any other day that Congress was in session. Committee staffers and staff assistants to senators who worked in the building were scurrying to their office desks to deal with the unending amounts of paperwork, phone calls, and corporate visits to the bevy of senators who awaited them. The Senate members and their staffers were anxious for agendas, appointments, and activities to be completed as soon as possible so the new year's calendar could be finalized, at least in draft.

The sense of urgency to conduct the nation's business had at least two and probably three levels of importance. One, get the appointments and meetings on the schedule so they could tell the requestor it was finished; two, get the urgent, time-sensitive meetings completed because it was important to their senator's agenda and to the country; and three, finish the meetings so they were no longer on anyone's agenda and day-to-day business could proceed unimpeded by e-mail or telephone harassment.

The Russell Senate Office Building rose three stories above ground on its Constitution Avenue side. On its other sides it rose five stories above ground facing C Street. The architect of the capital deliberately kept any design of the building simple to avoid any detraction from the grand architecture of the Capitol Building. The exterior of the building was lined with a colonnade of Doric columns and faced with white marble and limestone. After many repeated efforts to modernize the building over the years, it had finally been equipped with all of the modern conveniences of central heating, air-conditioning, and ventilation. It had also been outfitted with the latest twenty-first-century real-time satellite surveillance reception. All frequencies of audio and video communications could simultaneously transmit data, both open and secure, and access national archived information. It also had the capability to conduct two-way verbal conferencing communications with political, diplomatic, and national security recipients around the world and in space.

The cornerstone of the building had been laid without fanfare on July 31, 1906, and the building admitted its first occupants on March 5, 1909. Originally, each senator received a suite of two rooms, one for the senator and the other for the senator's personal staff, which included a secretary and a messenger. Each senator's office contained a fireplace and a large window that faced onto the street or the inner courtyard. Consolidation of rooms was ultimately undertaken to make room for committee meeting rooms and a chamber on the third floor. The Senate Caucus Room was set aside for party meetings and larger public hearings. The caucus rooms became the site of some dramatic Senate investigations, including regarding the sinking of the *Titanic* in 1912, the Teapot Dome investigation in 1923, the Army-McCarthy Hearings in 1954, the Watergate investigation in 1973, the impeachment of President William Jefferson Clinton, and later, the investigation into the Blackthorn Conspiracy in 2017.

Because of the building's concrete and marble structure, it lent itself to subdividing entire suites and private subcommittee business meeting rooms into very secure compartments. Over the years the increasingly secretive nature of many meetings had made the Russell Senate Office Building a natural for the location of the sometimes classified meetings of the Senate Armed Services Committee, the SASC, and its subcommittee activities. The committee met regularly in Room 228 in the building.

A companion committee, the Senate Select Committee on Intelligence, the SSCI, also met in regular, secure sessions to evaluate newfound intelligence data and to collaborate with the SASC on decisions that affected the national military force structure needed to counter a specific threat. The SSCI, however, met in Room 211 of the Hart Senate Office Building. The Hart Building also was of a construction that allowed and facilitated the secretive nature of all intelligence-related information that the committee reviewed. For the sake of continuity between these two key committees, many senators served on both committees in an attempt to ensure minimized preparation time for those national security issues that oft-times required quick decisions. The SSCI almost always met in closed-door sessions because of the classification of the agenda items.

Beginning in February 2018, a great deal of time was spent on internal domestic housekeeping issues. There was more to pumping the bilges of the ship of state, and to rebalance the workload to a comfortable center of gravity, than one could imagine. Many executive orders from the previous administration still needed to be rescinded with urgency. Groups of immigrants and citizens in distress needed to be helped with dispatch. Governmental agents such as the border patrol, the U.S. marshall's service, and the Secret Service needed immediate new leadership and mission focus. Revisions to tax laws governing business required revision, recision, or wholesale rewriting to bolster the economy. Foreign relations and national security needs were shredded and lying about the floor in a multitude of governmental agency offices, and the pieces needed to be recovered and restored to assure national sovereignty was again seamless. None of these tasks could be accomplished with a mere wave of the hand. They needed wise, thoughtful, patriotic, and articulate citizen civil servants to restore the nation's laws, pride, self-respect, and will to succeed. All the while, intelligence, surveillance, and reconnaissance continued unabated in a continuous and fruitful stream of pertinent data to talented military and civilian analysts who knew and understood what they were seeing.

While domestic recovery was underway all across the United States and new diplomatic bridges were being built between the United States and all her allies, close attention to global events continued to be monitored for tipoff to potential catastrophic activities. One of those events was the fall and the reconstitution of government effectiveness in French Guiana.

16

New Conquests

Washington, D.C., March 2018

Nearly four months after the safe extraction of the hostages from the tyrant's bunker near Isnard et Priane, French Guiana, there was still mild euphoria among the Senate and House office building staff. Some staffers knew why there was exuberance, but many more did not. But those not in the know were upbeat because those who were in the know were very celebratory. The enthusiasm was contagious, even though many staffers didn't know why the atmosphere was so exhilarating. But not all of the emotion was based on a completely victorious outcome. Yes, the hostages had been extracted without injuries. Yes, the nuclear-tipped missiles had been neutralized. Yes, the mission had gone as clockwork with no friendly casualties. And yes, the operations of the tyrant had been terminated and the command and control of national assets had been returned to the rightful and duly elected government officials.

Those in French Guiana who had come to believe they were doomed and had limited options, actually couldn't believe they were victorious. In point of fact, they still had limited options in the near term but were counseled and briefed rapidly after hostilities. They were informed by U.S. State Department diplomats who acted as a quick response political recovery team under the leadership of seasoned Department of State Assistant Secretary Marcia Vargas, an apolitical civil servant. They were quickly and temporarily placed ashore from the USS *Truman*, so the Guainía president had a small window of opportunity to make things right again in his country. But he and his ministers needed to act quickly, decisively, and with resolve to put their country back on a course of independence, democracy, and fair equivalency if they expected to survive in this new world of vulnerability to predators.

Unfortunately, the tyrant himself and one of two senior officers had somehow miraculously and mysteriously escaped. One of the senior advisors and three junior advisors were in custody and were being interrogated by CIA, DIA, and French DGSE specialists before their extradition to France. Curiously, the interrogators were focused on not only asking questions about tactical and governing policy matters, but also on personal questions about the tyrant himself. Where did he go? How did he escape? Was he warned in advance? With whom did he frequently speak? Who of influence did he know? Did he leave the country? If so, how did he leave? Where was he now? The answers to these questions, if anyone knew, were to be covered behind closed doors. Classified testimony from Phantom Force leaders was scheduled in the committee room of the SASC as preliminary afteraction reports. If the tyrant did indeed escape, the details of how and where he went needed evaluation to see if there was third-nation involvement or if a cover-up was unfolding. The SASC and the HASC needed to take immediate action before the scent of the tyrant's trail grew ice-cold.

Pyongyang, North Korea, and Beijing, China, February 2018

"Mr. Defense Minister General Quan, I am sorry to report that our common operative in French Guiana has failed to achieve his goals," stated Defense Minister General Yang of the DPRK into the private and secure tabletop conference phone on his desk.

Minister General Quan of the People's Republic of China was silent for a brief few seconds. Some of the silence was for dramatic effect in part to show his country's disappointment, and part was to show his personal contempt for the failure of this joint mission with his North Korean counterpart, who, in his personal opinion, was obviously either incompetent or innately stupid. In either case, his instructions were to make the best of every situation that might come from this liaison with his North Korean counterpart. After all, efforts to make any support offered by the United States or its allies to look paltry and insincere would take only a small amount of diplomatic tinkering to make the United States appear incompetent.

The United States had done this repeatedly for the last eight years under an inexperienced and poorly advised president. Heretofore, this was uncharted territory, but now it appeared safe for ambitious nations, large and small, to be militarily adventurous.

He continued, "General Yang, there is no need to proceed further with a description of the events. I have been briefed. What is important now is to ensure that our contact individual there has escaped with his resources and influence lists intact. We should do whatever is necessary to ensure his transit to a friendly nation elsewhere, so that his, ah, relationships remain strictly confidential."

"I understand, Minister General Quan. I will see to it and ensure it occurs without disruption."

"One more thing, Minister General Yang, our counterpart in Russia has indicated an interest in our program of mentoring promising young leaders in emerging nations, especially in the Middle East. I trust you can facilitate the advent of at least one new sponsor of burgeoning programs of national independence around the world."

There was a tone in the voice of the more senior PRC defense minister that made the more junior defense minister become somewhat more humble and a bit uncertain about his own security and the decisions for which he had a responsibility.

"I understand, Minister General. I assure you, any suggestions or participation by Defense Minister Colonel General Vukovich will be welcome and handled with the greatest of care by my security forces. The Democratic People's Republic of Korea welcomes his participation and the donation of pertinent assets." Both men knew this meant money, weapons, and transportation vehicles to ensure designated tyrants would have every opportunity to succeed.

17

After-Action Report

Senate Armed Services Committee, Washington, D.C., March 2018

In the Witness Well of the SASC Committee Room, Rear Admiral Ray Andrews stood quietly talking with the committee chairman, Senator Mark Dorner of Virginia. Colonel J. W. "Bud" Patrick talked in hushed familiarity with Senator Denny Smith of Oregon and Senator Phil Crabtree of Alabama. Patrick knew that Smith was his patron and single most important congressional advocate. Crabtree was his home state senator and college classmate for many years, before they took separate paths for their state and country. Ray and Bud were there to provide classified testimony on the Project TEMPEST activities.

The SASC had not yet been gaveled to order, but as was customary, the members of the committee took a few minutes outside of protocol to informally greet their witnesses, especially when the committee liked and understood their witnesses, and most especially, when the committee endorsed what the witnesses had just accomplished.

With the cordialities and courtesies completed, the meeting took on a more formal and structured air. It was gaveled to order by its chairman, Senator Dorner, a three-term veteran of the Senate. Much of his constituency was related to military and national defense issues that resided in Virginia. Since the Department of Defense, along with certain agencies of the intelligence community and a number of important military installations, also were located in Virginia, Dorner was the natural chairman. Dorner announced, "Would the sergeant-at-arms secure the room for closed session testimony?"

Denny Smith slid into his chair on the SASC dais to the left of the chairman. Denny had met many interesting people in the course of his life, men, women, and children alike. Denny was always graceful and poised. He seemed drawn to individuals whom he found intellectually stimulating or who were involved in professions and skills from which he could gather newfound information. Those he gravitated toward were considered intellectual superstars in their own rights, and he gave them unspoken respect. In return, he was regarded by them as also one to whom respect and civility should be given. These people knew who they were, because Denny always kept an open phone line, and they in turn knew the communications channel could be used to exchange thoughts, ideas, concepts, and constructive criticism. Denny and this circle of professional friends, colleagues, and acquaintances all knew the tie would be severed if a confidence was broken or an uncomplimentary comment was made publicly by any of them. This relationship allowed Denny to make the best-thought-out arguments among his colleagues and allowed his friends to make better professional decisions for their corporations, agencies, or practices.

Since the Senate was ruled by a Republican majority, Senator Smith's background, experience, and congressional ranking made him the perfect choice to be the vice chairman of the full committee, an appointment that was soon to come his way, and chair of the powerful Special Operations Subcommittee. He also served as the vice chair of the equally powerful SSCI.

Denny had spent six years as a freshman, a subordinate and an understudy to many members of the Senate. He had learned how to be humble in the most exclusive gentlemen's and gentlewomen's club in the world. He had endured the flurry of requests for passes to the White House from his constituents and the voluminous requests for him to speak at club luncheons, political action committee meetings, women's and men's clubs, church functions, and an unending stream of cocktail parties in and around the Washington, D.C., area. He resisted most of the invitations with the excuse of "schedule conflicts," when in reality he wanted to focus on a subject in which he strongly believed and which could have a far-reaching influence on the international standing of the United States, and on America's domestic and financial well-being. He took personal interest in and participated on debating panels that dealt with a change in national military strategy. These policy development seminars and think-tank sessions had been grappling with concepts and the effects of how to move forward with a multi-service special operations covert strike force concept.

For the last five years, the full committee, in concert with the full SSCI, had been debating the question of how the United States could avoid being the 911 office of worldwide crises. Until six months ago, the debate had been just that—verbal jousting. The Blackthorn Conspiracy that unfolded in the Middle East and resulted in a major holocaust in lives, antiquities, and valuable cultural treasures and international relationships, now brought the issue to the front and center. The moderate Republican president and first Native-American woman to hold that office had quietly urged members from both political parties and both houses of Congress to address the pros and cons of the options that would significantly and irreversibly change and strengthen the military standing of the United States. The quick and simple answer to the question of how the United States could continue to protect and defend nations of the globe from attack and takeover was that it couldn't. The more complex question was what the United States should do to protect and defend its own global interests, perpetuate its sovereignty, deter adventurous countries from daring to confront the United States, and assist its closest allies. That answer had become politically unsavory and elusive.

Senator Dorner looked to the right and left of the committee and was pleased to see that thirteen of the twenty-three senators were in attendance at the opening. Smith and Crabtree of course were there. But he was also pleased to see Senator Wes Clark from West Virginia, Dick McLeod from Colorado, Matt Kimble from Alaska, Bill Hamada from Hawaii, Fred Shoemaker from New York, Sam Hernandez from Arizona, Brenda Joyce from Tennessee, Sylvia Black from South Carolina, Gill Williams from Texas, and Debbie Gage from Georgia. In all, there were thirteen senators present for this critical meeting.

It was enough for a quorum in the event a decision needed to be made. The agenda was billed as a Forces Status Update. The title was general enough to be just another boring briefing to discuss budget requirements and expenditure of money for routine day-to-day military forces upkeep. The committee members, however, knew this to be a special meeting to summarize what had gone well and what didn't on a well-planned and orchestrated clandestine, covert mission.

Dorner reached up and covered the microphone in front of him to block the recording of his off-the-cuff remarks. He leaned to his left to whisper to Denny Smith, who rose from his seat to approach the chairman to listen and respond so no others could hear. "It looks like everybody wants to be in on this issue and will be choosing sides soon," said Dorner. It was meant both as a social comment and a warning to keep clear mental notes on the implied opinion of each member present.

Denny responded, "I think you're right, Mark. From what I'm hearing, some members have already broached the subject with their constituents and they begin to sense a major base closing and reduction in forces across the country. This is liable to be tough on defense-related production businesses." Dorner nodded affirmatively, and Denny returned to his seat.

Senator Dorner had five witnesses for this morning's testimony, but he let it be known to the Pentagon and the State Department that he really only wanted to hear what three of the witnesses had to say about the mission. One was Rear Admiral Andrews, who was aboard the *Truman* during the mission. The second was U.S. Army Colonel "Bud" Patrick, who was on the ground in the midst of all the lead that was flying through the air. There were two backup military witnesses: Brigadier General William P. Mitchell, U.S. Army, Commander, 2nd Regiment, Special Operations Command, and the other was Brigadier General Oswald O'Malley, USMC, Commander 3rd Regiment, Special Operations Command.

The fifth key witness and the only other witness the committee needed to hear from was Assistant Secretary of State Marcia Vargas, who was responsible for Middle-Eastern affairs. Her job was to follow up military actions with civilian government reconstitution activities to ensure a smooth transition to balanced government operations on behalf of the people of the target nation. So far her actions had put French Guiana back on an even keel, using indigenous political figures and power bases. The committee needed to hear her assessment of what it took in terms of effort and resources to reestablish a legitimate government in a vanquished nation. This was something the president really did not want to become immersed in, but she knew it would be a necessary adjunct to stopping tyrannical activities.

Andrews, Patrick, and Vargas were the key components of the covert operations strategy that was unfolding and could be the model for all future U.S. geopolitical activities. If there was going to be another similar mission elsewhere in the world, Generals Mitchell and O'Malley could be future witnesses before this committee. But the office of Vargas would always be on the hook for cleanup and reconstitution actions.

Denny Smith and Mark Dorner privately and behind closed doors shared the view that the very reason for such missions was in response to the way the world seemed to be politically unraveling. The presence of Andrews and Patrick and their support staff, as well as Secretary Vargas, had been deliberately kept secret and unannounced.

Dorner then began, "Ladies and gentlemen of the committee, today's agenda is for your information. It will address matters of serious and important national security as well as topics relevant to near- and far-term funding for Department of Defense assets and resources. We soon will be considering appropriations for national security forces of the United States and how they can be more efficiently managed to support our country's strategy of deterrence and protection of foreign assets of vital importance to us, and to our friends and allies. I plan to suspend any further remarks in deference to the reports by our special guests, who have status reports on recent military operations."

Senator Dorner then turned to the minority party ranking member in accordance with longstanding protocol and asked, "Does the Ranking Member Senator Blakely from Connecticut have comments for introduction?" Blakely, in whose state the Groton Ship Yards resided, responded, "Mr. Chairman, thank you for recognizing me, but I will defer my remarks at this time in order to hear what our guests have to say."

"Thank you, Mr. Blakely." Dorner said to the other members of the committee, "Ladies and gentlemen of the committee, since all of you have received personal classified briefings on this operation previous to this meeting, I will presume you have already had opportunities to question what occurred. I, therefore, will suspend the usual formality of allowing each member in turn to ask a series of questions and make relevant comments. Instead, I encourage each of you to ask questions that have come up subsequent to your personal briefings as the subject matter requires. Please interrupt the speakers as the occasion arises and ask your questions. Brevity and candor are preferred to ensure that we all have an opportunity to speak if need be and to thoroughly vet the subject."

Senator Dorner then directed his attention to the witness table and said, "Admiral Andrews, would you begin please."

18

Mission Assessment

*Senate Armed Services Committee,
Washington, D.C., March 2018*

Rear Admiral (Lower Half) Raymond Farragut Andrews was a fourth-generation naval officer. As a 1986 graduate of the U.S. Naval Academy in Annapolis, he was a died-in-the-wool professional sailor and had many assignments and commands that prepared him to be where he found himself on this day. He had been a U.S. Navy SEAL and a planner and programmer on the staff of the Chief of Naval Operations, the CNO, in the Pentagon. He had also been a strategic and tactical planner with the Joint Chiefs of Staff, the JSC, and served three commands at sea and two shore commands at installations both in the United States and overseas. Before this current command, he was the naval attaché to Ambassador Brad Williams, who was killed in the Blackthorn raid, and later to Ambassador John Woodard in Tehran, Iran. His background and experience prepared him both to recognize radical Islamic terrorism when he saw it, and to know how to deal with it to prevent it from spreading.

With the entire world changing both politically and militarily, he was now in the right place at the right time to guide the implementation of a new United States strategic plan, intended to save lives and money, and help decide if going to war was going to be justified when and if a decision was required. As the regimental commander of this Phantom unit, he had more than a personal stake in a successful operation. He was a "Plank Owner." In the U.S. Navy, this referred to the planks in the deck and it meant he was one of the original members of the crew when the vessel, in this case the Phantom Force unit, had first been commissioned. He automatically became a member of the original history and heritage of the organization. He knew his actions and those of the unit would result in a strategic counterbalance that would reverberate globally.

Admiral Andrews looked at Senator Dorner and responded by saying, "Thank you, Senator Dorner. I would indeed like to give you my perspectives on how the tactical action unfolded, what items worked well during the action phase, and what few things might need to be changed for future deployments, if they present themselves. I might also offer some perspectives about the force we might need, if we are to move forward faster."

He continued, "In summary, our tactics were sound, our training prepared us for any eventuality, our weapons and equipment were just right for what needed to be done, and the resources we had at our disposal from the navy, army, air force, and the augmentation from our allies and comrades in Canada were appropriate and fully employed. We worked extremely well together.

"Mr. Chairman, ladies and gentlemen of the committee, it was well executed and supported by the national command authorities and by our political leadership. Knowing that President Chenoa, Secretary of State O'Donnell, and the prime minister of Canada were on the line with us every step of the way, and knowing that they had our backs, was reassuring. It was obvious as we got into this that it needed to be done, it was worth the risks, and we hope the payoffs will be evident.

"While training for this assault, we employed the best combination of shoulder-fired and handheld weaponry to ensure we had superior and decisive firepower. We made a few adjustments in the lethality of some weapons to ensure that once they were fired, the enemy could not fire back. Communications connectivity was superlative. Our up-and-down links to overhead assets, intelligence-gathering satellites, and comms to and from the B-2 and B-3 aircraft and to the Ghost Hawk choppers worked perfectly. We had no dropped calls."

There was mild chuckling from the committee, because, to this day, cell phone calls still got sent out into the ethernet or just suddenly were disconnected for no apparent reason.

"The real-time video and night-vision cameras met our expectations, and I'm told that our coverage was as efficient and timely as the coverage of each play in the Super Bowl.

"The tense moments took place during the neutralization of the transporter erector launchers and the short-range nuclear missiles. The closest this nation had ever come to a nuclear exchange in this hemisphere was during the Cuban Missile Crisis in 1963. We were determined not to allow those weapons to be fired and thus create a horrific tragedy. We owe our success in this mission to superior personnel, quality training, and the finest weapons in the world, as well as the expert execution of the operations plan.

"Unless there are questions, I refer you to my detailed remarks submitted in the record and would defer further comments to Colonel Patrick, who was on the ground with our Phantom Force troops and made this operation a success."

Senator Dorner responded, "Thank you, Admiral." He looked to his right and left to see if there were any comments or questions. Senator Smith said, "I have one question, Mr. Chairman. Were there any injuries to our personnel or the hostages?"

"Thank you, Senator, for the question, and I'm sorry I failed to address that topic. The friendly hostages came through the ordeal without any problems. They are a valuable source of intelligence regarding our adversary and the effects of third-world-nation incarceration practices. There was only one minor scrape. Colonel Patrick tripped over a tree root and fell during the extraction. He received a scratch on his forearm. I'm expecting a request any day now for a Purple Heart medal for his injury."

The committee chuckled, and Colonel Patrick's face turned a little red in embarrassment for being so clumsy.

The admiral then said, "Ladies and gentlemen of the committee, I have only one additional comment to offer for your consideration. In 1887, Alexander Tyler, a Scottish history professor at the University of Edinburgh, had some words about the fall of the Athenian Republic two thousand years earlier. And I'm paraphrasing. He said the majority of people in a besieged nation support the candidates who promise the most benefit from the public treasury with the result that the eventual government will collapse over loose fiscal policy and the lack of commonsense oversight. It almost always results in the emergence of a dictatorship. That is what has happened in French Guiana. And I believe it will happen again, somewhere else where our national security interests are at stake.

"I would add that if the forces of reason must go into a country to help with a course correction for that nation, and the chances of success are good, the risks are worth it. The price we must pay to help is low in treasure and blood and less than a massive invasion, then we stand ready to help. But going into a dysfunctional country with the intent of making it functional is not a reason to invade, otherwise we would be faced with another Iraq, Afghanistan, Libya, Brazil, or Syrian situation."

Smith responded, "Thank you, Admiral. Those are some of the central themes that are the basis of what many of us on this committee, and other committees in the Senate, believe can be a possible new United States strategy concerning being the conscience of a troubled world. We can't possibly help everyone while our own interior fabric is being shredded with problems of excessive taxation, crumbling infrastructure, financial inflation, and indecisive oversight of the industries that are the foundation of American ingenuity. The committees will talk more of this soon. Thank you for your sincere concern and your thoughts. I believe we will meet soon for further discussion on these issues."

Denny Smith turned and nodded to his chairman, indicating he was finished with his questions. But he added the observation, "Mr. Chairman, what we are seeing here today is a new paradigm in military strategy. It behooves us all to try to understand both the near- and far-term impacts of these kinds of operations. I would like to address this issue later with the committee still in closed session, with your permission."

His request was granted.

Senator Dorner then said, "Colonel Patrick, the floor is yours. Tell us how the operation unfolded."

Bud said, "Thank you, Mr. Chairman. I have submitted a detailed written copy of our activities for inclusion in the record. So my comments will be selective and will serve to embellish what has already been said.

"We found our adversaries far outmatched and undertrained. They seemed to believe they had more lethality in their hands with the Russian Kalashnikov rifles than was really there. Like most forces in third-world countries, when they are faced with a trained, dedicated, and determined armed adversary, the first thought they have is to turn and run. The army we faced liked having guns and uniforms and enjoyed being respected by farmers and peasants. But against a more formidable opponent, they were ineffective. We were there to fight and win. They were there to maintain the peace and not fight unless they had to. Our mission was clear and just. We prevailed.

"It was almost a shame for us to confront these citizen-soldiers and expect them to fight like a trained army. Yes, they possessed the tools of war, but they were emotionally and logistically ill-equipped to exploit them. While I denigrate the performance of our adversaries in this confrontation, I would not be so boastful to generalize that we are so well trained and they are so poorly trained that they didn't have a chance. No, there were a few instances when an individual soldier would stand his ground and fire back with everything in his arsenal. Their army had a few heroes who were not afraid to die.

"Ladies and gentlemen of the committee, I, my colleagues, my planning staff and soldiers, sailors, airmen, covert ops specialists, and coalition comrades know that sooner or later we will meet a formidable force that is intent on killing all of us, and they may survive to fight again."

There was an eerie silence across the committee chairs. They knew Patrick was right. They each had known for some time that this nation could not dispatch U.S. servicemen to go into harm's way and never suffer casualties. "We were lucky this time. I have been lucky on twelve previous similar missions around the world. I don't know if my 'luck bucket' is bottomless. Time will tell. But for now, we focus on planning, training, rehearsing, and perfecting each of our personal skills. Perhaps being overprepared is the better term. But next time, if there is to be one, and it appears as though there will, no amount of training or preparation can avoid injuries or loss of life on our side.

But everyone knew this time that our cause was just."

Bud went on to say, "Senators, I can't add much about our performance and the manner in which we carried out our mission. It was done with precision, dedication, and professionalism. Any nation that faces our Phantoms is at a distinct disadvantage. We are the good guys, and we all know it.

"Let me say a few words about our primary adversary. General Francois Ricardo De La Plane is a much better politician and soldier than I had given him credit for. His forces were deployed in unusual and unexpected diversionary locations; his command post operations were organized and disciplined; the weapons of the close-in protective forces were of the latest-generation Russian and Chinese caliber; and his escape and evasion procedures seemed well rehearsed. Yes, he got away somehow, this time. His tactics and deployments were reminiscent of Chinese and Russian procedures I have seen before. He has had some very experienced and skillful instructions from somewhere. My sense is that we will see him emerge elsewhere on the South American continent, or in an overseas region of conflict. We know several things about him. We know who his friends are, what nations financed him, what sort of training his soldiers have received, and who he relies upon for support.

"We also have some clues about his personal habits. We know what he likes and dislikes in people, we know some of his more carnal desires, and we know what he likes to eat and drink. On this latter point, we know he likes Remy Martin French Napoleon cognac, very old, very rare, and very expensive. For the record, I found an unopened bottle of this cognac on a table next to the sealed door leading to an escape tunnel in the underground bunker. It was almost like a signal that said he knew we were near, that he would see us again, and that he was toasting us on this victory, but next time we would not be so fortunate."

The Rayburn House Office Building,
Washington, D.C., March 2018.

At 3:00 p.m. that same day, two long blocks away from the Russell Senate Office Building, was the Rayburn House Office Building in which the House Permanent Select Committee on Intelligence, the HPSCI, met on regular dates each month. They were not in session then, but the Subcommittee on Intelligence and Special Operations was meeting. It was chaired by Congresswoman Doolin and was meeting also to hear the testimonies of Admiral Andrews and Colonel Patrick. The subcommittee's goal was the same as that of the SASC, but it was more pointed toward the efficiencies and effectiveness of tactics, equipment, and personnel performance.

The opening statement by the chairwoman was more bellicose than that of her SASC counterpart and more constructively critical, as well.

"Ladies and gentlemen of the subcommittee," she began. "The room is now secure and the testimony we are about to receive and our discussions are classified Top Secret." Each subcommittee person's chair was filled. There were even seven members of the full House Armed Services Committee present who normally would wait for the edited report to reach the full committee. But all the members present wanted to hear the unvarnished and unedited report from the men who had completed the mission.

Congresswoman Rosemary Doolin, chairwoman of the very influential subcommittee, began her opening remarks. "Since April 1972, after a false alarm was called in from an Islamic mosque in New York that was known to be extremist and hostile to the United States, first responders were butchered in an ambush that murdered police and fire officers. The shooters were later confirmed to be terrorist jihadists and faithful practitioners of the basic precepts of Sharia law. In modern recollection, that was the first of sixty-four-plus events between then and 2017 that are either believed to be, or are proven to be, deliberate acts of savagery against the United States. In those events, more than 4,677 Americans have been killed and more than 1,592 have been permanently injured. Tactics by the jihadist terrorists have run the gamut from shootings, to stabbings, to political assassinations, to bombings, to hijackings, to family killings. The point is, members of the subcommittee, Islamic extremist jihadists have been at war with the United States for forty years, and we either didn't recognize it as such, or in our precious Judeo-Christian attitude, we just turned the other cheek. The nature of war has clearly changed.

"Each year since the mid-1970s, the United States has donated aid relief, medical help, educational support, and billions of dollars in aid to countries who have deceived us, whom we politically and militarily supported, and who all this time hated us for what we have and who we are. Over the last several years, we have given Hamas more than four hundred million dollars. They hate us. We have given Russia more than 550 million dollars. Their government hates us. We have even given Mexico, one of our closest neighbors, over 750 million dollars. They have never liked us. We have given Pakistan more than 2.5 billion dollars. They hated us even before we found and killed Osama bin Laden on their territory. We have given the Sudan, Nigeria, Uganda, Ethiopia, Senegal, Iraq, and Tanzania over 6.5 billion dollars over the last five years, and they all immensely dislike us. Yet we continue to buy their friendship in the hope that some small measure of appreciation will be shown to America. They continue to hold us at arm's length with their hands outstretched to receive the cash.

"Unfortunately, there is nothing we could have done about changing their attitudes. We tried to be a good international neighbor and sympathetic to their plights. No matter what we did, however, it was never enough. From now going forward, we can and should find ways to establish common ground and be more deliberate about what we want in exchange for our continuing support. If they decline to offer a quid pro quo, they should look elsewhere for financial handouts.

"I will yield the floor to the minority leader for his opening remarks. Mr. Minority Leader."

"Thank you, Madame Chairwoman. I'm afraid I can't top your comments, so I will defer to you." There were muffled chuckles both in the subcommittee and from the floor.

Rosemary then continued, "We are going to hear testimony today of a classified operation that was approved by the National Command Authority to curtail a direct threat to the national security of the United States. It occurred three weeks ago. It sets the stage for examination and evaluation by all of us, to recommend to the full committee a different force structure and creative use of our national security forces and agencies. I urge each of you to communicate within secure channels your impressions and conclusions to me and the subcommittee so that we can decide how to approach new threats to the United States and its most cherished allies.

"Admiral Andrews, will you proceed, please?"

19

The Aftermath

Downtown Washington, D.C., April 2018

The streets and blocks of downtown Washington were full of reputable restaurants and bars where government workers, Hill staffers, and lobbyists met frequently. They met not only to socialize, but more importantly, to exchange rumors and tidbits of information that might give someone leverage over others.

One block south of Union Station and five blocks west of the Capitol Building was Johnny's Half Shell Restaurant at First and North Capitol Streets. It was an upscale restaurant and bar in the CNN Building that, for practical purposes, had a larger bar area than seated restaurant space. This way, more people could be encouraged to stand around the bar, buy more drinks, and seek out information that might be useful. The place was frequented by many staffers, newspaper reporters, industry moguls, foreign embassy workers, and military attachés.

On this evening in mid-April 2018, Hill staffers began showing up at this and every other bar around Capitol Hill to vent their frustrations with their congressman or congresswoman's operating procedures, or to complain about Senator so-and-so's idiosyncrasies, or more precise, his mistress's. In any case, this was a time to unwind and meet people who had valuable information, or to meet someone who could enhance one's career.

Consuela Vera Cruz was standing at the bar talking with a tall, very good-looking "stud" who had more on his testosterone-energized mind than business. At that moment, a soft-spoken, gentlemanly individual of apparent American-Asian descent walked up to Consuela and said, "Excuse me, aren't you Consuela Vera Cruz? I recognized you from one of your recent visits to our publishing offices."

She was somewhat taken aback by this surprise recognition, but being skilled in American quasi-aggressive business practices oriented to not publicly embarrassing a potential ally, she said, "Why yes, I'm Consuela, and you are from…?"

"I'm Bill Loh from Veritas Publishing Company."

"Oh yes, I was there yesterday morning." She then turned to the stud, who was obviously irritated that his plan for the night had been unceremoniously interrupted, and said in her most gracious business tone, intended to allow her to escape but to also leave the door open to a later liaison if time would permit, "Please excuse me, Stan, but business is calling. I have your card and will be in touch."

She then turned to Bill from Veritas. "Hello, I'm pleased to meet you." She extended her hand.

They shook, and he said, "May we sit at a table in a more private area of the bar?"

They slowly walked to an area to one side of the bar where there was a table covered with a cloth set for two, with a candle and a flower in the center. He assisted her to one of the chairs and took the other for himself. While curious about his intentions and the subject of his presence, she was at the same time comforted that he was quietly aggressive, self-assured, and positive in his remarks and moves. He also seemed to be honest and legitimate. She was curious in a business way, as if he had by his gestures said, *"I have a business proposition for you,"* which was exactly what he had.

His real name was Bong Wang Guanzhong, and he was from an organization she had never heard of—the general staff of the People's Liberation Army, in the People's Republic of China. Bill Loh was a convenient, easily remembered name that she would recognize from a future phone call. She couldn't know this now, but she would never see him again after tonight. She would, however, answer phone calls from him and give detailed reports to him. The generous deposits into her checking account at her chosen Bank of America would reinforce his company's interest in her expertise in recruiting.

He began their casual conversation by exchanging small talk about competitive publishing companies and corporate executives they knew in common. He then began discussing prospects for future opportunities in the worldwide publishing enterprise. He then revealed a program that supposedly had been sponsored by his company that offered two hundred thousand dollars over a two-year period for promising young business executives to study for an all-expense-paid doctoral program in business management in Canada, Venezuela, England, Italy, China, or Egypt. He said she demonstrated the qualifications for such a business executive candidate.

The word *Venezuela* sparked immediate attention by Consuela and evoked memories of home: hillside villages, her mother and father, her Catholic school classmates, and the moderate, non-aggressive climate.

Their first fifteen minutes turned into an hour and a half and four glasses of Duck Pond pinot noir from the state of Oregon. As time went on, it became apparent that "Bill" knew more about Consuela than he had initially revealed.

In the end, he wanted her to remain closely connected to Washington, D.C., to political connections here, and specifically to other bright, up-and-coming candidates for his company's program.

One such person was a young man, approximately the same age as Consuela, who worked in a senator's office on Capitol Hill. "Bill" would arrange for a meeting between them and would periodically seek her opinion about the young man's capabilities to be a candidate for the advanced degree program. She would, of course, not reveal her true motives to this person, and she was encouraged to be as persuasive as she thought necessary to determine his true potential. She also would be handsomely reimbursed for her opinions and evaluations, without needing to reveal details of how she drew him out.

She eagerly agreed. "Bill" thought to himself that she was ideally suited as a candidate for surreptitious extraction of critical information. She was sufficiently quick and bright enough to believe this was a legitimate screening program, but also "ditzy" enough not to know where her information was going. Time would tell.

20

New Challenges

Portland, Oregon, July 2018

Denny Smith was walking down the hill on Southwest First Street in Portland. It was a rainy summer evening. The weather was mild but cloudy and dreary. Congress was in a summer recess. It had been four months since the after-action report to the committees. He had just left his very private two-bedroom condominium apartment at the top of the hill and was headed for a quiet dinner at the Veritable Quandary Restaurant, or the VQ as the locals referred to it, at 1220 Southwest First Avenue, just west of the Hawthorne Bridge. He had liked this small, friendly neighborhood watering hole for many years. He entered the restaurant and was escorted to his usual table, where he sat quietly by himself, at the back of the intimate glass-walled dining room overlooking the outdoor patio. Here he would not be recognized by anyone except the maître de, Fred Martin. Denny had come to know Fred in the last eight years as a person who respected Denny's privacy, but at the same time who wanted Denny to feel comfortable in the solitude of his own thoughts. Fred always gave Denny a table in a far corner against the wall, away from the hustle and bustle of the business crowd that came and went hour after hour. Fred knew Denny always had one Chopin vodka martini before dinner, chilled, and stirred, not shaken with two olives. He also knew Denny would have a glass of Duck Pond pinot noir wine with dinner from their vineyards in Dundee in the Willamette Valley, just south of Portland.

Fred was the maître de's maître de. He watched over his special customers like a mother duck watched over her ducklings. He kept the other waiters away, and if someone said to him, "Is that Denny Smith? Would you introduce me?" Fred always said that Mr. Smith (never "the senator") was waiting for an appointment. He protected Denny's privacy, and Denny knew it. Denny always inquired about Fred's family. He had a mother on Medicare and a daughter with a perpetual eye infection and visual acuity problem. Fred always received a more-than-generous tip at the end of Denny's dinner evening. Fred, of course, was a generous man like Denny, and he placed the tip in the general tips collections that was shared among all the wait staff that evening. Denny knew it but never said anything. This was Fred's domain, and he knew what was best.

This evening Denny sat at his table alone, as usual, reading a ten-page paper by the Heritage Foundation, in Washington, on how to deal with countries who slaughtered their own population for no apparent reasons other than to demonstrate a show of force, to feed the ego of a maniacal would-be dictator, and to try to entice an Asian foreign country to believe they could gain a foothold in the godforsaken wasteland. Denny was starting to lose his appetite.

The article was well written, current, and factual, but it had a desperate attitude about it that screamed, "*SOMEBODY SHOULD DO SOMETHING ABOUT THIS!*"

Denny thought, *You're right, but who? Where is the African Union? Where is the Muslim Brotherhood? Why isn't Islam policing itself to rid it of the barbarians that are giving all of Islam a bad name? Where is the United Nations? Where is Russia? Where is China? Yeah, I know, they're waiting to see who wants weapons and if they have any money to pay for them.*

Those scavengers! Why is it that the people of the world can't see this? Man, oh man! I suppose the phone is going to ring, and the United States is going to answer the nine-one-one call again.

It was a good thing that Denny's thoughts were just that. Most Portland residents, specifically, and many Oregonians in general, were liberals in political persuasion and Democrat in party affiliation. Denny knew he was not elected by a majority of the voters in Portland. The vast numbers of other Oregonians in the east, in the Willamette Valley, along the coast, and in the southern part of the state were strong conservatives who believed in a central government that spent less and left citizens to make their own decisions. Outside of Portland, the state's population worked hard at their jobs, and those in agriculture needed hundreds of temporary aliens to harvest their Oregon crops, but they wanted them to go home when the job was done. These constituents advocated less government spending, and put parenting responsibilities on the backs of wage earners and mothers and fathers. Denny was a true conservative. But he also knew there were some people who simply did not know how to take care of themselves and their families, and they needed help and guidance.

He was about halfway through the paper and his Chopin vodka martini when his cell phone vibrated. Very few people had his personal cell phone number. When it rang, he usually knew who was calling. This time the caller ID said "SAE."

He thought, *I haven't heard from them...her...in some time. I wonder what's up.*

He pressed the Answer button and said, "Hello?"

"Denny, this is Joanie. Are you busy? Can you talk?" It was Joanie Ann-Marie D'Arc, corporate executive and lawyer for the SAE Corporation and an intellectual business confidante to a select few company executives in the United States. Denny knew her information in the past had been accurate and pertinent. She might now have additional data of use to him.

In his usual cryptic manner used to dispose of frivolous conversation, he said, "No and yes. I haven't heard from you in some time. My chief of staff, Jason, did, however, tell me you had left messages with him for me two months ago and again one month ago. I'm very sorry I haven't exactly been accessible. What has SAE gotten you involved with now?"

"Oh, it's just the usual. Profit-and-loss statements, business practices that don't work, employee relations, and international agreements that are more of a hindrance to good business than a benefit. But there are some interesting international events unfolding that seem innocent enough, but are taking on some curious twists. I'd like to discuss it over dinner tomorrow if you're free."

"I'd love to, but I'm having my drink right now. I could gulp it down and catch a cab to wherever you are. By the way, where are you?"

"I'm in my room at the Willard Hotel in downtown Washington."

"Oh," Denny said. "Then it might take me a little longer to get there in a cab. I'm in Portland, Oregon, three thousand miles away from the Willard."

"Oh," Joanie said. "I knew when I left Toronto yesterday and New York this morning I should have called to see if you had plans. I called your office, and Jason simply said you were not in the office. Somehow my intuition told me I needed to ask more questions, but I decided in favor of discretion."

"Joanie, I'm sorry. I haven't talked with you for many weeks, since you were in Washington for the annual Association of the United States Army Convention. I don't get to exchange thoughts and observations with you as much as I would like to. And I would like to do so sometime soon if the opportunity presents itself. There are a number of international imperatives unfolding in the Middle East again that I would like to discuss with you, and there are some national domestic issues emerging here that I would like your views on." She was invariably very well in tune with domestic U.S. and a broad range of international topics.

Denny did indeed enjoy intellectual jousting with Joanie. She always was very well-informed and articulate about her perspective on the impact of foreign events on the United States. She was attractive enough, but Denny never thought of her in a romantic way. Besides, it had been rumored there was a significant other in her life in Paris, and Denny thought it would be considered prying if he broached the subject, so he didn't; and neither did she.

"Maybe it's a carryover of the Independence Day activities, when patriotism is so ebullient, or maybe it's the fleeting moments we have together, but it would definitely be good to get together, even if it's only for lunch. Unfortunately, I have recess appointments with my supporters and constituents in my Portland office over the next two weeks and won't be back in Washington on a regular schedule until after Labor Day. Where will you be then?"

"Hmm, well, I think I'm scheduled to be in Paris for a September strategy development meeting that is expected to take five or six days. After that, I may be back in New York."

"Well, can we connect later in September then? Let's make a plan and try to make it work. I'll talk to Jason and tell him you will be calling. I'll tell him he should make a concerted effort to make our schedules come together. I have a couple of thoughts I'd like to get your opinion about."

"Thank you, Denny. I would like for us to talk. There are also some general joint industry—government professional ideas that have been rattling around in my head I'd like to share with you. I need your opinion."

"Okay, we'll make it happen. Meanwhile, don't be a stranger. Even if you'd just like to say hello, call my cell. You know I'll answer."

"Thanks, Denny. You are a very kind and thoughtful man. I promise I will call."

Denny decided it would be best to set the wheels in motion now, rather than wait till later and risk that some detail would be forgotten. He dialed Jason Foster's cell phone number. The phone rang once. The voice on the other end was Jason, who sounded a little out of breath. That was to be expected late in the evening in Washington, D.C.

"Yes, sir, Senator. Is there something I can help you with?" was Jason's response.

"Yes, Jason. I'm sorry to interrupt, and I know it's three hours later in Washington than it is here. I hope I'm not interrupting anything."

"No sir. I'm out with friends, and we're having a small, quiet celebration of one of my friend's late August birthday. We are just winding down now and will be leaving soon."

"Good, Jason. I hope you're with a really nice young lady who has all the fine tastes of life that you do."

"Yes, sir. We met a few weeks ago, and she and I are very much in tune with one another and like many of the same things. All is well here. How may I help you, Senator?"

"I'll be brief," Denny said in his usual direct and businesslike way. "Ms. D'Arc of SAE Corporation will be calling right after the recess, and I want to ensure you get her scheduled to see me as soon as is practical. I wanted to make sure you knew it before I forgot to tell you. So just file that away, and we'll revisit my spring schedule in a week or so. Anyway, Jason, have a nice week and I wish you the very best of all good things in the coming year. I hope the future is bright for both you and the young lady. By the way, what is her name?"

"Thank you very much, Senator. Her last name is Vera Cruz. She came here from Venezuela a few years ago. I hope all is going well in Portland this month. I know some of your most loyal constituents were anxious to have you back in Portland for a few weeks."

"Thank you, Jason. I'll talk to you soon. Enjoy the rest of your evening."

21

Pushback

Portland, Oregon, August 2018

The private office phone on Denny's desk in his downtown Portland office rang the next morning at 10:00 a.m. He picked up the handset and said, "Good morning, this is Denny."

The voice on the other end was that of Fred Shoemaker, senior senator from New York. Shoemaker was a liberal Democrat but hawkish on national security matters. He was a strong believer in constitutional principles, and bullish on plans and interests of defense contractors across his state and in the successes by each of the military services, especially when they used materiel made by aerospace contractors who resided in New York State.

"Denny, how are you? Are you having good constituency visits? I know I am, and boy, am I getting an earful from my people on defense and economy issues. " Denny knew the disarming tactic of asking about one's well-being was a ploy. He had used it himself. But in Fred's case, he knew there was an agenda item Fred wanted to share with Denny, or that he wanted to test Denny's perseverance.

"Fred, hello, it's nice to hear from you. I am well. Visits with children, grandchildren, and constituents always make time at home memorable. Office work keeps me busy and the problems of my constituents are never-ending. I know you are encountering the same challenges."

"It sounds like we're on the same schedule even though most local public events slow down. But not in politics, I guess. It's cold and rainy here, but family time makes those discomforts insignificant. Listen, I know you're busy, so I'll get straight to the point."

Just as I thought, Denny silently said to himself. *There indeed is a reason for this call.*

Fred continued, "I just wanted to touch base with you about the last SASC meeting. I won't talk details, but I did want you to know that I've spoken to Sylvia Black of South Carolina and Bill Hamada from Hawaii. I think the three of us and possibly six others are in agreement about the long-range national security plans you are advocating for the country. I can't speak to the details of the changes because we have not yet been informed of the full scope and depth of them. But from what I know at this juncture, we all support the national security objectives of the president, but we are concerned about the details. I can't speak just yet for the other six since they are out of pocket for the next few days. But we three have major investments in military service and force sustainment and deployments. In addition, we all have questions about the relevance of Executive Orders 11905 and 12333 on neutralization, which we can't get into on this phone."

Denny knew immediately Fred was making political-speak for "we are making a lot of money in our states from the DOD industry." He also knew the Executive Order references were associated with assassinations, which didn't apply and which the president was expressly strident about and would not violate. Fred was looking for reasons to not do what needed doing. Politicians frequently found reasons to avoid doing things that a simple majority believed was a cause worth fighting for. The citizenry, on the other hand, could assemble a consensus to go ahead and do what needed doing when the crisis required it.

"So far, none of us has seen any real domestic or foreign impetuses to alter the force levels in our states, and in turn, support for the concepts you are advocating for the future," Fred continued.

"I understand completely, Fred. The army, navy, and air force have a significant presence in at least twenty-five states, and another five have very large national security defense contractor sites in them. Debbie Gage from Georgia, Gill Williams from Texas, and Ed Syring from

Florida have similar constituencies in their states, as well. Ed Syring's challenge is particularly daunting. He hosts all the services and an equally diverse set of missions. He supports missile launch operations, drug interdiction in the Gulf, covert operations training, surface and subsurface naval maneuvers, tactical and strategic air operations, and many other activities. He works hard and plays hard. You recall the two-day committee off-site meeting in Gulf Stream, Florida, where we had such vitriolic exchanges on force strengths? But when the day ended, he sat at the piano and played 'Tangerine,' and we all joined in to sing. We were unified.

"He and the others thoroughly understood and accepted that changes in both our military force structure and appropriations must sooner or later be adopted to protect the economic base of the country. But none of those changes should impact readiness and the hardware they use. So far those changes have been non-specific and will remain so until field assessments of requirements and capabilities are proven."

This statement was a risk for Denny to verbalize. If Fred wanted to pursue details on the "field assessments," he might be compelled to reveal what the Phantoms were doing, how they were preparing to conduct covert operations, and he might be forced to cite sources and methods used. This, therefore, was Denny's way of circumventing further details of the force structure changes being contemplated by the president until successes were proven.

"Now, insofar as the Executive Orders are concerned," Denny continued, "we can say on this phone line that nations may act in self-defense, and that in wartime, countries have the right to act against terrorists. I look forward to a debate on the justification for our actions after we reconvene." Fred, then knowing he was lacking some intellectual background on this subject, decided to concede for now on the issue.

Denny then said, "As you know, the defense budget authority for the year 2018 is over five hundred eighty-five billion dollars. And that's without the war costs of the various police actions we have going on around the world. Those add about a billion dollars to those annual figures. It's expected that 2019 expenditures will be five hundred ninety-five billion dollars, or more if we continue on this path. We just simply cannot afford to kick the can down the road and avoid taking some sort of positive action to significantly reduce these expenditures.

"Fred, I know all of us in the Senate have received correspondence from the taxpayers expressing anger at the extravagant spending that is being supported in Washington. We all are concerned that something *must* be done."

"I know, Denny. You've got some persuasive data and cogent arguments put together to support financial investment changes and our country's spending habits. For the record, I'm not averse to listening to your justification. Hell, I'm in agreement on several of the ideas. But the real issue for me and others is that it's a matter of timing and identification of certain resources in our states that makes your ideas a tough sell. But many of my constituents have a major reliance on the military services stationed in my…er, our states. Besides, the chairman of the Joint Chiefs of Staff is a resident of the state of New York, and I'm certain he would not like to see unjustified reductions in any of the services at this time."

"Fred, again, I understand the lay of the land." This was Denny's way of admitting he knew he had a long and difficult argument on his hands. "There are at least forty-five members of the Senate to be convinced that the country is in real financial chaos and can no longer continue to provide foreign aid in the amounts given in the past, and that we cannot finance large-force deployments to countries halfway around the world and keep them there for five to ten years."

Denny, as well as many others in the Senate, also knew there were a bevy of generals and admirals in all the services who liked the status quo of their respective services. And they all knew a reduction in the total numbers of troops would be quickly followed by a reduction in flag rank billets and possible forced retirements.

Denny regarded the discussions with the uniformed services to be a hard fight. But he also knew that once those generals and admirals had their say, they would salute smartly and get behind the secretary of defense and the president, who were already convinced, and they would make it work.

"Fred, I have already spoken to the chairman, Admiral Nagle. He is on board with the concept. In fact, he revealed to me that the services began to examine the Phantom Force concept five years ago because they sensed the financial handwriting on the wall. He also added that such a concept might make span of control and command awareness much easier with a smaller, more flexible, and resilient force."

"Denny, I want to remind you that the three of us and probably as many as eight others face reelection next year, and trying to explain to our voters that there may be fewer troops in their areas, spending valuable dollars, and the possible loss of orders for defense-related products will make reelection very, very difficult."

Aha, Denny thought. *Now we're getting to the core of the problem: reelection.*

"Fred, again I understand. I also appreciate that you are as aware as all the members of the Senate that if we don't do something, the United States will be in the same circumstance as Greece and Portugal. Their unemployment rates are as high as twenty percent in portions of their countries, and the workforce and military services have been reduced to bare minimums to just keep the governments running. The unemployment rate in Oregon is eleven percent, but I'm prepared to be more persuasive about this than I have ever been before."

Fred now took on a more conciliatory tone. "Denny, you have taken on a terrific fight to get the ship of state to make a ninety-degree, or more, turn in national policy. But out of respect for you, I need you to know there are many in both houses of Congress who want to bring this concept to a full stop. At a minimum they will try to amend or delay changes in the forces until a more favorable political climate presents itself."

"Fred, I really appreciate this phone call and your guidance. I really do. But I sincerely believe this country can no longer delay a major change in the way we support our friends and allies and reinforce our policy of not negotiating with tyrants and terrorist-led governments. If we don't confront the issues now and avoid the passive responses that were given in the past eight years, when will we do it? As for amendments to this idea, a lot of us would welcome thoughts on the creation of a homeland infrastructure workforce to identify jobs and increase the production levels for building materials, highway improvements, bridge reconstruction, and many other parts of our economy. Hell, we could re-create the Civil Defense Corps and have wardens on every street corner to keep the peace as we did in the 1940s. That would take the pressure off the active duty forces and the Department of Homeland Security, but even that is not enough.

"Just look at Hiroshima and Nagasaki, Japan," Denny continued. He was getting revved up now. "Most scientists said that after the atomic bomb was dropped, no one could live there for hundreds of years. Just look at South Korea. Everyone said that after the Korean War they would need many generations of support from the community of nations to even begin to be self-sustaining. Now, just sixty years after those cataclysmic events, look at where those nations are. They each began their recoveries by turning their attention inward and lent only a modicum of support to external international priorities until they could afford to do so. There are other foreign policy considerations, as well, and I would like to discuss them with you and the others when the time is appropriate."

"Well, thank you, Denny, for this conversation. I now know how formidable you will be when this idea is ready to hatch. Let's keep the dialogue open, and we'll discuss it more as time goes on. We are both busy, so let's leave this for now and plan to stay in touch as time moves forward."

"Thank you for calling, Fred, and I hope the rest of the summer recess goes well for you. Please say hello to Mary Beth for me."

After hanging up the phone, Denny sat for a moment reflecting on the exchange between the two senators. "So now it begins," he uttered out loud. "I guess I need to turn up the heat on getting my arguments and counterarguments clarified."

He pushed the button on the interoffice communications system and rang Jason Foster's phone in Washington. Jason didn't always travel between Washington and Portland. This time, however, he chose to remain in D.C.; Denny now knew why.

"Yes, sir, Senator." Jason was always respectful of the senator, not just because of the position he occupied, but because he genuinely respected Denny as a person.

Denny replied, "Jason, pull the classified folder on Force Structure Changes please, and call me back. I want to pass you some notes to be incorporated into it. We need to start working on the section entitled 'Rationale'."

U.S. Department of Education, Washington, D.C., August 2018

Consuela Vera Cruz was just leaving the offices of a lower echelon education executive, after conferring on middle school curricula on U.S. history. As she closed the office door behind her and headed down the hall to the elevator, her cell phone rang. She answered, "Hello?"

"Consuela, this is Bill Loh. Can you talk a moment, and are you free at 5:00 p.m. today? I hope the answers are yes."

"Why, hello, Bill. The answers are yes and yes." She liked it when business associates were polite but direct in their interests. She believed a great deal more positive business was conducted when parties were succinct. She judged that Bill believed the same thing based on their previous meeting, which had been direct and to the point, and on the way he sandwiched three thoughts together into two very brief sentences.

"Good. I have a lead on a fellow who comes to me highly recommended as a potential candidate for our international executive training program. I would sincerely appreciate your evaluation and a report back when it's timely for you. His name is Jason Foster, and he plans to be at Hamilton's in the two hundred block of Second Street northwest just off C Street. He'll be there at five o'clock today. Do you know where it is?"

"Yes, I've been there before. The drinks are expensive, but the atmosphere is nice. I'll be there. How will I know him?"

"Good. One of my colleagues was in the DOE a short while ago in a meeting on middle school curricula. He reported on the meeting results. So to check up on our publishing competition, I asked who else was there. He gave me three other names and yours was among them. I took the opportunity to ask how you were dressed so I can pass it to Jason. My representative described you as wearing a dark green dress with a beige business jacket and carrying a soft-sided brown briefcase. Jason will be looking for you, too."

Consuela stopped, looked down at herself, and thought, *Am I that distinctive? If I stand out like that to perfect strangers, I'd better tone down my profile and become a bit less visible, or more transparent.*

"Yes. That's correct. What do I look for in Jason?"

"He's wearing a dark blue business suit with a ridiculously bright fuchsia, turquoise, and yellow necktie with black dots sprinkled on it." They both took a brief moment to chuckle.

"Okay, I have it. I'll call later with a report on both Jason and the necktie. Is this a good number to use between seven and eight p.m.?"

"Yes, it is perfect. I'll await your call."

22

Developments

Al Hudaydah, Republic of Yemen, June 2018

Muhammad Al Yamani looked across the table of abundant food choices at the tall, lean man seated opposite him. The man was tanned and athletic-looking, but he also appeared tired and older than his thirty-eight years. He seemed detached from the present surroundings. Yamani sensed that his guest was disturbed and angry about the events of the last few months. This was obvious by his physical reactions and by the monosyllabic responses to the host's comments; answers such as "yes," "no," "hmm," "oh?" and "right!" were signals to Al Yamani that he should get to the point.

"So, my friend, my sources tell me you and your plans were solid, your intentions honorable, and your support clear-cut from your people. But my sources also tell me you might have been betrayed by members of your own staff and some trusted confidantes."

The tired, bearded man across the table was Francois Ricardo De La Plane, far removed and still smarting from his defeat in French Guiana six months earlier.

"Your sources, my friend Al Yamani, may be correct, but as the last few months have gone by, I have had ample time to review my actions and those of my commanders. Some subordinates failed to double-check action plans; some I trusted to be brave and committed, turned and ran like frightened dogs; and still others immediately surrendered when faced by the surprise force of foreign troops. If I personally failed, it is because I trusted those closest to me too much and failed to imbue them with the fear that Allah would punish them unmercifully if they shirked their duties. I lacked information. I myself would not have escaped had it not been for a last-minute call on my personal cell phone that unknown forces might imminently arrive to stop my activities. As it turned out, they were American military forces who were very well-equipped and even better informed. As I have rolled all the events and preparations over and over through my mind, maybe I didn't have a longer-range, more global view in my mind of where I wanted to go and what other allies could have been better partners in my plans. My world, at that time, was rather narrowly focused on my country, my goals, and the limited capabilities of my potential adversaries to my east and west. I respected the weapons I had at my disposal and did not fear what the opposing forces had for retaliation. I felt invincible."

"I promise you, my friend Francois, I have learned from your misfortune. I very much desire for you to stay here with me in Yemen, to right the wrongs done to my people. I prophesy that my future, and the future of those closest to me, will be very bright. The destiny of my people and those of this region will also be filled with success, happiness, and prosperity. It would be an omen from Allah if you would consent to stand at my side as my closest advisor while I move to change the direction that the drug-crazed, so-called leaders of this country have chosen for us. Loyal experience is difficult to find. I hope you will consent to stay."

"Yamani, my good friend, you embarrass me with your praise. I would like very much to stay awhile, but I fear there may be a stigma attached to my presence since I have failed to save my own country. So, it is I who has much to learn from you. I have come to know a tried-and-true ideology, like that found throughout the Muslim world, though Sharia law has never captured the imagination of the liberal countries of the Western world. They have resisted Sharia, the teachings of Mohammed, the structure of a Taliban or Al Qaida–led government, and strong believers such as you who can bring these teachings to people and liberate them."

Yamani then said, "My friend, Francois, there is no stigma. There is wisdom to be gleaned from your experience. You can be valuable in recognizing paths of strategy we should and should not follow. You know what the Americans and their Western lapdogs can or will do in response to our activities. They are a threat to our cause, and you have learned how to deal with them and are a living example of experiencing their weaknesses. There is good and sufficient reason for you to stay. You have insight into who, among my supposed friends, are not my friends at all. You will be able to see that more clearly from a vantage point distant from my seat of power. Again, I hope you will consent to stay."

De La Plane allowed his gaze to drift toward the window and the palms slowly waving in the soft, warm breeze from off the Red Sea. Al Yamani sensed De La Plane was thinking, evaluating what had been said, and weighing the alternatives. Francois had not given up hope that he would one day return to French Guiana and reclaim his place as a majority land owner and the leader of the caliphate. But he could not see a pathway forward at this time and needed to buy time to gain a constituency to support his future actions, even though they were ill-defined right now.

Though many minutes of silence went by, three years of experiences whisked through Francois's mind and rushed toward a decision that he believed might result in a means to an end.

He said, with a sound of resignation in his voice, "Yes, my friend, Yamani, I will stay for a while. If either you or I detect that my presence is detrimental to your plans and the Cause, then it would be appropriate for me to quietly withdraw. All I require is a place to lay my head, a place to kneel and pray, and a laptop computer to search the world for opinions that are vulnerable to change, and those that intend to seek us out for more information."

Yamani beamed with excitement and approval. "Good. It is settled, then. Yes, your request is wholeheartedly approved. You will become my closest confidante and advisor. Over the next few months, I want you to meet my family members and certain friends who have been fighting the diplomacy, ideas, and emissaries of the Great Satan nations of the Western world. They will come to be as comfortable with you as have I. There are also some other individuals whose ears I have impressed with my plans for the Republic of Yemen and beyond.

"I have a grand design for Yemen and this part of the world. It is my plan not to take this country as my own. It is not my plan to take this region or even the entire Middle East over as my domain. As I am a devout Houthi of the Zaydi Shiite sect, we traditionally do not want or seek complete and total power in our nation. We do, however, demand a religious and unified state in which we share power and influence. We are closely allied with the Shiite forces in Iran. We are becoming stronger and more influential in Yemen and are rapidly supplanting the Saudis as the dominant power in this region. Yemen is a strong country if we can unite all Shiite sects. To allow our people to fragment the country behind the Saudi-led coalition of Sunnis is not in our best interest.

"If the people want singular, stable, anti-Western government, I will give in to the whims of fate and to the grace of Allah on the direction of my destiny. If the public clamors for my leadership, who am I to resist?

"In confidence, my friend, Francois Ricardo, my plan and strategy are narrowly focused…for now, but my vision is global in nature. Ultimately my plan will create a theocracy unmatched by anything the world has yet seen. I can envision a caliphate led by an all-powerful caliph. Your scheme was well intentioned. Here in the Middle East, we are wary of many more variables and human dynamics. Each tribe, country, government, and military force has objectives and resources that can defeat any man's plan to be the singular leader and visionary for all of Allah's people. Let me use a metaphor that flaunts yours and my Western collegiate education. We must play this region of Allah's symphony like an opus from Bach or Beethoven. Every region and every tribe has a significant solo to play, and they want it to be heard. I simply must read the notes of the music and know when to direct allegro and when to direct adagio.

"In my dream of the future, I can see this caliphate will ultimately reach from Pakistan in the east to Morocco and Mauritania and beyond in the west. I plan to direct allegro then. The caliphate will be one all-encompassing nation without international borders. It will not be like the caliphate of the Islamic State, created four years ago, which suffered a slow death because of its timidity. The dreams of my caliphate will subsume the caliphate of the IS and will exist with one religious mind and one political and military purpose. It will be one jihadist nation living in peace with the people of other continents. I would call it the Free Islamic Yamani Empire, or FIYE. Does the name sound too self-indulgent? I believe it must have a familiar name in its title to give it personality, character, and an identity. Our peaceful message will be adopted by nations and cultures as far away as England, Norway, the Americas, China, and Japan. We will make them believe our way is preordained for them and is just. Opposition will not be allowed.

"It is my plan that the best and brightest of Al Qaida, Houthis, Taliban, Islah, Salafist, Boko Haram, Hezbollah, and Hamas will come to me as a safe haven here in western Yemen. I want them to see it as the place to refresh themselves and quietly and deliberately prepare for the jihad on the Western world. In time, I will reveal my plan and my battle cry, which will rally all of Islam around me and embrace Sharia law as the vision for the entire globe. I ask you to bear with me and believe in me. For those who seek to oppose Sharia, the free and diverse cultures of the West are anathema because Islam prohibits diversity in Islamic lands. Only conformity is acceptable.

"I propose we license and encourage anything Sharia permits, and that we forbid and prohibit anything Sharia does not allow. This means we expel or dispose of Western Christian groups and missions. We, of course, should ask them to convert to Islam. The supremacist construction of Sharia, deeply rooted in Muslim Scripture, exhorts Muslims to drive out or kill Westerners even if those Westerners who believe their missions in Islamic countries are for the humanitarian benefit of indigenous Muslims."

Francois listened as Al Yamani spoke. He noticed that as Yamani continued to explain and reveal his goals and visions, his voice increased in pace and volume. Yamani was becoming so excited by the thoughts racing through his mind that Francois knew he was beginning to live his dream, and he was probably implementing facets of the plan now, to take advantage of the indecision and disorganization that had marked regional and cross-border politics for hundreds of years. Francois could see that Yamani believed that he, and only he, was going to bring Yemen and its neighboring countries into the twenty-first century as a unified, fearsome, and if need be, militarily decisive army crusading to eliminate Israel, the United States, Canada, and any other nation that refused to do his bidding. For a brief moment, Francois thought he recognized a Hitlerian megalomania in Yamani's exclamations, which were gradually becoming rantings. Just as suddenly as Yamani's explanations began and built to a bolero-like crescendo, however, they slowed and then stopped.

Al Yamani took a deep breath and said, "You see, my friend, Ricardo, there is much to do, and repeated opportunities for us to move forward have occurred and then vanished. I would like to seize each opportunity as the door is opened."

Francois hesitated for a split second when his friend, Al Yamani, called him "Ricardo." He'd had less of a reaction earlier when Al Yamani called him "Francois Ricardo." It was a bit distracting then. But now it was almost as if Yamani had ceased to recognize Francois as a friend of many years and many eons of religious thinking. But he quickly dismissed it as a fleeting lapse of memory, a scintilla of enthusiasm that pushed all reality aside in expectation of future goals.

Al Yamani continued speaking thoughts of direction the movement would take. "The Americans, the British, the French, and the Israelis, their military forces and their political diplomats fail to grasp events as they confront them. They are hesitant, indecisive, and even reluctant to enforce their own foreign policy plans. They would rather defer to their politicians and ambassadors, who are charged to ask us how much money we need to move forward on programs they have decided we need. Of course, I encourage my so-called political leaders here in Yemen and in our neighboring nations to respond tentatively, apologetically, and even ashamedly when large dollar or Euro amounts are offered to them. The West thinks we are backward and stupid. But I say we are designing and crafty, and they will one day feel the wrath of Allah in a sudden and devastating reprisal that will bring them to their knees, begging for mercy. They will one day find themselves drowning in their own blood."

Al Yamani hesitated for a brief moment and gazed at the sunlight outside the window. It was as if he had a sudden awareness around him that his ranting was being wasted on only this single individual. He seemed to be struck with the thought that he needed a larger, more adoring audience. He took a short, deep breath. Then in what appeared to Francois as recognition that he needed a more thoughtful and calmer tone, Yamani continued, "All that is the grand scheme. But for now, my friend, Francois, the near-term objective is very simple and easy to understand and adopt. I do not covet Yemen at this time, nor do I want to be its president. Neither do I want to be the commanding general of its armed forces."

Francois thought again there was a hint of too much enthusiasm in Al Yamani's voice and actions. He took a quick mental note to be balanced in his suggestions and advice to him. He didn't want to appear critical, but he did not want to appear condescending either. *A critical balance is needed here,* he thought to himself.

"But if the time was right and it was to come to a choice of leaders and the people wanted only me," Al Yamani continued, "if they wanted me to be the standard-bearer of our cause, how could I refuse? The FIYE will be the shield of Allah in this hemisphere.

"Let us take this a phase at a time," Yamani continued. "There are nations who possess technologies, money, and strategies that they are prepared to commit to us. They have clever new explosive devices, new chemical alternatives, they use unmanned aerial drones to give them extended-range vision; they have air-to-surface missiles and new ideas to neutralize civilian airliners belonging to infidels of foreign nations.

"First, all I want is the western part of Yemen that borders the Straits of Hormuz to embrace my visions. I want independence, autonomy, and a friendly, but influential relationship with the Yemeni presidency. As time goes on, you can become a part of this dream of peace and tranquility. I know you will understand this much better than others with poorer insight, as time goes forward."

De La Plane thoughtfully looked at Al Yamani and said, "Your dream is well sketched out, my friend." Francois thought to himself that he needed to tread lightly here and choose words carefully and softly, words that were certainly palatable; because he might have to eat them later.

"If I can be of assistance in fine-tuning some of the features," he said carefully, "I would be pleased to do so. There are some foreign powers that must initially be dealt with rather gingerly. The Americans can be unpredictable. The French like to be enticed with the romance of a long-term close relationship with the Middle East. The British want permanent political agreements that give them a feel of a firm foundation. The Germans, the Russians, the North Koreans, and the Chinese all deal with the Middle East with ulterior motives. They all have a secret shopping list in their pockets, which they share with no one. We must outsmart them. We must always foresee and plan ahead before we seek them out to talk. I think I can help with that aspect of the plan," Francois concluded.

"Good, good, that is excellent," said Al Yamani. "Those kinds of thoughts are exactly what I want from my advisors. But for now, our focus must be on solidifying our ties with our Islamic brothers and neighbors." Then, with a sneer and a slight chuckle of personal delight, Al Yamani said, "An occasional public beheading can always be a persuasive bargaining argument." They both began to chuckle, then laughed energetically out loud.

23

A Eulogy for the West

Al Hudaydah, Republic of Yemen, September 2018

For the last three months, Al Yamani and Francois were seen as inseparable, and they traveled together over the full length and breadth of the country. They were noted taking momentary respites to huddle and quietly discuss matters that appeared to be serious, important, and private. These trips were interspersed with periodic cross-border visits to tribal leaders in Oman, Somalia, Qatar, and the United Arab Emirates. There were single trips to Iran and Iraq with invitations for return visits and promises from Al Yamani that it could be sooner rather than later.

While in Yemen, they traveled frequently northeast to the capital at Saana with stops in towns and villages throughout the region to recruit supporters and advocates. As always, Al Yamani would have a private closed-door conversation with local strongmen, mullahs, chieftains, and police chiefs. He always gave them a gift in a plain, small box of something valuable. Initially, Francois didn't know what the gift was. While en route back to the confines of Al Hudaydah and the security of home, their personal concubines, and the perceived security of Al Yamani's villa fortress, they would discuss plans to expand their "goodwill" tours, as Al Yamani liked to describe them.

When in Sanaa they met with politicians and industrialists alike.

During each visit Yamani presented his host with a more ornately hand-carved box, a bit smaller than a briefcase. The more important the person they visited, the more ornate was the box. After a period of time, Francois didn't need to be curious about the contents. On some occasions he saw what went into them. In some cases, it was a million or more in U.S. hundred-dollar bills. In other cases, it was a million or more of hundred European Euro bills. The amount varied according to the importance of what Al Yamani wanted.

In all, Yamani delivered at least fifty such "gifts" to his hosts, some of whom made no secret that they were loyal to Al Qaida and to some Houthi principals. In the Middle East, all leaders were unabashed in their support for Islam and opposition to the Great Satan. They were less publicly vocal about which sect was paramount in their lives. They would only admit that when someone wanted to take some of their personal property from them.

Before each visit, Yamani would always remark to Francois, "I have spent a few weeks preparing our paths to our host's doors. I want to look them in the eyes and see and hear their commitments of support. When I am before them looking into their hearts and souls, it is impossible for them to lie to me without me knowing it. If later I discover they have been duplicitous, by the grace of Allah, they will cease to exist and could be beheaded. Besides, I always like to offer a gift to influential patrons to ensure I have their promise of fealty and their undivided attention."

Francois knew he had to restrain his thoughts that the progress of takeover traditionally moves slowly; more slowly than he thought was needed for this endeavor. But he dared not question Al Yamani's strategy because this was his turf, these were his people, these were his hallowed grounds. He knew Al Yamani was carefully sowing the seeds of unity and solidarity. But it was a bit too deliberate and too careful for De La Plane's desire for positive results.

In nearly all cases, the recipients never opened the ornately carved boxes, as if they already knew what was inside. Before Francois ever came to this part of the world, he had started to develop a keen sense of judgment about people. He had failed in his judgments about his supporters in French Guiana. But even in that failure, he had learned something. Being here, now, among unsophisticated and unworldly commoners who had not learned the skill to obfuscate, to be devious, and to stretch the truth, he found a fertile ground for analyzing those who would actually support Al Yamani and those who would say they would support him, but have other intentions. The days and weeks honed that judgment to a fine edge. He quickly and accurately became able to determine what an individual thought or might do based on their expressions, gestures, eye movements, and the tilt of their heads.

Without ever describing this private interrogation intuition to Al Yamani or anyone else, Francois closely watched the actions of the recipients who opened the carved wooden boxes, to see if they registered surprise at the contents or opened the boxes based on skepticism. None of them showed surprise. Francois carefully filed away the reactions of those few who, in fact, opened the boxes as potential allies who still needed confirmation before they committed assets to Yamani's yet-to-be-publicized master plan.

Where there was a sense of doubt by the recipient, Al Yamani sweetened the deal with a promise of some new lethal, technical "toy" that the tribal leader could employ to make offers to other tribes and villages that they simply could not refuse. De La Plane regarded all whom they visited as interested, mostly supportive, but in need of additional later persuasion. Mohammed Al Yamani commented to Francois in private, after each meeting where appropriate, that the individual just visited was indeed "on board" and that the host they had just visited would make a good and loyal military general in the master plan. On occasion, he likewise would indicate when a certain leader was not particularly enthused but would have a sincere change of heart in less than a week after a visit by Al Yamani's "cousins." Francois was not convinced this would work, but he was willing to see it employed in practice.

Yamani reminded him that diplomacy required a certain bedside manner. Leadership and action required the ability to strike fear into the hearts of followers. Yamani knew leaders, potentates, tribal chieftains, and self-proclaimed generals in this part of the world could be extremely strong in their beliefs, and hard to sway. But he also knew that the use of certain barbaric reprisals, such as cutting off fingers, toes, feet, or hands, and even a selective head, could be convincing.

Francois never vocally disagreed with Al Yamani, and he certainly was never argumentative in the presence of Yamani with potential allies. De La Plane knew this was a terrific training ground for a benevolent dictator, or even an impatient tyrant.

24

The Education Continues

Al Hudaydah, Republic of Yemen, November 2018

As time and events moved forward, Al Yamani continued to be the teacher and De La Plane the pupil. In many instances during provincial and tribal visits, Al Yamani was both physically and verbally abusive, depending on how obstinately the host responded to the visit. Yamani's contacts, tribal chieftains, political friends, military officers, and general contributors gradually came to anticipate Al Yamani's deportment on arrival and adjusted their responses dependent on the size of the gift he presented. They also became comfortable with having Francois present in both open and sensitive closed discussions.

Among the sensitive conversations that were held, a few included promises of weapons and munitions deliveries to clandestine locations, from unidentified benefactors. Also, a commitment was made of warriors, professionally trained soldiers, and percentages of tangible territories if conflict should break out. Al Yamani was certain conflict would erupt. He was certain because he was going to make it occur.

One visit by a foreign Asian emissary, obviously Chinese, accompanied by a foreign emissary who was obviously North Korean, promised extremely lethal and formidable munitions that would cause massive widespread destruction. A missile delivery system was also promised. It was implied that nuclear and chemical assets could cause a nation or region to quickly capitulate. Of course, cash and technical assistance to further Al Yamani's cause were also offered.

Al Yamani continued Francois's transformation into a recognized advisor. As the weeks progressed, the full scope of Al Yamani's plan to secretly overthrow the current Yemeni regime was complete. The timing was such that everyone knew the present Yemeni leadership would go quietly. At the same time, not so coincidentally, Oman, Qatar, and Bahrain were experiencing uprisings, and certain governing officials in those countries were reported as missing, fleeing, or resigning from their posts. Francois had deduced the components of the plan from the many conversations he witnessed and saw all failures in the governments around the Yemeni peninsula as opportunities for the grand plan to take a more solid form. He offered periodic comments, bits of constructive criticism and suggestions for changes in tactics and strategies. He also became Al Yamani's consultant on matters of international diplomacy and political contacts. As each week and month went by, Al Yamani became more powerful and wealthier. He possessed more sophisticated weaponry and began to show his power to rule and reward those who were committed to him, or to savagely punish those who opposed him. One by one, his detractors and critics began to disappear and failed to arrive for crucial appointments. There was a dark side to Al Yamani's leadership that most never saw. He commanded a small army of secret service assassins recruited from the Dawlat al-Islamiyah fal-Iraq wa al-Shamthat, or DAIISH for short. They were a violent militant arm of the Islamic State, populated by al-Qaeda in Iraq, and they did his bidding when an opponent failed to agree with him.

Francois came to know that a massive exodus of thousands of Yemenis, Omanis, Qataris, and others from the south, the northeast, and west, who had participated in the previous two decades of hostility between the states, did not go unnoticed by Al Yamani's regime. In fact, it was clear Al Yamani saw them as targets of opportunity for recruitment to his side. He was simply waiting for the proper time to strike. He wanted them to be so desperate and demoralized with the current state of affairs that they would welcome the entrance on the scene of a savior, a sympathetic ear, an agent of change—a Messiah.

Those among the Yemenis and neighboring countries who disapproved of Al Yamani's changes suffered reprisals and were silenced before their voices could be heard in public forums. They were annihilated, and not with quiet execution. Many times it was with very public, gruesome displays of brutality.

Fighting in the northwest between the Yemeni government and rebel tribes and jihadist extremists had gone on for more than nine months—and it continued. Minor resistance to all these events of discontent was provided by the Caliphate of the Islamic State, which had been active since 2014. At its creation, then known as the Islamic State of Iraq and the Levant, or ISIL, or its Islamic acronym, DAIISH, it was under the savage, but shortsighted leadership of Abu Bakr al Baghdadi. In Al Yamani's opinion, the DAIISH were doomed to failure; their minimal and sporadic successes were turned to Al Yamani's advantage. Out of fear of the mission of the DAIISH Caliphate to first annihilate domestic resistance from the governments of Syria, Iraq, Iran, Lebanon, and Jordan before confronting the Christian and Jewish infidels, it was marginalized. The very threats espoused by the DAIISH Caliphate drove these Islamic states into an agreement with the United States and other Western nations to cripple the DAIISH with air strikes, ground attacks, curtailment of financial sources, and destruction of their war materials.

Francois conferred with Al Yamani and encouraged him to patiently wait until resistance to his dream diminished. And it did, in a matter of only three months. Government forces did not move without Al Yamani's approval. Houthi rebels, a group seeking a return to traditional Zaydi Islam, had begun more than ten years earlier and resulted in fighting that finally ended with a precarious ceasefire. Public rallies continued off and on for two years, and Al Yamani turned a blind eye to it. He did so because Francois suggested the United Nations was watching and it was politic to appear sympathetic with the rebellion. Globally, human rights took on new meanings as long as demonstrations were peaceful and the demands of the demonstrators were not too militaristic, such as asking the leader to resign and slip away with his tail between his legs.

In the late autumn of 2018, with Francois's strategy design, Yamani was discreetly, separately counseling the warring parties to destroy their tribal opponents. His hope was that they would thereby destroy themselves. Al Yamani's plan was then to step in as the voice of moderation, authority, and reason and automatically be elevated to a preeminent position of political leadership. Unlike De La Plane's strategy in French Guiana, Al Yamani was encouraging the warring parties to tear the present corrupt governments to shreds, aided by subtle and not-so-subtle torture and annihilations that Al Yamani had bought and paid for with his visits earlier in the year.

Years earlier, there had been complaints to the Yemeni and neighboring Omani, United Arab Emirates, and Qatari governments. The complaints were of joblessness, high taxes, conscription of young men in the protective forces, and subjugation of women to Sharia. Restrictions and corruptions became intolerable to the people. Later, some protests resulted in violence and the demonstrations had spread to all the major cities in the Saudi Arabian peninsula and beyond. Over a short period of time, the opposition had hardened its demands and was unifying behind calls for the ouster of the current regimes in each of the countries.

De La Plane knew that most actions behind the changes and reprisals were carried out by the few remaining squads of the Caliphate of the Islamic State. These included Al Qaida terrorist groups, DAIISH butchers, Taliban, Boko Haram, Kurds, Muslim Brotherhood, Islamic Maghreb, Sunnis, rebels from the Islamic Front, Hamas, remnants from Hezbollah, and other ragtag forces. There was no central leadership and no overarching strategy dedicated to supremacy of the Sharia code. These factors had not escaped the sight of Al Yamani, Francois, and the newly created council of advisors to Al Yamani.

Western nations appeared alarmed at the rebellious events in the nations of the Arabian Peninsula, bordered by the Red Sea in the west and the Persian Gulf in the east. They had observed the population's disaffection with their governments but somehow thought they were local disagreements that didn't affect all the nations of the Middle East. Offers of assistance from Western nations went out to governments teetering toward collapse. In fact, Al Yamani remarked to Francois on more than one occasion, "The stupid Westerners, especially the Americans! We have appealed to them that our military forces need counterterrorism and counterinsurgency training. They quickly respond to our requests with advanced weaponry, tactics, money, and advice. They don't seem to have learned that they are giving us inside information that we, in turn, will use against them at every possible future opportunity. We will defeat the infidels with their own methods, money, and equipment."

The Gulf Cooperative Council, or the GCC, in late 2018, in an attempt to mediate the crises all across the southern Saudi peninsula, proposed an agreement in which the presidents or prime ministers of each nation would step down in exchange for immunity from prosecution. Any president's refusal to sign an agreement led to heavy street fighting and his injury or death in an apparent coup attempt. All the regimes in the region called for a single regent or sovereign to be their representative in the community of nations. The dream of a caliphate would soon become a reality.

The UN Security Council passed a resolution calling on all sides to end the violence and complete a power transfer deal. Unfortunately, they could not achieve agreement on a process to monitor and enforce their decree. Al Yamani used this as the catalyst to launch his quiet, unifying diplomacy measures, making himself the only one who continued to have influence in Saudi Peninsula society. With that influence came his promise that he would enforce compliance by all the parties if the council would appoint him the chairman of the Gulf Cooperative Council. They agreed. The participants in the GCC gave him cautious approval with no dissent by any of the members. Neither were there any enthusiastic accolades at this time. Many of them knew Yamani commanded obedience from his relationships, but the price was always high in blood and treasure if the parties reneged.

In the late summer of 2018, beneath all this regional political maneuvering, Al Yamani and De La Plane conducted private negotiations with representatives from Al Qaida, DAIISH, and gentlemen from China and North Korea. The Asians promised more weapons and money in exchange for naval basing rights in the seaports around the coastal shores of the countries around the Arabian Sea.

The Asians also requested territorial grants for the placement of air base construction materials they said were for the commercial access and logistical transport of petroleum drilling equipment. In addition, Mohammed Al Yamani guaranteed he would pave the way for exchange agreements to take effect within sixty days. The negotiating personalities and the perceived payoffs were very familiar to De La Plane. The materiel would be delivered well enough, but the return on the investment was to be profits for the Chinese, the North Koreans, and the Iranians, not the Yemenis. It was intuitively obvious to Francois that the long-term agreements would eventually give the Asian nations exclusive rights to future petroleum and mineral assets. Francois could see a scheme of initial collaboration emerging but also a potential for a conflict in ownership of natural resources. He could see the schemes of the Asians unfolding; Al Yamani apparently couldn't, or wouldn't. Francois chose to say nothing now, but knew there would soon come a day of reckoning when he would have to voice his suspicions.

The reprisals, annihilations, and atrocities continued around the peninsula. Groups of workers and their corporate entities began to be taken over. Ultimately they simply and quietly disappeared. Their former structures gradually became state-owned and state-run entities. The puppet governments in Yemen, Oman, and the UAE feigned authority and control over all internal events. But, in fact, the government agencies did not act without first quietly meeting with Al Yamani and his growing staff of brutal Al Qaida and DAIISH operatives. Of course, Francois was always in the shadows.

It was obvious that Al Yamani, Francois, and a small group of Saudi, Yemeni, and Syrian advisors were financially and strategically inseparable. They jointly shared in the unspoken agreements to rid the peninsula of foreigners who thought of themselves as controlling national government policies. All this was done while accepting monetary aid from well-meaning countries who offered cash to "help" Yamani assist Yemen and its neighbors in remaining democratic. His ties to Al Qaida, DAIISH, Houthi, Salafist, Taliban, and other tribes made him a force to be reckoned with, and a regional threat to the leadership of central and eastern Africa. Of course, he commanded a small army of well-equipped, well-trained soldiers who knew who their benefactor was.

To date, two Germans, three Americans, one Englishman, four Frenchmen, and two Saudi diplomats had been assassinated or taken hostage by "unknown" Yemen or Somali Islamic terrorists—at least "unknown" to the outside world. Three Americans, two Frenchmen and their wives, and four children had been beheaded in very public, televised ceremonies for crimes against Islam. Al Yamani, Francois, and their Al Qaida henchmen took false comfort in believing they were "unknown" to the Middle-Eastern public and to the outside world.

Beijing, China; Pyongyang, North Korea; Moscow, Russia; November 2018

Defense Minister General Quan Ying Mang of the PRC was connected via a secure telephone conference with Defense Minister Alexandrovich Vukovich of Russia and Defense Minister General Yang Dong Phun of the DPRK. All the conferees knew this was a crucial strategy call and that the results of the tactics to be employed in the next few months had to be successful.

The nations of Central Africa and the Middle East were ripe for assisting and leveraging. *Leveraging* was a more palatable term for *exploiting*, and all the persons on the call knew it. They were all on the same wavelength. They all salivated for more footholds in Africa and the Saudi Peninsula, and they all wanted to displace the United States, Britain, Germany, and France as the dominating forces in the area. They believed this was their chance to do so. The Blackthorn incident had failed them. The French Guiana incident had failed them. Now Yemen was the prize on which they had their sights set. They all vowed they would not make the same mistakes with this small, but geographically pivotal nation.

25

Global Unrest

Washington, D.C., November 2018

There were several venerable institutions in the United States. Among the less venerable incidents were the discovery of gold, the history of the discoveries of Lewis and Clark, the east to west railroad, the creation of moonshine, Prohibition, the crimes of Bonnie and Clyde, and others. Among the more elegant institutions were the White House and the Washington and Lincoln Memorials, Arlington Cemetery, Mount Rushmore, the Grand Canyon, and certainly the gentlemen's club of the U.S. Senate. Right behind that was the United States House of Representatives.

The House assembled for the first time in 1789 in New York. It moved to the U.S. Capitol Building in 1807. Invading British forces burned the building in 1814, and it took many years for it to be restored. The Representatives moved into it in 1857 and began running the government from those chambers.

The House's first African American member was elected in 1870. The first Hispanic member was elected in 1877. The first woman came to the chambers in 1917. The first African American woman was elected to the House in 1969, and the first woman to be Speaker of the House took her place in the annals of history in 2007. There have been innumerable "firsts" for the House, and its history is rich in changes, events, and horrific instances when chaos and confusion were the rule of the day. But the House continued to stand.

In previous decades and previous near-term years, House members were to have certainly uttered the words, "The House has never been through anything like this before." Now, in 2018, House members could say the same words and they would be as true now as in years gone by. It is a different place and time; events are as chaotic as they have ever been in the past. Even solutions to challenges appear as elusive now as they have been in the past. This generation of problem-solvers, however, is better-informed than those of the past. They have better educations, more maturity, more means of instantaneous communication, and bright young staffers who are more creative and inventive than their predecessors. After all, they have two hundred years of history and precedence to lean on.

This day begins a new direction for the House. One woman is vested with the mission, the confidence, the political support, and the perseverance to change the direction of the nation. She simply must reach down deeply into her convictions to find the compelling rationale to turn the ship of state ninety degrees to the right.

"The Chair recognizes the Gentlewoman from Florida, for fifteen minutes," said Representative Andrew Wolf from the state of Michigan. He was the designee to be the stand-in Speaker of the House, to maintain decorum and civility for the day.

Congresswoman Rosemary Doolin, from the Seventeenth District of Florida, politely and with the proper protocol acknowledged her recognition. "Thank you, Mr. Speaker. I reserve the right to revise and extend my remarks submitted for the record.

"Mr. Speaker, I have been a member of this august body for more than a decade. I was elected to this position in 2002 and have seen so many policy changes that I can't count them all. I have seen marked changes in White House administrations that have made me fear for the safety of my constituents. I have seen changes in the course of our country that have made me fear for the American people, and many that have made me proud for the oppressed."

Congresswoman Doolin had taken as her sacred mission the personal request from President Sally Marie Chenoa, POTUS 46, along with Senator Denny Smith from the other body, to support a new strategic military direction of the United States that involved a complete reorientation of the strategy for employment of the military forces of the United States. It was now late September 2018. President Chenoa has delivered two State of the Union messages to the Congress in joint session and to the American people. Her message declared that the state of the union was on a firm and steady foundation, but counseled that certain repairs to the nation's infrastructure were essential. So it was appropriate that Rosemary would be asked to speak, since she served on the House of Representatives Armed Services Committee, the HASC, and she was a key member of the House Permanent Select Committee on Intelligence, the HPSCI. She knew what worked, and what didn't.

"My friends and colleagues, I am a Churchillian Republican. The Middle East, like the Russia of the twentieth century, is a riddle wrapped up in a mystery inside an enigma. I say that because of the activities we now see inside Yemen, Somalia, the UEA, Libya, Oman, Syria, Lebanon, Saudi Arabia, and those erupting from mid-Africa. The unrest began in cities, then moved to countries, then consumed regions, and is now on the verge of sweeping across continents. People of these former sovereign states seem to want different destinies. Their discontent is ripe for dictators and tyrants."

There were 221 members of the House out of 435 seated at this point of her presentation. Many were there simply for discussions and votes on off-shore petroleum drilling and tax increase legislation. But prior notice on a national security presentation by the congresswoman from Florida was added to the House agenda, which sparked increased interest. As only a political hack could know, the congresswoman knew something that the other members hungered to know. She was an insider. She knew the president intimately. Things in national security, in economic policy, were changing. If one wanted to be a Washington insider, one needed to be knowledgeable about some important person's thinking. The word was out to the entire junior and median representatives: "Doolin from Florida is on the floor; you'd better be there!"

The other members also had heard rumblings of a Phantom Force that was rumored to be operating out of MacDill Air Force Base, in Doolin's district. It had never been confirmed, but all the members were hoping for some insight that they could turn to their advantage in their own districts. In this respect, they would be disappointed.

Rosemary continued, "In 1848, Thomas Babington, a Whig member of the Parliament in England, a poet and historian, said the experience of many ages proves that men may be ready to fight to the death, and to persecute without pity, for a religion whose creed they do not understand, and whose precepts they habitually disobey.

"We are seeing that in the Middle East now, and it may be coming soon to a community near you. They have a belief that they think should be ours. They have a barbaric attitude that they believe we should adopt here for our women and children. They think beheading, torture, rape, and acceptance of an ideology that is abhorrent to us should be accepted, unequivocally and completely. Certain tyrants and tribal caliphs believe that line of thinking is right and acceptable. Do we want that? *No!* We do not.

"Tyrannical activities are unfolding in the Middle East. We almost saw them come to life in French Guiana. But they were suddenly curtailed, suppressed, and destroyed in place by the coordinated action of our military forces and our highly effective intelligence resources.

"Members and colleagues of the House, World War Three was declared upon the United States of America as long ago as 2001. We initially took restrained action to oppose it. Later administrations, in 2009, chose to ignore the threat, and still later in 2014, the Administration decided that the Atlantic and Pacific Oceans would keep our land safe and pristine. As a result, most Americans think we are at war with no one. But there are forces out there that want the hearts and minds of our people, our children, and our grandchildren. For us to assume the ostrich position with our heads in the sand is unforgivable, reckless, and irresponsible.

"I'm not just standing here suggesting we be irate! I'm saying we should be here advocating a force for good. I'm advocating we have forces that protect us. I'm advocating a streamlined, multi-service military force that is equipped to know the locations of the enemy. I want a force that can spring into action *before* terror strikes us, our embassies, and our allies.

"I'm suggesting that it is up to us to give the men and women of our armed forces the needed strategic agility. They need the benefit of the best tactical thinking, training, education, equipment, and transportation we can offer. They need a realistic budget, goals, and strategies. My friends, it's time for institutional reform and a reevaluation of our force structure, improved capabilities and contingencies, and certainly better intelligence, surveillance, and reconnaissance, or ISR.

"But that strategic agility will not come without your help, your support, and carefully programmed funds. I can assure you the president is behind this concept and so are the joint chiefs of staff. I can assure you we have already begun to address these needs in my subcommittee, and the full HPSCI has it on their agenda for early finalization.

"I am soliciting your support and hope you will offer a favorable vote when this measure comes before the full House for a vote.

"Mr. Speaker, I yield the remainder of my time." With that, Rosemary turned and walked away from the dais and proceeded up the center aisle, intending to return to her office. Representative John Billings from Alabama and Representative Carla Carlson from Nebraska, both members of her subcommittee, awaited her departure from the chamber and arrival in the cloakroom outside the chamber doors.

"That was a fine introduction to the way ahead," said John.

"It was excellent!" Carla acknowledged. She then added, "We've got our work cut out for us. As you were speaking, I was watching the reactions of many of the members on both sides of the aisle." Rosemary, John, and Carla all started toward the elevators that took the members to the basement of the Capitol Building under the House side. They were headed for the underground tunnels that led to the Rayburn Building. Rosemary's offices were in a third-floor office where they could discuss sensitive political and military information in a secure environment.

As they walked through the tunnels toward the basement of the Rayburn Building, Rosemary graciously responded, "Thank you both for your help in putting the remarks together. I sincerely appreciate your support and edits. What was your sense of the members present?"

"Everyone seemed intent on your words and the meanings behind them," noted John. "Not everyone in the chamber is aware of the events unfolding in Yemen and the belligerence being shown around the Red Sea."

Carla interjected, "There are still a number of members who have blindly accepted the jihadist extremist political ideology of the two caliphates that currently rule large portions of territory in that region of the globe."

They reached the Rayburn elevators and pushed the button to the third level. They continued to talk in general terms, exited the elevator on their floor, and headed toward Rosemary's offices, where they could continue to talk in detail about reactions and next steps.

"There is a rumor that another caliphate may soon emerge. Some of our more liberal friends haven't fully accepted that these extremists may be civil when we are all in diplomatic sessions with one another, but they have always regarded us as infidels, and they always will."

"You're right, and that's why I say we have plenty of missionary work ahead of us," observed Rosemary. "There are some troubling events occurring in an increasing number of countries that used to have sovereign borders between them. The incursions across borders, the unrest among the people, and the sadistic activities of certain rebel forces are abhorrent."

They reached Rosemary's suite and proceeded to her secure office to further strategize. Her administrative assistant rose as the members entered.

"Hi, Michelle. Everything went well and no one threw any tomatoes. We'll be in my office for about forty-five minutes. Please hold all my calls for that time. However, if there are any calls for Congressman Billings or Congresswoman Carlson, please announce the calls on my private line so that they can decide if they wish to take them."

Michelle responded, "Yes, ma'am, I will."

They entered and closed the door behind them. The three took seats around the small conference table, and Rosemary began by saying, "I wanted to take some notes on your observations and share my plans on this subject for the next week or so." John and Carla opened their small notepads and in the name of efficiency and time-saving, they made no comments. They, just like Rosemary, had always been businesslike and succinct in their meetings. All three of them found anecdotal experiences and small talk counterproductive and a waste of valuable time when there were decisions to be made or actions to schedule. That was one reason they were so closely linked in sharing congressional business with one another; they shared the same mental rhythms.

Rosemary said, "I resonated with your comments about some members blindly accepting the Middle-Eastern political ideology. In late 1789, Thomas Jefferson and John Adams returned to Washington after a series of political meetings in London. They are said to have remarked that they met Tripoli's Muslim ambassador to England, while trying to negotiate actions to cease attacks on English and American ships by Barbary pirates. They noted that the ambassador spoke of a prophet who followed the teachings of a book called the Koran. They were astounded to hear that the Koran stated that any nation or peoples failing to submit to Islamic authority were sinners and infidels, and it allowed Islam to declare war on those infidels and enslave them, or kill them. It is indeed unfortunate that things have not changed much since 1789. If anything, they have grown worse. Let's get down to the business at hand."

26

Recruiting Report

Atlanta, Georgia, November 2018

"Bill, this is Consuela. I'm in Atlanta on business, and I want to tell you about a person whom I think could be a candidate for the executive training program."

"Great, thanks for calling. I was going to touch base and see when you were returning to Washington. Your reports about the potential of Jason Foster are superlative. Keep them coming. Now, whom are you suggesting?"

"I have been hesitant for several weeks to offer this person's name, because she is a distant relative and is in a position of trust with the government. She is located at MacDill Air Force Base in Tampa, Florida. She has broad management skills and, as near as I can tell, works a number of multitask subjects in a balanced way. Her name is LuAnn Hernandez."

There was a slight silence on Bill's end of the phone. However, it was so imperceptible that only Bill knew it was there. Bill sat at his desk in the embassy of the People's Republic of China in a small, well-appointed office befitting a senior military officer in the PRC. He held the phone to his ear while at the same time quietly turning pages in a folder marked U.S. Special Operations Forces. He turned to a section entitled "Phantoms." He knew the name LuAnn Hernandez from some source, but he had very little data on the subject.

"Well, being a relative of a U.S. government employee does not necessarily exempt one from consideration. In fact, the government teaches its employees certain disciplines and skills that cannot be found anywhere else. Who is she, and what do you think are her qualifications?"

At the same time, Bill sat at his desk thinking he might be on the verge of filling in a solution to a personnel and organizational puzzle that had evaded him and his superiors for some time. He turned to a page entitled *Admiral George Andrews, USN*. The page showed a picture of the admiral acquired from a public media source, along with a biography. The next page showed a picture of Colonel J. W. "Bud" Patrick with a simple biography, also from an open source outlet. The next page was entitled *Administrative Staff*, and it pictured Master Chief Petty Officer Reed Barrett and a fuzzy picture of a woman and a man walking down a street. Bill whispered to himself, *"Kowabonga,"* a central African expression freely translated meaning, *"Holy shit, we may have found an inside contact!"*

Trying not to show too much interest, but enough to encourage Consuela to gather more data, he said, "Why don't you approach her with our follow-on education concept and the financial rewards to make a tentative early commitment and see what she says. If there is reluctance and she appears to be a particularly excellent candidate like you are, maybe we can devise something to entice her further. Please let me know how it works out, and give me a report in a few days. Thank you, Consuela. This is terrific work. You are an especially good catch for us. I have to run to a meeting now, so please call back soon."

Bill looked at a statuette of Buddha on a shelf across his office and reverently bowed his head in a thank-you gesture for seemingly thinking divine intervention had given him the intelligence data he had long been seeking. He then turned to the secure phone on the credenza behind his desk, picked up the receiver, and said, "Get me General Defense Minister Quan." There was a moment of silence. Then someone on the distant end of the call responded. "Mister General Defense Minister Quan, this is Colonel Bong. I have a small bit of good news to report that I hope will please you."

27

Changing Events

Washington, D.C., November 2018

Rear Admiral Ray Andrews and Colonel Bud Patrick opened the outer door to the offices of Senator Denny Smith in the Russell Senate Office Building and entered. The office receptionist and one of the more senior aides to Denny Smith was Julie Wood, seated at the desk in front of the door. Standing next to her at the moment was Jason Foster. She nonchalantly looked up at the two bemedaled military officers and did a quick double-take. The uniforms, the emblems, the brass and braid were a bit intimidating and yet comforting. She immediately recognized them from the office rumors and quiet stories about recent escapades, and she shouldn't have been startled. But seeing them in person was, indeed, momentarily surprising and caused her to take in a slight gasp, which she very carefully disguised. She had been told these mythical, but very real officers were scheduled to see Denny today, but she hadn't been told a time. The admiral and Bud Patrick were exactly on time. She recovered nicely by saying, "Admiral, Colonel, I'll tell the senator you are here."

Jason said, "Good morning, gentlemen. Thank you for being so generous with your limited time."

Julie buzzed the senator's office and said, "Senator, your guests are here. Yes sir, I'll show them in." She stood from her desk and walked to a large oak door on her left, gave two soft knocks, and opened it.

Denny was already on his feet, walking to the open door toward the two officers. He said, "Gentlemen, gentlemen, welcome. I'm very grateful you could take the time to be here for this short discussion." With that, Julie quietly walked backward, pulling the door closed, and latched it.

Denny said, "Ray, Bud, thank you so much for coming." Denny turned slightly to his right and extended his right hand to acknowledge the presence of another person in the room. "I think you have met Congresswoman Rosemary Doolin." The admiral strode forward and extended his hand to her, followed by the colonel.

"Good morning, ma'am. It's always very good to see you," Andrews said. Bud followed and said, "Hello, ma'am. We certainly appreciate everything you do for all of us who reside in the MacDill area."

Rosemary responded with her usual grace, saying, "Good morning, gentlemen. Believe me when I say the pleasure is mine. The services you provide are invaluable and deserving of much more support than you have received thus far. Be assured, Denny and I are continuing to do what is necessary to keep you safe and well equipped to do your jobs."

Denny then stepped forward and said, "Please, gentlemen, be seated. We have some new news to discuss, and I need your opinions. The world as we thought we knew it is rapidly changing, and I want to confer with you two first, since I think the Senate, the House, the White House, and the intelligence community is beginning to process rapidly changing events."

Admiral Andrews responded, "Senator and Congresswoman, the secretary of defense has said we were to be at your beck and call as circumstances dictated. He asked only that we back-brief him quickly when and if it was necessary."

Bud Patrick interjected, "Senator and Ma'am, in earlier meetings we've had with you, we were aware that there were several agendas at work here, and we know we are somehow a part of the scheme of things. The secretary and the chairman have alluded to potential major changes in the way the United States will conduct future strategic business. We know we and our people are part of a team, and we're ready to help wherever we can."

"Thank you both for understanding," Denny said. "Yes, you and your team members are indeed a part of a larger vision that many of us in government know is the right course of action. First, though, I want to assure you that my office is a secure vault for the display and discussion of classified material, up to and including Top Secret Specially Compartmented Information. We have a lot to talk about, and it may take a few more closed-door meetings. For now, let's take this a step at a time. The strategic force changes recommended by the president are classified to protect the concept and the changes from being revealed to our international adversaries. The changes and the force numbers, missions, and equipment employed we will be discussing are code-named Project RESOLUTE. When the time is right, the changes to be adopted will be declassified and implementation will follow thereafter. Any future individual missions that will be conducted, like the raid into French Guiana, which was named Project TEMPEST, will have separate and distinct code names. Our discussion here today will be classified TS-SCI because a new threat has been uncovered that we may have to deal with. I'll get to it in a moment."

Denny continued, "I know I have not told you all that is in the offing for several reasons. One is that the Project RESOLUTE plan needed to be completely developed so that President Chenoa could evaluate, revise, and approve or deny parts or all of it. That step is now complete, and she is in total agreement. The guidance from the president is to go slowly, methodically, and deliberately. She wants us to be sure of our facts and principles. I know I'm still being a little vague, but I'll explain in a moment."

The admiral then said, "Senator, evidently some bits and pieces of the Project RESOLUTE national strategy have leaked out in quiet back-channels at the Pentagon. I have been called to the office of the chief of naval operations and have been asked by the chief to tell him what's going on. Fortunately, I didn't know anything, so I couldn't tell him about any plans."

Bud Patrick then said, "I, too, Senator, have been asked by the army chief of staff the same questions."

"Gentlemen, I sincerely apologize for putting you both in an awkward position with your superiors. While a few in your respective chains of command are aware that Project RESOLUTE involves major military force restructuring, very few know the depth and breadth of the president's plans. Some of the plans are merely the germ of an idea at this point."

Denny then said, as sincerely as he could, "Time and secrecy are imperative. The secretary of defense, the chairman of the JCS, Congresswoman Doolin, and I have been given the green light by the president to proceed with the first phase of a multi-phase program. The first phase seeks to get key military and administration officials onboard with a plan to dramatically downsize the entire national security defense department structure. It is intended to reorient military activities to perform the kind of secret strikes you recently carried out in French Guiana, but on an international basis and when U.S. national security is in jeopardy. For now, those types of missions are to be conducted without warning to most of the administration and certainly without tipping off the target foreign government. You can imagine what the Russians, the Chinese, and the North Koreans would prepare themselves to do if they knew of our intentions. For them to know of any portion of our plans would most certainly be sending you on a suicide mission."

Ray Andrews and Bud Patrick stole quick glances at one another, as if to confirm what they already knew, or at least had guessed, were the changes and the potential future missions.

Ray Andrews said, "So far, Senator, that coincides with what Bud and I have already guessed. So I'm hoping Phase One will inform the necessary service secretaries and respective service chiefs who have some strong preconceived notions about the sizes and force structures of their services. They will not take kindly to reductions in forces of numbers approaching fifty percent without some very cogent factors to support size reductions."

"You're absolutely right, and you should be concerned about all the services in the Pentagon. I'm just as concerned about the members of the Senate and House of Representatives who have large constituencies of defense-related businesses in their states. Premature notices and alerts that something in the way of major reductions in government procurement of materiel could create economic havoc and alarms of concern across the country. Such notices could cause the markets to take a nosedive and sabotage most or all of the president's plans for a strong national recovery of the U.S. economy, which has been just limping along for more than five years."

Denny's voice then took on a different tone, as he shifted to a new but closely related subject. "We have another problem. International events are pulling us in another direction. We have two choices: We can either do nothing, and wait for the desperate nine-one-one call when things have gotten way out of hand. Or, very simply said, we can be proactive. As you know, I chair the SSCI, and my close confidante and colleague, Senator Wes Clark from West Virginia, has identified several intelligence community sources who will be presenting some closely held data about a potential threat to U.S. security. You also know that I, my committee, and a few selected members in the House and Senate collaborate with Assistant Secretary of Defense Mullaney in the DOD. All fifteen members of the committee are expected to attend a meeting. We will be reviewing recently received foreign intelligence that has been filtered through the ASD SO/LIC and the JCS, and will provide a classified recommendation to the Armed Services Committee for relay to the White House and the Secretary of Defense.

"South America is stable—for now. The Project TEMPEST raid into French Guiana got the attention of Jorge Chavez in Venezuela, and he is scaling back both the rhetoric and his active support for revolution in neighboring countries that he learned from his father, Hugo. North Korea and China are still acting out like sibling rivals, but make no mistake: They are collaborating in efforts to trans-ship missiles and munitions to whoever wants to demonstrate resistance to a world order. Iran, Afghanistan, and Pakistan have recently signed what they thought was a secret mutual defense pact, to avoid another Blackthorn Conspiracy. Our friends in Jordan have finally secured the last of the chemical and biological weapons of mass destruction out of Syria that we have found. That little caper has taken five years to complete. I haven't heard yet whether or not we have found all the WMD munitions. I also don't know at this time what is the latest target set of the Islamic State of Iraq and the Levant. We'll know more in a few days, but I have tentative information that they are acting out savagely against other Islamic nations and diplomats from our allied nations."

Denny continued in a matter-of-fact professorial tone, "In spite of the role China is reported to have played in the reconstruction of Iran and the Middle East following the Blackthorn disaster, they continue to surreptitiously and unabashedly infiltrate and hack the lowest to the highest levels of the U.S. and other allied governments. They continue to pilfer and rob us of as many strategies and technologies as they can get away with. Just last week they allegedly stole copies of a new, advanced-design stealth Indian submarine, and they will certainly begin designing countermeasures to thwart it. It's painfully obvious that they plan to emulate American national security strategies by building a second aircraft carrier, to extend the reach of their navy. They are building more bomber aircraft to employ stand-off cruise missile launches. Those aircraft are rumored to reflect the latest stealth and supersonic technologies available. No doubt they stole them from us. They are improving their intercontinental ballistic missile arsenal to give them a first-strike capability. They are slowly but surely moving toward an intercontinental triad strategy, involving long-range aircraft, ICBMs, and missile-equipped submarines that someday will no longer be second to ours. And geographically, as you know, they are encroaching farther and farther into the South China Sea. Their obvious intent is to cordon off that portion of the world to prevent anyone from seeing what they are doing. In addition, as you also probably know, there have been recent close approaches to some of our most sensitive spacecraft by Chinese reconnaissance satellites. It is my view that we are quietly and inexorably heading toward a future confrontation with the Chinese."

Denny sat back in the overstuffed chair in which he was seated and exhaled an audible breath of mild exasperation. He continued, "For now, however, either fortunately or unfortunately, the threats to U.S. national assets and policy are easier to see and to predict. The girth of Africa is suffering from a six-year drought; the countries of Mauritania in the west to Yemen and Oman in the east are disorganized, dysfunctional, and ripe for revolution. They are teetering on bankruptcy; they need food, water, transportation, and infrastructure; but most of all, they seek leadership. Whoever comes along and offers something to those people who have nothing will have an automatic following. To complicate matters, that someone appears to have arrived."

The admiral and Bud Patrick had seen this week's intelligence update from around the world, and they had briefed the entire team at Mac Dill Air Force Base just two days earlier. Since their training and readiness plans were always to be ready to launch on short notice, it paid to remain abreast of where the hotspots were around the globe.

Bud was reminded that he had said on numerous occasions, *"I have never liked intelligence briefings. They never tell me what to do; they only tell me how bad the crisis is. But I go to those briefings anyway. To their credit, they have told me whether I need to pack foot powder for tropical climates, or Muk Luks for the Arctic."*

Now, as Ray and Bud were about to find out, the briefings at Mac Dill had left out some very important facts.

"To avoid boring you with minutia right now and to circumvent telling you something you already know, let me cut to the chase," Denny went on. Both officers sensed what was coming, and a small knot began to grow in each man's stomach; another Phantom strike mission was becoming a necessity and they each knew the cost. Rosemary had already been briefed on what Denny was about to say, one hour earlier.

Denny went on, "In the last six months, one name keeps rising to the top of every list as an influential, Western-educated, charismatic, and well-funded leader in Yemen. He is Mohammed Al Yamani." Denny rose and walked to his desk, where a dark blue canvas satchel with a key-locking zipper latch lay under some papers. It was the standard courier pouch, and it had been delivered earlier that morning from the CIA. Denny took a key from his pocket and opened the pouch. He took out several sheets of classified paper on which had been printed the words *TOP SECRET—Project RAMPART* across the top and bottom of the pages. He handed both Ray and Bud copies of the papers.

"I've taken the liberty of ensuring that the Defense Intelligence Agency has transmitted these pages to each of you, over secure lines, to Mac Dill. They are there now, marked for your eyes only. It is essential that you know now what Rosemary, I, and soon, our committees and the president will know. The detailed background of Muhammad Al Yamani of Yemen, his connections, his financing sources, his atrocities, his weapons caches, and his probable plans are contained in these pages. He needs to be stopped.

"Another more or less interesting fact uncovered by HUMINT sources, depending on one's perspective, is the name of one of his intimate advisors. He is a general, and I use the title loosely, Francois Ricardo De La Plane. Does that ring any bells?"

"Holy shit, er... Excuse my language, ma'am, Senator," Bud said. "But try as we might, we could not uncover where he slipped away to after the French Guiana raid. Nor could we determine how he was alerted to our presence."

Ray Andrews just stared at the data and the photographs in the packet.

Andrews then said, "We gave De La Plane short shrift the last time. We regarded him as just another up-and-coming dictator who was full of himself. We will not underestimate him again. Now, as for our next actions, I think I already know the answer to my next question, Senator, but I will ask it anyway. How would you and the president like for us to proceed?"

"Ray, my answer is, do what you do best. I'm certain official authorization to proceed will be forthcoming within seventy-two hours, and if we're lucky, we'll have thirty days to prepare. Gentlemen, I suggest you mount up, get back to Mac Dill, and await imminent word."

Julie and Jason sensed the meeting was over. They knew not so much by the end of the conversation, but more by the *click* of the door handle as Denny opened the door for the admiral and the colonel.

Andrews and Patrick left as quietly as they had entered. Denny stood in the doorway for a moment as the two Phantoms left.

Jason said, "I hope it went well, Senator. May I assist you with anything?"

"No, Jason, but thank you anyway. There will be more action for us later. By the way, how are things with Ms., ah, Ms. Vera Cruz?"

"Fine, Senator, very fine. Thank you for asking. " Denny knew right away that things were going well, not only by Jason's responses but by his nonverbal actions. He knew instantaneously that Jason was on the verge of confiding in him, on some enthusiastically emotional level, that things were going really, really well. That was TMI for Denny.

"Okay. So all is going well for all of us right now. Let's stay focused on all of our actions and make sure all of our troops continue to have our support."

28

The Next Mission

Mac Dill Air Force Base, Tampa, Florida, November 2018

The admiral and Patrick arrived back at Mac Dill by 1815 hours. One of the perks of being on a special high-priority assignment meant that nearly everything was taken care of, to include assignment of quality personnel, enough resources to complete any task, support from all the services, and transportation—especially transportation. The C-38A flight from Andrews AFB to MacDill was in keeping with the mission priority: nonstop. Lieutenant Colonel "Duke" Westcott and Master Chief Barrett met them when they arrived. During the flight Andrews and Patrick mapped out the near-term training plan, the possible timelines, and an estimate of the resources needed to accomplish this mission. Everything was tentative, of course, in the first stages of mission planning. They both knew the only thing they could count on for certain was change. Before leaving the flight line, Andrews and Patrick briefed Westcott and Barrett on the meetings and probable guidance they would receive. They would convene at 1000 tomorrow, with the entire squadron, and inform them of their tentative plans. Details would follow over the next five days. Project TEMPEST was now history. Project RAMPART was now beginning.

Bud went to the refrigerator in his kitchen and took the bottle of Gilby's Gin out of the freezer compartment, for his martini before dinner. He took his usual ten-ounce martini glass from the cabinet above the sink, wrapped a napkin around the glass, filled it halfway with ice cubes, and placed three queen-sized olives in it on a toothpick. He then filled the glass with frosty, near-frozen Gilby's and sat down in his favorite recliner next to Barbara, or Barb as he preferred to call her, in her matching recliner with a glass of white wine. They both sat for a moment staring at the television program with the volume muted. Another moment went by, and then Barb spoke. "Where to this time, and for how long?"

At the same time, half a world away, Francois De La Plane was just awakening from a fitful two-hour sleep. It was 1:15 a.m. in western Yemen in the village of Al Hudaydah. The town was safe enough; the climate on the coast, and the serenity in the villa one-quarter mile from the beach of the Red Sea, was pleasant enough. The home and its rooms were comfortable, spacious, and safe. The walls of the villa were at least a foot thick. They resisted the cooling effects of the ocean breeze at night, and yet they retained enough warmth from the hot daily sun. The grounds around the large villa were open in all directions for at least fifty yards, giving unobstructed views of anyone who chose to approach. Curiously, there were groundskeepers who worked around the clock, innocently grooming gardens, fence lines, and berms on the landward approach sides, the pathways, and the roads leading to the house. Most curiously, Francois noticed, they were all armed with large, high-powered pistols under their robes. He deduced that they were not groundskeepers at all. The roving small bands of groundskeepers around the facility, twenty-four hours a day, could make a casual walk precarious, to say the least.

The things he had seen evolving were somewhat distressing. He saw chemical and biological weapons and cases and cases of C-4 explosives. He saw nitrates and ingredients for non-metallic explosives. But most distressing was what he did not see. There was little talent and expertise apparently present for handling such sensitive and explosive weaponry. All this unpreparedness kept him awake most nights.

In the nearly six months he had been in Yemen, he had not had a full night's rest. He slept for an hour and a half, then was awake for two hours, then slept for an hour and awakened again. He found himself dozing in twenty-minute segments. He worried almost constantly.

He prayed daily to Allah; he confided in the resident imam that he feared for the lives of Al Yamani and his three wives and family members who resided in this opulent home and compound. He thought often about French Guiana and how he could have missed the signs of traitorous activity, and where he failed to plan or consider shortfalls in his infrastructure.

Occasionally, a fleeting thought about Jesus Christ and his Catholic upbringing went through his mind. He asked himself, *Have I been too quick to condemn? Have I been too quick to compare and decide? Have I moved too fast? Am I happy?* On this last question, he invariably hesitated, then said to himself, *Yes, I am happy! I am alive. I have friends who care for me very much. I am where I am supposed to be.*

Francois believed himself to selectively be a loyal friend and ally. He always tended to judge the intents and commitment of friendships quickly. He believed his ties and bonds with Al Yamani were strong, lasting, and unbridled. And, too, he had the support and understanding of Allah. Two concepts of Islam, however, gave Francois pause. The two concepts were the doctrines of kitman and al-taqiyya. The first was the command to deliberately conceal one's beliefs. It was a clever form of lying, intended to save the devout Islamist from mental or physical injury.

The second doctrine, al-taquiyya, was a form of deliberate lying and deceit in personal conduct, diplomacy, and negotiation. It was preferred mostly in dealings with non-Muslims. But it had its uses in dealing with others of the Muslim faith, as well. Al-taquiyya taught that any ends justify any means, and that included using conspiracy, murder, and treachery to get what the Muslim wanted. Both doctrines were acceptable in the eyes of Allah.

A third doctrine Francois had seen that was less openly discussed was the use of violence, savage liquidation, and physical maiming to command obedience. He had seen this used by Al Yamani on several occasions when he said it was necessary. He had also seen it used with thoughtless abandon by members of the Islamic State caliphate and DAIISH, who were steadily growing in numbers and strength.

Francois had seen his friend Al Yamani use these tools effectively in his negotiations with representatives of adjacent tribes and countries over the last six months. Francois came to recognize when Al Yamani was conceding issues, principles, and territorial gains with plausible reluctance. He sensed, but never commented, that Al Yamani never had any intention of complying with an agreement—he was covered by al-taquiyya.

Because of his strong moral obligation to friends who gave him shelter and sustenance, Francois believed his friend Al Yamani would never subject his longtime friend and brother, De La Plane, to these doctrines—or would he? Nonetheless, he constantly worried that he might fail his friend Al Yamani. He also came to believe that Islam was not an organized national or international religion; it was a political ideology shared by two billion Muslims around the globe. Even though only 10 percent of those were regarded as super-patriots, or extremist, as the Western world preferred to label them, they carried the burden of perpetuating the prophecy of the Koran and would rid the world of infidels and non-believers. Then, and only then, would there be peace in the world.

Francois took heart in the words of the late prophet Al Awaki, an American convert to Islam who had believed in leaderless jihadism—acting alone in performing acts of violence, rather than joining a team effort seeking to inflict greater violence. Francois knew it was forbidden to give one's own interpretation to the words of Allah. Individuals were not to think for themselves. Insights into Allah's words and intent were intended for only the mullahs, the imams, and the ayatollah. Therefore, the frontline of jihadist extremist Muslimism would be fought by those who sacrificed themselves in the name of Allah to achieve perpetual life and happiness. Suicide bombing was regarded, therefore, as the ultimate sacrifice any Muslim could make.

Francois sat in the dim light of the room in front of his personal copy of the Holy Koran, wanting to believe in himself and believe in his friend Al Yamani. He had conceded many months earlier he needed more time to reconcile all these contradictory thoughts and forms of guidance before he could be an unquestioning convert. For now, he would believe in what he could see, feel, and hear that kept him alive. He was convinced his destiny was to emerge as a world leader; he just didn't know yet how it was to come to pass—or where.

It was now 2:00 a.m., and he had just worked his way through chapter 9 of the Holy Koran. He reread the words "to fight and kill the disbelievers wherever you find them." He felt enlightened, somewhat buoyant and optimistic that all would be well.

Suddenly, but very quietly, there was a soft knock on his door. He rose as the door slowly opened and his good friend and brother in Allah peered around the edge. "Francois, may I come in?" Al Yamani quietly said. Francois quickly answered as though relieved to have someone in whom to confide, to break the monotony of the darkness and nighttime silence. "Of course, of course. I'm glad you are here. I have been reading the Holy Koran and am heartened by its words of encouragement and guidance."

Al Yamani said, "Ah, then it is fortuitous that our lives have been synchronized to blend at this coincidental time. It means that we are to be here together, now, in this place, at this moment. I have many things to seek your guidance on and to talk with you about. One thing is to tell you how very happy I am that you are here and that you share our goals and objectives. You have been a valuable strategist, confidante, and loyal brother. I don't know how I can ever repay you."

Francois thought, *Al-taquiyya? No, no, no. It is not possible.*

Yamani continued, "I have brought you a small gift. We all have our individual and unique vices, and I happen to know yours. I am embarrassed enough to not tell you what mine is. But please accept this small token of my appreciation for all the sacrifices you have made." Yamani handed Francois a paper-wrapped package that felt like a bottle. Francois accepted it, unwrapped it, and saw that it was, indeed, a bottle. But not just any bottle. It was a bottle of fifty-year-old Remy-Martin Napoleon cognac, and it brought a rush of fond memories to François's conscious memory. He expressed his profound thanks and set it aside. He said, "Al Yamani, you are more than kind. You are most genteel."

Francois was somewhat humbled by the tribute of the gift and the statement of loyalty from Al Yamani. He thought initially that he was trying to bring him solace after the disaster in French Guiana last year. They reminisced about their college days, the buffoonish professors and the misguided philosophies being taught in universities today. But Francois sensed Al Yamani had more on his mind he wanted to share, so he eased back in his chair, deferring to his friend.

Al Yamani began softly, as if to impress Francois that he was about to relate some of his innermost thoughts and secrets, and also those of the imams and elders of the region. Francois had read that correctly.

"My friend, Francois, I have not been completely forthcoming with you about my plans for this region of the world, and my role in it. I hasten to add that I have not lied to you, but I have not fully explained the plans in detail either. That is because the plans and dreams I shared with you many months ago have been developing for many, many months, and it has taken long hours, days, and weeks of discussion to prepare to make them materialize. There are many countries and tribes involved, and it has been necessary to achieve the proper responses from our brothers in Allah, Saudi Arabia, Somali, Iran, Iraq, the caliphate, and Ethiopia to finalize our efforts."

Francois was excited, thinking that after all the time he had spent assisting Al Yamani in various negotiations and in traveling throughout the Middle East, finally he was going to hear the results of their efforts. He also had the somewhat uneasy feeling that he was to be given a role in forthcoming events that would be key to the success of the plan, but that might not be an event over which he had complete and total control. Nonetheless, he listened intently and enthusiastically. After all, this was his longtime friend, who had given him safety and security, and who had confided in him. Francois sensed he was going to be given a key role in finally organizing this chaotic country and region into a functional, respectable nation.

Al Yamani continued, "My friend, Francois, it was indeed fortuitous that Allah brought us together. I believe you will be pleased that your name and reputation will go down in the annals of history in not only Yemen, but in all of the Middle East. But before I tell you how that will unfold, let me tell you of the plans that are soon to begin.

"For many decades, the United States, England, France, and Germany have had colonial influence in this area of the world. From the very beginning of their arrival in this region, we have resented them. They took our riches, they conscripted our best people, and they subjugated us to their rules and habits and gave us nothing in return. For many decades, our brothers in Allah across this great region have been quietly planning and waiting for the proper time to stand up to them. That time is now at hand."

29

Almost a Security Breach

The United States Senate, November 2018

"Mr. President, I rise to speak to all members of this distinguished body on the subject of the Constitution of the United States of America."

The chair of the president of the full Senate was occupied on this day by the Democrat senator from the state of Mississippi, Senator George Washington Carver Sanders. Senator Sanders was a skilled attorney-at-law, serving his second six-year term in the Senate. He had done this temporary chairmanship duty on five previous occasions, and he enjoyed the sense that he was, in essence, running the country. He didn't aspire to anything greater than his Senate seat from Mississippi, at least for now. But who knew? Maybe someday someone would ask him to fill a cabinet position, perhaps as secretary of housing and urban development, or perhaps vice president; a Supreme Court appointment would also be really great. But for now this job was very rewarding. He enjoyed the power of the chair, and he wielded the gavel of authority with conviction and, in his mind, impartiality.

The senator who had requested and been granted twenty minutes was Denny Smith's good friend and formidable intellectual adversary, Democrat Senator Fred Shoemaker from the state of New York.

Shoemaker continued, "Mr. President and distinguished members of this august body, the Constitution of the United States of America is under assault again, maybe not directly, but certainly indirectly. Attacks come in many forms. If it's not an irritant from the American Civil Liberties Union, it's a disagreement by the libertarians on the right to vote. If it's not an issue with the Atheists of America, it's a disagreement by the evangelicals of the country. If it's not a disagreement by the media across the country about stifling their freedoms in the press, it's about too much data being leaked to the public, which puts the entire nation at risk.

"Well, this time it's an issue with national security—either too much or not enough. The defense spending plan is scheduled to be submitted to Congress as part of the administration's full 2019 budget, on February 13. Prominent in the Chenoa Plan is a renewed focus on Asia, where China's rapid and continued military modernization has worried U.S. national security experts and our allies; on eastern Africa in Sudan, Somalia, and Yemen; and on the critically serious events in the Middle East that never really went away after the Arab Spring in 2011 and 2012, and the Blackthorn Conspiracy in 2017.

"The Pentagon has embraced a proposal by the secretary of defense, the chairman of the joint chiefs of staff, and the chiefs of each of the services that is woefully short of what this great nation needs to support our strength abroad. Even the chief of the multi-services special operations command has submitted only a conservative request for more manpower and equipment for worldwide 'Theater Special Operations Commands,' to strike back wherever threats arise. The administration and the Pentagon claim they need speed, agility, lethality, and instantaneous command and control. Well, I for one have seen the equipment requirements for this force structure and the technology needs, and I believe they fall woefully short in meeting our force projection plans.

"The strengths exhibited by our national security forces have always been, and should continue to be, second to none. But they cannot continue to maintain such status if we continue to whittle away at our defense needs and the abilities of our defense industrial partners to meet the needs of our forces. Why, even my colleagues in South Carolina, Hawaii, and Connecticut have indicated their serious concerns for the preservation of industry in their states. I would imagine that even our colleagues from Georgia, Texas, and California are alarmed by the draw-downs in defense products being ordered by our national security forces in support of the constitutional mandates under which they are operating."

At this point Shoemaker knew he had the support of at least four senators from those first three states, plus his own state of New York, but not all. The other senators from the latter three states still needed to be won over. He could only speculate about those remaining senators would vote. He thought he might be able to capture the one senator from Georgia and maybe one from California. But he needed a few more weeks to spin his political web and recruit a number of others who were more oriented to social issues and less to leaner, meaner, rapid in-and-out force strategies. He believed he had a formidable, winnable argument to support the defense contractors in his state and others who would bring lucrative donations to his reelection campaign. After all, he was a professional politician and lobbying and cajoling was what he did best.

The next part of his address needed to be done more carefully, more delicately. It was directly related to the mission of the Phantom force, and nearly everything they did was not only highly classified, but was specifically related to the national security of the United States and to the "support and defend" clauses of the Constitution.

He began in a slow, deliberate manner, so as to slowly awaken the twenty-two senators who were yawning and waiting for Fred to finish so they could be recognized, and to also alert those senators in their respective offices conducting daily business with constituents and who had Fred and the chamber proceedings on CSPAN-TV in their offices. Some of those senators were "in the know "about the existence and tactics of the Phantom force, and others knew there was another side of the Senate that was concerned with domestic and selected foreign policy issues. But they were not involved in national security problems, and they preferred it to stay that way. Fred Shoemaker was hoping that he might recruit some converts to his ideas to grow the defense industries, or that he might awaken others who might think, *Holy shit, it sounds like he's about to say something we haven't discussed in open session yet. Maybe I should get down there and support Fred, or at least, ask some questions.*

Fred thought he was on a roll, and he internally vacillated between excitement and hesitancy. "There are those in this august body, and indeed, in the other body and in the executive branch who think a more efficient, smaller, less-equipped force can do the job that a three-hundred-ship navy, twenty-two fighter and bomber wings, a seventeen-corps multi-national army can do. Well, I for one am not convinced smaller is better. I think smaller is a lesser number of body bags and fewer regrets and apologies."

Denny Smith's national security legislative assistant was watching the proceedings, and he picked up on the "...smaller is better..." line. He quickly passed a note into Denny's office, through Julie, that "Denny should go to the chamber and be prepared to speak, extemporaneously if necessary." Denny quickly read the hastily scrawled note, put on his suit coat, and headed for the chamber. At the same time, the LA for Debbie Gage from Georgia, who was also "in the know" about possible impending action, graciously excused herself from a meeting of political action committee members and headed for the chamber.

Senator Sanders, who sat in the president's seat and was presiding over what he thought was a routine session, began to yawn and then looked over the rest of the agenda. Many of those thought that what they had to say was of an urgent national priority to convey, or they knew they were facing reelection next year and needed face time for the folks at home. When Sanders heard the words "smaller is better," however, he sensed a stirring in the Senate chamber, and casually but deliberately, he began scanning the chamber for some indication of activity. It wasn't as if he was anticipating activity, but he had a responsibility to preserve decorum—after all, he was impartial, disciplined, and always adhered to the rules of the Senate; he never strayed from the rules and was known as a purist in conducting the business of the most exclusive gentlemen's and gentlewomen's club in the nation. His senses didn't fail him.

"Mr. President, will the gentleman from New York yield five minutes to the gentleman from the state of West Virginia for a parallel and complementary subject?"

One of the twenty-two in the Senate chamber was Senator Wes Clark from West Virginia. He, too, was one of those "in the know" and was fully aware of Project RESOLUTE. He wasn't dozing but had one ear tuned in to what Shoemaker was saying. His other senses were focused on his notes and what he was going to say regarding support to the pay and allowances of government civil service workers and a 2.5 percent pay raise to the military men and women in uniform. He also was a member of the Armed Services Committee; he was aware of the key words "smaller is better" and knew about the Phantom force. When he heard the words "smaller is better," he was one of those who thought, *Holy shit, this guy is about to step on his schwantz and reveal information that is privileged and classified.* That's when he stood to be recognized.

Shoemaker was at the same time startled but relieved. He knew he was probably about to say too much for the record, and for CSPAN, and that he was treading on unverified ground that needed more spade work.

Fred Shoemaker looked up from his prepared remarks and said, "Yes, I will yield five minutes to my good friend and colleague from West Virginia." He slowly retreated to the speaker's chair behind the podium to await the expiration of the five minutes. At the same time, Wes Clark, physically confident, strode to the podium, but intellectually he was not certain what he was exactly going to say. It had to be something to divert Fred's inevitable course away from covert operations and the inquisitive eyes of senators and CSPAN viewers who didn't need to know right now what was going on. Wes was also aware of the curious staffers who thought some added knowledge would make them look good in their offices, and then there were always the investigative reporters always lurking in the hallways looking for the next "Watergate" that could get them a Pulitzer Prize.

Wes knew and believed that the United States had been fighting World War III for many years, since the storming of the American Embassy in Tehran, Iran, in 1979, by Islamic extremists. There were some in the Senate and House who concurred. But not many in the executive or judicial branches of government agreed. He had never had an opportunity to discuss his evidence in a large forum. But now was as good a time as any to address it.

"Mr. President, thank you for concurring in this request to address the senate, and my thanks go to my colleague from New York for affording me this time. I want to concur with and support my good friend and gentleman from New York in the facts he was addressing."

Fred Shoemaker was visibly relieved to actually hear someone say they agreed with him. But he was enough of a veteran of these proceedings to know that there was probably a "however" in the remarks about to be made.

Wes waxed eloquently and succinctly for nearly two minutes about the importance of industry, technology breakthroughs, and the effective employment of weaponry developed by skilled American innovators. He knew Sanders was watching the second hand of the five-minute clock tick away precious time he needed to advocate more industry involvement in national security, but at the same time protect secret operations and not tip off potential adversaries of U.S. intentions.

"In conclusion, Mr. President, I want to remind my colleagues that we have lost four distinguished ambassadors overseas to terrorist activities: one in Afghanistan in 1979, one in Pakistan in 1988, one in Libya in 2012, and one in Iran in 2017. Between 1981 and today there have been more than eighty, *eighty* I say, terrorist attacks on Americans or American property or assets abroad, and in this country, by terrorist extremists. They have been encouraged by dictators, tyrants, and self-appointed despots in various nations who have made it their goals to assassinate Americans and neutralize American technology whenever and wherever they deem it necessary. The battle lines have been redrawn; they are without borders, without rules, and without restraint. Terrorist jihadists believe non-Islamists are infidels. They believe buildings, cities, governments, women, and children are all legitimate targets. They believe beheading Western journalists and aid workers makes them appear strong and unified. They believe any gender, any age suicide bombers are the weapons of choice.

"The nature of global warfare has been changed forever. Single, two, or three terrorists with a high-powered rifle, automatic weapons, or a suicide vest packed with explosives are intended to cause us to cower in fear and capitulate to the threat that they will strike when we least expect it. This form of leaderless jihadism has become the new normal for radical Islam. Therefore, I concur with my distinguished colleague from New York that selective technology, improved surveillance and intelligence techniques, and advanced lethal weaponry are urgently needed. Improved weaponry produced in controlled quantities from our elite American manufacturers is essential to the survival of our American way of life, the protection of our Constitution, and the national security of the United States. Therefore, a thoughtful, measured, and affordable national budget to support our troops and motivate the technical innovative sectors of American industry must be supported. Thank you, Mr. President, and I yield back the remainder of my time."

Fred Shoemaker looked at his watch and then to Senator Sanders, and they concurred in their mutual glances that Senator Clark had used thirty seconds more than his five minutes. Fred concluded that he couldn't have said anything better at this time about support for American industry, but he could only conclude that he wanted more of it for his state of New York. He also felt he might be digging a deeper hole that would be difficult to climb out of later this year. He decided to declare victory and go back to his office interpreting Wes Clark's comments as a consensus from other key members of the Senate. He solemnly thought to himself that he would return later in the month, when he had more ammunition. He rose to face Sanders in the president's seat and simply said, "I yield back the remainder of my time."

As Wes Clark returned to his desk in the chamber, he looked up to see Denny Smith, Debbie Gage, and four other members of the SASC each with a single thumb pointed up. He knew it was a quiet and nonverbal vote of "well done."

30

Deploy—Again

Tampa, Florida, December 2018

Bud Patrick drove to MacDill Air Force Base near Tampa. He enjoyed this five-mile drive because it allowed him to sort out his tasks for the day, and it gave him a few minutes to displace himself from the tactical military missions he faced regularly. At 0515 each morning he also received an encrypted cell phone briefing that lasted anywhere from three to six minutes and included his daily schedule of urgent activities, rendezvous times and places for events, and updates on potential targets the Phantoms were planning to visit at some near-term future time and place. It also gave him a few minutes to relish the drive from home to the base in his 1965 red Ford Mustang convertible that he had completely restored himself. Bud was as precise about his hobbies and personal family projects as he was about his military authorities and operations. So, needless to say, the Mustang ran like a fine Swiss watch.

MacDill Field, as it was called in the late 1930s, was established in 1939 as Southeast Air Base, Tampa. It was eventually named in honor of Colonel Leslie MacDill, who was killed in 1938. A World War I aviator, Colonel MacDill was killed in a crash of his North American BC-1 on November 8, 1938 at Anacostia, in the District of Columbia. During World War I, he commanded an aerial gunnery school in St. Jean de Monte, France. Though the south end of Interlay Peninsula, south of Tampa, was used as a military staging area as early as the Spanish-American War, the land at the end of the peninsula was not formally declared a military installation until it was given to the War Department in 1939, by the state of Florida and Hillsborough County.

MacDill Field was later dedicated as an Army Air Corps installation on April 16, 1941. Since that time it has been the host base for multitudes of bombers, fighters, aerial refueling tankers, and reconnaissance aircraft, and was even considered as the strike base from which aircraft would attack bases in Cuba during the Cuban Missile Crisis in October 1962.

Today the main gate to the entrance of MacDill is a Mediterranean-style stucco-finished gatehouse, perched at the bottom of a traffic circle that hosted two inbound traffic lanes and two outbound lanes. It has a tasteful terra-cotta tile roof with beige stucco-cement walls extending from the right and left of the entranceway. The outward-facing walls are adorned with the military emblems and insignia of the military units located on the base. One of the emblems is the insignia of the Phantom force, but it didn't identify much about the unit unless one looked at the logo very closely and knew military heraldry.

Bud drove through this gate every day he was in town, which was most of the time At this time of day, there were always two airmen on duty to either halt incoming traffic for inspection or to wave through authorized personnel. The airmen rotated duty at the gate at varying times of the day; they all recognized Colonel J. W. Patrick, Phantom force commander and his antique 1965, red Ford Mustang convertible. Bud slowed as he approached the gate and stopped at the gatehouse, as he always did. Airman First Class David Polson snapped to attention, rendered a sharp, snappy salute, and said, "Good morning, Colonel Patrick. How is the 'tang running this morning?"

Bud returned the salute and said, "Good morning, Airman Polson." Bud knew all the guards by their ranks and last names. "Old Betsy is running just fine today. She knows better than to misfire on me. How is your day going to go today?" Bud asked.

Polson responded, "Just fine, sir. Several of us are going scuba-diving later this morning and inspect an old sunken ship beyond the Bay."

"That sounds terrific. I wish I could go along. Watch out for barracuda among the rocks."

"Yes, sir. We'll be careful. Have a great day, sir." And he saluted again. Bud returned it and slowly drove to his office quarters.

Bud walked into the suite of offices occupied by the command and administrative personnel of the unit. There weren't many admin personnel assigned since this was an operational unit that spent nearly all its time training, physical conditioning, practicing marksmanship on the firing range, swimming fully clothed in battle fatigues with small military backpacks and weapon, or practicing parachute or ground assaults on a dummy compound located several miles from the base in a secluded sector; or they were gone, and no one ever knew where they were, as happened during the assault into French Guiana.

Master Chief Barrett was already in the office, making ready to go to weapons qualification at 0715. He was wearing his heavily starched navy battle fatigue, camouflaged uniform. Bud Patrick always wore his army battle fatigue camouflaged uniform when at the Phantom's home base. Each service member wore the battle dress uniform assigned to his individual service. Each was a slightly different color of camouflage to differentiate his service affiliation.

Barrett had been in the navy nearly twenty-nine years and was planning to stay for thirty-five. He had seen service in Granada, Iraq, Afghanistan, and seven SEAL Team assaults in various locations around the globe. He had been to Pakistan, Uganda, Malaysia, North Korea, and now French Guiana. He could handle himself in a fight, and he was an excellent planner and leader. He had served with Bud Patrick for three years and had seen Bud win a hostile hand-to-hand combat fight, led troops in tight battle situations, and save two young enlisted men from certai-death firefights. He saw Bud enter and said, "Good morning, Colonel."

Bud responded, "Good morning, Master Chief, we've got a busy day ahead of us. Is all well at your house, with you and Fran?"

"Yes, sir. She asked this morning if I needed anything laundered. Somehow she knows I may travel soon. How do they know that?"

"I don't know. Barb asked me the other night how long I would be gone this time. All I did was have a drink, sit in my favorite chair, turn on the TV, and mute it. Maybe next time I won't sit in my chair; I'll stand up. They seem to have a sixth sense about world affairs, don't they?"

Barrett chuckled. "What's up this morning, Skipper?" Skipper was a long-respected naval term for "the boss." It was rendered by subordinates in the maritime services for those whom they respected, and to whom they gave unquestioned loyalty. Bud knew that, and in this multi-service unit with a presidential mission priority, he encouraged service and uniform traditions.

Bud answered, "At thirteen hundred hours we'll do our fifth rehearsal assault on Target A from the Zodiac Boats, out in the Bay. We'll walk through the attack on the dwelling, then practice going back to the Bay with stand-in hostages and prepare to board the waiting simulated submarine."

Bud continued to look through the pages attached to a clipboard labeled, *TOP SECRET HOURLY UPDATE*. Bud hesitated a moment, then exhaled a breath that appeared more out of exasperation than submission. Then he continued, "Admiral Andrews has an industry technologist scheduled to be here at ten hundred hours, to show and install a new piece of technology for our snipers. Please get word to Lance Corporal Hall to be here with all three of his M-107 rifles, for refitting, installation, and calibration. This is something new that will give Hall precision from GPS, and video from the new Phantom eye drone aircraft. All this will be visible through his targeting scope. We'll need this new toy in our next mission, and Hall will need to be proficient."

"Aye, aye, sir. I'll ensure that he's here."

31

The Sniper's Girl

MacDill Air Force Base, Tampa, Florida, December 2018

At 0952 hours, Lance Corporal Darrin Hall strode into the headquarters offices and walked up to the reception desk. He was low-key, erect, and proud, and in his starched Marine Corps battle dress uniform. He had three rifle cases over his left shoulder, and he carried an accessories satchel in his right hand full of scopes, day-vision and night-vision devices, and tuning equipment.

The receptionist was LuAnn M. Hernandez. She was twenty-eight years old, tall, shapely, and very attractive with long, strawberry-blond hair that hung down over her shoulders in brushed, loose curls. She had a bright, friendly smile, blue-green eyes that made constant contact with those whom she was talking to, making them feel she was intent on and genuinely interested in their inquiry and their problem. She had been in this position for three years, and she knew each of the "Ghosts" well, but not personally. She knows much of the content of their unclassified records. She knew their hometowns, where they trained, what decorations they had earned, when they were wounded, and whether they were single or married. But all of their individual accomplishments since being assigned to the Phantom force were classified and not discussed in their personnel records. Instead, those records were secured in a *Top Secret* vault and only a few people had access. Luann was not one of them.

She was pleased to occasionally see team members in the office to handle routine administrative matters. Then she could associate a name with a face. She had been single since she left South America eight years earlier. She had earned an associate of arts degree in business administration, and she spoke fluent English, Spanish, French, and German. She had worked for Shell Oil Company in Texas, as a program administration assistant in the international business sector, before learning of a need for administrative support specialists at a federal government facility in Florida. She interviewed for the job, was hired, and three months later was granted a *secret* security clearance. Her work record showed nothing but punctuality, expertise, skill in interpersonal relations, and success as a translator of the written and spoken word. With less than a year on the job, she had become an integral part of the small staff that coordinated logistic and travel arrangements for team activities. She never knew where the team was going or when, but she planned the movement of pre-positioned assets for use by the team at least two weeks in advance of the team's D-Day—Deployment Day. Sometimes she became aware of a midpoint stopover and had to make arrangements for overnight stays or access to meals and showering facilities. It was in those instances that she became exposed to deployment factors that sometimes included dates or a code-named maneuver. No force member's name was ever mentioned in these *secret*-level orders, and locations were always code-named site Alpha, Bravo, or Charlie. At other times they might simply be numbered as Site 1, 2, or 3. The who, what, when, and where data were always contained in Top Secret Code Word orders handled through encrypted channels to a limited number of recipients.

No one knew much about Luann Hernandez or her past family ties, but she maintained occasional contact with a cousin somewhere in South America. Once she was granted her security clearance and welcomed into the Phantom force front office, no one ever pried into her family ties or her life outside the office.

"Ma'am, I'm here to see the colonel and the master chief." LuAnn looked up into piercing green eyes. There was an instant connection, and the mood seemed to immediately soften, become less structured, and take on a friendlier, personal tone, when LuAnn said, "Well, hi.

You must be Lance Corporal Hall. I'm Lu Ann, and I'm so glad to finally meet you. And please don't call me ma'am. I'm too young to be saddled with that name."

She extended her hand, Hall extended his, and they stood there for what seemed like an eternity, but it was only about three or four seconds that they spent holding each other's hands. Darrin stood ramrod straight. He was the consummate professional marine, very military in thought and deed. He was always polite and proper. He was always cool under fire and used to spending incessant hours on the firing range, where he invariably would go through two thousand rounds of ammunition a week to perfect his skill. But something inside him melted a bit in this meeting with Luann. She, too, saw and felt a sense of magnetism toward this man, something she had neither felt nor seen in any other man who had crossed her path.

Hall finally broke the awkward silence and said, "I was ordered by the master chief to be here now with my equipment. Umm, I've been here several times before and have never seen you. Are you new?"

"Goodness, no. I've been here for almost three years, but I frequently run errands for the office, or pick up visitors at the flight line, or do filing of records in the admin filing room. But I've never seen you in here before either."

Then Hall, who was normally guarded, deliberately low-key, and very military, spontaneously said, "Well, I am normally in assault training or on the firing range and don't make it to the headquarters unless I'm ordered to be here. Umm, by any chance are you available sometime, for coffee or lunch? I mean, do you sometimes have a free hour in the day to get out of the office?"

Luann also was a dedicated professional and seldom had personal or social dates. There had never been any permanent man in her life, and certainly no romantic involvement. But somehow she knew and felt that this man, and this moment, was different. She said, "Well, yes. Today or tomorrow are good for me."

"Okay, then. Maybe when I finish here we can talk about—"

From down a short hallway behind Luann came the commanding voice of Master Chief Barrett. "Hall, let's move out!"

"Yes, sir, Master Chief," Darrin said in a loud voice. Then he whispered to Luann, "I'll see you in about two hours or so."

For the next three weeks Luann and Darrin spoke on the phone nearly every day. Between daily periods of assault training, firing range exercises, physical conditioning, and classified session briefings, Luann and Darrin managed a coffee hour or a late afternoon snack. Hall never revealed the Phantoms were in training and preparation for a deployment. Even if he had, Luann would never have mentioned to anyone anything she might have suspected or known.

Luann spoke once in this three-week period on her cell phone with her cousin Consuela Vera Cruz in South America, who was in Peru on business. Luann told her cousin she had met a wonderful young man who was a United States Marine; who, she lied, was in an inconsequential specialty. She believed she needed to protect his role in whatever mission the Phantoms were involved. Luann did, in fact, know that Hall was a special rifleman, but she didn't know what that entailed. Neither he, nor his records, discussed what he actually did for the team. She lamented to her cousin Consuela that she would have liked to spend more time with Darrin, but that he was in what was called "Intense Familiarization Training," or IFT, and sometimes went away for two to three days at a time. They were readying for some kind of inspection or short trip somewhere, right now. With that, the two began discussing Consuela's career, and her own relationships that seemed interesting.

Consuela revealed to LuAnn that she, too, had met a wonderful young man in Washington, D.C.

"He's bright, he's well educated, he's got responsible employment, and I think he loves me."

"Consuela, that's wonderful! I hope one day soon we all can get together and share our mutual good fortune."

"I hope so, too, LuAnn. He's so good to me, and he is so excited when we get together every other week or so. Our work schedules are so restrictive, but I hope it will not always be so."

They also talked about relatives in Venezuela, French Guiana, and events in South America. They both wished they could participate in the happy holiday ceremonies that occurred in South America, but not frequently enough in the aggressive business atmosphere of the United States.

As time went on, Luann and Darrin yearned to be with one another more frequently and with as much regularity as their busy schedules would allow. They came to know each other intimately, and became dedicated to one another exclusively. But they seldom discussed work; when they did, they never talked specifics.

The day that made a permanent difference in their lives came ten days before the end of December. Luann and Darrin had gone out for pizza, and they returned to her apartment in the early evening. It was a small two-bedroom apartment on the second floor of a three-story building situated on a low hill in the western part of Tampa, less than six miles from MacDill. It was quiet in that neighborhood, and most apartments had small balconies that allowed views of parts of the city, but what was best was its view of the spectacular sunsets over the Gulf of Mexico.

They sat in a love seat side by side as the golden disc of the setting sun just touched the horizon of the earth. The wind was calm, the temperature was warm, and the mood was mellow. They held hands and made small talk.

"The pizza was good. I like the mild, white mozzarella and Venezuelan gonzo cheese they put on it. The black olives and sage-flavored sausage they used was good, too," she said.

"It was good, but being with you made it especially a pleasant meal and a wonderful evening. I hate for our times together to end. But I must admit, after being with you, the next morning and afterward is always easier to face," Darrin replied.

Luann leaned over and kissed his cheek, and he was at the same time flattered and a little flustered. No one had ever made him feel so important and needed before. He turned and kissed her lips with a tenderness he knew he could show if the right person brought it out in him. She was the right person.

32

Consensus

Mac Dill Air Force Base; the Atlantic; the Mediterranean Sea; January 2019

The time was now 0300. The gunmetal-gray MC-130J Super Hercules had arrived at Mac Dill Air Force Base the night before at 2130 hours, with three air crews on board. It had been serviced and refueled with 10,724 gallons of fuel. It was then rolled into a hangar on the flight line, away from the prying eyes of seemingly innocent visitors to the base and out of view of Chinese and Russian imaging and infrared detection satellites overhead. It was outfitted with twenty thousand pounds of cargo that included ammunition for hand-carried weapons, medical supplies, eight Zodiac boats with attached outboard motors all wrapped in 1,000-pound para-droppable bundles, and rations for up to ten days for forty personnel. It was then declared ready for the 9,500-mile flight to a special rendezvous in the Mediterranean.

Four days earlier, the aircraft carrier USS *Harry S. Truman* had departed the U.S. naval base at Norfolk, Virginia, on what had been advertised as a routine rotational mission to the Middle East, to replace the aircraft carrier USS *George H. W. Bush*, in the Gulf of Aden. The *Truman* was accompanied by two destroyers and one oil tanker, and it was to be followed in transit overhead by three joint stars command and control E-8Cs on rotational flight plans, which would sequentially relieve one another on the 11,000-mile voyage. Each aircraft was equipped with an MS-177 camera to provide real-time visual target data, side-to-side and forward-to-back, as events unfolded. The flotilla was under constant surveillance for its entire voyage. Once on station, it would resort to autonomous control. Then, along with its own support vessels and those left behind by the *George H. W. Bush*, it would become the seven-hundred-pound gorilla in the area. But for now, it was destined for the Mediterranean Sea with planned passage through the Suez Canal, into the Red Sea, past the Straits of Hormuz, and into the Gulf of Aden. This was not only the best and most efficient navigational route to the Gulf to relieve the *George H. W. Bush*, but it was the best route to show the American flag and to quietly say that the U.S. was not shrinking from its responsibilities in the Middle East. It also was the best route for a special, unpublicized rendezvous off the south coast of Italy.

At the same time, but with no fanfare at all, the nuclear-powered Virginia class, fast attack submarine USS *Montana*, SSGN 795, was deployed. It was equipped with 154 tomahawk guided cruise missiles, two collapsible-winged UAVs, and a bevy of sophisticated communications gear that could serve as a forward-deployed command and control center. It also had a special pressurized cargo blister built onto the spine of the submarine filled with covert operations assault equipment, inflatable Zodiac attack boats, medical supplies, and weapons. It was quietly being temporarily redeployed from the South China Sea to a point six miles off the north coast of the Seychelles Islands in the Indian Ocean. The *Truman* and the *Montana* would later rendezvous in the Red Sea, near the Straits of Hormuz, as the carrier was preparing to exit and as the submarine was entering.

Bud Patrick arrived at the flight line hangar where the Super Herc was secured only two minutes before the three covered six-bys carrying twenty-four members of the elite Phantom force ghost soldiers. They had all trained in secret for four weeks together in a scenario that simulated a large, multi-roomed, two-story stucco-covered building located somewhere in the Middle East. It was a seventy-five-foot-long building that faced the north and was aligned between two other sets of buildings oriented north and south. One faced east and the other faced west. In all, the buildings, for practice purposes, were arranged exactly like the buildings in the target area; they were in a U-shaped configuration nearly three-quarters of a mile from a large circular arrangement of in-ground structures that looked curiously like missile silos. The actual target was specifically located in Al Hudaydah, Yemen, on the coast of the Red Sea, but none of them knew that at this moment.

Bud, the admiral, the master chief, and a few selected members of the Senate, the House of Representatives, the DOD, the CIA, the DNI, and of course, the president knew where this two-story house was located. Unbeknownst to the inhabitants of this dwelling at this time, it was under constant surveillance from a high-altitude RQ-170 Sentinel, stealth-drone aircraft and a pass overhead in low earth orbit every ninety minutes by the Air Force's secret X-37B orbiting intel collector. When the X-37B was not overhead, there was an image intelligence Guardian spacecraft flying by at 310 kilometers' altitude. Both the *Truman* battle group and the Al Yamadi house near the Red Sea coast, in Al Hudaydah, were in each sensor's coverage.

Muhammad Al Yamani, Francois De La Plane, and even the Russians and Chinese didn't know the United States was secretly monitoring every phone call, trip to the marketplace, visit to local tribal locations, conferences at the Al Hudaydah compound, and tribesman visits to Al Yamani's fortress. Many among Al Yamani's advisors suspected that someone was monitoring their moves and conversations from within, and they thought there was an infiltrator, a mole, or a traitor who had been talking to the infidels in exchange for money or safety guarantees.

One week earlier, Francois and his mentor and confidante, Muhammad Al Yamani, were engaged in a respectful but heated disagreement about atrocities committed by Al Yamani's jihadist forces.

"My friend, Francois, my plan here in Al Hudaydah is to create a new state for all of Islam. It begins with a new caliphate. We cannot advance our cause in our war against the UK, France, all of western Europe, and the United States if we cannot convince our brothers in arms here in Yemen, Iraq, Iran, Afghanistan, Somalia, Oman, Syria, Egypt, and Pakistan that our cause is just, well funded, carefully thought through, and requires unswerving loyalty for what Allah wants us to do, if we do not make examples of tribesmen and infidels who oppose us. Hence, as you have noticed, our friends from North Korea have provided us with medium-range ballistic missiles and appropriate small-yield nuclear warheads. I have also created an underground, hardened command post and control center near the missiles that I know our adversaries can see. Since they can see them, they know we are serious, formidable, and a force to be reckoned with. Are not the over flights of drones and incursions by covert operations soldiers not enough to convince us we should redouble our diligence to defeat the satanic efforts of the Western infidels? They see us and they fear us! They want, no, they demand that we cease and desist for the good of international peace. They want us to consent to occupation and submission. No! I will not do so. We have come too far in preparing for war, and I will not wilt under Western threats of serious reprisals."

"Al Yamani, I do not question your motives and strategic goals. I agree with and support you. But I have learned in my beloved French Guiana that the actions of the so-called superpowers will show no mercy in persuading us to alter our goals. They have no vision of what is best for us. But we cannot continue to mercilessly slaughter hundreds of our own people just to prove a point. Our brothers, Al Assad in Syria, Quaddaffi in Libya, Mubarak of the Muslim Brotherhood in Egypt, Abdullah Ben Mushini in Mali, Abu Al Asiri in Sudan, and many others since 2012 and 2015 have learned that message the hard way."

"Ah, but Francois, we cannot lead if we lose sight of the goal. Likewise, our people will not follow if they do not fear us. I have worked many, many months to persuade and bring the tribes from all of Saana, Shabwah, Abtan, Al Jawf, and the Hadramawat provinces into our fold. They gave me their solemn vow they would follow when Allah decreed it was time to do so. Many responded to our call, but some did not. Those who didn't were publicly beheaded for breaking their promises. We have even had to venture east into Oman, north into Saudi Arabia, across the Red Sea to Eritrea, Ethiopia, and Somalia to show them we are serious. They have acquiesced to our plan. They are now committed to us. They have committed people and treasure to us. We are now prepared to make offers to Riyadh, Cairo, Khartoum, and Addis Ababa to create a united nation of Islam."

"My friend and brother in arms, Al Yamani, I have seen this attitude before. We have beaten their bodies into submission, but I fear we have not yet captured their minds. We have sent quiet Al Qaida armies and crazy warriors from the Islamic State caliphate into their countries in the name of Allah and world peace, but I sense they are not convinced. We have given them no assurance of future rewards other than the hope of seventy-two virgins in the hereafter. We have also not convinced them that we are going to create a great Islamic nation, of which you will be the caliph and grand Imam. These are great and wonderful goals, but the groundwork is incomplete. All we have done is bring worldwide notice upon ourselves that the methods we use are atrocities. We have killed forty thousand citizens who have disagreed with us or have intellectually or physically opposed us. The world has noticed. You and I have been noticed and branded as opportunists and leaders, yes; but also butcher-sadists and demons who will stop at nothing to achieve our conquest. Our Muslim brothers in Turkey, Iraq, Iran, and Afghanistan have internal turbulence and can be counted on for little support. Our Omani brothers to the east and our Somali brothers in the west are weak and have indecisive leadership. Our Turkish brothers in the north value their NATO ties as much as their allegiance to you. My friend, our power base is, at best, uncertain right now. We need just a little more time."

Francois continued, "Al Yamani, if we do not stand down for a short period of time, even just for three months, to assess our victories, evaluate our failures, implant our own loyalists in each of these countries, our tactics and our goals will surely not be met and we will fail our Islamic jihadist brothers. Or worse, the infidels from the West will send forces to oppose us. I guarantee, if they do, they will strike without warning and with decisive firepower, much greater than we can repel. They will appear among us as ghosts. They will come quietly and without warning and destroy all that you have built, in an instant. We must reconsider and reassess our plans now, for at least a month. I beg you!"

Al Yamani sat back in his chair and thought for a long moment before he spoke in slow, measured tones.

"My brother, Francois, I understand what you have said. Further, I believe that much of what you say is sage advice. But I have established a timetable for many events. Those events and the actions to energize those events have been completed or are nearly complete. Too much has been started and too many events have been set in motion for us to slow our pace now. We may not have agreement from selected leaders in all the countries you cite. But the people, military generals, tribes, political parties, and religious societies have committed to me. I think we are on sound footing. Now it is time for you to play your role for our cause that will be the keystone to our success."

"Yes, of course. I will do anything you ask."

"Yes, I know you will. A grand diversion is required to make the Great Satan look back instead of forward. I want you to go to Riyadh, Saudi Arabia, to the American embassy there and attend an evening social event on the tenth of next month. The ambassadors to the United States, England, France, and Germany will all be in attendance. I have already arranged for your credentials and your unquestioned attendance. Only five of us know of this plan. Under your clothing you will be wearing a new, undetectable vest design of massive explosives that will take all the lives within a radius of seventy-five meters of you."

Francois visibly inhaled in surprise.

It was now 1630 hours this same January at MacDill Air Force Base, Florida. LuAnn Hernandez was straightening up the papers and printed forms on her desk, preparing to go home at the five o'clock hour. She took a quick glance at a small photo in an obscure corner of her desk. It was a picture taken at a happy moment, weeks earlier, of she and Darrin Hall holding each other and smiling at the camera. A subtle, happy expression came over her face as she remembered the place and the moment the photo was taken. She also remembered that Darrin had told her last night that he was going to be involved in some special training for a week or so and would call her when he returned. She had come to realize that the words "call when I return" meant that a telephone would not be available to him for a few days. She also had come to know that he could say no more than that about his absence and she should not ask any questions about his "training." She accepted it, and she knew that she was in his heart and he was in hers.

At that moment the phone on her desk rang, and the caller ID window illuminated with the words "Unknown Caller." She knew instinctively it must be Consuela; it was. Despite her intuition, she answered with her professional office response in the event the caller turned out to be someone other than her cousin.

"Operations Administration," she said in her usual bright voice that would make the caller feel welcome. "Lu Ann, this is Consuela. How are things in paradise?"

"Hi, cousin! Things are really great, and it's just another terrific day in paradise. How are you, and where are you this week?"

Consuela was her usual bubbly self and had more things to say than the phone time would allow, and she said so to LuAnn. "This evening I'm in Toronto, Canada, and just finished a very productive business meeting with the local ministry of education. They are very pleased with our proposal for classroom books for grade-school children. So I'm really excited that it's been a good day. I'm leaving in a few hours for a stopover in Washington, D.C., to see 'you know who'. How are things with you? Is that new man in your life waiting outside for you to leave the office?"

"Things are moving in a positive direction with him and me, if you know what I mean. He and I are really tuned in to each other. Things get better and better as the weeks go by. I hope it's that way with you also. Although I don't think either of us has a clear picture yet about where this is going, but our feelings about each other seem to be the same. And no, he's not waiting for me outside."

"Well, I hope he's not far away and will be close tonight," Consuela said. LuAnn was not uncomfortable with Consuela's comments about herself and Darrin, but she didn't want to discuss Darrin's whereabouts, which were irrelevant for this phone call and were, frankly, none of anyone's business. She did, however, want to ask more questions about the new man in Consuela's life. But she felt as though she might be prying.

So LuAnn simply said, "No, he's training for a few days and we have plans for a home-cooked dinner at my place in a few days." Then in an effort to redirect the conversation to Consuela, she said, "Where are you off to after your visit to Washington? When will you be coming to see me?" From there the conversation focused on Consuela's travels, bosses who were irritants, an occasional "hunk" who would pass by, places to visit, and more business trips to cities in both North and South America.

The time in al Hudaydah, Yemen, was 0230 local time in early January. Francois lay in his bed half-asleep and half-awake, just as he had been each night since he had arrived in Yemen, nearly eight months earlier. The Yemeni national government was in chaos, as it had been since 2014, the prime minister had resigned, and the presidency was temporarily being filled by a reluctant vice president. He was known to be politically weak and poorly connected to his cabinet and to surrounding countries. The people of Yemen had come to believe Al Yamani was their true leader. They knew he had the most influence and international connections to get them the food, the water, the medical treatment, and most importantly, the internal stability they so urgently needed. They respected him because of his political connections. But moreover they also feared him and his army of so-called advisors who were heavily armed, humorless, short-tempered, and ruthless. The people also hadn't realized yet that he was a classic tyrant, and in spite of what he said, he didn't care a whit about their plight.

Francois heard a buzzing sound in a drawer of a small cabinet. It was a sound he hadn't heard in many, many months. It was his personal cell phone that he had brought to the Middle East from French Guiana. For some reason, maybe sentimentality, he had kept it and maintained its charge because it was the lone tie he maintained with his beloved country and his family. Even though he had never, and would never, publicly admit it, he still had a yearning to someday return to French Guiana.

He heard it buzz and vibrate against the bottom of the cabinet drawer again. He rose from his bed in the dark, went to the drawer, found the phone, and pressed the Answer button. "*Oui? Oui! Oui!* When? Tonight? Tomorrow? This weekend? Next week? Ah, so there may be time. *Merci.*" The line clicked on the other end, and the call was terminated. It had lasted no more than one minute. He replaced the phone in the drawer and quickly looked at the door to his room. There was no one there. There were no sounds from the hallway outside.

Francois returned to his bed in the dark, lay down, and stared at the ceiling in the light of a small dim lamp on a table. A warm breeze blew through the open window from the west, from across the Red Sea. A brief chill came across his body.

He thought, *My God, what does this mean? This was an unclear and unspecified warning. This was a call from a source whom I thought had forsaken me. It comes at a time when I'm being asked to sacrifice everything I have and everything I am for Allah. And yet, am I to think that there might be more to my destiny than seventy-two virgins? What do I tell my benefactor, Al Yamani?*

His racing mind grew still for a moment while he tried to weigh the messages he was questioning. He consciously became aware of the silence that had fallen over the room. His mind drifted for another thirty seconds, and he suddenly concluded, *No! I will say nothing for now.*

33

Hostile Operations

The White House, Washington, D.C., January 2019

President Chenoa sat, leaning on the front edge of the Resolute desk in the Oval Office of the White House, in Washington, D.C. It was 0700. She was not seated behind it with her feet disrespectfully propped on it, like her predecessor had done so many times before her. She was in front of it, not hiding behind it. She looked at the secretary of defense, Arnold P. Stoddard, a former defense industry CEO, and the chairman of the joint chiefs, Admiral Charles "Chet" Nagle, and said, "What are our chances of success?"

Vice President Henry Caldwell Smith, the former governor of Alabama and a former electronics surveillance equipment manufacturer, knew and understood the risks of the mission they were now discussing. He believed in the mission. The national security advisor, retired U.S. Air Force General Thomas Mossman, a careful man with broad military and political connections, had conferred with the vice president before this meeting and assessed the risks and benefits. Mossman, too, believed in the mission and the personnel who would carry out the operation. General Mossman spoke first. "Madame President, the vice president and I have spoken extensively with the chairman, and we have concluded there is abundant evidence that if we don't act, the situation in the Middle East will be beyond restoration. The result is that confidence in the ability of the United States to negotiate and support any political agreements with any nation in the Gulf or the eastern Mediterranean will be seriously eroded. We are already facing a situation where our friends don't completely trust us and our enemies no longer fear us."

Senator Denny Smith and Congresswoman Rosemary Doolin sat quietly among the group, fully knowing this was both a threat briefing update and a decision-making meeting. They had specifically been invited by President Chenoa so that they could continue to lobby for and defend the new national security strategic plan, Project RESOLUTE, offered many months earlier by the president. They did not have a speaking part in this meeting unless specifically asked to input comments. To clearly represent the president's new strategy meant that they needed to have access to the unfiltered, current thinking of the key members of the administration, so that their speeches and comments before their respective committees and subcommittees in both congressional bodies would not be interpretations relayed by someone's press secretary or staff assistant.

A meeting such as this would normally be held in the Situation Room, but too many White House reporters from the print and television media might notice the unusually high number of black staff cars entering the White House gates and leaving their high-powered principals at the West Wing doors to the building.

The director of national intelligence, the DNI, Dr. Gary L. Hollen, PhD, a former six-term congressman from the state of Washington, with a sterling record of effective and affordable support for the aerospace industry in his state, and a respected former member of the House Armed Services Committee, then interjected, "Madame President, I remind all of us that this operation is classified Top Secret—Project RAMPART. The number of individuals briefed into this project total only one hundred and three. I agree with the vice president and General Mossman. If no one acts, neither we nor our closest allies will retain any credibility. We are receiving hourly reports on the whereabouts and movements of Muhammad Al Yamani and his terrorist jihadist force commanders, and we have confirmed that six hours ago he captured and beheaded two tribal leaders, one from eastern Yemen and one from western Oman. We have confirmed that he is in his compound, in the city of Al Hudaydah, near the Hodeida International Airport. His underground command post and bunker there controls six of the fifteen intermediate range ballistic missile, IRBM, launchers that are on the launch pads and have warheads in place and they are fueled. We don't yet know what the warheads are, but missiles that size can accommodate small nuclear, toxic gas, or extremely high-explosive materials. Missiles that size also have a range of up to 1,250 nautical miles.

"We also have a report that the Italian consulate in Saana, Yemen, is under siege by hostile demonstrators who have surrounded it. The siege has all the same characteristics of the attack on the American consulate in Benghazi a few years ago. This attack has all the earmarks of a preplanned and organized terrorist onslaught. So far, the select Italian Carribianeri guards and contract security people are holding the crowds and the few violent demonstrators at bay. But the guards are lightly armed. If the Yemeni, Islamic State, Al Qaida, and Al Yamani soldiers show up with heavy weapons, which is predicted, the Italian embassy will fall. The embassy workers, their families, and their children will not be treated kindly."

The DNI took a short breath. It was not clear whether it was merely a pause for a transition from one part of the report or if it was because of his sadness about the apparent hopelessness of the situation or the exasperation with the situation the diplomats in Saana found themselves. In actuality it was the latter. This was a situation in which the United States had found itself in so many times in the past twenty years. These situations seldom ended peaceably. He checked some notes on one of the pages he was holding, and then continued.

"It appears that the Italians in Saana are not the only embassies or consulates that are encountering confrontations. Our embedded operatives on the scene tell us more serious lawlessness appears imminent. The Italians, British, French, and Germans have been alerted that we have certain forces in the area and that we are vitally concerned about events in Yemen. We passed this on to the Israelis in Tel Aviv also. Without being more explicit with the Israelis, they have acknowledged they know exactly what we mean by our message to them. They support us and are sending a clandestine demolition team to disable the missile silo operations since it appears as though Tel

Aviv is their target. They are standing by to act on our command.

"It has been confirmed that jihadist forces loyal to Yamani possess the access to and have the capability to deploy toxic and poisonous gases formerly owned by the government in Syria. Yamani also has the ability to deliver these WMD with long-range artillery shells and short-range missile systems capable of reaching territories close to the southern border of Israel. But use of the IRBMs seems more likely."

"We have also intercepted communications reportedly from Yamani's Number Three that some sort of catastrophic event is planned against Western diplomats in Saudi Arabia. But we have not yet confirmed the target, locations, or dates. We do know, however, that it could be carried out in celebration of the Muslim Eid al-Adha holiday in late February."

"There is one other disturbing bit of news," the DNI continued. "Friendly intelligence agents say that either the Chinese or the Russians have provided the Yemeni Air Force the capability to fly drone aircraft with some first-generation intelligence collector aboard, and possibly a weapons launch capability from the drone. The Yemeni Air Force, meager as it is, reports to whoever pays it the most attention and treasure. In this case, the first reports of battle results go to Al Yamani. Copies of those reports eventually end up in the prime minister's office, but he resigned last week. Our Humint reports say the intel collector on the drone is primitive, by our standards, and is an infrared camera that can image ground-based troops and equipment with next to no granularity. That means the analyst can see moving shapes but little else. Over the last few years we have lost some drones in that region, and we think the Yemenis, Somalis, Libyans, and Algerians have been offered the technology in exchange for some as yet undefined quid pro quo. We have no information about any other munitions or weapons that may be in the possession of Al Yamani or his forces. We're continuing to watch this development."

The vice president then spoke up. "Madame President, in my view we need to act, but with caution, careful intent, and precision. It appears as though we don't have much time. Perhaps one to three days, maybe five days, if we're lucky, before events begin to unravel and get worse, if that's possible. I would think we should act sooner rather than later."

The president responded, "Thank you, Henry. Your suggestions to me on all activities are always valuable. I take comfort in knowing you'll agree with my final decisions. Now, I know your helicopter is here to take you to the bunker, so you should be on your way. We'll stay in touch. If this goes wrong, all this will be yours one day." This parting shot was meant in jest. Henry Caldwell Smith and Marie Chenoa were longtime friends and confidantes. There was an unquestioned trust between them. But there was some serious intent in the president's comment. If things were, indeed, to go south badly, that could mean a global jihad had been unleashed in many major cities of the Western world, including Washington, D.C., and the White House. And that would mean she was no longer available to be president, and he knew it. Henry quietly arose and left.

Director Hollen then added, "We also have confirmation that Francois De La Plane, who escaped capture in French Guiana a year ago, has been in hiding in Yemen and is secreted in the personal home of Al Yamani. He is reported to be assisting in the development of broad-based terrorist plans that include possible attacks on U.S.-owned assets in Qatar and Saudi Arabia. There may be other collaborators who are also there in Al Haydudah, offering resources and weapons assets to the Al Yamani regime."

"Tell me, Dr. Hollen," the president asked, "is there unequivocal evidence that there is involvement in Yemen, or the region, by the Russians, Chinese, North Koreans, or any other nation, that they are supporting Al Yamani or elements of his regime?"

"Yes, ma'am, we have in-transit documentation on weapons movement by sea lanes through the Suez Canal and into selected ports on the south coast of Yemen, from both China and North Korea. We have rifles, grenade launchers, and IRBM components that were pilfered from crates aboard those vessels. We also have records, weapons, and IRBM fuel canisters that came into Yemen through overland routes from Russia. We have irrefutable names, dates, places, and hard evidence of collusion by our 'friends'."

President Chenoa said, "Thank you. I will need those details." She then turned to Secretary of Defense Stoddard and Chairman of the JCS Admiral Nagle. "Arnold and Chet, have you been in contact with your counterparts in Saudi Arabia about the need for a stabilizing influence that will be needed after we pass through the Suez?" Both men responded in the affirmative, and indicated that select special operations military and medical personnel were on standby in Jiddah, on the south coast of Saudi Arabia, for an unspecified cleanup and governmental reconstitution mission.

She continued, "I have been in contact with Prince Sahfajah in Riyadh, and he is prepared to act when you give his defense minister the word to go. The prince was not overly curious, but he seemed to know some action was going to take place imminently. He and his closest advisors don't know exactly what we are doing, but they understand and trust us."

President Chenoa then turned to Denny Smith and Rosemary Doolin, raised her eyebrows, and gave a slight nod. The gesture was the same as saying, "*Comments?*"

Denny took the initiative to speak before Rosemary did. He was representing the senate majority leader, the chairman of the SASC, and the SSCI. Rosemary was representing the speaker of the house and the chairmen of the HASC and the HPSCI. The principals of each of those bodies had been deployed to classified locations to ensure continuity of government actions should things go awry as a result of the operation. This was a normal, secret protective measure when the United States was involved in a potentially provocative activity. There was no fear that Yemen, or any other small Middle-Eastern country in the region, would deal a deathly strategic blow to the United States in retaliation. However, no one was clear or certain how the Russians, the Chinese, or the North Koreans might react.

"Madame President, selected members of the Congress have been in close contact with, and are supportive of, the actions by the secretary of defense and the chairman. The armed services committees and select committee on intelligence of the Senate are supportive of covert action to defuse a growing national chaos in the Middle East, and the hostile activities going on in Yemen, Somalia, Mali, Oman, Saudi Arabia, Iraq, and Iran. There may be other countries that are teetering toward radical Islamist forces. If so, they are included in this authorization support statement. Just as you have, we have been briefed on the tactics and targets of the Phantom forces that will depart Florida a little under twenty-four hours from now. You have bipartisan Senate support for a region-specific, preemptive tactical strike action to defuse the impending chaos that will result if Al Yamani and De La Plane are not reined in."

The president then looked at Rosemary and gave the same nod to solicit her comments. President Chenoa knew Rosemary didn't mince words when asked for an opinion and she never used a tome or even a paragraph when a sentence would suffice. Rosemary said, "Madame President, the speaker and the chairs and members of the appropriate House committees also concur and support a region-specific preemptive strike."

Denny then returned to a subject the president had expressed concern about earlier, requesting an answer for herself and the administration representatives gathered here.

"Madame President, certain members of Congress have expressed concern about Presidential Executive Orders 11905 and 12333 from previous years. But none of our targets are legally constituted leaders of foreign nations. They assumed their positions as a result of coups, a hostile takeover, or by conquest. Besides that, our forces are only dispatched when it is determined that U.S. national security is in imminent danger or there are threats to sovereign national U.S. territories, embassies, U.S. citizens, or those of our closest allies."

"That's reassuring, Senator. I don't want to be regarded as a Reagan-esque 'cowboy,' but I don't want any nation to take the United States for granted, either, and erroneously conclude that we are indecisive about our role in the world. The sequestration decisions that took effect in 2013, 2014, and 2016 had serious, adverse impacts on our nation's ability to have a decisive global impact in diplomatic and military capabilities. I'm optimistic this covert approach will make a point with our friends and adversaries, once they determine unequivocally it was done by us. I say the mission is a go, but I want to be advised when the *Truman* reaches Sigonella, Italy, and all the Phantoms are safely and secretly on board before they enter the Suez. I will give my final approval after receiving your reports. Please let me know if there is any change to any nation's political or military posture. I would normally declare a change in our defense readiness condition to DEFCON 4, but that telegraphs to our so-called friends and adversaries that something is up. So let's go to Alert Orange for the National Security Council and to Alert Red before the landing. That way only our highest-ranking field commanders will be in their command posts, ready to act if necessary, and no other administration officials outside those of us gathered here will be involved and risk an inadvertent leak of plans. It is going to be difficult enough to explain the absence of the vice president, the speaker of the House, the secretary of state, and other key administration officials as it is. The cover story is that they are in an offsite conference exploring foreign and domestic policy options for introduction to the Congress early next year. We have advertised that I, and other government leaders, will be joining them later this week for study updates and possible strategy alterations. Thank you all."

34

A World Far Away

MacDill Air Force Base, Tampa, Florida, January 2019

Nineteen hours after the presidential meeting, the MC-130J, Commando II, Super Herc was still parked in the last hangar on the flight line. The aircrew had completed all preflight checks, the Phantom force was on board and was as comfortable as they could make themselves on top of, under where accessible, and around the cargo pallets containing ammunition, weapons, survival gear, appropriate uniforms, and wetsuits thought needed for the mission. The logisticians who supported the Phantom force wanted to ensure that the troops did not want for anything to do their jobs. Some of the Phantoms were still milling around in the cargo bay when the aircraft commander announced over the PA system, "Stand by to taxi. Please strap in or be seated while we are moving. We'll be airborne in fourteen minutes."

It was 0350 hours on this mid-January morning. The aircraft tug was already attached to the nose wheel of the aircraft and began to pull the heavily loaded Super Herc onto the ramp for engine startup and taxi. The Super Herc started engines and requested taxi approval from the tower, which came immediately. The aircraft taxied to the right on Taxiway Echo, headed for Runway 22. The tower approved the aircraft for immediate takeoff, and the lumbering MC-130J entered the runway at taxi speed. The aircraft commander increased the throttles to full military power as he aligned the aircraft with the center line and gently pulled back on the yoke. The time was 0404 hours. Flying time to Sigonella Naval Air Station, Italy, was to be eleven hours and fifty-two minutes. They would rendezvous with the KC-135R tanker in six hours over the Atlantic, just southeast of Iceland.

At eight hours into the flight, Colonel Bud Patrick awakened everyone so they could get coffee, open their eyes, take a leak, grab a sandwich, or brush their teeth. They were at least four and a half hours from touchdown at Sigonella. He intended to pre-brief everyone one last time before they landed, to refresh their memories on the details of the mission. He would have two more brief opportunities to update them aboard the *Truman*, and one last time aboard the *Stingray*. But those would be abbreviated remarks, having to do with mission execution more than profile summaries. After touchdown in Sigonella, it would be mid-afternoon and daylight. Their movements would be visible to anyone who might be watching or who were just curious about people around a newly arrived MC-130 on the airport ramp. So they were to remain on board the aircraft after landing, and the plane would be quickly towed to a maintenance hangar on the flight line. The massive hangar doors would be closed behind them once they were inside. Then the Phantoms would be allowed to deplane.

While there waiting for the *Truman* to slowly pass by Sigonella, three miles out to sea, on her way to Suez, their schedule was hectic but secretive, so everyone needed reminders of what they were to do. Cell phone use, mailing postcards, and finding food vending machines were not on the calendar, and they all knew it.

Patrick and Master Chief Barrett had the lead on this mission. Duke Westcott accompanied Admiral Andrews, who was aboard the *Truman* in the Combat Information Center, the CIC. Bud Patrick's air force communications specialist was establishing comms from the airborne MC-130J to the carrier so that Andrews could listen in to the pre-brief and add late-breaking details if needed.

Air Force Staff Sergeant Norm Davis turned to Patrick and said, "Sir, the link is up and comms are encrypted and are five-by-five. The admiral is on the line."

"Thanks, Davis. Admiral, we are a little under four hours out of destination Alpha, the first stop on our course. All Phantoms are listening on receive-only links." Patrick continued with the pre-brief, "Gentlemen, I don't need to tell you, but I will, we are a long way from home—again. This time we have two targets to retrieve. The hard-copy handouts that are now being distributed to each of you show the latest photographs we have of our two targets. The first is Muhammad Al Yamani, who claims citizenship in Yemen, France, and Switzerland. For political invisibility purposes, he could claim he is a legitimate citizen of any one of these countries and could be given sanctuary for any reason he could think of. For our purposes, he is a citizen of Yemen who has committed international crimes, is not protected by any rule of law that our Department of Justice lawyers have been able to identify, is regarded by the United Sates and the United Nations Security Council as an outlaw, and is not a legally constituted elected official of any government in the Middle East. He is a self-appointed cleric, political party leader, community organizer, tribal council chief, military commander-in-chief of disparate forces, and honorary Middle-Eastern prime minister who has limited diplomatic immunity and is recognized as an ambassador-at-large for general Yemeni affairs. I will add that our clandestine agents inside Yemen have verified his credentials as self-initiated and self-proclaimed. He has no legitimacy! He is a ruthless killer! We have visual evidence that he has murdered at least twenty-six elected Yemen and Omani government officials! We have additional visual and eyewitness personal reports that he has been responsible for, or has been directly involved in, the murder of 1,256 innocent Yemeni, Omani, or Saudi Arabian civilians—maybe more by now. Gentlemen, he is a bloodthirsty killer with dreams of authoritarian rule, and he has at least a six-month record to prove it. Are there any questions about this man?"

Patrick looked down both sides of the cargo bay to see if any of the team leads had questions. Captain Sid McCauley, USAF, raised his hand. "Colonel, should we assume he has a loyal army of followers we'll have to face?"

"That's a good question, Captain. There's a long answer to that question and a short answer. The short answer is that if anyone gets in the way of trying to prevent us from taking him prisoner, or if he himself resists, then you are authorized to use lethal force, and if they seem to want to die—accommodate them. I will not sacrifice any one of you in place of one of them."

Bud continued with his pre-brief. "Al Yamani is being assisted by someone we tried to apprehend a year ago. He is Francois De La Plane from French Guiana. He has been on the run for more than a year, and we are informed by reliable sources he has been advising and consorting with Yamani on tactics, strategies, and international policies. He is a very smart man, is well educated, and is a superior tactician. He scrupulously avoids painting himself into a corner, and has undefined ties to persons or nations that want to help him survive for some reason. Both of these gentlemen are wily, are well protected, are probably armed, and should be considered dangerous. They will have surrounded themselves with a few henchmen who will be willing to sacrifice themselves for these two tyrants, but their level of commitment and loyalty won't be known until you stand in front of them with your M-14s pointed at their noses.

"Our orders are to attempt to take these two tyrants alive and to bring them back to civilization to stand trial in an international court. They have not only threatened the national sovereignty of the governments of Italy, France, and Germany, but more importantly, they have killed two American CIA agents, a family of four American tourists, and they have bombed the American embassy in Saana, where three embassy workers were killed. They have also threatened to do some as yet undisclosed harm to our ambassador to Saudi Arabia. We hope to have more detail on that in the next eight hours.

"Meanwhile, we have a small amount of confinement and misery to endure after we arrive at Sigonella. After landing at the airstrip, we will remain aboard this aircraft until it can be towed to a hangar on the flight line and the doors to the facility can be secured. It will still be daylight there when we arrive. We won't want to see or be seen by any voluptuous, mysterious, and hungry Italian women who rove around the flight line in search of horny Americans."

With that remark the Phantoms erupted into loud, raucous laughter. Even the admiral on the other end of the line aboard the USS *Truman* chuckled aloud.

"Once we're safely locked in the flight line hangar, we'll disembark from the aircraft and have free access to hangar facilities for approximately four hours while awaiting transport to the *Truman* after dark by Ghost Hawk helicopters. There are sleeping quarters in the hangar, showering facilities, hot and cold food buffet lines, weapons cleaning and checkout tables for your M-14s, and Glock pistols and knife-sharpening tools for your use. Just don't shoot yourselves in the foot or cut your finger on any weapons. If you do, you'll have to go on this mission anyway, because we are short-handed and you will be slightly impaired while doing your jobs." The men chuckled again.

"Gents," Bud continued. "We have a slightly tricky sequence of transfers over the next hours to go through to get our mission accomplished. Our paths are deliberately laborious and hard to track because Al-Qaida, the Taliban, Islamic State soldiers, a bevy of undercover foreign agents, and even some people out there who say they are our friends, want to know what we are up to. They have their own reasons in this part of the world to talk to some not-so-friendly governments, tribes, or warlords. Everybody in this part of the world is ready to cut a deal to save their own skins. If it also means cutting your throat and delivering your head for a bounty, they'll do it. For those reasons I want all of you to be fully awake, to be completely informed, and to know where each of us is located from your point on the ground."

Then, for emphasis because of the criticality and complexity of the mission, he said, "I say again, be aware, be awake, and be ready. Everyone who is here now is going home with us when this is over." He thought about adding the words "*living and breathing*," but both he and they knew he could not guarantee that. So he moved on.

"While on the ground at Sigonella, I want you to rest, eat your fill of food, work out to stay limber, and make sure all your weapons are working with maximum efficiency. Make sure you are ready. Under cover of dark we will transfer to the deck of the *Truman* and innocently, quietly, and invisibly transit the Suez Canal into the Red Sea."

Bud then added facetiously, "I'm sure the navy knows how to make an aircraft carrier look insignificant and innocent. There will be a final intel briefing on all aspects of what is known and unknown about the mission, and specifically the targets, once aboard the *Truman*. As we briefed back at MacDill, at a specified rendezvous point in the Red Sea we have an option to transfer to the attack submarine USS *Montana*. They will put us ashore at the proper time and place, depending on the target circumstances at the time. We'll get updated final briefings aboard the *Truman* before going ashore. Questions?" There were none. "Admiral, can you add anything at this point?"

"Thank you, Colonel Patrick. We have two living targets to bring back, if possible. Al Yamani and De La Plane are currently in buildings three and four of the compound on which you have already been briefed. As we get closer to your landing, we hope to have a more specific location of those two individuals of interest. You'll know where they are before you arrive ashore.

"I anticipate the landing at the beginning of the mission and the egress after Mission Accomplished, the MA, will be done just as we have practiced it in the last two months. The *Montana* will pick you up at the rendezvous point and shortly afterward you'll transfer back aboard the *Truman*. I'll see you all when you arrive back in a few hours. I wish you Godspeed and protection. Andrews out!"

Bud Patrick then wrapped it up by saying, "Get some rest and get ready. I and the master chief will let you know when it's time to make ready to go to the *Truman*."

There was the sound of the four turboprop engines on the Super Herc being throttled back and a slight lurch forward as the massive aircraft began a gradual descent. They were fifty miles west of Sigonella Naval Air Station, over water, and approaching the island of Sicily, Italy. They were lined up with Runway 10 Left and would be on the ground, on time, in five minutes.

35

In Transit

Washington, D.C., January 2019

Senator Denny Smith opened the door to his office in the Russell Senate Office Building after leaving the West Wing office of General Mossman, the national security advisor where he and Rosemary Doolin had been given a thirty-minute threat update and Phantom status briefing. The previous morning he had been in the president's office for the decision briefing of the Project RAMPART mission. POTUS had received this same morning briefing only one hour earlier than Denny and Rosemary. As he entered his office, he was greeted by his receptionist, Julie Wood.

She said, "Good morning, Senator."

"Good morning, Julie. How was your weekend?"

"Just fine, sir. The weather was perfect for sailing on the Potomac. We had a great time."

"That's wonderful. I wish I could have joined you, but duty called. Do I have any messages?"

"Yes, Senator. You have three calls from Ms. D'Arc of SAE Corporation; Senators Shoemaker, Clark, and Gage; the chairman of the joint chiefs, and Admiral Andrews. The chairman and the admiral called on your secure line and asked that you use it to call them back."

"Okay, Julie, thanks. Please get me Ms. D'Arc first. Then I'll call

Admiral Andrews and the chairman. I'll get to the others afterward."

There was one ring on Joanie's cell number. She immediately recognized the caller ID number and picked it up quickly. "Ms. D'Arc, this is Julie in Senator Smith's office. Are you in a place where you can talk with the senator for a moment?"

Joanie responded by saying, "Yes, of course. Now is an excellent time."

"Thank you. I'll put the senator on now."

Denny then came on the line. "Joanie, are you there?"

"Yes, Senator, thank you for calling me back."

Denny began his queries immediately because time was now of the essence. But he couldn't allow Joanie to know that. "The subject of our last call regarding gold has turned out to be extremely useful. Thank you for that. I just wanted to follow up and inform you that in addition to the transfer of the commodity discussed, there has also been a transfer of some military hardware that could change the balance of things even more in the area we discussed. I don't want to be too specific about the information on this line, but I trust that you and I are understanding one another."

"Thank you, Senator. I understand what you are saying perfectly. It's always gratifying to know that our sources of information are correct. I would amend that information with a data point that is only six hours old that says there has also been a transfer of a small amount of U-235, weapons-grade nuclear material in that region, as well. I know you can make the connection between all the types and amounts of transfers and what a final product might look like."

"Hmm. Yes, Joanie. I am aware of all the unusual movements in that region of the world. I appreciate your confirmation and hope we can stay in touch."

This was Denny's way of confirming what he had been told only two hours earlier by U.S. intelligence sources. But he had wanted to ensure he was on firm ground by validating what was reported through classified channels, with what was now known in the open source channels. He was certain he and Joanie were communicating about what was said, and unsaid.

"Thank you, Joanie. Please stay in touch." They then hung up their phones. He stood at his desk and started to move toward the door.

Denny looked at the door of his office that stood open a crack and said, "Julie, I'm ready for Admiral Andrews."

"Yes, Senator. He's coming up on the line in two minutes."

Denny retreated to his desk chair and sat down. The secure phone on the credenza behind him buzzed with a familiar sound, and he knew he was connected to Ray Andrews. He picked up the phone and said, "Ray, are you there?"

"Yes, Senator. This is a Project RAMPART update. We are slowly transiting the Mediterranean and will be within range of Sicily and Sigonella NAS in about one hour. I talked to the chairman about fifteen minutes ago, and he has briefed the national security advisor and the president on our status and progress. We are still a go. I spoke with Bud Patrick and he says they are as ready as they'll ever be. Once he and the Phantoms are aboard the *Truman*, we'll do an updated intelligence briefing and make whatever small tactical changes are required before launch of the mission. The *Montana* is confirmed in place, as well."

"Ray, the DNI whispered to me that the Yemeni national forces there are supported by some Asian-looking fellows who have access to drone technology, but it's not supposed to be as sophisticated as ours. We think all they can do is take pictures. There is also a small possibility they may have access to streaming video, but they can't fire weapons at ground targets with any known precision. So be sure the Phantoms go stealthy. Also, I'm told the Yemeni and Somali governments have issued a decree at the insistence of Al Qaida and the Islamic State caliphate, that a bounty of the equivalent of fifteen thousand dollars will be paid for any local troops or tribesman who can bring in the body of a European soldier. They have offered the equivalent of twenty-five thousand dollars for an American."

"Thank you, Senator. This is helpful information. Training and precision execution go a long way toward the survival of our people. Being tipped off to something we didn't know is added insurance and preparation. We may have to make a few minor changes to our battle plan. I'll give you a follow-on update as we get closer to going ashore."

"Thanks, Ray. I'll be standing by."

Denny placed the receiver back in the cradle, but he didn't take his hand off of it. He stared at it for a brief moment, then dialed the chairman's secure number in the Pentagon. He knew he wouldn't be getting any better information than what he had just received from Admiral Andrews. But following protocol and remaining connected to the few players in this crisis would ensure the channels would remain open. Besides, Denny was the conduit between the White House, the Pentagon, and the skeptics in Congress who could jeopardize lives, plans, and possibly the destiny of future U.S. foreign relations.

For now, Denny decided he would keep the line open to the chairman but would talk face-to-face with Fred Shoemaker, the loudmouthed, self-serving so-and-so, and with Wes Clark, whom he knew he could rely on when things started getting testier. Wes sat on the other side of the aisle, but he was a team player and believed, like Denny, that the United States needed another strategy in order to remain the guardian of freedom.

Denny heard the secure line buzz as it rang in Admiral Nagle's office in the basement of the Pentagon. The voice on the other end answered in a curt, businesslike manner, "Nagle!"

"Admiral, this is Denny Smith. I wanted to confirm that I have spoken to Admiral Andrews and I am fully aware of the status as of about thirty minutes ago."

Chet Nagle responded with, "Great, Denny. I wanted to inform you we are tracking a spurious piece of intel and are working feverishly to verify it. Intercepted comms have tipped us off that Dense Sal Khandar, the notorious Somali pirate and longtime personal friend of both Al Yamani and De La Plane, may be in the compound when we get there. We're attempting to verify that tidbit to determine if he's bringing an entourage. That could be a force multiplier for Yamani, but we can handle it."

"Thank you, Chet. That's good news, I think! If we can capture all three alive, we may have a treasure trove of strategies and plans for the entire Middle East for the next five years."

"You're right, Denny. But let's wait on verification. We're also doing backgrounds on all three tyrants to assess their willingness to allow themselves to be captured. We'll know more in two to three hours."

"Thanks, Chet, that's interesting news. I, too, have some information that at this time is probably classified as RUMINT. I received some data from a confidential open source from U.S. industry that says there's an amount of weapons-grade U-235 that has arrived in that area within the last six hours. It might be worth you running it to ground through your secure sources, to see if it's valid."

"Thanks, Denny. That's valuable information. It could be a game-changer depending on its configuration. I'll check it out and make sure Ray Andrews and Bud Patrick know about it. If it's there, and we can get a sample, we'll know who's supporting terrorist operations there and beyond Yemen. Thanks again, Denny."

"You're welcome, Admiral. Let me know if there's anything I can do from my end to help."

"Will do, Denny. More to come in the next few hours. I'll stay in touch. Nagle out!"

Denny replaced the handset in the secure phone cradle but again left his hand on it, staring in reflection and thinking consciously whom he should talk to next, if anyone, to ensure the loop was closed. His active military experience and his time spent in close quarters with intelligence analysts and strategic planners had taught him the more all players were of one mind for an operation, the better the likelihood that they would succeed. It was a team effort!

He dialed the secure phone of Rosemary Doolin in the Rayburn Building, and she answered immediately. Denny and Rosemary spent the next thirty minutes exchanging information on conversations and updating one another on what impact of impending actions, and what next legislative steps, might be essential to realize the president's goal. Rosemary ended the conversation by saying, "Denny, I think we're as ready as we're going to be for this next phase."

36

Tyrants Galore

Al Haydudah, Republic of Yemen, January 2019

Dusk began to settle over western Yemen at 5:30 p.m., Arabian Standard Time. The weather in Al Haydudah, next to the Red Sea in Yemen, had been hot, dry, quiet, and predictably unremarkable. It was always like this at this time of day and at this time of year. In fact, the weather here and now was like this every day of every month of every year in this region. So this day had been like all the days in this region. Al Yamani would not have it any other way. He insisted on controlling matters dealing with money, politics, religion, women's rights, military deployments, people who needed to disappear, and the availability of food and health care. If he could control the weather, he would do that, too. He unquestionably controlled all the activities in his compound. It was located south of the city he controlled, which was west of the international airport he controlled and next to the Red Sea, where he controlled access. He also controlled lands three hundred miles west across the Red Sea into Eritrea, one hundred miles north into Saudi Arabia, three hundred fifty miles southwest into Ethiopia and Djibouti, and another three hundred miles due south. That southern control extended into parts of Somalia, farther south through the narrow sea lane through the Bab el Mandeb and into the Gulf of Aden and the Arabian Sea. It had been many months since the governments, if that's what they could be called, of Oman to the east, United Arab Emirates, Qatar, Bahrain, and Kuwait in the northwest had conceded that Al Yamani and his soldiers and "advisors," well-known members of Al Yamani's organization, known as the United Islamic Yamani Empire or referred to as the UYIE, knew what was best for the people. More than 3,650 citizens, soldiers, and policemen had been publicly assassinated in these countries in the name of Allah and Al Yamani's new, as yet to be announced UYIE caliphate. His long arm of control indeed extended almost as far as the old Roman Empire in 27 BC. Even though his subjects were not completely loyal to him, they feared him and thus obeyed him and did his bidding.

The UIYE caliphate grand opening had not yet been held, but rumors of the consolidation of nations and people had already begun. Roving bands of cutthroat bandits and barbarous jihadi terrorists roamed the cities and local farmlands, threatening and butchering people to force them to bow before the new caliphate—to give it their allegiance, money, and loyalty. The structure and hierarchy of the caliphate had already begun to take shape. Like most caliphates of the past, it was built upon the slaughter of infidels, fear of authority, and unequivocal allegiance to a theocratic leader. Many nations had already capitulated, and the people had already surrendered to the perceived attraction of peace, stability, free living, food, water, medical care, and education. All the people had to do was to cease resistance, work at any task, and pay 60 percent of what they made to the caliphate in tithes and offerings.

The landlocked tribes of those regions would answer to Al Yamani, as did tribes and provinces to the east in the Yemeni heartland. Many, but not all of the Somali pirates, six hundred miles to the south, knew of him and believed he would be their theocratic leader one day. Because a caliph was supposed to be descended from Muhammad himself, they awaited word from one of their own to direct them to follow Al Yamani. For now, they continued to raid and plunder vessels in the waterways and sea routes bordering those areas, purloin their cargos, and demand ransom from owner-nations. They bowed to the almighty Euro and the dollar. They did so now, and until told to do differently, they would continue to do so under the leadership of and at the behest of their own leader, Dense Sal Khandar. Al Yamani knew of the influence Sal Khandar held over these common sailors and plunderers.

Sal Khandar had become legendary as a pirate and had garnered more than money from ransoms of foreign-flagged vessels plying the Indian Ocean and Arabian Sea shipping lanes. He had accumulated money in amounts equivalent to three billion American dollars in the last five years and six hundred million in the last two years. He distributed prudent amounts of cash and booty from the ship cargo holds and the ransoms to selected people and tribes in Somalia to ensure their loyalty and compliance. He had indiscriminately annihilated more than one thousand people in the last year and a half who questioned his motives, or who wanted to change his procedures, or who requested a piece of his pirating processes. He also had murdered several captains of commercial vessels who resisted his orders to surrender their cargoes, cash, and ship crews.

Dense Sal Khandar was himself a tyrant. He had all the characteristics of the traditional tyrant. He was well connected, well educated, well funded, and well supported. The difference between him and tyrants like Saddam Hussein, Al Assad, Quaddaffi, or Al Yamani was that he had no designs on becoming a regional or world leader, a caliph, or a potentate. He loved money, adoration, sex, and happy people to whom he gave money to ensure his anonymity and personal security. Any violation, however, that exposed his persona or location meant instant death, mutilation, or public beheading. His dislikes were dealt with quickly and violently. He had left several hundreds of mutilated and dismembered individuals, families, and foreign visitors in his wake. His loyal followers knew these rules and followed them precisely and religiously.

Officials in the government of Somalia appreciated the treasure Sal Khandar's activities brought to them and had come to expect secret personal and private payments each month. In return, Sal Khandar remained elusive, unrecognizable, untraceable, and was never where adversaries thought he was supposed to be.

Sal Khandar and Al Yamani had stayed in close contact over the years after being classmates and students at the University of Zurich. But Khandar never had an address, a permanent phone connection, or a place where he could usually be found. This was deliberate and was done for the purposes of personal survival and anonymity. Al Yamani liked that. When he wanted to talk to Sal Kahndar, he simply told one of his "advisors" to contact Kahndar's people so the two could talk. The request was passed by word of mouth until it reached the proper ears. It took a day or so, but it always worked.

On this late afternoon weekday in January 2019, Al Yamani quietly knocked on the door to the suite of Francois. De La Plane had nearly completely resigned himself to the notion that he would be a Sharia martyr who would be immortalized after the upcoming international summit in Riyadh. It would be his presence, his action, his suicide vest, that would send more than one hundred high-ranking international guests to the feet of Allah. But only Francois would be presented with seventy-two virgins as his reward.

"My friend, Francois, may I come in?"

"Of course, Al Yamani, you needn't walk so quietly. I am alone reviewing this spring's plans for territorial expansion."

"Good. I am pleased. They do indeed need thought and refinement. We must move swiftly but with deliberate thought. I wanted to see if there's anything you need. Since you will soon be immortalized, there is nothing you should be denied while you are at my side. I have given you the best food, the finest feminine company, and the best literature available to our world to ensure you continue to plan and leave me with your strategies and objectives. For my…er, our goals must continue to live even after we both have passed on."

"Do not despair, Yamani. I have written plans, intelligence estimates, political assessments, and identified selected individuals who will pledge you undying loyalty to keep our dream alive."

"That is good. We must discuss those plans soon so that our way forward is clear. One thing bothers me, however, and I request your opinion. I am somewhat concerned that our North Korean friends have been overly accommodating. They have given us everything we have asked for, and more. Your experience in dealing with them is critical to ensure they don't become permanently imbedded in our culture.

"But enough of this for now," Yamani said in a more jovial tone. "I have a small surprise. Do you remember Dense Sal Khaddar from Somalia and Benjo Adama from the Cameroons in our graduate school days in Switzerland?"

"Yes, of course," Francois responded with pleasant surprise. "Dense has been instrumental in accumulating large sums of money, treasure, and influence in the region. I have not heard much in the last year and a half about Adamo, but I believe he has risen to a position of power that will allow him to make a difference in the Cameroons. Allah has looked upon Sal Khandar with favor. In fact, you and I lamented on more than one occasion that if we could only persuade him to subjugate himself to you, it would extend the range of your influence to nations like the Sudan, Mali, Libya, Nigeria, and even Kenya. But he has been reluctant because his forces have been so successful. He has had no incentive to concede. If we could offer him protected and unopposed access to the Red Sea, the Gulf of Oman, and the Persian Gulf, he just might find an arrangement with us extremely attractive."

"Yes, that is true. You are thinking like the strategic planner I admire you to be," Al Yamani agreed. "He has not been resistant, just unpersuaded. But he is now willing to discuss the future with us. He will be here day after tomorrow and will stay with us for two days. He says he has social, political, and business reasons to come now. I sense an alliance in the wind. Adamo has communicated with me that he must send his regrets and is tied down with affairs of state and some military tasks. But he sends his respects to you and repeated his invitation for you to visit one day. He has also invited Dense Sal Khandar to visit, as well. I only wish we could all go one day to visit. I understand the Cameroons is a country of contrasts."

Francois responded favorably, "All of this is great news. They both have certain strengths, loyalties, and territorial relationships that we can easily assimilate, if they were to agree. Dense has been a friend for many years. I for one welcome his resources and have no reason to believe he will lend us nothing but more success in our quest for the supremacy of Allah."

De La Plane continued his strategic thoughts in spite of Yamani's visual excitement that an old friend was to grace his opulent surroundings. Francois continued, "Beyond the Middle East lies Europe and North America, who are gradually pivoting our way, with internal help of course. In two to three years, these regions will welcome us to their homelands as the allies they have long needed at their sides.

Once we annihilate their hierarchy and they willingly submit, there will finally be peace."

Al Yamani smiled and agreed. "Yes, indeed. All will be ours. But for tonight, I wanted to share this good news with you so we can rejoice in a possible new, very formidable alliance."

Seated at his breakfast table the next morning, Al Yamani barked at his administrative assistant, "Ruhani! Get me my chief of security! Get me my operations command center director! And get me my chief caliphate advisor!"

Al Yamani mumbled out loud as he sipped his espresso and fruit juice. "I can't read these reports. They are gibberish. They tell me nothing about the status of air, land, and sea activities!" Then he thought to himself that if he did not provide the security and invisibility to Sal Khandar and himself during the visit, it could be some time before another opportunity presented itself to unify the caliphate.

The air surveillance site controllers who monitored the airborne comings and goings into the region secretly reported the activities of commercial and military flight plans. They all pay him homage in one form or another in information, gold, or silver. Al Yamani was such a controlling personality that he had come to believe he did, indeed, control all those resources. He is convinced they work only for him and would never betray him by reporting vessel, aircraft, or ground transport movements to someone else or some government bureau before reporting to him.

There still, however, were international oversights that could not be easily avoided. Any sleazy official who was on the take had to protect both of his loyalties to ensure the candle burned evenly at both ends. He must appease his international authorities while at the same time pass favorable data to local officials to make sure they felt informed and secure. Francois, as Al Yamani's tactician and alter ego, orchestrated this control mania, too, and had himself come to believe that it all worked perfectly. He was too myopic.

Since the 1520s this southern region of Yemen had been invaded by the Ottomans, the Italians, the Saudis, the British, and even tribal factions from within Yemen. In later years the Russians, the Germans, the Chinese, and the Americans tried to woo the Yemeni leadership into their camps. They came bearing money and construction designs that would serve to improve Yemen as a major seaport and gateway to the southern Arabian region in the hope that the Yemenis would suddenly have an epiphany about these "Greeks bearing gifts."

Now the North Koreans had come offering more sinister, insidious gifts of military security and items that translated into political leverage. They built missile launch emplacements from which to launch fifteen missiles. If they were SCUD-B mobile missiles, they could hurl up to one ton payloads more than three hundred kilometers. If they were No Dong-1 medium-range ballistic missiles, they could launch a 1,200-kilogram payload up to 1,300 kilometers. It was presumed that Al Yamani had selected the weapon that could assuredly reach the mouth of the Suez and Israel beyond.

But the North Koreans had also provided underground command posts, state-of-the-art physical security detection equipment, and thirty days earlier, delivered toxic paralytic gas agents and small-yield nuclear warheads with no-cost military advisors and consultants. They even constructed a secret, one-mile-long underground trolley system to connect Al Yamani's opulent private quarters and command center to an underground bunker twenty meters from the end of the airport runway. In exchange, Al Yamani served as the go-between to negotiate land use agreements and reciprocal trade treaties for cotton, corn, dried fish, and the addictive marijuana-like chewing gum called madak or used a hookah to smoke hashish, shisha, or argile used by most nations in the Middle East.

Using this massive network of source data terminals interconnected to his status computers by the Internet and buried cable, Al Yamani received continual status reports in his subterranean command post. Some of the reports, like today's, were prepared by technicians who were poorly trained or simply didn't know what they were seeing and failed to grasp its relevance. The reports were normally very comprehensive. They included daily total numbers of converts to his cause; money received, rather, taken for his cause; numbers of tribal dissidents eliminated; the transit of seagoing vessels moving north or south through the Red Sea; international military force movements; vessels maneuvering in the Gulf of Aden; and the air traffic that overflew the domain he claimed as his imamate, his caliphate, his new country that would fold into the new United Islamic Yamani Empire.

Only Saudi Arabia and Egypt were missing from his kingdom. But even they were teetering with transitional caretaker governments, becoming more vulnerable to Al Yamani's style of subtle but permanent Islamic persuasion: "Join me and receive abundant monetary rewards, or continue to resist and risk widespread annihilation."

In a year or so he planned to make those two nations, and several other smaller countries, an offer they could not refuse. In time he would achieve his status as a major economic, military, and nuclear center of sharia academic thought, action, and practice recognized by all the Middle Eastern nations of the world. Over the last four years, he had established himself as a power to be reckoned with. He believed no one would dare challenge his authority. Francois De La Plane came to believe that Al Yamani was becoming invincible.

Political leaders in the region and a variety of tribal elders believed as Yamani and De La Plane did. They feared Al Yamani's wrath if they failed to react to his commands. Yamani's spies were everywhere, and they dutifully reported and were paid handsomely for reporting the smallest of infractions and disloyalties to Yamani's doctrine. But Francois knew what it was to become so enamored with one's accomplishments that one could begin thinking one was immortal. He tried mightily to put these thoughts of doubt and humility out of his conscious mind.

37

Good Intel

The Mediterranean Sea, January 2019

Fifty miles west of Sigonella NAS, Sicily, Italy, Captain Bill Chandler of the USS *Truman* ordered the helmsman to direct All Ahead Slow at six knots. He then ordered the XO to prepare the ship to receive as many as ten helicopters to the flight deck in nighttime operations beginning at 2030 hours. He added, "These operations must be done swiftly, efficiently, and with as little light and as little notice as possible. Operations are going to be accomplished while the *Truman* is underway so as to attract less attention. A seven-hundred-pound gorilla has difficulty in not being noticed."

Ashore at Sigonella NAS, Bud Patrick's secure satellite phone rang. It was "Duke" Westcott. "Colonel, this is Westcott with a RAMPART update. The admiral asked that I establish initial contact before the transfer operations begin."

"Thanks for calling, Duke. We're all getting a little restless on this end, and as soon as we're aboard the *Truman*, I know everyone will be ready to launch. The chopper flight crews tell me all ten Ghost Hawk birds are ready to load and head for the IP."

"Yes, sir, I understand and am ready to execute with you when we get the GO code. Speaking of which, we received word that everyone in Washington is leaning forward, there are no dissents so far."

"Thanks, Duke, that's excellent news."

"We have some additional intel to cover when you arrive onboard that will help in launching. One tidbit is that we've heard there may be a hostile, armed drone over-flight, so we've brought aboard an air force two-man aerial surveillance and warning team to neutralize it if it happens. They'll be on the beach before you get there and will remain on the beach when you go inland. We also have an update to the physical security measures installed at ground zero. They're intricate, but we have someone who will land sixty minutes before you penetrate and she'll neutralize their systems. There are other items to cover, but we'll wait till you and the Phantoms are onboard to cover them."

"Okay, Duke, it sounds like you have your finger on the pulse of all the operations. Don't let those swabbies co-opt you into moving permanently aboard that carrier. All that rocking and rolling will make you seasick."

"Not a chance, Colonel. The air force chow, the family quarters, and the golf course at MacDill are too good to give up. One more thing, Colonel. We've received back channel intel that Dense Sal Khandar, the Somali pirate chieftain and longtime close friend of Yamani's and De La Plane's, will be visiting while we're there. We'll be inviting him to accompany us, too, when we depart."

"That's terrific news, Duke. It sounds like we have tyrants galore for this mission. That will clean up a lot of the Middle East, at least for a while. I'll see you soon. Patrick out."

Master Chief Barrett, like all master chief petty officers in the navy, command chief master sergeants in the air force, and command sergeant majors in the army, know their enlisted subordinates intimately. They knew their families, their financial problems, their problem children, their difficulties in the bedroom, and much, much more. The master chief in this outfit kept the communications channel open between all the Phantoms and was intentionally discreet enough to protect confidences and little-known information that could make a key man distracted.

The master chief of the Phantom force walked a delicate line between operational mission perfection and home life tranquility. For the Phantoms to operate at maximum efficiency, both mediums had to be in balance. At that moment U.S. Navy Petty Officer Third Class

Bill Hubbard was quietly confiding in Barrett that his wife was expecting their second baby while he was on this mission. Hubbard was worried and his wife was nervous, anxious, and sometimes had been mildly hysterical about his absences. He said, "She is probably bipolar and her thinking is not clearly rational at times. She's fearful of being alone at this time of her greatest need."

"Master chief, I think she may not make it through this birth," Hubbard confided. "I talked to her a lot before we left MacDill, and she seemed to understand that everything was going to be alright. But I don't know if I got through to her."

"Hubbard, I have been through this in my own life and in the lives of twenty or thirty of my friends. I assure you, she's going to make it. My wife, Fran, is with her as we speak." Hubbard looked up at the master chief in surprise.

"I didn't know that. How could you have known this was going on, Master Chief?"

"Son, do you see all these stripes? I didn't just get them at the blue light special at Walmart!"

Just then Air force Staff Sergeant Brandon Forshaw walked over to the master chief and Hubbard. "Hey, Bill, I just got a receive-only text from my wife. All the wives from the squad are at your house on a continuing Water Break Watch they're calling it, for the next week.

The master chief's wife is there, the XO's wife, Pam Westcott, is there, the colonel's wife, Barb, is there, and so are six others. They've got a pool started on the date and time the water will break. I put you in for ten bucks on February two at two p.m. That's two-two at two. That has to be lucky. I hope you win. If you do, you owe me a ten-spot. The pot is already $175 bucks. Hang in there, buddy!"

Hubbard looked at the master chief with wide-eyed amazement. "I never realized anyone knew or even cared."

The master chief looked back at Hubbard with an expression that only a crusty old military careerist, husband, father, and grandfather could generate. "Of course we knew and of course we care. There are two other members of the force with us here tonight who also have problems that need tinkering with at home. The deal is, I take care of all of you here and you do your job the very best that you can. There are people on the home front who have our backs and things will go smoothly there. Keep your head on straight, Hubbard, and focus on the mission. Everything else is going to fall into place."

"Thank you, Master Chief. I had a lot of uncertainties about this mission this time. I don't know how I can ever thank—"

Barrett deliberately interrupted, knowing what was coming next. It was not time for thanks or promises of repayment or any other words of appreciation. Besides, the child wasn't even yet born. "Forget it for now, son," Barrett abruptly said. "That's the way a military career works. Just focus on what's ahead. When there's news from home, someone will get it to you as soon as possible. Got it? Just do your job. You're excellent at what you do. We're all counting on you."

Just then Bud Patrick's voice echoed close behind the master chief and Petty Officer Hubbard. "Master Chief, can I have a word with you?"

"Yes sir, Colonel," Barrett responded.

"I've received some target data and we'll get more details when aboard the *Truman*. Do you ever get a sensation that some things are not all that you think they are? Do those little hairs on the back of your neck stand up and tingle a bit sometimes?"

"Yes, sir, Skipper. I get them all the time on these missions, and even at home before my first cup of coffee in the morning when I haven't made the pot myself. What's up?"

Bud then spoke in low, quiet tones. "I get a sense that this landing will be a challenge for us. I want everyone to have their heads on a swivel and beware of tripwires and booby traps. These bastards are wily and savage. They are not the normal terrorist assholes we've encountered in the past. If we lose anyone, I don't want it to be because I forgot to tell someone something."

"Right, Skipper! I understand and know what to do."

38

Restless Constituents

Washington, D.C., January 2019

Julie Wood knocked softly at Denny Smith's office door. "Senator, Senators Fred Shoemaker and Cynthia Black are here to see you."

"Thanks, Julie, show them in."

"Denny, Cynthia and I are headed to the senate dining room and wanted invite you to join us for a bowl of that famous bean soup."

"That's very kind of you, but I have back-to-back appointments this morning and have only a ten-minute window to wolf down this tuna sandwich here at my desk before my next appointment arrives."

Cynthia quickly responded, sensing the urgency in Denny's voice. Both she and Fred understood that it took a few minutes for an update before each and every appointment to ensure senators were fully witting of all but the unpredictable issues a constituent or a government visitor might bring up. She said, "Sure, Denny, we understand. We've been in that predicament, too. But very quickly, we hear there's a change to a current operation pending. Can you share any details with us?"

Denny was not surprised at the request. Word traveled fast in the whispers around the cloakrooms of the senate committee chambers. "I can't tell you much that you don't already know. We've all had status-of-forces and status-of-operations briefings either in our secure offices or in committees and subcommittees. As you also know, only twenty-two of us are privy to operational details on a strictly need-to-know basis. Yes, the Phantom force is quietly under way right now, and details about target parameters are surfacing by the minute. What you may not know is that now there will be three Middle-Eastern terrorist leaders meeting at zero hour. The plan is to deal with them with the hope that we can bring them back."

Fred reacted with amazement. "Wow, Denny, that's interesting news."

Cynthia said, "Can you keep us apprised of any other late-breaking intel?"

"Yes, of course. But we have to be careful we don't have a breach of security or commit any information to one another via electronic means. I'm still skeptical about the communications security of the senate's secure e-mail system. So update data will be passed through subcommittee channels in the secure committee rooms or by face-to-face voice."

"Yes, yes, of course, Denny," said Fred. "But, Denny, you know many of us, while supportive of our military forces and especially the covert operations concepts, are yet to be convinced that it would or could supplant a large, well-equipped, and formidable military force. You recall the haggling that went on back in 2014 when the president said he wanted to 'degrade ISIS' and he was going to do it with only air strikes. That didn't work then and it won't work now—"

Cynthia then interjected, "Denny, let's be frank, many of us have large defense industry constituents who supported us to come here and do what's best for everyone. That includes keeping our military as ready as possible with state-of-the-art technology, supplies weapons, and special tools. We want to honor that philosophy of support."

"Fred, Cynthia, since our time right now is short and an operation is pending, let me be blunt. We have discussed this before but never in the full senate. That debate is coming—and soon. We all agreed to a period of operational mission practicality applications before a classified review of results and costs by both houses was to be conducted. The posture of our armed forces since the sequestration actions of 2013, 2014, and 2015 is precarious. We haven't as yet recovered from layoffs, closed production lines, stretched-out procurement schedules, and so-called forward funding practices.

"We can no longer serve as the nine-one-one call center for the world. We can no longer expect a smaller military force to struggle through back-to-back deployments to global hotspots. We can no longer burden the American people with a tax-and-spend policy advocated by previous administrations. At the same time, we need to support the triad national security strategy to offset the two or three countries that have nuclear forces equivalent to ours.

"There is an increasing potential as time goes by, for the unconventional delivery of WMD by either a state or, more probably, a non-state actor. We have to expect it to grow to adversely impact the United States. Conventional covert operations are probably the most militarily efficient and cost-effective way of addressing that conflict. Something has to change the way we do business today.

"I hope you both agree. I also hope you agree there are some things more important in United States national security than keeping our defense contractors afloat and getting ourselves reelected." Both Fred and Cynthia blushed at that last comment with a bit of offense as well as embarrassment and guilt.

"One thing that can change that will yield immediate results is to support these small covert operations forces that can get in and get out of international crisis locations instead of sending in a nation-building defense force that makes us an army of occupation for interminable periods of time. Hell, the current covert ops force is about thirty GIs of the most highly trained and most elite members of the armed forces of this country. They are armed with more lethality per man than a small army of suicidal Al Qaida terrorists any potentate in the Middle East can muster. They have air cover from several C3 aircraft, one sea-based vessel that can annihilate anything within a five-square-mile area, space surveillance from low earth-orbiting satellites, IMINT from stealthy space planes with real-time down links and small but highly lethal backup forces with equivalent capabilities. They are to get in and get out in less than two hours. Now, tell me that is not better than an eighty-thousand-member international force to do the same but taking two to five or more years and ends in a compromise that installs a temporary caretaker government that doesn't like us when we arrived to save their bacon and will like us even less when we draw down our forces to a hundred advisors and leave.

"What we can do is change the response to crises created by tyrants who believe they are untouchable and who believe they live in a domain that is sacrosanct. We can take back the initiative and use it in our favor. We can decapitate their illegitimate leadership and let the people of those nations choose their own leaders. If they choose someone we don't like, we can register our displeasure and try to diplomatically work with them. If they turn against us and pose a national security threat to this nation and its interests overseas, we can deal with it at the time. But providing an army of occupation to make them adopt our way of thinking is a strategy that is passé. What can change is the strategy to deal with these tyrants who no longer fear or respect the United States and have come to think of themselves as immortal and untouchable and think of us as a paper tiger. This is a change we can afford and that our military forces can sustain.

"Now, I wish we had more time to talk because I want and need to hear your opinions. But the chairman of the JCS will be here in five minutes, and I haven't even taken a bite out of my tuna sandwich. After this week is over, we need to schedule discussion time in and out of committee to vet this fully. The White House supports this concept, but both houses of Congress are taking a wait-and-see attitude."

Fred said, "You're right, Denny," in an unconvinced tone of voice. "I know you're passionate about this and there are some components with which we all agree. But we need to talk soon, very soon. Elections are coming up at the end of this year for many of us. My defense contributors, er...I mean, constituents are looking for answers to questions about our actions."

"Mine, too," Cynthia added. "And so, too, are the supporters of twelve others of our colleagues."

"Thank you for understanding," Denny said. "And especially for understanding our short timelines. When we have American troops in harm's way, I think we first need to support them in whatever way is needed. After the mission is over, we need to hear their assessments and then weigh our options. We'll talk more soon."

Denny's phone then rang from Julie's desk outside. "Senator, Congresswoman Doolin and the chairman are here now."

39

The Pre-Brief

The USS Truman, The Mediterranean Sea, January 2019

The loading aboard the eight Ghost Hawk helicopters at Sigonella Naval Air Station and subsequent transfer to the deck of the USS *Truman* went off without a hitch and was complete by 2110 hours. All twenty-eight Phantoms in full combat gear were disembarked from the choppers on the darkened flight deck. Their added ammunition, medical supplies, and Zodiac assault boat packages were unloaded and moved to the hangar deck of the carrier. The giant ship and its battle group escorts moved quietly toward the entrance to the Suez Canal without incident. It was a dark, solemn night, but everyone aboard the ships in the task group knew they were being watched from the shore. So all lights were out, and open deck activity was kept to a minimum. But all personnel were at Ready to Move to Battle Stations if the command were to come.

Duke Westcott and one other officer met Bud Patrick when he touched down in the first Ghost Hawk to arrive. The night was quiet. The sky was dark except for one billion stars in the night sky. All that could be heard was the continual *swoosh, swoosh, swoosh* of the bow wave of the *Truman* moving forward at a deliberate six knots of speed. The wind over the southeastern Mediterranean was mild and came across the bow with a mild fishy and seawater odor. If one did not know they were at sea aboard a ship, one would think they were at a seaside resort at night with the tiki torches burning along the beach, awaiting the bartender to arrive quietly with a tray of margaritas, pina coladas, or mai tais. But there would be no drinks on this night. This was war.

When Bud stepped off the Ghost Hawk chopper, Duke saluted his boss, Trigger Lead, and said, "Welcome aboard, sir. All the Phantoms will be met and escorted to their temporary quarters. While aboard the *Truman* they can settle in for just under forty-eight hours while we are in transit to the Gulf of Aden."

"Very well, Colonel. All of our people are spun up about this mission, and we all have high expectations for its success."

"Yes, sir, I understand. I have set up a senior staff meeting in one hour in the flight crew briefing room. Admiral Andrews, the captain of the *Truman* and selected members of his staff, you, me, the master chief, and a few others will attend."

As Westcott and Patrick started walking toward the side of the flight deck, they stopped at the hatch leading to belowdecks. Duke said, "Colonel, I want you to meet someone who will be with us while we are in transit to the IP. He is fully briefed on RAMPART. Sir, this is Colonel-Chaplain Norm Derossier. He is an Episcopal chaplain sent out from the Pentagon. Please forgive him, he's air force."

Bud then said, "Chaplain, I have to say I'm glad to see you. We haven't had any spiritual reinforcement in any of our previous deployments, and I think it's long overdue."

The chaplain said, "It's nice to meet you, Colonel. There are a lot of good stories floating around the services about you and the Phantoms. You're doing a hell of a job. This is tough work, and I know it takes its toll on the minds, bodies, and spirits of the best of men. And with regards to my service, God loves all His children, regardless of the color of the battle dress uniform they wear."

Bud then replied, "Chaplain, I think you and I and all the Phantoms are going to get along just fine. Thank you for taking us under your wing."

Westcott then interjected, "Father Norm used to do covert ops deployments in an earlier enlistment, so he knows what we're up against and will keep a low or high profile as the situation demands. He'll be going aboard the *Montana* after we go ashore and will meet us there when we return."

"Father Norm, thanks again. This one could be a challenge for us. This is going to be a tough and tight time-constrained deployment. Please stay close and visible. This operation is by no means a Christian crusade. But if we can save a few Middle-Eastern friends and protect our Phantoms, I'll consider it a victory. I hope you'll attend the senior staff briefing and all the briefings before we launch. I want all the Phantoms to know you're here and that they can each privately talk to you if they wish."

"That's what I'm here for, Colonel. An army Muslim cleric will be coming aboard later in case he's needed when you return. But I'm here for you and all the Phantoms." Bud made no response to the chaplain's remark about the Muslim cleric. Everyone then knew that if any Muslim captive arrived who was seriously injured and could not be medically saved, the prisoner's religious last rites would be respected and administered, just as had been done with Osama bin Laden in 2012.

One hour and fifteen minutes later, Master Chief Barrett said in a loud and commanding voice, "Attench-hut!" All the Phantoms, four members of the *Truman* senior battle staff, Patrick, Westcott, and Father Norm all stood crisply to attention. Lance Corporal Hall, his spotter, Lance Corporal Willoughby, Army Specialist Miller with his sniffer dog, Fritz, and the air force air surveillance team, Master Sergeant Sue Beaner, and her technician assistant were there. Admiral Ray Andrews strode into the briefing room also wearing his battle dress uniform and curtly said, "Seats!"

The admiral and a navy lieutenant commander intelligence officer were there to cover all aspects of the situation to the point of disembarking from the *Truman*. The admiral spoke first with the task of making the point that this operation had been practiced over and over. Even so, he also wanted to caution that this operation was to be extremely hazardous. "Gentlemen, this operation will be conducted just like the practice drills held at MacDill. The beach will look the same; hostile fire, if any, will be as we simulated it; the buildings will look the same; the physical security will be the same; and the resistance will be close to how we practiced it. There are two things that will be different."

With that last comment, the anal pucker factor of all the Phantoms increased, including that of Bud Patrick, and the master chief thought, *Holy shit. What did we miss?*

Admiral Andrews continued, "The only things different are that the targets may have gotten a hint that something is about to happen that they won't like, and certain guard posts, numbers of adversaries, or weapons may be different and we lose the element of surprise. The second thing that we now know is different is that there is a third hot target person present we had not planned on. He has the same 'Capture Priority' as the other two. He just doesn't know we have accommodations for him, as well. His wives may not have packed a bag for him this morning, but we have a straitjacket and a brig cell for him where we have left a light on in the window." These opening remarks seemed to settle any anxieties the Phantoms might have had about the mission.

Admiral Andrews went on to cover all the actions in timed sequence before going ashore. "While the *Truman* is in transit heading south through the Red Sea, the attack submarine USS *Montana* will escort us on a parallel course with all her detection sensors at high alert. She'll make the pickup when your work is done. We'll launch from the *Truman* at approximately 0200 hours, less than forty-eight hours from now. The Zodiac boats you'll use to go ashore and all the extra portable supplies and munitions you'll need are ready to be put over the side of the *Truman* fifteen minutes before you climb aboard them. The Z boats are equipped with long-lasting low-noise battery-powered motors so the bogeys won't hear or see you coming. There will be six boats with five Phantoms aboard each one. After you clear the stern of the *Truman*, which will be barely moving at the time, it should take you twenty-one minutes to arrive on the beach from time of launch from here till your boots are on the beach. I'll now turn the remaining part of the brief over to Lieutenant Commander Alvarez, the *Truman*'s intelligence officer, for a short threat briefing, and then Colonel Westcott will cover landing and assault plans. Commander?"

"Thank you, Admiral. Gentlemen, I'll be brief and succinct about the possible threats you could face. We have sufficient intercepts, HUMINT reports, and IMINT photos to substantiate that the enemy has a full weapons suite to draw upon. They have what appear to be up to fifteen intermediate range ballistic missiles, six of which are loaded, have the targets uploaded into the flight and impact geometries; the launch circuits are continually at the ready; and all can be fired in less than ten minutes. We don't know at this time if the missiles are old Russian SS-4 or SS-5s or are shorter-range North Korean NO-Dong 1s or even a few SCUD-Bs, which have a lesser range. We may know soon. We do know they have all the components for small nuclear warheads, or sarin and VX toxic gas agents or seven-hundred-fifty-pound high-explosive munitions warheads. We just don't know which missiles are uploaded with which warheads. We are, therefore, assuming they have some of each uploaded. We are also assuming they are able to rapidly upload the same munitions on the 'Stand By' missiles to be used in a second salvo. They also have short-range tactical missiles with anti-personnel explosive warheads powerful enough to blow a hole in the side of the *Truman* in the middle of the Red Sea. They have Kalashnikov automatic rifles, rocket-propelled grenades, or RPG, launchers, multi-shot automatic Chinese forty-four-caliber pistols, grenade launchers, miniature short-range tactical drones for photo coverage, night-vision surveillance optics, at least twelve sniper rifle marksmen, six rapid deployment armored personnel carriers equipped with thirty- and fifty-caliber machine guns, and lots of knives." This last comment brought laughter among the Phantoms, because bringing a knife to a gunfight had never worked for an adversary.

"I think you are more than equipped to counter most all of these capabilities and have the tactics to support you. Even so, gentlemen, be careful out there. Shoot straight and kill with the first and each subsequent shot. Colonel?"

Duke Westcott stood up and took the podium. "Thank you, Commander. Gents, while in transit to the shoreline you'll be arrayed twenty yards apart as you move landward. You all will hit the beach at the same time. You'll have all the supplies you need in small floatable containers. You'll beach the Z boats, unload your gear, turn the empty boats back out to sea, and activate the silent scuttle mechanism. After ten minutes the boats will be in fifty fathoms of water, and all systems will be flooded and will go silent. Then only the bottom-crawling sea crabs will know where they are.

"When that's done, you'll set up surveillance and communications positions and notify Trigger Lead when set over the secure, encrypted comm channel and wait for the Go Code." Westcott moved to a large video screen illuminated behind him. It was a daylight picture of the beach line on which the Phantoms were to land. The resolution was very precise. The center point of the photograph was Al Yamani's opulent mansion twenty yards east of the main north-south highway, now seldom traveled, that ran from Tiazz twenty miles to the south and to Jazan, twenty miles to the north. Fifteen yards west of the highway was the clear, sandy beach of the Red Sea where the Phantoms would land and wait.

Bud Patrick sat in the front row of the audience being briefed. He sat with his elbows on the arms of the seat with his fingers interlocked under his chin. He was in an alert, but pensive mood. He was taking in all the data but was also trying to think of failure points, faults in their thinking, points where they might be unprepared. He hadn't lost any Phantoms so far, and he didn't want to start now.

This beach reminded him of the Omaha Beach in Normandy, France, on D-Day, June 6, 1944. In the Army War College and the National War College, he had studied the D-Day assault, the tactics used by both the Allies and the Nazis, the landscape landed upon, the broad expanse of flat, sandy beach reaching shoreline vegetation, the sloping hillside leading to the tops of the small cliffs accessible from level land and a paved highway ten yards away, and an open space of land between the highway and the targets. The open spaces, the vantage points atop the beaches, the openness of the area between the beach and the missiles, the command buildings, the opulent residences of Al Yamani, De La Plane, and Target Number Three, all taken together bothered Bud tremendously. If the Phantoms were to storm the beach and move uphill, they would be exposed for up to six minutes. Each of the Phantoms would be vulnerable and open to annihilation by an enemy, who, if he had his shit together in a defensive posture, could end this operation and near-future Phantom ops for some time. It could be over before it ever got started—much the same as what nearly happened on June 6, 1944. The setting was similar to that historic battle, albeit on a smaller scale. But a massacre here could have major and lasting ramifications to the United States if it were exposed to the world.

Bud raised his hand, and Westcott took immediate note. "Colonel Westcott, may we request an overhead daylight and nighttime infrared over-flight of the landing area eight and two hours before the assault?"

"Yes, sir. I will ensure that is laid on." Duke Westcott wasn't sure why his boss requested that extra mission sortie, but he knew Bud well enough to know it was not an arbitrary or whimsical requirement. That happened in the Pentagon all the time. But this was a battle zone. He was an expert tactician himself and could offer an educated guess as to why Patrick requested one last look-see. He knew he would find out later. The need for more data also had intangible value to the Phantom unit. The public nature of the request told all the Phantoms their commander saw a possible flaw that had been overlooked before and that he cared that his troops might lose a position of superiority.

Duke Westcott then continued with his presentation. He knew they had been in this briefing room for nearly forty minutes and that some attendees probably had to pee, write notes to be delivered home later, or needed food; after all, these were high-energy, positive-action, continually-in-motion people who didn't do well when sitting in one place or position for long periods of time. So he picked up his pace.

"You will be spaced fifteen yards apart while on the beach located at the points one through six identified on the chart. Points A, B, C, and D on the chart are the positions of the intelligence, surveillance, and reconnaissance technicians, the intrusion alarm defeat team, the tac control team who will orchestrate your departure, and the communications systems controllers. The medics will be collocated with the tac control team, but we won't be using them." Duke made this last comment as a throwaway line, as if to say that no one would be in need of anything more than a Band-Aid at egress time.

"As per usual, audio and video feeds will be active, and Trigger Lead will control any chatter on the circuit. No one transmits unless he needs clarification or assistance. The team will await the Go Code from the *Truman*, Hammer, and it will be transmitted to all via Trigger Lead as the Code Execute Plan A—GO. Changes in the plan will be passed as Execute Plan B—GO. An abort command will come from Hammer as code word LINCOLN-LINCOLN used twice, as I just said it. You then Hold in Place to await commands for the next moves."

Al Hudaydah and Al Yamani's command center lay in the center of the aerial photo that Duke Westcott was using aboard the *Truman*. It was in such detail that one could make out trees, shrubs, male and female pedestrians, guard posts hidden in tree growths, and other relevant details.

Westcott continued his operations pre-brief. "We've got other assessments that say the property is excavated for small missile launch capabilities as well as the known IRBM launch silos. They seem to be prepared for both tactical and strategic defensive and offensive operations. We need to be prepared for quick and decisive strikes to preclude a launch of any of these weapons.

"While ashore at the tyrant's command post, the extraction procedures after the mission will be complete and ready for execution. All will be in readiness for the loading aboard the escape Zodiac boats that will be air-dropped to the beach area, already inflated and ready. I'll cover that in a moment. *Montana* will be standing by for the rendezvous one thousand yards offshore and ready for escape."

The Phantoms had practiced this routine over and over again in Florida and offshore in the Gulf of Mexico. They knew what was to happen, where each of them was to be, and what the extraction routine was. They each knew what their individual tasks were to be, what armaments they were to carry, and what the Al-Qaida guards and soldiers they were going to confront, would be carrying.

Westcott tried to be specific about mission hazards, tasks, and objectives. He said, "We have a physical security defeat specialist who will be on the ground before you, and he will disable all the devices and networks he can find. But be aware of undetected tripwires, landmines, and pressure plate devices in front of doors, out-of-place scents and aromas, and IEDs in pathways leading to buildings.

"Since there will be a third target to capture, I expect the existence and placement of additional bodyguards and sentry posts to be at least half again as many as we originally thought. So take three extra clips of ammo for your MK-18 CQBRs. The *Montana* will be on station while you are ashore, an Air Force MC-130J Ghostrider will drop your Zodiac escape craft, and the surveillance operator will steer the Zodiac chutes to the beach area and have them already inflated as you arrive on the beach with, hopefully, your 'guests.' The MC-130 Ghostrider is equipped with twin electro-optical day-night sensors, thirty-millimeter cannons, a day-night synthetic aperture radar, and low-yield precision weapons such as small-diameter bombs and Griffin mini-missiles to cover your egress. It can also neutralize any UAVs detected in the area. We'll all be receiving real-time down-linked imagery from the JSTARS and low earth-orbiting satellites and an Air Force X-37B spacecraft in low orbit at the time you arrive ashore. We have issued a bogus UN message that says to all nations in the area that an international geodetic survey aircraft will be in the area taking coastal depth, wind, and tide readings. He will be our guy. He will loiter in the area while you are ashore. You will be well covered.

"We will be clearing the Suez Canal four hours from now and will be leisurely headed for the open waters of the Red Sea. Most aircraft and all Ghost Hawk choppers are already stowed below in the hangar deck so that the *Truman* will look unassuming and will appear as though she's just out for a harmless vacation cruise.

"You will be given a final update status briefing before you leave the *Truman*. We will commence preparations for operations in twelve hours under the cover of darkness at 2100 hours Red Sea time. We leave the *Truman* at 0100 hours. Rest up, recheck your weapons, ensure that all your weapons have fire and noise suppressors, and be sure your night vision equipment is working.

"There will be a short update briefing and equipment check just before we disembark the *Truman*. Rest assured you will have all the latest information before getting aboard the Z boats. Are there any questions?" There were none. "Admiral? Colonel? Do you have anything to add right now?"

Andrews and Patrick shook their heads. "Then that will be all for now, gentlemen. You are dismissed to your quarters for food, showers, weapons checks, and sleep for the next nine hours. We'll pass the word to muster when it's time. Dismissed!" The Phantoms all stood at attention in unison and then filed out.

40

Forward Motion

Al Hudaydah, Republic of Yemen, January 2019

Al Yamani sat on the vine-covered patio on the north side of his villa grounds. Like all mornings when he was in residence, he took his coffee, figs, pomegranates, bread, and fruit juices in the courtyard immediately outside of the main house. He repeatedly lamented in gruff tones that he "can't read the reports!" "There is nothing of importance in the papers!" "There are no aircraft or ship movements in the reports!" "The reports contain nothing!" "The ones who brief me don't know anything of importance!"

To avoid this frustration and to force the Al Qaida warriors to learn to report to Yamani in clear and succinct terms, Francois coached certain of the apparently "brighter" soldiers to prepare the reports and to present the details in understandable terms. It had worked with only modest success. The soldiers were not technical whiz kids, were not computer-literate, and were not familiar with possible military applications of what appeared to be civilian capabilities. They didn't understand the strategic implications of what they saw. They knew that what they were reporting was important, but they didn't see how it mattered to protecting Al Yamani. The learning curve for these former camel drivers was very steep indeed.

Nevertheless, Al Yamani was visited each morning by four or five young men dressed as servants. They were trying very hard to please Francois and hopefully, Al Yamani. The visit schedules and discussion times were regular and consistent. The soldiers were coached in advance by De La Plane to ensure that Al Yamani could understand what was transpiring in his yet-to-be announced caliphate. In reality, the briefers were trained Al Qaida soldiers, two of whom had recently arrived from two years on the front in Afghanistan. Only weeks earlier, they were concerned only with killing people, torturing farmers into revealing information, and planting IEDs beside roads. Weeks earlier they were killing buffoons, but killing buffoons with a little more intelligence than the ordinary sand soldier. So they were plucked from the desert to a higher calling, the house of the soon-to-be caliph. Francois coached the soldiers that this was a formal situation and that no one publicly addressed Al Yamani with any other title than "My Leader," "Imam," or "My Caliph." Al Yamani completely enjoyed and relished this newfound adulation and respect for titles that reinforced his statements of personal power, his so-called preordained crown of anointment from Muhammad, and his downright enjoyment for butchering people in public.

The soldiers in turn quietly discussed with Al Yamani what they had been told to say about political events in the region and the movement of American forces as far south as the Seychelles and as far west as Mauritania. They told him, as best they could, of new offers of assistance from distant Eurasian and Asian nations they believed existed but were not certain of. They reported to him that the North Koreans had declared that their Taipo Dong II long-range missile was now operational with a small nuclear warhead and could now launch it as far as 2,800 miles or more if need be. The soldiers had no idea what a North Korean was, let alone a Taipo Dong. But they reported it anyway. It was reported that the North Koreans also quietly said they had enough weaponized plutonium for ten to twelve bombs, and they had offered one to Al Yamani and to Pakistan. The soldiers could not know what this meant, but Al Yamani and Francois did. Another soldier told him that an equivalent of $950 million American dollars in gold and silver had been placed in the vaults in Sanaa in his name. The soldier comprehended the exact value of this information and knew it had to be important. He thoroughly understood the words *gold* and *money*, and the location of Saana. It had come as a joint gift from the Russian Federation and the People's Republic of China. The soldier didn't care about the source of the gift or what its meaning was. What he did care about was the word *gold*?

Another man told Al Yamani that Al Qaida had solidified its complete influence over the Islamic Maghreb and now controlled all operations in the Sahara. He reported that the emir of Al Qaida had implemented Sharia law throughout the region and was inviting Al Yamani to join in alliance and support of them. This soldier knew what that meant without an explanation from anyone.

At that moment, Francois was close, as he was nearly every morning for these discussions. He overheard what had been said and stepped close to Yamani to say, "My Leader, this fits superbly into our plans to create an Islamic state in Azawad in northern Mali, in Chad, and in Kenya, as well. Your participation will solidify relations between the jihadists, the Islamists, Boko Haram and the Tuaregs. You should consent to go there and be conciliatory."

"You are right, Francois. This could be a very convincing factor in making our friend Dense Sal Khandar finally see things our way and bring his Somali pirates and legions of followers to our camp. He will arrive this afternoon and stay for two days. We must discuss this subject first and foremost with him."

The next young jihadist soldier had only a few short comments from the command post on foreign forces movements and what observers had seen. "My Leader, there are three American warships transiting the Suez. It is advertised as a routine transfer of ships by the Americans into the Gulf of Aden. They seem to pose no threats and will not be in the Red Sea for long. There is also a message to all nations of the Red Sea that a United Nations coastal geodetic aircraft will be in the area late tomorrow night taking tide and current measurements. They will not be in the region for more than two and one-half hours."

Al Yamani looked pensive for a moment, looked at Francois, then back to Hakeem the soldier, as if seeking a comment.

Francois took the moment to report, "My Leader, I have taken the initiative to post one sentry on a point of high beachfront to watch through the night as the ships pass. If anything untoward occurs, he will sound an alarm. Otherwise no additional action is to be taken. I believe this is a prudent action."

Al Yamani, seeing no other interesting gestures, and hearing no other amplifying comment, said, "Thank you, Francois. Hakeem! Let me know immediately if anything of interest occurs." Then he said, "Francois, join me for a few moments of reflection on Khandar's visit before he arrives tonight."

Phantom Headquarters, MacDill Air Force Base, January 2019

The phone on LuAnn's desk rang. "Hello, this is Special Operations, LuAnn speaking."

"LuAnn, this is Consuela. I'm in New Orleans on business and thought I would just check on you. How are things going for you and the new man in your life?"

"Consuela, how nice to hear from you. Things are well, thank you. They are a little quiet right now. You know how it is. Sometimes there are lots of activities and sometimes none. I'm in the 'none' phase right now and have been for five days. It will get busy here in ten days or so."

"Oh? Why is that? Are the troops out on the town or out of the country?"

"I can't say, Consuela, they never tell me anything. They are a wonderful group of young men who train all day, every day, and talk only to one another in foreign languages all the time and then laugh at themselves. They are a lot of fun to be around. One of them said something to the group in Yemeni last week and they all burst out in laughter. How are things with you and the man in Washington?"

"Well, it sounds like a fun job for you. Things in Washington are very warm and friendly. We enjoy each other very, very much. I believe we are becoming closer and want to be with each other more frequently. Things are unchanged, however, back home in French Guiana, Surinam, and Venezuela. I believe government activities are stabilizing considerably. There is a more friendly air about the country again. The old family estates are getting along better now. The Chavez family in Venezuela has instituted a new university executive education program for citizens like me who have gone abroad to find better jobs. In fact, that's how I met Jason. Both he and I have been recruited by the company that is managing the educational program. They will eventually facilitate our travel to Venezuelan locations of our choosing to fill governmental positions of responsibilities. The goal of these jobs is to improve trade programs. I'm enrolled in it."

"Wow, it sounds like you might be the president of Venezuela or Surinam one day. That sounds like a terrific opportunity," LuAnn said.

"LuAnn, I have taken the liberty of telling my recruiter about you and how important and well educated you have become on your own initiative. His name is Bill Loh. He has asked me to tell you about the program, and he may call you sometime soon. I hope that's alright?"

"Yes, that's fine, Consuela. I'll think about it and might discuss it with him, but I think I've found a nice place here in Tampa. You must come see me sometime and stay with me in my little apartment. It's just outside the base on Bayshore Boulevard overlooking Tampa Bay. I want you to meet Darrin, too. He speaks Spanish very well and knows a few Middle-Eastern phrases, too. He's really smart." Just then LuAnn's internal desk line illuminated and the phone rang. "Consuela, my phone is ringing up a storm and I have to go. Please call back very soon. There are so many things we need to talk about. Bye-bye for now."

Washington, D.C., January 2019

The secure phone in Denny Smith's office in the Russell Senate Office Building rang. Denny looked at the digital caller readout window and saw that it was General Tom Mossman, the president's national security advisor. "Hello, General, this is Denny."

"Denny, I just thought I'd call to tell you the president has just said 'go' to the *Truman* and the *Montana* for the Project RAMPART Mission. Ray Andrews and Bud Patrick should be getting the message about right now. Fifteen minutes ago I received a scrambled message that said they are in a state of Ready. So I guess we are all on the same page."

"Thank you, General. I have high expectations for this one. I've just read the intel reports about new atrocities in the region committed by Al Yamani's people. He has set up military-style boot camps in Yemen and is turning out minimally trained recruits who have more interest in killing infidels than they have knowledge of how to do it. They are driven to fight and have no capacity to be objective about what they are doing. This training has been going on for five years, and it's clear that radical Islam is bent on taking over all of the Middle East and Africa. I fear Europe is on their 'to do' list. I see where they have claimed the lower one-third of Saudi Arabia, all of Oman, the United Arab Emirates, Qatar, and are on the move toward Bahrain. Their forces are taking city after city in Djibouti, Ethiopia, and parts of the Sudan. They are overwhelming unarmed civilians, infrastructure institutions, governmental buildings and their staffs, and they are butchering or maiming any civilians or timid para-military groups that get in their way. They seem to be on a rampage. We also have two unconfirmed reports of the use of chemical warfare on some of the civilian population. We need to confirm that. If it's true, this sheds a whole new light on the situation and lends some urgency to corrective action. I'd say we are none too soon in trying to put a stop to these activities."

"Denny, you've just told me everything I was calling to tell you. You are very well attuned to the deteriorating situation over there. You're also absolutely right in your assessment about doing something to stop them. The State Department filed a formal protest with the UN Security Council late yesterday afternoon. The forces of Al Yamani's caliphate seem to have the Suez Canal, the Persian Gulf, and the Gulf of Oman in their sights. None of the nations of the region want to take them on without one of the major nations of the world to cover their backs—more correctly, to confront the ground forces of the caliphate alliances first and whittle them down to size. So, without a U.S. or NATO presence, the Yemeni Alliance and their new undeclared UIYE caliphate may soon control strategic accesses and major oil refineries in most of the Middle East.

"By the way, the president wanted me to thank you for your words of support and those of Congresswoman Doolin to your colleagues in the Senate and the House in support of this covert concept force and for the modified future budget. We're on the right track here in advocating smaller, more lethal forces to deal with threats to U.S. national security interests abroad."

"Thank you, General. I still have more arrows in my quiver to use in support of the concept. Call if you think I can do more."

"Rest assured we'll be calling. I'll get you an update on the current ops as soon as I know something. The president will be in the Situation Room for the landing and the exit. She would like you and the Congresswoman there, too. I'll call Ms. Doolin and pass the same message to her. I'll get back to you."

Denny then said, "Thanks, General. I'll await your call."

Pyongyang, North Korea, January 2019

Yang Dong Phun, defense minister of the DPR, spoke into his encrypted hotline phone to Quan Ying Mang, defense minister to the People's Republic of China. In the last three months, they had spoken at least once a week about circumstances in the Middle East. Some of the conversations had been about Iran, Iraq, Afghanistan, Syria, and Israel. But slowly, yet inexorably, the conversations have been more and more oriented to the situation in Yemen, Oman, Djibouti, Kuwait, Ethiopia, Somalia, and all the nations who had vested interests in those countries.

Minister Yang opened the conversation with the comments, "Mr. Minister. The events in Yemen have more than met our expectations. Caliph Al Yamani has acceded to all our wishes and has put all the resources we have put at his disposal to very good use. I am happy to report that the people are believed to be very satisfied with the communal support they are receiving from Mr. Al Yamani. My observers report that they have more food than they have ever had before, their medical care has improved markedly, and their educational opportunities have opened new horizons to those who have availed themselves of the classes. They all seem to know that the peace-loving nations of DPRK and the PRC are assisting in improving their lives."

"That is indeed rewarding to hear, Mr. Minister," responded Mr. Quan. "My president had received what he described as a confused report from the director general of Hezbollah in Lebanon via a roundabout message circuit, that military and political arrangements were somewhat, shall I say, disjointed. You, we, and the Russian republic gave those five hundred million Euros in gold in the hope that it would, first and foremost, provide Al Yamani bargaining power to gently persuade his neighboring countrymen to see things his way. Instead, my reports say he spent the funds on chemical, biological, and nuclear systems that, while making him formidable, will also make him dangerous, potentially unpredictable, and certainly visible to Western intelligence. If that is true, it could make you and me culpable in undermining a plot of insurrection. It could instantaneously destabilize the entire Middle East. Please assure me that our involvements are invisible to any casual observer."

The conversation continued for another thirty minutes, with each assuring the other that their tracks were covered, that the sources of missiles and nuclear and high-explosive munitions for Al Yamani were appropriately diffuse, and while Al Yamani knew who his benefactors were, their identities were so subterranean that no one would ever unequivocally uncover the involvement of North Korean or Chinese government officials in this blossoming international catastrophe.

Mr. Yang ended the conversation by summarizing, "My contacts in Washington, D.C., have confirmed that the White House may be oblivious to happenings in that region and they are conducting business as usual in that area. In fact, I am told a flotilla of five U.S. warships is transiting the Red Sea as we speak and show no signs of increased readiness."

"Thank you, Mr. Minister," replied Minister Quan. "That is comforting news. Over the next two weeks, as events unfold in Yemen and the surrounding areas, we must stay in close contact to see where we can build more lasting bridges to our Islamic cousins to ensure our firm and decisive presence is felt."

41

Possible Bugs and Gas

The Suez Canal, January 2019

Aboard the USS *Truman*, one could look up and see the first rays of sunrise to the east and the fading stars of night in the west. The night had been moonless, and at least four more nights were forecast to be equally dark during the assault. The nights in this part of the region were ideal for star-gazers and astronomers. The warm, arid desert air had no aroma and no sense of the presence of mountains, forests, or rain. It was just bland, dry air. The *Truman* was on battle stations with lights out. She was accompanied by two guided missile destroyers and two cruisers. All were at the same battle station alert status with absolute minimal illumination. All ships quietly sliced through the waters of the north end of the Suez Canal, past Stations Number 1 and Number 2, past Isma'ilya, Station 3, Station 4, and into the Gulf of Suez. The canal poured out into the Red Sea, and it was 1200 hours when the task force cleared the canal and began to regroup into a defensive phalanx, not to meet an attack, but to be prepared for random gunshots that were regarded as a distraction and an irritation from the shore. Such shots could be met with absolute destruction, resulting in the annihilation of the shooter and everyone in his surrounding vicinity. But now, here, at this time, it would bring unwanted and unnecessary attention to the mission.

Al Hudaydudah was 875 nautical miles to the south through the Red Sea from the *Truman* battle group's current position. At the current speed of the battle group, it would take slightly over twenty-one hours for it to reach a point directly abeam of the target at Al Hudaydah, Yemen, with an hour or so of slow-forward loiter time to provide cover for the infiltration team.

At 1700 hours Saudi time, the next day, Bud Patrick, John Westcott, all squad leaders and team members, and, of course, Father Desrosiers were assembled in the Ready Room next to the *Truman*'s combat operations center, the COC. The room was lined with seven rows of theater-style seats. They were arranged in two separate sections; there were six seats in each row, three seats in each of the right and left sections. A briefer's platform was located at the front of the room on a small riser. A small podium was located at the right-hand corner of the riser. Three large forty-eight-inch television screens were placed at the front of the room. One was on the center of the front wall, and one was located diagonally on the right and one on the left of the center screen. Current regional weather briefings were continually portrayed on the left-side diagonal screen. Current and near-real-time overhead intelligence from satellites, JSTARS, AWACS, Ghostrider aircraft, or UAVs could be accessed and shown in split-screen format if required. Most importantly, the team could see on the center screen a display of the current target from a low-orbiting stealth UAV directly over the target grounds. Resolution of the video from this sensor was so clear and precise one could see the details of a handheld weapon or an explosive device that an individual was holding.

"Gents," Bud began, "we're here for the first of three update briefings on the status of the mission. As you have heard many times before, we have good news and bad news. First, the good news. The sequences we practiced are still current. Two of the characters we are after are, as of this time, in place as we have been informed. The third character is en route now and will be there before we launch. We are informed as of this hour that those three targets will be in the same location at the same time in about fifteen hours from now. We'll continue to monitor COMMINT for changes. Our mission is to take them alive, but not at the risk of compromising mission secrecy or of losing one Phantom.

"I had asked earlier for daylight over-flight of the target area at least eight hours before our assault, and that has been done. There is no change in the battle space. We are due a nighttime view in two hours to see if there are any last-minute changes to bogey deployments. As soon as I get it, I will pass it to all of you. If there are dramatic changes in the enemy's deployments, I'll make alterations to our plan.

"Now the bad news. We are going in with six five-men teams. We all have our work cut out for us. Fortunately, we have the most comprehensive picture of the battle space. We have reason to believe chem-bio munitions are in the hands of our adversaries; if pressed, they will use them. So we need to isolate and contain the situation.

"Phantom Trigger Team One will cover the north end of the assault area. We are getting an assist from our counterparts in the Israeli Special Ops Command since we have confirmed that Al Yamani's missile targets are in Israel. They have a vested interest, so they have been entrusted to neutralize the silos. Overhead sensors have confirmed the presence of small, low-yield nuclear warheads on the pointy end of the MRBMs in the silos. We have shared that with our Israeli comrades. We have given the Israeli team all the same info we have, so they are just as well informed as we are. The Israelis know what they're doing and they have our backs, just as Trigger Team One will have the backs of the Israelis. You will cover their deployment to the six silos from the east edge of the north-south highway. You'll also cover their egress from the area after the silos are blown.

"Trigger Team Two will be led by Navy Lieutenant Senior Grade Clark Moore and will be made up of three snipers and their two spotters. Sniper specialists Hall, Willoughby, and Johnson will back up Trigger Team One and will also cover Trigger Team Three. They will take out any enemy sentries or observers placed on the beachside ridges before we come ashore. Sniper specialist Johnson will lay down suppressive fire on my command to neutralize enemy reactions. The sniper teams will position themselves at twenty-yard intervals from each other. Lance Corporal Willoughby will cover the advancement from the north side of the compound with his new MXT 135 Punisher battle rifle to cover Trigger Team One. Lance Corporal Hall will be the lead shooter to neutralize resistance around Team Three with his MXT 135 Punisher.

The MXT 135 gun's sight uses a laser range finder programmed to position the heavy destruction round to a point centered on GPS coordinates designated by the laser. It is a highly accurate weapon with an equally precise explosive charge that sends destructive shrapnel in all directions out to ten meters from the point where the munitions detonates, two meters above ground.

"Sniper Specialist Johnson will also cover the advancement from the south end of the compound by Trigger Team Four. Watson and Baker will be the spotters for Team Two. If need be, they each will take out the targets, but only on my command. You sniper teams have a big role in this to cover all our asses. So, keep your heads on a swivel.

"I will be Trigger Lead with Trigger Team Three, which will advance from the Red Sea shoreline directly toward the villa. Each member of my team has a full description of the three targets. We know their height, weight, places of significant scars, tattoos, and marks, and can verify we indeed have our targets. Our job will be to bring out the targets if possible. Once we have them in tow, Team Three will be collecting as many hard drives, documents, flash drives, cell phones, memos, logbooks, encryption devices, and letters as possible in the minimum time we have. I'll be watching the targets and the clock. When I say go, we head for the rendezvous point back on the beach.

"Two members of Trigger Team Three will also immobilize the launch control center located within and below the residence on the compound since we'll already be there to escort our three guests out of the area. The Israelis will very much appreciate the control center destruction.

"Trigger Team Four will be positioned thirty yards from the northwest corner of the villa and will lay down suppressive fire on the north side of the villa and on its west side. Team Five will position themselves thirty yards south of the villa and on its southeast corner. They will lay down suppressive fire on the south and east sides of the main compound house. Both team's missions are to neutralize defensive fire by the enemy soldiers.

"Our goal is to not let individual enemy soldiers get off more than one shot before they are dropped. Zero shots are even better. As more soldiers emerge from underground billets, which are very likely, resistance is expected to be heavy, with lots of wild firing until they figure out what's happening. Reports tell us the protective platoon around Al Yamani is made up of al Qaida and ISIS veterans from Afghanistan and Syria. Expect them to be vicious, tenacious, and persistent.

"Smoke, anti-personnel grenades, and flash-bang explosives will be used to maim and confuse the enemy. I expect them to seek routes out of the compound facilities out the front and back doors. There may even be tunnels or secret doors we don't know about that lead to a taxi stand to downtown," Bud said facetiously. "Be alert to booby traps, tripwires, or pressure plates in walkway stones or stairs. They'll probably also try to use feints in an attempt to draw you out so you will be a target.

"Trigger Team Six will be positioned east of the highway next to the west perimeter of the villa compound facility. Their job is backup firepower, interception of enemy forces who think they are going to outflank us on the west side, and to detonate the two ammo storage bunkers on that side of the compound, which are marked with large red flags. You'll also back-fill any team that has its integrity breached and cover our exit with our guests.

All the phantoms knew what Bud meant when he said "integrity breached." It meant there were unexpected casualties in a team because fleeing and defending forces could overwhelm some Phantoms. They also knew that no Phantom would be left behind, no matter what his status.

"Hammer, will continue to steam south toward the Gulf of Aden at all-ahead slow, just as if they didn't know any of this activity was happening. Although, once our assault commences, the noise and the bright explosions will alert every nation within a hundred miles. We're hoping everyone in the Middle East will think Al Yamani mishandled one of his rockets and it misfired.

"The other four vessels of the battle group will remain close in-trail at full surveillance, black out, and at battle stations. We will rendezvous with the USS *Montana* just abeam of Al Hudaydah, where it will be loitering offshore after we deploy. They will be continuously ready to pick us up as we exit the target. The *Montana* will be semi-submerged four hundred yards offshore awaiting our arrival. The sub's deck crew will assist you aboard as quickly as possible, and they will scuttle the Z boats with remote controls if you don't have time to do it yourselves. There will be an extra Z boat for our shore-based spotters, and they will be armed to assist in covering your egress. The Israelis have their own way out of the area. They have a high-speed Bladerunner speedboat capable of making eighty miles per hour. They'll be met on the beach north of the villa and due west of the silos. Their boat will rendezvous with the last ship in our battle group, the USS *McKinley*. Their speedboat will also be scuttled, and no one will ever know that any of us were there. All our brass expended from your weapons is specially made and has no identification or markings on it. So there is no need to pick it up as you shoot.

"We now have continuous stealth UAV coverage to collect ELINT, COMINT, and IMINT. We also have streaming high-resolution imagery from satellite scanning, which is being down linked to the *Truman*'s combat ops center. So we know what is going on in the target compound right now and continuously. Our activity is also being relayed to the White House Situation Room. So check your makeup before we leave and don't use swear words out loud." All the Phantoms broke out in laughter with this comment. It indeed was a tension reliever.

"The AC-130J Ghost Rider gunship orbiting above, while we are on the ground, will also have a battle picture. Three five-man teams of Phantoms from the Second Regiment will be ready to launch from the gunship to augment us if the situation goes south. The Herc will drop our seven Z boats in para-drop configuration to land five yards off the beach when needed. If we need him to chop up the grounds with his Gatling guns, he can do that, too. The air crew is programmed to lock on to a beacon from the *Montana*, which will pick us up. We will have a para-guidance officer on the beach to make sure the boats come down where they're supposed to and will be inflated when we arrive. The Ghostrider will be squawking a neutral IFF transponder code, and will appear as harmless. It is in the area posing as a UN flight mission mapping currents, tides, and winds for the Egyptian government, who, as you know, is responsible for Suez and Red Sea navigation. Once the missile silo or silos blow, the gunship will send a message in the clear over an unsecure UN frequency while still posing as a UN measurements flight and will report what looks like a massive accidental underground explosion. That will lend credence to the detonation cover story.

"Colonel Westcott will follow me with weather briefings. He tells me his update will be short. The weather is predicted to be clear, hot, and dusty, just as it is every day and night. Chaplain Desrosiers will remain behind for anyone wanting personal time with him. We'll assemble on the hangar deck on the starboard side of the *Truman* in two hours to move to the Z boats. Follow the master chief to that disembarkation point. We'll meet the chaplain there, too. He'll have some good luck charms for each of you. We'll begin moving to board the Z boats at twenty-two-hundred hours."

Al Hudaydah, Republic of Yemen, January 2019

The attendees at the late-evening festivities were prepared for a jovial, friendly, and possible slightly raucous party that was expected to last at least five hours. The long banquet table in the spacious dining room of the villa was heaped with fresh fruit and sweetmeats from local goats and lambs. There were pitchers of beverages from local vats that were identified as fruit juices from the hills of Yemen, although there was a distinct aroma of fermentation that was usually avoided for public meetings but offered in important private meetings. This was no public or local meeting. It was, rather, a meeting of two powerful, influential clans that had similar designs on the people and the wealth of the region. They each also coveted the treasures that certain Asian countries were funneling their way in the hopes a merger of sorts would occur, with one clear leader who could command the most tangible property over oil and natural gas assets, the best seaports and airports, and who showed a superior management ability that promoted growth, strategic position, and influence. Both leaders showed most of these characteristics, but perhaps Al Yamani commanded more diplomatic skill, territory, and international wealth than did Khandar. Both men knew that. Both men also recognized that together they commanded a greater percentage of wealth and territorial resources than did the Egyptians or the Saudis. Both men also knew that a merger between them and their forces could easily make the Egyptians and the Saudis irrelevant and no threat to further expansion to the north toward the Mediterranean and to the west toward central Africa. All that made these two men extremely formidable.

Both men were surrounded with three or four of their most trusted advisors, all of whom knew they were present to witness the birth of a new dynasty and a power base for the Middle East that would, within six months, be the dominant force with which any infidel would have to reckon. Al Yamani had the edge on forces and wealth and benefited from the worldly view and advice of Francois De La Plane. Dense Sal Khandar held the edge in numbers of forces, seagoing ships, and stolen high-tech weaponry that caused large ships and crews to cower from shots across their bows. In short, Al Yamani was long on intelligence and ability to plan. Sal Kahndar was long on brute-force sailors who were one-dimensional.

Each leader was not fooled by the other's polite show of force. Each knew of the other's strengths, weaknesses, and shortcomings. At this point, Al Yamani didn't know it, but Khandar had no worldly view or sense of immortality and was prepared to capitulate, as long as the percentage of his take on any treasure was to his advantage and he could protect his freedom to move around the region in secrecy and anonymity. But he didn't want it to appear as surrender. He wanted it to appear as a friendly agreement between longtime allies, close friends, and forthright business partners who trusted one another implicitly. He wanted an agreement that looked like a regional alliance of brothers who trusted each other without a shadow of a doubt.

"My longtime good friend and classmate, Dense Sal Kahndar," said Al Yamani in a sweeping and overly lavish show of appeal for solidarity, mostly for the consumption of the less personal individuals gathered around them.

Only Francois was so familiar with both individuals and their cultures that maybe only he and Al Yamani knew there was more pressure to capitulate to come.

Yamani continued, "It has been too many years between our visits with one another. Your precious time here honors me, Francois, and my plans and dreams for my future caliphate." We are brothers in a sacred bond that few in the Middle East can know and appreciate."

"My dearest and longest-time friend, Al Yamani," replied Khandar.

He was less a politician and more a businessman. He wanted to get directly to the point. "We have been friends for too many years to be evasive and indirect in our thoughts and dreams. I am familiar with yours, and you are familiar with mine. Your thoughts, dreams, and actual resources combined with mine will make us the most respected and feared religious, political, and military force in the hemisphere. No country or region in this part of the world will be able to resist us, not even the Great Satan. Beginning next week I am prepared to follow your lead and your plan for conquest of middle Africa, southern Europe, the Persian Empire, and beyond. I am a businessman and a loyal ally. Let us get on with it. But tonight, let us revel in our alliance, friendship, and capabilities. Tomorrow we shall plan how to take over the Western world. They will wilt before our power and our fierce beheadings that will foretell our allegiance to Allah. But tonight, let us enjoy our time together and the life we have come to enjoy."

This was music to the ears of Al Yamani and Francois. The man got right to the point. Yamani was ecstatic. Francois was encouraged by what he heard, but failures in arrangements such as this in which he had been engaged in the past, could be a humbling experience. He would much rather choose to appear overjoyed, but he was inwardly cautious. He needed to read and see the details of the agreement. Much chaos, death, and destruction lay ahead, and he knew it.

42

Stand By to Launch

The Red Sea, January 2019

The USS *Montana* silently, without lights or fanfare, in the pitch-black darkness, surfaced fifty yards off the starboard bow of the USS *Truman* as expected. Her forward speed was the same as that of the *Truman*. The captains of both the *Truman* and the *Montana* each knew the other was there at the appointed place and time. The *Truman*'s deck crew was lowering six Z boats into the water six feet below the lower hangar deck access to the sea. Father Desrosiers stood at the hangar deck hatch opening. He had in his hands what appeared to be a stack of five-inch-by-seven-inch cards. He handed one to each Phantom as they passed him and said, "Go with God." Everyone knew what the card represented; it was a "blood chit." The top half of the card appeared blank, but in reality an American flag was printed on it that could only be revealed under ultraviolet light. A Yemeni flag appeared next to it, but it was visible so that even an ordinary Yemeni citizen could recognize it. The words beneath the Yemen flag, written in French, Arabic, and Persian, read that "the holder of this card is a foreigner who speaks neither French nor Persian nor Arabic but means the finder no harm. It guarantees the finder fifty thousand American dollars for the safe return of and aid to this fallen soldier with no questions asked." The card was less intended to identify the soldier's nationality, even though it might be obvious to an educated citizen, and more intended to help in the return of a lost or captured soldier. As an added benefit, Father Norm and the DOD had locator chips embedded into the cards that could beep out a location within a radius of three miles of the card holder's location. Each of the Phantoms tucked the cards into their undershorts for safekeeping.

Bud Patrick, Master Chief Barrett, and U.S. Coast Guard communications specialist, Petty Officer Third Class James Chavez stood at the hatch seeing Trigger Teams One and Two down the gangway to the water and their respective Z boats. The backpack of Chavez held not only forty pounds of several different types of defensive weaponry and explosives, but it had thirty-five pounds of communications electronics in it, as well. Team Three approached, and Bud and his two-person lead and communications element fell in behind and disappeared down to their Z boat. Three more teams, fifteen Phantoms in all, quickly moved down to their respective Z boats. Father Norm stood at the hatch, made the sign of the cross with his hand, then held up his hand, palm outward, in a gesture of nondenominational blessing to all of the Phantoms. Lieutenant Junior Grade Michael Coles then said quietly to the priest, "Father Norm, we need to make ready to move down the gangway to transit to the *Montana*." Father Norm and Coles moved to the hatch.

Once the Z boats cleared the stern of the *Truman*, all boats assumed a phalanx formation with Bud and Team Three at the point. Three minutes away from the *Truman*, each boat then moved to a position that would put it on the beach at the appropriate landing point closest to the team's appointed beachhead firing position. The boats were approximately fifteen yards apart, and their powerful advanced electric motors were quietly humming and moving the boats steadily toward the shoreline. There was very little wake and practically no churn from the outboard motor props. They were almost five hundred yards offshore, and everyone had engaged their NVGs, or night vision goggles, to scan the shore for movement.

Bud quickly looked down at his left wrist control keypad and engaged his comms to perform a communications quality check back to the *Truman* and over the horizon to the White House Situation Room. All the Phantoms were also connected, but were in Receive-

Only mode. They could hear everything that was going on between Bud and the command channels and the chatter between Bud and the shore spotters. This made for quick reaction or none at all, easy to anticipate.

"Trigger Lead to Hammer, Teton, and Deer Hunter. Comm check!"

"Trigger Lead, this is Hammer; read you five square," came the response from the *Truman*.

"Trigger Lead, this is Teton; read you five square and standing by," came the response from the USS *Montana*.

"Trigger Lead, this is Deer Hunter; read and see you five square," came the response from the White House Situation Room. Bud simply clicked his mic switch twice in quick succession to acknowledge he had received all responses. This kept chatter to a minimum and let all who were on the line know that two-way comms were working fine. But Bud thought to himself, *Shit, I was hoping everybody in Washington was out having a beer instead of watching us. Oh well, this will be a much better show than* Dancing with the Stars.

Three hundred yards offshore, Bud's command channel clicked and a low voice came on the line. "Trigger Lead, this is Ice Breaker, Tally Ho!" Bud expected this call. It was the defense systems operator ashore who had just validated that all enemy shore electronic detection systems had been spoofed, overridden, or disabled with no response from Al Yamani's perimeter defense lookouts.

Bud simply responded, "Roger, Ice Breaker." He and all the Phantoms knew the coast was clear—so far.

It was nearly 2300 Arabian Standard Time. Earlier in the day, Hakeem Ali Abdullah had briefed the Leader that some vessels were moving through the Red Sea but that nothing more was known. His leader, and Sheik De La Plane, as all the soldiers called Francois, said, "Go out tonight and call if you see anything unusual." It was now approaching an hour before midnight, and Hakeem had been chewing the "magic root" for three hours. He was feeling no pain or urgencies. He did, however, remember his charge, "Let me know if you see or hear anything." So here he was in a daze from the magic root, believing himself on a mission for Sheik De La Plane, Al Yamani, and Allah, staggering up the north-south highway next to the villa in search of something, someone, or anything that would allow him to sound an alarm and make him the hero that saved the caliphate, or something like that. He had a Kalashnikov automatic rifle with twenty rounds of ammunition in the clip slung loosely over his shoulder and down his back, where it would be impossible to get it to firing position if necessary.

He walked or, more correctly, staggered for nearly twenty minutes north on the road toward the secret rocket pits, as they were called by his fellow soldiers. They didn't know exactly what was in the rocket pits, but they were told they didn't need to know and if they did, they would know too much.

Bud and all the Phantoms had just come ashore and were quietly and slowly downloading from the Z boats. They were all then preparing to turn the boats outward and set the automatic scuttling mechanism for ten minutes later into one hundred fathoms of Red Sea water. Bud's comm channel clicked.

The quiet voice on the other end said, "Trigger Lead, this is Eye Ball. A strolling sentry due east your position. I have him in my scope. Standing by." This was Air Force Master Sergeant Sue Biener and her spotter, the other scouting team sent to hide, observe, report, act if required, and cover the evacuation at the end of the operation. Biener was always tough, ready, and never wrong; Bud knew this.

"Roger, Eye Ball, stand by!" Bud looked to his right and to his left. He held up a clenched fist, which all Phantoms could see through their NVGs. They all went down to one knee and froze. Bud turned to the master chief and whispered, "What say you?"

Barrett replied in as cryptic an answer, "There's no rush. Let's wait five to eight." Both men looked at their watches. Bud clicked his mike to all Phantoms and the command elements. "Stand by for five minutes!"

The Situation Room, the White House, Washington, D.C.

When President Chenoa, General Mossman, Admiral Nagle, Denny Smith, Rosemary Doolin, and the others gathered around the Sit Room table saw the team on the beach and heard the exchange, there was a quiet collective intake of breath and concerned glances exchanged around the room that the mission could be compromised. Chenoa broke the silence. "The Phantoms know what they're doing. Let's wait with them for the five minutes. Colonel Patrick knows what's at stake."

The Red Sea

Captain Bill Chandler of the USS *Truman* and Captain Rod Blake of the USS *Montana* both heard the short exchange and both thought the Sword of Damocles was hanging over the heads of the Phantoms with the stroll of this one drunken sentry who seemingly had no purpose other than to walk around. Unfortunately this walkaround could jeopardize a critical mission whose outcome could save countless lives in a variety of countries. Both captains looked at their watches—four minutes to go to a decision.

One minute later, Bud Patrick looked at his master chief and pointed to his watch, then held up three fingers. The gesture was meant to say three minutes to a decision. Bud knew Eye Ball, his spotter who had been in the area for twenty hours already and was not only a spotter, but a very decent sniper for close-in targets. After one and one-half minutes, Bud looked at the master chief, who nodded his head in consent. Bud clicked the mic button.

"Eye Ball, Trigger Lead. Status?"

"Trigger Lead, Eye Ball. Subject is drunk. Fell down and is now taking a leak in the bushes. Subject is twenty yards away and moving to me. Subject in sights for immediate departure."

There were chuckles all around the Sit Room, aboard both vessels, and among the Phantoms. Bud again looked at the master chief, who nodded in the affirmative. Bud depressed the mic button again and said, "Eye Ball, Trigger Lead; go on my command in thirty seconds."

"Roger that, Trigger Lead."

After thirty seconds, Bud again depressed the mic button and said, "Eye Ball, Trigger Lead, go!"

Trigger Team Two, closest to Eye Ball's position and the staggering Hakeem, heard a muffled *thunk*, but saw no flash or heard cries or mumbling that could be construed as an attempt to radio a warning.

All the Phantoms and the listeners on the channel awaited the next transmission. One minute went by and then, "Trigger Lead, this is Eye Ball. Subject is silent and out of sight."

"Roger, Eye Ball. Trigger Teams complete housekeeping and be ready to move out to your tactical positions in three minutes on my Go Command."

There was a collective sigh of relief among all the listeners on the channel. The mission was now again moving inexorably toward a conclusion. It meant among many possibilities that threatening nuclear devices would be destroyed, chemical weaponry would be neutralized, atrocities in the region would diminish significantly, and so-called caliphs, leaders, self-appointed presidents and generals, and fools who thought they were immortal would vanish from Yemen and this region of the Saudi Peninsula.

43

BOOM!

Al Hudaydah, Republic of Yemen, January 2019

Bud Patrick depressed his mic button and said, "Trigger Lead and Trigger Team Three in position. All teams start roll call when ready." He then waited, knowing it could be up to ten minutes before he heard the teams check in with their Ready status. Some had to creep unseen farther than others. But in no case should it take longer than ten minutes, if time and distance calculations were correct. Everything so far had gone without a hitch. There were no confrontations, no one had tripped on anything, and everyone moved like the Phantoms they were. Even so, operations like this usually had at least one hiccup and sometimes two. Bud knew he would have to deal with them when and if they occurred. Then he thought to himself, *This has gone too smoothly so far, so we need to be on our toes.* He knew he would pass that alert when all checked in.

Al Yamani Villa, the Banquet

Francois had just enough to eat and drink to feel euphoric and encouraged by what had been said and agreed to in the last four hours. He secretly harbored misgivings about the mission Al Yamani had tasked him with in Riyadh in February. He had come to believe, one way or another, this was not to be his destiny. He had learned over the years to hide certain feelings, certain gestures, and certain ways of responding to comments and questions. Yamani's task for him was placed in a mental file that he seldom accessed. If he needed to go to this file he could, but he knew, somehow, it would not be anytime soon. Sacrificing himself seemed a noble cause to Al Yamani. But Francois had the peculiar feeling that Allah, or God, had another calling for him. The conversation between all the old schoolmates was lively, animated, and exhilarating to all of them.

De La Plane spoke in bitter terms about how they believed the Middle East had been ravaged and economically raped by the United States, France, England, and the other members of the NATO alliance. They spoke jokingly and a bit drunkenly about how they would like to hang all the leaders of Western nations in effigy in downtown Riyadh, Saudi Arabia, or Cairo, Egypt, to show the strength and power of the caliphate. They laughed aloud about how they had emasculated the political power of the United States and England in the Middle East and how American soldiers had run like frightened boys from Iraq, Afghanistan, Kuwait, and Qatar only three years earlier. The three were indeed on an ego trip about the force, speed, and ferocity of the brutal and sickening devastation they left in most countries in the Middle East. Now they imagined and fanaticized about moving to central Africa and north to the Mediterranean and into Spain, France, and beyond. Their lieutenants yelled in glorious exhilaration at the thought of European women and the great bounty they would conquer and own.

There were at least thirty mid- and high-ranking Al-Qaida soldiers and more than twenty women who laughed and screamed in joy at the debauchery that was unfolding. It would not be an exaggeration to say that most of Yamani's and Khandar's men were distracted.

Outside the Villa

Bud turned to his comm specialist, Petty Officer Chavez, and said, "Unlock the transmit channels to all teams and keep them open."

"Aye, aye, sir. It's done."

A green light was illuminated on the small handheld comm channel control keypad in Chavez's hand. The same green light came on at each of the team lead's keypads. They knew the channel was now hot for their roll call and would remain so throughout the operation. The helmet cameras for Bud, Barrett, and Chavez were also activated. Each Phantom knew he should only transmit messages if he had something urgent to say. Otherwise, they were only to listen for commands or requests for aid or redirection of mission instructions. Then the cryptic reports started to come in.

"Team One, ready."

Bud clicked the mic button twice.

"Team Two, ready."

Click-click.

"Team Three, ready."

Click-click.

"Team Four, ready."

Click-click.

"Team Five, ready."

Click-click.

"Team Six, ready."

Click-click.

"David, Ready." This was the Israeli commando team who were also on the same frequency and ready for the Go Command. Their code name referred to the Star of David.

Click-click.

"All Teams, be alert to traps and hidden bogeys." All the Phantoms recalled Bud's warning earlier about tripwires, traps, pressure plates, unusual aromas, bogeys hiding in closets or toilet rooms, and unfamiliar lights or beeps.

"Proceed on my Go Command in five." They all knew they had five minutes to check themselves over for weapons locks, holsters, ammo clips, and anything else that might be dangling that they could lose or trip on. The Israeli commandos were also on the frequency, and Bud, the master chief, Chavez, and Team Three were going right into the lions' den. Their target was the banquet room itself, where the raucous activity was taking place. They weren't sure if there would be anyone sober and armed. If so, he or she was dead. Bud looked at the master chief and gave him a knuckle bump. Then he looked at his watch. Four minutes to Go Command.

Al Yamani Villa, the Banquet

Francois had learned to control his intake of the powerful Yemeni beverages; they had a paralyzing effect. His conscious mind drifted to the late-night anonymous and obtuse cell phone warning him to be observant, to listen carefully, and to sense all aspects of how a target opportunity would appear. A sudden clarity hit him just then, as if he had been struck across his back by a large object; he looked around, saw all his friends, noticed sensitive documents, saw computers carelessly up and churning with names, plans, and places, money scattered around with abandon, much food and drink to cast a fog over everyone's laughter and banter, half-naked women rolling on carpets and pillows around the room, and a careless attitude among the guests. He whispered out loud, "My God, it's tonight! We are vulnerable, and we are going to be hit tonight by the ghosts."

Francois quietly excused himself to go to his room down the corridor. He moved past the steel door leading to the underground tunnel to the airport runways, where he knew Al Yamani always had an executive jet ready for any last-minute whimsical flight to a neighboring country. He knew the pilots would respond to Yamani or himself, if need be.

For now, he believed he needed to retrieve several maps and cryptic notes on plans for the next six months. If there was no assault, he would return and stay with the raucous group and rejoin the party. He could put the papers back in his room later. He quickly entered his room, gathered his papers, and headed for the door. He stopped for a brief moment, then opened a small cabinet next to his bed. He removed the unopened bottle of very rare Remy Martin cognac, placed it on the nightstand, and headed back to the banquet.

Unbeknownst to anyone except Francois, Al Yamani planned to launch six of the IRBMs within four weeks. The targets were to include Tel Aviv, Cairo, Damascus, Ankara, and Khartoum. A sixth target had not yet been selected but was being held in abeyance as a bargaining chip. Al Yamani knew where he wanted it to go, but he was waiting for the reactions of the West. Francois didn't know for sure, but he believed the sixth target was to be the Suez Canal entrance with a U.S. warship in it.

Francois sensed that these missiles would be tantamount to poking a sleeping tiger with a very sharp stick. He knew such actions would most certainly mean the rapid annihilation of the UYIE caliphate, the ISIL caliphate, and their plans to quietly consume all of the Middle East, its people, its treasure, and its power and oil.

44

GO! GO! GO!

*Outside the Villa, Al Hudaydah,
Republic of Yemen, January 2019*

"This is Trigger Lead, two minutes," Bud said quietly into his mic.

Inside the Villa

Francois slowly, though thoughtfully, walked back toward the banquet room. He passed the steel door to the tunnel, quickly turned the dead bolt to unlock it, and continued the ten paces toward the banquet room. This short walk to his room and back served to crystallize in his conscious mind that something terrible was about to happen. He stood in the doorway and called to his friends, "Muhammad! Dense! Come with me, now!" He had never called these men by their first names since their days in the university. To do so now imparted a sense of alarm Al Yamani and Sal Khandar were not used to hearing. Yamani looked up with surprise, and then a grin spread across his face.

"Francois, my sheik of strategic plans. You are too serious, and our beverages have made you delirious."

They both looked up through the haze from the hookah pipes, through the odor and vapor of the fermented coconut milk and date juice.

Sal Khandar said, "My longtime friend and schoomate, come sit so we can chat about your future."

"No, my friends, you must come with me, now," said De La Plane.

"No, Francois, you are being too emotional for our guest and his men. We cannot break up the festivities now," said Yamani.

Outside the Villa

The local time was 0145, January 27, 2019.

"This is Trigger Lead, one minute; stand by for my Go Command."

Inside the Villa

Al Yamani and Sal Khandar had more drink and food than usual because of the successful discussion. The two of them were reveling in their graduate school experiences and protest marches and still feeling giddy about the peace followed by lack of action of those events. The time between then and now seemed to be a lifetime compared to the force and progress of their current conquests. Yamani and Khandar believed they had more to discuss, and they decided to ignore "the Sheik" for now.

Outside the Villa

"This is Trigger Lead. Go! Go! Go!"

Inside the Villa

Patrick, Barrett, and Chavez burst through the large double doors at the narrow end of the banquet hall. At the same time, three Phantoms from Team Three crashed through the smaller entry door on the west side of the larger double doors, and two Team Three members crashed through the smaller door east of the main doors.

One Phantom on the right and one on the left were equipped with Mossberg twelve-gauge shotguns. The gun and the shooter could always be guaranteed to clear a room when the quarters were tight. The others in the team were equipped with M4 rifles with 223-caliber ammunition or M-14 rifles with 7.62 rounds that destroyed a target the first time, every time. All of these weapons combined with the skill of the Phantoms to use them made the Team Three warriors nearly invincible.

Eight feet from the entrance doors stood a four-foot-high ornamental stone wall extending at least ten feet across the width of the broad hall. It served as an ornamental greenery planter and was a perfect shield for the bullets that were about to be fired their way.

Then there was loud gunfire and a flash-bang stun grenade was hurled by a Phantom into the center of the room. Two Phantoms followed with another grenade around the right flank of the ornamental wall, firing well-placed shots into four Al Qaida soldiers. The shotgun blasts opened a wide swath down the right and left sides of the room. A second Phantom hurled a smoke grenade to the far end of the long room. A quick look around by Bud, the master chief, and the other Phantoms showed very few of the Yemeni or Somali party guests or their Al Qaida and Taliban guards were in any state to fight at this moment. But they were about to awaken from their dazed euphoria. Up to this point, they might have thought they were happy, but now they were not.

The room was large, perhaps twenty-five feet by forty feet, and dimly lit with low-wattage ceiling lights and candles. In addition to the ornamental wall at one end, there were sufficient pillars and corners to shield the Phantoms from wild bullets in the smoke-filled area. Bud motioned two Phantoms to begin flanking moves down each of the right and left sides of the room. Overturned tables and furniture items were plentiful to serve as shields. The Phantoms had them all claimed. The Al Qaida and Taliban soldiers were not so lucky; they were in the open, looking for clear targets. There was little for them to see in the hazy room. Team Three members were carefully but quickly picking them off.

From the second the Phantoms came crashing through the doors at the end of the room, Francois knew what was unfolding and quickly backed several steps down the hallway to the steel tunnel door, opened it, and went through, locking it behind him.

Four Taliban soldiers then emerged from a small doorway at the end of the room connecting a food preparation kitchen to the banquet room. All were armed and equipped with spare ammunition and small anti-personnel grenades. They entered firing wildly through the smoke. Bullets were ricocheting off the walls and floors. Barrett was grazed by one of them in his left thigh. He fired at one of the soldiers, and the man went down. Then he fired at another; he, too, went down. The soldiers were bent on protecting Al Yamani and the Somali occupants of the room. They had been pre-briefed that in the face of a threat they were to do so at any cost, even their own lives. But there was so much haze, smoke, and scattered debris around the large room, they couldn't find the men they were to protect.

When the first soldier from each of the three groups entered the room, they began firing wildly at shadows, draperies, and rugs, mistaking them for camouflaged battle dress uniforms. They then fired their weapons toward voices speaking English and at real and imagined targets in the room.

Bud yelled, "Yamani and Khandar, freeze! Stay where you are or die right here and now." There was no opportunity to frisk them for weapons at this moment without exposing a Phantom warrior to direct gunfire.

Then gunshots started to ring out from every direction. One Phantom tossed another smoke grenade into one hallway, and another Phantom tossed a Sun-Brite Flare farther into the room. All the Yemeni and Somali fighters were temporarily blinded. The Phantoms were all wearing light-sensitive tinted glasses for just such an occasion.

Two Al Qaida guards suddenly appeared as if out of nowhere. They were wildly firing their automatic weapons in the direction of the ornamental wall. But Patrick, Barrett, Chavez, and the remaining Phantoms had already moved down the side walls.

There was panic and confusion in every corner of the large room. The only ones in control were the Phantoms. They shot three to six rounds into the ceiling to cause most of the Yemeni and Somali soldiers to crouch down and make it difficult to get into a firing position, if they had weapons.

Yamani yelled, "Who are you? You have no right to be in my home or my country! Get out! Get out! I will have you shot!"

"Shut your mouth and keep your head down," Bud yelled back. "Where is De La Plane?"

"I don't know what you are talking about! Get out!" screamed Al Yamani.

Sal Khandar just knelt on the floor, watching the camouflaged soldiers and the Al Qaida and Taliban guards firing back at any and all shooters. He was starting to emerge from his drunken stupor and realized what was happening.

One soldier on one side of the room pulled a pistol from beneath his robes, and the master chief shot him squarely between the eyes. Six soldiers came running from some buried bunker down the hallway beyond the opening through which Francois had just exited. Two Phantoms along with Bud and Chavez picked them off as they entered the room.

Barrett had his back to Bud and Chavez and was looking for Al Qaida soldiers to enter the great hall through the large entry doors through which the Phantom team had just entered. He didn't have to wait long.

He yelled, "Four bogies at our six o'clock, Skipper!" Barrett fired and got two of them. Bud whirled around and fired two shots from his Glock pistol into the other two.

"Stay locked on to the doors, Master Chief, I'll cover forward," Bud yelled.

Three deafeningly loud explosions could be heard at the far north end of the compound. The buildings and ground shook as if a massive earthquake had just erupted across the countryside. The David Team had blown three silos and irreparably destroyed three North Korean missiles. The sky was as bright as day outside for several minutes. The David Team then moved to Silos 4, 5, and 6.

Six beturbaned soldiers came racing down one of the hallways into the large room; each carried an automatic Kalashnikov and spare ammo in belts or bandoliers. Each also had two small pistols in shoulder holsters or belt holsters. They entered the room with the firing sequences set on their rifles at automatic, and they didn't know what or who they would find. But immediately they saw the vague outline of eight Western military-style uniformed soldiers with weapons pointed at them. They each pulled their triggers and fired eight to ten shots in all directions.

Six more Al Qaida soldiers arrived from behind a curtain on the opposite side of the room through a hidden door that matched the stucco wall surface. They were all firing at vague targets in the large smoke-filled room.

The Phantoms were arrayed all across one end of the room with clear vantage points of the full length of the room. They were behind cover and could see robed and turbaned fighters all around the great room. This would have been a difficult position for an untrained warrior. But the Phantoms were all skilled in close-in combat, low-visibility quarters, and low-light or sudden bright light events. They trained for just this kind of firefight. They were ready for this battle.

Outside the Villa

Phantom Team Six was in position just outside the villa along the highway between the villa and the beach. They didn't expect any activity until the teams were ready to egress the buildings. They were surprised when a large trapdoor sprang open in the field fifty yards north of the villa but south of the missile silos. Twelve guards dressed in Al Qaida and Taliban garb rushed out of the opening like ants from an underground nest and took up a circular firing formation from prone positions to apparently determine the size and makeup of the threat. This was an unexpected maneuver, but the Phantoms were prepared.

Just then another trapdoor opened twenty-five yards farther north toward the silos. Another fifteen guards emerged and took up the same circular observation-defensive positions. It wasn't clear whether they were attempting to escape the force of the silo detonations and feared for their own safety, or whether they were making ready to defend the compound. They all must have been placed in the underground launch control center buried in the center of the massive compound grounds.

This was a situation tailor-made for Darrin Hall. He had been scanning the field through his NVGs when the door in the ground opened and the fighters emerged. He sighted-in the center of the first group of twelve through the scope of his new MXT 135 Punisher Battle Rifle.

Twenty-five yards to the north, Lance Corporal Rick Willoughby was following exactly the same procedures for the fifteen fighters who emerged from the second in-ground hideaway. He, too, sighted in his MXT 135 and was preparing to fire.

Hall fired one round, which exploded over the heads of the twelve soldiers. He scanned the grounds through his NVG scope at the point of detonation. He increased the magnification to see details; he saw at least two faces. They were Oriental. There also was no movement. To be safe, he fired a second round.

To the north Willoughby fired his first round, scanned the area of detonation, and saw one soldier get up and charge toward his position. The soldier looked Oriental. He set the laser finder and the GPS precision locator and fired a second round. The shot burst right where it was supposed to. There was no movement in the target area.

Inside the Villa

Meanwhile, of the sixteen Al Yamani henchmen who rushed into the great hall to defend their "caliph," ten were down. The others were behind shields in the room, and Yamani and Khandar were still cowering in the center of the room on the floor. One of the Al Qaida soldiers threw a tear gas grenade into the room toward four of the Phantoms. One Phantom was bleeding down his right arm. But he was still firing. A second Phantom took a bullet through his left shoulder, but he was still able to fire his M-14 with his right hand using his left forearm to support the rifle. All the Phantoms pulled up their inter-nasal re-breather filters and inserted them into their nostrils to counter the tear gas. They had all been through tear gas defense measures training and knew not to touch their eyes.

"Master Chief and Chavez, are you still in one piece?"

"I'm okay, Skipper, let's move," Barrett said.

"Yes, sir, Colonel, I'm ready to roll," said Chavez.

Bud knew his team was up against the clock. There were a few more bogies than were anticipated, so this was taking more time than expected. Bud knew he had to lock down this building and begin collecting his prisoners and tactical intelligence evidence.

He said, "Good, let's move around to our right and head for that pantry kitchen."

45

Dead Captives

The Situation Room, the White House, Washington, D.C., January 2019

General Mossman said, "Madame President, the recall code is Lincoln-Lincoln. If you say the word, we'll abort now and reduce possible casualties."

"No, General. The team knows what they are doing and are sensitive to the injuries and the clock. It appears as though they may have this just about done. Give them more time. We need the papers, the cell phones, and the computer hard drives," said President Chenoa. "Please send a back-channel to the *Montana* that there are minor casualties so they'll be ready," she continued.

"Yes, ma'am. Right away," said Mossman.

Inside the Villa

Just then, there was another detonation at the far north end of the compound at Missile Silo 4. Then there was a secondary explosion, and both detonations lit up the sky and the surrounding area for ten miles in all directions. The explosions perforated missile number six and rendered it useless, even though it was not fueled or armed. All that was left of the five silos and the missiles were craters, twisted metal, concrete chunks, and gravel.

The David Team was already headed for the beach, away from the fires and burning rocket fuel and toward the safety of the Blade Runner fast attack boat that would take them safely to the USS *McKinley* and whisk them on to safer waters. Team Six and their embedded sniper covered their exit to the beach. There had been so much noise, massive amounts of destruction, and so much fire, that none of the Al Qaida and Taliban fighters had dared to come out from their cover for fear of more massive explosions.

Teams Four and Five and the embedded team snipers from their positions on the northwest and southeast corners of the compound fired very few rounds of suppression fire. Those corners had no more than eight or ten Al Qaida and Taliban guards to provide protective cover for the tyrant. They were quickly dispatched as soon as they became visible. Resistance by Al Yamani's guards was minimal.

Meanwhile, Patrick, Barrett, Chavez, and one Phantom went down on one knee to survey the path ahead. They each aimed at moving targets and dispatched them in rapid succession. They fired with carefully but quickly aimed shots from their M-14 automatic rifles. Bud led Barrett and Chavez down the side of the room, picking out targets while at the same time looking at the computers, the cell phones, the papers, the loose cash, and especially the Chinese and Russian weapons that could serve as evidence of sources of support to the al Qaida and Taliban butchers.

Just then Khandar reached behind his back and pulled a forty-five-caliber pistol out of his belt and pointed it at Bud. In a split second, Chavez raised his M-14 and put two bullets into Khandar: one in the chest and one in the head. Yamani looked in horror at his old friend with blood all over him.

Bud Patrick, squatting next to a pillar, looked at Sal Kahadar with half his head blown away for what seemed like several minutes. It was, in fact, a long second. He then looked at Chavez for another long second and realized what had just happened. A key tyrant was gone, but he, Colonel Bud Patrick, was still alive and not a statistic.

"Thanks, Chavez. I'm glad you came along. Make sure all comm channels are still open."

"Aye, aye, Skipper. We are five square on all comms," replied Chavez.

While clicking his wrist-mounted mic button, Bud said, "Deer Hunter, I hope you're getting all this video. These guys have had a lot of help. Confirm Sal Khandar is a Splash and De La Plane is a No Show."

"Roger, Trigger Lead," came the reply from Deer Hunter.

"Yamani, you son of a bitch, you stay right there and don't make a move, or I personally will send you to see your seventy-two virgins along with that hookah pipe next to you shoved up your ass!" Bud said clearly for all to hear. The master chief knelt next to Al Yamani for less than thirty seconds, yanked his hands forward, and slipped a Flex-Cuff around his wrists to partially disable him.

There were bodies and blood everywhere, so the scene was very convincing to Yamani that he had failed. Bud looked around and quickly counted all the Phantoms in Team Three. All were accounted for.

Yamani had always said he would never be taken alive by any adversary. But because of his exalted position and the army of ISIL, Al Quada, Houthi, Al Shabab, Sunni, Shiia, and Boko Haram fighters, he believed himself invincible. Now, however, he began to think he was not so immortal after all. He thought if he could only find a weapon on the floor, he would deny these infidels the prize they seemed to want so badly.

Yamani momentarily reflected that only minutes earlier, he, Khandar, and De La Plane had spoken in bitter terms about how they believed the Middle East had been ravaged and economically raped by the United States, France, England, and the other members of the NATO alliance. They spoke jokingly, and a bit drunkenly, about how they would like to hang all the leaders of Western nations in effigy in downtown Riyadh, Saudi Arabia, or Cairo, Egypt, to show the strength and power of the caliphate. Now, Yamani concluded, that all was now over and his dream of immortality was gone. A wave of despair came over him. He wished he could put an end to this hopeless situation.

From his position on the floor, he looked around for anything that could serve as a weapon. He saw Khandar's 45-caliber pistol under an overturned chair. He quickly looked around to see if anyone was watching him. No one was at that second. Even though his wrists were bound, he lunged for the pistol, hoping it had a full clip. He quickly put the barrel in his mouth and pulled the trigger. The back of his skull blew away into the room.

Bud and the master chief quickly turned when they heard the shot. They saw what was left of Yamani.

"Shit!" said Barrett.

"Damn it all anyway," said Bud. "I was hoping we could get some more intel out of the bastard. Son of a bitch!"

"Deer Hunter, this is Trigger Lead. Yamani is a Splash by his own hand."

"Roger, Trigger Lead, we saw it! Expedite data gathering and exit."

"Roger, Deer Hunter."

All the soldiers and Taliban fighters were down. No more shots were being fired. Nothing remained to be done except to gather information, computer hard drives, cell phones, some of the Euros, Chinese yuan, and Russian rubles for evidence of foreign support. There were even nearly two dozen small gold ingots with North Korean DPRK logos imprinted on them. The Phantoms began stuffing each other's backpacks with the loose items.

Chavez pulled out a camera and took several photos of the carnage, the evidence, and the weapons. The master chief took out his combat knife and cut the Flex-Cuff off the wrists of Al Yamani. To have shot himself while having already been captured would be too hard to explain to the radical Islamists who would eventually discover the carnage. Chavez directed his photographic task on the bodies of Al Yamani and Sal Khandar and several of the Al Qaida and Taliban soldiers who were wearing turbans and scarves with their identifying tribal colors and designs. The analysts back at Langley could figure out where they came from. Right now, their origins didn't matter. He was careful to avoid getting any Phantoms in the background. After all, no Americans were ever there.

One of the two Phantoms, who had been charged to check and clear all the rooms of the villa, approached Bud Patrick. He held out an unopened bottle of very rare, very old, and very expensive Remy Martin Napoleon cognac. All the Phantoms knew what that meant.

Bud's eyes narrowed into an angry sneer.

Within another twenty minutes, all the Phantoms were moving toward the beach and the Zodiac boats with their evidence and the wounded Phantoms. None were left behind, nor were there any indications that they had ever been there. They left all their ammunition brass, but the casings and shells were unmarked.

It was 0225, January 27, 2019.

46

The Escape

Yaounde' Nsimalen International Airport, Yaounde', Cameroon, January 2019

Local time in Yaoundé was 0500 West African Time. The sleek Gulfstream G650 touched down on the 01 Runway after six and a half hours flying time and slowly taxied to the Executive Jet Parking Ramp at the extreme south end of the ramp area. A black Mercedes stretch limousine was parked on the ramp, and a lone greeter stood in front of the car. It was Cameroonian Foreign Affairs Minister Benjo Ahmadou Adamo, a longtime friend and school classmate of Al Yamani's and De La Plane's.

The jet slowly taxied to a parking spot in front of the Mercedes, and the jet engines were shut down. A few short moments went by, and finally the passenger door on the side of the fuselage opened, and the access stairs extended out of the belly of the aircraft and telescoped to the ground.

A lone figure appeared in the doorway. He turned and handed a small packet wrapped in cloth containing 150,000 Euros to the pilot. He then turned and slowly descended the steps. He was tall, tanned, sported a short black beard, and was wrapped in a white robe. His head was wrapped in a white Kafka-like turban. A dark canvas bag was slung over his shoulder from a wide strap. The bag appeared full of several bulky articles and appeared heavy. The two men met on the tarmac and briefly embraced and exchanged kisses in the air on each other's cheeks.

"Francois, my friend. It has been many years since we have seen one another. But our telephone conversations have been informative and fruitful. I am pleased you have finally accepted my invitation to visit Cameroon."

"Benjo, my good and loyal compatriot. It has indeed been many a year since we have had the opportunity to talk and reminisce about the past and dream of the future. I hope my short-notice visit has not disrupted your schedule."

"Of course not. I invite you to stay as long as you wish. In fact, the longer you stay, the more I can avail myself of your experience and ideas. I hope you are amenable to that. We face many challenges here in my country, and I am in need of assistance in exploring a variety of solutions to them. Unfortunately some solutions are distasteful and have long-range deleterious effects. But we have much time to discuss the future, and I'm sure you are tired from your long journey."

Both men turned and walked toward the car. Francois then stopped a brief moment and said, "I hope my aircraft and crew will be welcome here, as well. It is unfortunate, but they have nowhere to go from here. As I will explain later, their profession is unique, and their skills are finely honed."

Benjo turned to a man who was just exiting the car and said, "Achmed, see to it that our friends from the aircrew are fed, housed, and have all the conveniences we can give them. Ensure that the aircraft is serviced and towed to a hangar for safekeeping."

"Yes, Mr. Minister," replied Achmed.

Francois then briefly turned to look back at the aircraft, where the two pilots were standing at the bottom of the stairway. He gestured with a brief military salute. They responded in the same way, as if to acknowledge they knew they were to be welcomed and taken care of. At the same time Francois nervously scanned the immediate area, searching for small groups of people who seemed disgruntled or angry. He looked at the buildings suspiciously, expecting to see rooftop snipers. He quickly looked to his right and left, searching for trucks of soldiers or armored personnel carriers bristling with automatic weapons.

None of these visions were present. There were only three single individuals wearing robes opened at the front but with an embroidered collar on each. They were identical coverings and were obviously a minimum security detail for Adamo. They boasted shoulder holsters that became exposed as the men walked in the light breeze blowing across the tarmac. The men walked parallel to Benjo and Francois, perhaps five meters from them. As they approached Benjo's vehicle, the three men casually joined one another and turned to walk diagonally toward one of the hangars, presumably to return to an office in the building or to meet a waiting vehicle located elsewhere.

Francois said little as the two men walked to the waiting limousine. But his eyes and ears were attuned to the surroundings, expecting to see or hear the *zing* of ricocheting bullets or hateful shouts to discredit and disrespect him or Adamo. But he neither heard nor saw anything out of the ordinary.

"My friend, Francois, we have much to discuss. But it can wait until after you are rested, and later this week, we can have a private talk to review events."

They entered the limousine and drove the twenty-one kilometers into the city. The road to the city was peaceful, and there was very little traffic on the road at this early hour. A small carafe of strong Cameroonian coffee and two cups on saucers had been placed on a center table between the seats occupied by the two passengers.

47

Now What?

The Minister's House, Yaoundé, Cameroon, January 2019

It was now midmorning and approaching 9:45 a.m. Cameroon time, two days after the arrival of Francois. An arrival in Cameroon from that compound of conflict was not unexpected. Within an hour after the assault on the Al Yamani villa grounds, word of trouble had flashed around the Middle East and central Africa. Presidents and prime ministers in many nations, some who were strong supporters of Al Yamani and others who disapproved of him and his methods but respected his goals, began receiving reports that he had mishandled very sensitive explosives and even some very large medium-range missiles. Most everyone knew Yamani had those types of munitions, and therefore, they believed what they were told, heard, and read.

Some said, "If he had only called, I would have sent experts and security forces who know about these things." Others said, "I knew he was too adventuresome and was moving too fast. If he had asked me, I would have told him he was going to fail."

But like most presidents and prime ministers in the Middle East and central Africa, they each had their own set of unique problems. Had the call actually come from Al Yamani for assistance, most would have feigned serious internal political or population problems. That would certainly excuse them from sending resources to Yemen. Since no call was ever received from Al Hudaydah, and no resources ever sent, the status of Yemen in the Arabic community and in the Gulf Cooperation Council (GCC) countries was now in doubt. It was assumed, however, that since Saudi Arabia and Egypt had, at this point, maintained more control over their respective countries, they would be assumed to be instrumental in changing the government in Saana, Yemen, to a more centrist point of view. That was thought to be good for some and bad for others. Those who thought it bad were groups like the Houthe tribes, Boko Haram, Al Shabaab, Al Qaida, ISIS, and a host of other pro- and anti-radical Islamist political groups who had their own objectives for the Red Sea region and central Africa and their places in the world of Islam. Those who though it a good move in a proper direction were in the minority in this region of the African continent.

"Francois, I hope your last two nights were pleasant and you rested well," said Adamo. "I was expecting someone from Al Huydaydah but was uncertain who it would be. At the most I was expecting Al Yamani, Sal Khandar, you, and maybe one or two others. I must say, I was a little surprised to see only you."

"You are very kind, Mr. Minister…"

"Wait, stop there! You and I and our classmates have known one another for many years. While we haven't always been close enough to visit frequently, we have stayed in contact and have sought honest opinions and thoughts from each other. My friend, Francois, we share secrets, lies, and stories about each other's families, victories, and defeats. We are as close as brothers can be. Please, when we are in private and among family, I am Benjo and you are Francois."

"Yes, Benjo," Francois said in response. "That makes honesty and clarity much easier. Thank you. I am so grateful for your acceptance of me in this trying time that I can only pledge my loyalty and allegiance to you for accepting me into your house."

"No pledges are necessary, but honesty? Yes. It is how I best relate to my friends and my adversaries. I would have been offended if you had not asked for refuge. Now, let us discuss the future."

"As you already know, Cameroon is a land of many ethnicities and religions found among its more than twenty-three million people. In our 184,000 square miles, divided into ten regions, there are many riches. We have thriving agriculture, petroleum drilling, and we export coffee, sugar, tobacco, rice, and valuable minerals from our mines. We have several hydroelectric power plants that provide energy for ourselves and neighboring countries, and we have hardworking people who make an adequate wage to support themselves, their families, and the country.

"Francois, I know these last two years have not been without strife in your daily life. These last few years here in Cameroon have been tumultuous for me, as well. My father and mother were brutally killed in a radical Islamist attack on the tribe they were visiting in the north of the country—in the town of Maroua, to be exact. The senior mullah betrayed them, and they suffered a quick but unfortunate and premature death. My father had been destined to be the next president, the successor to the current president, my grandfather. It now appears that I myself am in line for greater political responsibilities. But we will discuss this later. Now let's talk about your future.

"I know you lost your dream for what you wanted for your country. You escaped in spite of, what I hear, were overwhelming odds. Now you have lost whatever it was that Mohamed Al Yamani was seeking in Yemen and for his new caliphate. So, your history in French Guiana and in Yemen has preceded you. It occurs to me you may wish to find a place that is quiet, safe, and relaxing. It could be that you need a place to refresh yourself, to reflect and decide what is next for yourself. If so, Cameroon and my family are at your disposal. We neither want nor require anything from you. You are my friend and a guest in my home. That is all that my family and friends need to know or care about."

Francois had always been attentive when the person talking to him had something to say that he wanted to hear. If that person was not someone with a significant or useful message, however, Francois was known to often walk away—even in his university classes in graduate school. He had a reputation for not suffering those he thought were fools or who had a foolish message based solely upon generalities and beliefs to convey. His closest friends and allies always believed there was another, more introspective, and somewhat mysterious level to Francois. But he was always considered to be so morose that no one made the effort to probe his exterior façade in search of the real Francois Ricardo De La Plane. Part of this performance was for theatrical affect. But there was another part of his persona that was very private.

Francois listened carefully to what Benjo Adamo was saying; he had already calculated that this discussion was going to end with an invitation to stay in Cameroon indefinitely to help Benjo and his family develop and defend the country. Benjo was no fool; he firmly believed his cause was just and that, with the right allies, he could reach his goal of regional domination, albeit peaceful – as long as everyone did as he commanded. Benjo was also a man of some mystery, as well. The time was not right for him to share his goals for his countrymen or to reveal how he would govern when the mantel of authority was bestowed upon him. For now, however, his country was, indeed, under siege, and he, his grandfather, and the leaders of Parliament needed help in thinking through the country's national security. Francois knew he was right, that Benjo was going to ask for his assistance. But he wanted to hear what Adamo had to say. And after all, Adamo's family was his host and this was a safer place to be than any country around the Red Sea. For all Francois knew, there could be a bounty on his head from both known and unknown nations and caliphates.

"But if you are here," Benjo continued, "and if you want to help us in the challenges that face us, let me describe our circumstances. I don't want to bore you with situations you are probably already aware of, but these are facts you must take into account if you wish to help us maintain our sovereignty. Obviously, if you agree to do more, and if you want to be more involved, there will be things I will ask of you, and things that others in my country will ask of you also."

"My people have been fighting someone almost every year of their lives for the last two generations to protect their livelihoods and the security of the Cameroon. As I described, we have more than enough riches for the people of my country. Radical Islamic jihadists, like Boko Haram, the Houthis and their Shiite Muslim sponsors, the Sunni Muslim opposition, ISIS, Shia forces from Iran, and Al Shabab, supported by Syria and Hezbollah, would like to take what we have and make it their own. I have confirmed through various connections that they regard Cameroon as a strategic objective that must be conquered if a caliphate is to reach from the Persian Gulf to the Atlantic Ocean. Our soldiers and their families know that. Our army, our navy, and what we have left of our air force have stood and fought. Our resistance has so far been proven up to task. What we have done may not be enough. We seem always able to find weapons and munitions. But what we are lacking are battle-tested strategies and tactics for our self-defense."

Francois listened intently but in his usual stoic manner he was emotionally churning inside, trying to decide how best to respond. He was at the same time grateful to Benjo for granting him sanctuary, but reluctant to take on another national leader's battle, even though he knew it was exactly what he should do. He was especially reluctant because of what he believed this leader's reputation was; he was regarded by contemporaries across central Africa and in the Middle East as too soft on his adversaries. This budding leader needed a backbone of steel. He knew Benjo was obviously the heir apparent to become the next president of Cameroon, for which he was politically prepared. But Francois was convinced Benjo was no military genius who could defend his homeland without employing forceful and catastrophic bludgeonings, beheadings, and annihilations. Didn't Benjo know he could not win with diplomatic initiatives and peaceful meetings with his opponents?

He thought, *This is, indeed, a good man who will be a good president for the time he will serve, but he is not a fighter, so his presidency will be short-lived. His presidency will not be peaceful. He doesn't know how to exterminate dissidents and rodents. He doesn't know how to be ruthless and efficient.*

His mind raced through past events: confrontations, angry words with tribal leaders, disagreements with mullahs and chieftains, the need to avoid words of truth to military and religious leaders whose actions were bizarre but had to be dealt with diplomatically in face-saving manners. He was most upset by being betrayed by Al Yamani when he was told to wear a suicide vest to an international meeting. Was he not more valuable as a living, working advisor? Sure, there were some who thought he was valuable. That was obviously why he had been spared from certain death by the phone calls. Were all his strategy development efforts and advice not valuable to the global jihad and the growth of radical Islam? Perhaps it was time to speak his true feelings, but he would need to carefully choose his words so as not to reveal his most valuable skills. This would also include what he truthfully believed about the chaos being spread worldwide by both the naïve Western powers and the blind radical jihadist Islamist loyalists.

Hmm, Benjo is naïve and maybe a fool if he thinks he can win a war with the likes of Boko Haram and all the other factions of radical Islam that are undermining every nation in Africa and the Middle East. He is mistaken. Those forces placate unsuspecting nations. They give them false hopes and bribe them with money and offers of peaceful coexistence. I need to introduce him to the nations of Asia and Eurasia that will provide him weapons and wealth to personally empower him to meet his challenge. I need to persuade him that the global jihad, which is now underway, will undermine his governmental weaknesses and that he needs to strike back like a cobra at those who oppose him—both inside his government and outside. His people must become dependent upon him and his regime and come to believe that he and the state will protect and redeem them. He must win his people's hearts and minds. This country needs a powerful indoctrination program to make the people pay their taxes and become subservient to their leadership. I can help him with that.

"Benjo, I am, indeed, grateful for your warm and generous welcome," Francois began.

I must be careful what I say and how I say it, or he may suspect I am being disingenuous. I would like to reestablish my own reputation, and I need time to fit into another country to help where I can—as long as they do it my way.

"You and I have not yet spoken of my experience in my own country and how things developed and what I did for Al Yamani. I will share all of that with you now and as time goes by, and I will share what occurred at events and with certain people who proved to be useful in those activities. Be assured, you may do as you see fit with my suggestions and recommendations. You will not offend me if you reject my advice. Be forewarned, too, however, that gifts and assistance, especially from those from far-flung regions around the world, will be difficult to reject and even more difficult to keep at bay once they smell the scent of victory. But for now, with regard to your needs, I made some observations when we came here to your residence two days ago, along with things I observed this morning. I hope they become useful to you."

"Why, of course, Francois. I am not as well-steeped in tactics and security measures as you and many others who are fresh from the conflict. I would welcome your comments and would appreciate a future opportunity to hear your opinions as time goes on. But I sense you have not yet committed to your future plans. You, of course, are most welcome to stay as long as you wish, as I mentioned before. But I and my people must move forward in our dealings with Boko Haram, Al Shabaab, and ISIS, and we must confront pressures from the Western world. The threats they pose are real. Some are hostile, and some are delectable; some have destructive outcomes, and others are enticing. We must come to know the difference. They want our people to act as a workforce; they want our seaports for access to the South Atlantic; and they want our military hardware to continue their conquests. Right now I oppose everything both worlds stand for. You can help me buy some time to make the decisions I want for Cameroon.

"There is one more thing you need to know, Francois. My grandfather, the president of Camaroon, is gravely ill. If he passes away, as the first minister for state affairs, the presidency could pass to the current leader of our Senate. Senate Leader Doushambe is an old and longtime friend of my grandfather's. He does not wish to be the president and has said he will defer to me. He has asked me to privately and quietly organize my affairs and plans to accede to the presidency. I am doing so as surreptitiously as possible. But I find I am in need of an experienced, loyal, and competent national security advisor. I would like you to consider that position as you decide your own destiny. We can make the position as public or as private as you would like it to be."

"Benjo, or Mr. President-Elect—" Francois said with a wry smile. "I am flattered you have that kind of confidence in me. But I must honestly tell you, I am a difficult taskmaster. I have had two countries prematurely lost to me because of unexpected circumstances. I will not lose a third one. The phantom-like forces who arrived to dash my plans for the future were probably American, although I cannot confirm that.

"My current observations, for you to do with as you see fit, are as follows: Your guards and security forces are obese and inattentive; they do not have rounds of ammunition chambered in their rifles and pistols; they do not carry communication devices that connect them to you or to a central control point; and they speak little when spoken to and do not profess loyalty to you. You have no electronic physical security monitors to warn you of impending intruders, and I am unaware of any central government intelligence unit that monitors your national perimeter for invading forces. If Boko Haram is, indeed, a threat, you do not treat them as such. Individuals you believe are loyal who do not conform should be eliminated."

"Well, if by *eliminated* you mean killed, I need to first see a deliberate treasonous activity that results in indecision about what these people may believe. That may be a step beyond where I want the country to go right now—but I am willing to listen," Adamo responded.

"Benjo, you are idealistic. I once had those same guiding principles. But age and experience have forced me to take a different course. I have learned that if you don't set initial principles, values, and beliefs, no one will know the expectations required of them. I am one whose habit it is to set initial rules, directions, loyalties, national requirements, and conformity standards. If you want someone like me to assist your government, I am willing to help you, my friend, but you must also accept that I am structured, disciplined, and experienced, and that I have connections that can assist you. I know what to do, and I am driven to succeed—"

"I understand, Francois," Benjo interrupted, sensing that Francois was still distressed from the recent battle. "From all that I have heard, you may be just what we need at this time. To coin a Western term we both learned in the university, it may be *Providence* that you are here right now. But I want your head to be clear. I want you to understand our fight. I want your complete and undivided attention to our problem."

Benjo was slow at first, but he quickly shifted into a family mode and recognized the signs of battle stress and the need for time to separate the recent past from the present. He knew Francois needed some time to sort through all that had just happened. In spite of the seemingly disparate thoughts Francois was uttering, he had made some good points. He had made some observations that would be crucial to implement. Benjo knew, intuitively, that Francois had valuable knowledge, connections, and experience that could save himself, his family, and the nation of Cameroon from those who wanted all of those elements destroyed.

"Francois, you and your experience are valuable to my country. I need you," Benjo declared in a condescending manner, in softer tones than had been uttered before. He sensed and believed Francois was anxious, confused, distressed, but also a bit too certain. He wanted to calm Francois with the hope that he would come to be accepted. He was unique, different, and a longtime friend of Benjo's. Cameroon was a worthwhile country to Francois, strategically located, which in turn needed what De La Plane had to offer. Benjo believed he had to softly persuade Francois that he could be beneficial to Benjo's goals, although he had not yet been able to candidly articulate them to Francois, but first time to rest and reflect on their next actions was needed.

"Francois, I want you to take some time to understand what I want for my country. I want your insight and wisdom. I want to know what you think about our successes and failures. I want you to share your experiences with me and help save Cameroon from what we think lies ahead. I am thinking seriously of how best to implement what I believe needs to be the Cameroonian 'cobra bite'—that thing that convinces our people to conform, and that convinces our adversaries to keep their distance from us. Stay in my house; we'll talk frequently. I'll brief you on the status of events around us, then I'll ask your guidance on what to do. But first you need time to heal from the recent past events. Let's take it a week at a time, and if it takes two or three months, that's good, too. We will talk daily, okay?"

"Yes, that's a good plan," Francois agreed. "You know I will make plans, but I need a laptop computer to gather data and develop the foundation of those plans. I think ahead for the good of all those to whom I am loyal…"

"Yes, I know that. And I want the best plans you can devise for Cameroon. I will have a computer delivered to your quarters by tomorrow. We'll talk more then, and the next day, and the next week and each week after, until we know what we are to do—together."

Francois then said in a haggard and tired voice, "Yes, yes, together…next week."

48

R&R

Bayshore Boulevard, Overlooking Hillsborough Bay, Tampa, Florida, February 2019

It was 6:15 a.m. The rays of the morning sun were gently streaming in through the open doors to the small balcony. The air was warm and gentle. LuAnn lay in bed next to Darrin. She was propped up on one elbow, her head resting in her hand over her ear. She was looking at Darrin, whose breathing was shallow and restful. He lay on his back, beginning to rouse from a night of ecstatic pleasure and intimate sharing.

LuAnn leaned over, gently kissed his cheek, and whispered, "I love you. I missed you terribly. I want you to stay here next to me forever."

Darrin opened his eyes, and in a flash he thought, *This is certainly a far cry from Al Hudaydah, three thousand miles from here.* Instead he said, "I heard that. I love you, too. My thoughts of you kept me warm for three weeks. I don't feel complete unless I know you are near."

"Don't you think we should tell the master chief and the colonel about our relationship?" she asked.

"I think they already know" he said. "By the way, what's our plan for the day? I'd like for us to take a drive into Ybor City and do a little shopping."

"Shopping?" LuAnn's voice raised. "You don't like to shop—shop for what?"

"Oh, I don't know. Maybe we should go look for a ring?" he said casually.

"A-a-a-a ring? Hmmm, I'd like that very much." She paused for a moment and looked into his eyes to not only affirm her pleasure with his idea, but to give him a soft kiss.

Ministry of State Security, Beijing, People's Republic of China, February 2019

Minister of Defense General Quan sat at the end of an overly large table in an ornate, but secure room in the MOD Building in the middle of Beijing. He was a kindly, grandfatherly-looking man with graying hair at his temples. No one would ever guess he regularly ordered hundreds of military and civilian men and women to quick and decisive deaths for a variety of "crimes against the state." The minister was a high-ranking general officer in the People's Liberation Army who could unleash an explosive temper on his subordinates and was very direct with those of equal rank and position in the service of other nations. He was especially direct, and even curt, with those representing other nations who were to have supported him in a military venture that went poorly or failed. On this day, he convened a meeting to discuss just such an operation that had failed.

To Minister Quan's right sat the minister of defense of Russia, Colonel General Vukovich. General Vukovich controlled a large inventory of clean, low-yield third-generation Super-EMP nuclear weapons that had no counterpart in the U.S. inventory. These weapons gave Russia the escalation dominance, which meant that the Russians believed they could prevail over the United States in the event of a nuclear exchange. Vukovich also controlled a rather abundant budget of gold and silver assets that could be used in untraceable circumstances in clandestine foreign intelligence operations.

To Minister Quan's left sat Defense Minister General Yang of the DPRK. He, too, controlled a very large budget of fungible assets that could be brought to bear to purchase weapons, small-yield missile warheads, intermediate-range ballistic missile components, a full range of military weapon ammunition, advanced technology surveillance equipment, and large amounts of fuel and petroleum resources for a small, insignificant nation that wanted to become a large, fearsome nation. None of these assets and resources was indigenous to North Korea. The North Koreans took pride in having these assets available in their inventory to offer as persuasive gifts. They liked to have small, but aggressive nations come to them, showing humility and begging for military support. While the smaller nations were begging, the North Korean hierarchy knew the beggar was eager for power and would gladly negotiate away their seaport access, airports, military bases, and even natural resources just to get what they thought they needed. But at the same time, the North Koreans never addressed the origin of these resources, because many of them were given by the PRC and most of the remaining other weapons and components came from Russia or Pakistan. So, in fact, larger nations, like the PRC or Russia, were simply using North Korea as a conduit to export terrorism, chaos, orchestrated deaths, intergovernmental disloyalty, and the dissemination of anti-Western propaganda. The North Koreans enjoyed their position of synthetic power and influence, and they took real pleasure in distributing weapons and resources that temporarily empowered small nations to act like larger nations.

Each minister general had one aide seated behind him to take mental notes and to provide written evidence of one sort or another in case it was needed. The Russian and the North Korean generals sat in silence, waiting for Quan to speak first. It was, after all, his meeting. Vukovich and Yang sensed correctly that Quan was seething over the situation in Yemen.

After several long, silent moments, Quan finally spoke, first in low, calm tones. "Gentlemen, you know why I have asked you to come here. We have failed each other in the operation in Yemen. This was a carefully orchestrated operation, in which we all had invested a great deal of time and treasure. We all had anticipated gaining major military and political footholds in and around the Arabian Peninsula and into the Red Sea, the Gulf of Aden, the Ionian Sea, the Gulf of Oman, and the Indian Ocean."

His voice grew gradually louder, with angry, sharp edges to his words. His face reddened, and he increased the pace of his words, partially because he was sincerely angry, but also because he needed these officers to understand the political and diplomatic gravity of the situation.

"The People's Republic of China has invested more than either of your nations in this venture, and despite safeguards and promises by the two of you, you have each contributed to major losses and setbacks. My country is now confronted with a major embarrassment.

"You, General Yang, sent inexperienced and foolish officers to represent us, and as far as I'm concerned, they bungled every task you gave them. They should be shot in a public military tribunal to ensure this does not happen again.

"You, General Vukovich, generously provided Russian gold and weapons to incentivize the Yemen barbarians, who then chose to flaunt their newfound wealth and power. I had personal assurances from you that they would be properly briefed and warned that silence and frugality were to be exercised.

"For my part, representatives of the National People's Congress and the Party General Secretary have publicly humiliated me before the Central Military Commission and have charged me to conduct a full investigation of how this happened and who was actually responsible."

Quan's voice had become louder and more shrill as he became even angrier. "Within six hours after this debacle, I had investigators on the grounds of the Al Yamani compound. They could find no discernible evidence of who could have created this havoc. My guess would be the Americans, the British, the French, or the Israelis—or a combination of all of them. Even though a small American flotilla of ships was transiting through the Red Sea at the time, there was no evidence they were anything but observers of a massacre. No, the Americans have mostly withdrawn from any diplomatic and military presence in the Middle East. They have been emasculated by their former president, who had no stomach to fight.

"So, could it have been rival tribes or people from the ISIS caliphate who saw Al Yamani usurping their authority, and destroyed our plans? Do any of you know who did it? I think not!"

Quan was screaming again and pacing the floor, looking at his small audience as if daring them to challenge him with information he did not already have.

"In spite of all the intelligence collection assets we each had available, nothing out of the ordinary was identified. You and your sources have failed me."

"Comrade General Quan," said Vukovich, "I disagree with your assessment. Neither I nor anyone in my chain of command failed you or any one of our partners in this plan."

"If that is so, Comrade General, then where were your personnel when all this destruction occurred? Mine were in the underground missile launch command center and were exposed to pinpoint-accurate rifle fire. Nearly fifty of my most skilled and effective clandestine-operations personnel were killed by an unknown platoon of faceless marauders, by Shiite butchers, by Somali pirates, by Egyptian camel drivers, or by ghosts! Who knows? None of you do!"

Quan was now on the downward side of his tirade, and sweat was beading on his face. But he was even angrier and was now quickly becoming dictatorial and abusive.

"This is the third time my country has been humiliated and outmaneuvered by an unexpected adversary in recent years. The first time was two years ago in the Blackthorn incident. Then there was the debacle in French Guiana—now this!"

All those present in the room were familiar with the detonation of American cruise missiles in sensitive Chinese facilities and aboard a Mao Class submarine in the Pacific. They were familiar with the incident because all the same individuals now present had been involved in the planning of that mission. The same persons were involved in the events of French Guiana, and now in Yemen.

"I suggest you both return to your respective headquarters and demand the heads of anyone who cannot identify any of the perpetrators of this disaster. I demand that your staff be incarcerated, tortured, and killed if they do not have conclusive answers concerning this new threat to our dream of world domination. If you do not share my zeal for finding who is at fault for our losses, I urge you both to resign and take the only honorable path out for yourselves." He was, of course, suggesting they each consider suicide due to humiliation.

During this time General Yang sat silently, not wanting Quan's venom to strike him and his record of success in Pyongyang. Actually, after this tirade, suicide sounded like a respectable way out of this for himself. He knew a report of all aspects of this mission, including the vitriolic debriefing would be in Dear Leader's hands before the hour was up. His future was doomed, he realized.

Minister General Quan had one more parting shot for the two embarrassed defense ministers. "I am to inform you the People's Republic of China is ceasing all clandestine operations with your two ministries for now. When you two are replaced, we will entertain considering joint operations again. You are dismissed, Gentlemen."

The Oval Office, the White House, Washington, D.C., February 2019

President Chenoa had called for a small meeting of key individuals in order to briefly summarize her impressions of the results of Project RAMPART in Yemen. Those present included Vice President Henry Caldwell Smith, Secretary of Defense Stoddard, National Security Advisor General Mossman, Director of National Intelligence Hollen, Assistant Secretary of State for Middle Eastern Affairs Vargas, and Chairman of the Joint Chiefs Admiral Nagle. Rear Admiral Andrews, Colonel Patrick, and Command Master Chief Petty Officer Barrett were the focal points of the victory meeting. In stark contrast to the meeting in Beijing two days before, there were verbal "high-fives" all around the room.

"I'm pleased to have all of you here this morning to reflect on the favorable results of a very difficult military mission," the president said. "The results of Project RAMPART are still classified and will be for some time to come. Our sources of information are telling us that it is still a mystery as to who the forces were that conducted the raid. We want it to stay that way for as long as we can maintain plausible deniability, without actually lying about our involvement.

"While we can rejoice in the success of this battle, we cannot take heart that the war is over. It is not. There are some facts that clearly demonstrate the instability of our world and our international allied coalition's inability or unwillingness to deal with it. First, there will certainly be another Islamic terrorist jihadist tyrant sometime, somewhere around the globe who will again test the community of nations and attempt world domination. He will use some barbaric means that will make certain nations reluctant and unable or unwilling to confront him.

"Second, the tactics and strategies that seem to be most effective, both as corrective measures and as deterrents, are excellent intelligence and the use of covert operations to alter the behavior of certain societies in the world. We have shown that the most effective counterbalance to an army of occupation is proactive intelligence and a Phantom force. I dare say, however, that the more we are forced to employ our covert-operations capabilities, the greater the chances become that they will no longer remain phantoms.

"We in government are learning valuable lessons in national security and foreign relations. The withdrawal of the United States from certain areas of the world, where we had been a stabilizing influence, now makes those areas susceptible to takeover by terrorist groups. Another precept is that we have confirmed that the United States can no longer be the nine—one-one emergency response team for global crises. We can neither afford to, nor do we desire to send an army of our best and brightest youth to some far-flung nation for five, ten, or fifteen years. Our military forces are not nation-builders. That's why Ms. Vargas is here. Interventions must be conducted with an attendant plan to conduct reconstitution activities that foster stability operations after an attack. Our State Department and her office have done a superlative job in sending in foreign-service first responders to help countries get their elected, appointed, and legally constituted government structure reestablished after a tyrannical disruption.

"I have probably gone on too much about our national goals and policies for now. I want to congratulate Admiral Andrews, Colonel Patrick, and their team members for exceptional leadership in this experiment in democracy. I am sorry there will be no tickertape parades and no public ceremonies to applaud them. But the people who should know of their accomplishments do know how they have served this nation and our allies. I applaud their continued efforts.

"I would like to say that I will never again need to send them and the Phantom force into harm's way, but I can't say that with any assurance. So let me simply close with a simple thank-you from a grateful nation."

49

Where Did That Come From?

Congresswoman Doolin's Office, Rayburn House Office Building, Washington, D.C., February 2019

The intercom on Congresswoman Doolin's desk softly buzzed. It was 8:30 a.m., and Rosemary had already been in the office for more than an hour. Her work and the needs of her constituents were never-ending; there were never enough hours in the day to accomplish everything that needed attention.

Because of her seniority and her responsibilities as the chair of a major subcommittee, her office was spacious, befitting a person who required multiple meetings, strategy sessions, and secret debates to find answers and options to problems. Besides her desk and several easy chairs for visitors, she also had a long conference table at one end of the room that could accommodate up to ten persons. In addition, her office was secure, so that classified discussions, up to and including Top Secret ones, could be held.

"Yes, Michelle?" she said into the open mic of the communications system.

"Senator Smith is here, Congresswoman, and you will have two military visitors in thirty minutes."

"Yes, thank you, Michelle. Please show the senator in." She rose and walked to the door just as Denny entered.

"Denny, how nice to see you. Thank you for coming across the Hill to my place for this meeting. I'm genuinely elated about recent events, and I'm heartened that we may have made some positive inroads into our task."

Denny took her outstretched hand and said, "It's very good to see you again, Rosemary. How is John—and his golf handicap?"

"Oh, he's elated that he has so many golf courses to play in the Washington area, and he has a golfing buddy with a membership at each of them," she responded.

"I presume we are now secure."

"Yes. Once the door is closed, we are completely secure and the white noise begins even though we can't hear it."

"Good. It's been three weeks since we witnessed all the events from the Situation Room. Even though I was aware of what was going to happen, seeing it all unfold in real time made me feel as though I was there. Our guys did a terrific job."

Rosemary was equally excited about having been there and said, "Yes, there's always a chance some small thing can go awry and change the outcome away from our mission expectations. I guess the only thing that was disappointing to me was the loss of the three captives."

Denny shook his head in a gesture of mild disbelief. "I guess I'll never understand the Middle-Eastern mind-set that will opt for death and silence over life and truth. They could have left a fine legacy for their countrymen. I would have liked to talk to Al Yamani and Sal Khandar in Guantanamo, but I guess it was not meant to be."

"Well, their computers, cell phones, and all the papers and documents left behind are a real goldmine. That's a good thing. I haven't been told yet what's on them, but I'm sure all that data will be a real help to future U.S. strategy development, and our defensive plans and policies."

"Right," responded Denny. "Secretary Vargas moved right in with her State Department team, and I'm hearing that government offices are being quickly reestablished, infrastructure services are moving forward, and many of the citizenry are pleased that the U.S. is quietly helping to restore order."

"Is there any intel on the whereabouts of De La Plane?" she asked.

"No, nothing yet," said Denny. "I'm hoping Ray Andrews and Bud

Patrick may have some data points when they get here."

"Right, they're expected in fifteen minutes. They are always perfectly punctual, so the door will open precisely at oh-nine-hundred, and we'll see what new information they have." Rosemary poured coffee for both of them, and they made small talk about the task ahead—to garner more House and Senate support for the president's plan for a smaller, more lethal force.

At 8:59 and forty-five seconds, Rosemary's intercom buzzed. She simply pushed the Transmit button and said, "Thank you, Michelle, show them in."

At 0900 her door opened, and Admiral Andrews and Colonel Patrick walked in. The uniforms, the brass, and the medals changed the whole aura of her office. It was almost as if someone had suddenly turned on all the lights and the room took on a military brightness that could only occur when heroes arrived. The door was closed behind them, greetings were exchanged between all four individuals, and a friendly, family-like air descended on the room.

Rosemary said, "Ray and Bud, you both know that Denny and I are so proud of you and the team. As you know, we also were in the Sit Room, and we were all wringing our hands and praying for all of you."

Bud Patrick responded, "Well, we thank you, and whatever you did or said certainly worked. We want you two in our corner again, if there's ever a next time."

Denny then said, "Ray, Bud, we each will again sponsor a classified debrief to selected committees on each side of the Hill and you can tell our members how it went in whatever amount of detail you think is necessary. We'll be interested, of course, in what worked and what didn't. Is there any word on the whereabouts of De La Plane?"

Ray looked at Bud as if eye contact between them would affirm that Andrews would speak first. "Senator and Congresswoman, we don't have any clear data yet, but we do have some spurious clues we are trying to link together. Bud can cover that with you in a moment. We know how he got out and we saw his trail, but his destination is a mystery.

"Another part of the mystery is from where these two tyrants garnered so much support, military power, and wealth in such a short period of months? Initial findings from the computer hard drives and cell phones have been very helpful. The Chinese yuan, Russian rubles, and North Korean gold seem to indicate we still can't trust those international neighbors who go overboard in professing their lack of knowledge of these events and then are too eager to help the community of nations get to the bottom of this.

"The weapons, the foreign cash, the nationalities of the bodies, the tribal robes, and the Kufi and Kafia head covers tell us there's also a strong Middle-Eastern undercurrent of support for terror operations like this. There is also some direct military and political encouragement from Asian and Russian government officials who are desperate for footholds in not only the Middle East, but in Central Africa, as well."

Ray then looked at Bud as if on cue. Bud began with a partial answer to the first question. "I'm sure you know the story of the very old, very rare, and very expensive Remy Martin Napoleon cognac." Rosemary and Denny nodded.

"Well, when the bottle was left the first time, in French Guiana, I just assumed it could have been forgotten and De La Plane just didn't have time to retrieve it. I've had our clandestine ops support from the agency look into that brand of liquor in French Guiana. It turns out that it has a special meaning to De La Plane—it dates back nearly thirty years to his relationship with his father. They imbibed together on special occasions, and having it available is of sentimental importance to him.

"I guessed that leaving a bottle of this special elixir a second time was no accident—especially in a Middle-Eastern country where Western alcoholic beverages are forbidden. So, even though he didn't know who we were, he probably was trying to send a couple of messages. One was to remind us he has outsmarted us yet again. Another was that he's inviting us to catch him if we think we can. If he wanted to seriously protect his anonymity, he would never have left such obvious clues as to who he is or what his motives were. He has violated both of those MOs.

"Another point that may not have occurred to him, but certainly has to me, is that a mole may be warning him in advance of our arrivals."

Rosemary and Denny quickly looked at one another with an *Oh my God!* glance.

"Here's another set of facts that help me understand this fellow," Bud continued. "Fifteen minutes after our attack was complete and we were beginning our egress from the area, a Gulfstream G650-ER, owned by Al Yamani and his caliphate, was wheels up with a request for an immediate turn to the west and a climb to thirty-three thousand feet out of the airport traffic pattern. That airplane has a service range of over seven thousand nautical miles without refueling and could make it as far as the African West Coast in only a few hours of flight time. The aircraft, with tail number YN 613-1, requested a direct vector to Addis Ababa, Ethiopia. There was no request for a flight plan beyond there. So I asked my sources for further clarification of the aircraft's flight following. At thirty-three thousand feet altitude, it continued west toward the setting sun. After its arrival into the Addis Ababa airspace, the aircraft requested no further flight plan information and disappeared from the air route traffic control system.

"I know I'm belaboring this a bit, but I want to make a couple of important points. One is that the aircraft disappeared from the international ARTC system vectoring for the better part of an hour and a half. There was no report of it landing anywhere in Ethiopia. But it did renew its request for an in-flight plan filing in western Sudan and moving into the Central African Republic, with a final destination of Yaoundé, Cameroon. It was classified as a medical evacuation flight with a Cameroonian citizen aboard needing government attention there. The Ebola scare in that part of Africa means that any flights calling themselves 'medical evacuation' are allowed clearance to any nation that will accept them. All other nations give them a pass rather than try to accommodate them with en-route medical attention. Curiously, the Cameroonian government approved the flight to the capital without inquiry, and with the highest political category of approval for a foreign arrival.

"To make a long story short, I believe Francois De La Plane was the lone passenger on that flight. I suspect he was welcomed into Cameroon, where he will seek asylum with his old school chum, Benjo Ahmadou Adamo, who was supposed to be at the Al Yamani party but missed it. Adamo is rumored to be growing his own army of terrorists, or at least is pursuing his own plan for taking over the government.

Whatever he is up to, he may need a De La Plane type of strategist to help him expand and conquer.

"I don't have confirmation of any of this yet, but I am continuing to work on it. So regard this data for now as SPECINT."

Bud was a little embarrassed since he had seemed to monopolize the meeting agenda with his speculative status of De La Plane. "I apologize for taking so much time with this explanation of De La Plane's whereabouts, when there are other higher priorities and more urgent concerns about Project Rampart."

"Don't be so apologetic, Colonel," said Denny. "All the details you have about this raid and the related data are relevant. Africa is a continent ripe for tumult and chaos. Its riches are many. The people are pliable, and the ground is rich in oil, diamonds, gold, silver, and precious minerals. Of all the continents on the face of the earth where we might be able to confront and stop flagrant aggression, Africa is right behind the Middle East.

"So, rather than focus on what didn't happen, let's talk about what *did* happen," Denny said to reorient the conversation back to what was next. "The subcommittees and committees in both houses will focus on the question of *So what?* so our message needs to be oriented to the relevance of our actions, our objective in conducting this kind of covert military diplomacy, and the takeaways from this operation.

"First of all, let's look at the dollars and cents of these kinds of operations. The planning consumed nearly five hundred person-hours of labor over four weeks of time. The briefing, re-briefing, and pre-briefing took another six hundred person-hours to put the scenario together. The deployment of the *Truman* task force cost roughly two million dollars, and the deployment of aircraft and aircrews plus command-and-control personnel around the world cost about another two and a half million dollars. We expended about two hundred fifty thousand dollars in munitions and satellite communications connectivity. So all told, if we round off the numbers, we spent nearly seven million dollars to save one hundred million people from annihilation, and we avoided sending one and one-half billion dollars in U.S. troops and hardware in as an army of occupation for a minimum of five years, at a price tag of two billion dollars a year.

"On the more pragmatic side of the ledger, we also kept five million people from being enslaved or butchered, we stopped at least three Eurasian foreign nations from invading a small, peaceful country with whom we have had quasi-friendly relations, and we staved off a possible termination of transit through the Suez and kept worldwide oil distribution flowing to the free world. And one more thing: six intermediate-range ballistic missiles with horrific payloads were never launched. All in all, I would say that was a pretty good day's work. So far, it's United States two, the Bad Guys zero."

Ray Andrews looked at Bud and said, "And all this time I thought we were just killing some bad guys who needed killing." They all looked at one another and chuckled at the way military minds had a way of simplifying a complicated problem.

Throughout the remainder of the meeting, they discussed how Israeli-U.S. relations would quietly improve; how precise their intelligence was in identifying the nuclear warheads; and how the country and the region would hopefully soon recover from the near-disaster of Al Yamani's rule.

Ray and Bud also briefly addressed the presence of Chinese, Russian, and North Korean forces and equipment in the hands of an irresponsible dictator. The use of weapons and munitions from these countries was more commonplace than American politicians cared to admit. Andrews confirmed that even Mexico, Japan, and France employed an inventory of capabilities that included weaponry from these nations. Realistically, they were cheaper, most of the time were very reliable, and were relatively easy to acquire. What turned out to be a more serious concern to U.S. national security interests were the repeated and relentless efforts by China, Russia, and North Korea to gain tactical footholds in nations and territories that were former American allies, or at least reasonable acquaintances.

Rosemary said, "I hope in your testimonies before each of our committees you will address the export of terrorism to Islamic jihadist–leaning countries. The political targets of the Chinese, the North Koreans, and the Russians are countries that are in disarray, in political upheaval, and have a budding tyrant who is in need of hardware and allies to make him appear formidable. We unfortunately can't or shouldn't strike back at him unless or until he threatens the national security interests of the United States, or is on the verge of upsetting the international balance of power by introducing sudden chaos and man-made catastrophes.

"This seems to beg for an improvement in our strategic intelligence gathering mechanisms, and it underscores the need for a rapid deployment force of covert operations personnel who can quickly neutralize and defuse a precarious situation."

Denny added, "President Chenoa sees this new world order unfolding, but she knows we cannot get away with preemptive attacks to keep these events from spiraling out of control. Her plan is to move away from the United States being the first responder to an international nine-one-one call. The days of America providing an army of occupation to maintain a counterbalance in other regions of the world are over. But neither do we want to politically withdraw from these regions, then have potential adversaries moving in to backfill behind our departure. All nations need to know we will not stand for destabilizing influences that push unwitting countries into signing multi-use territorial agreements with governments like North Korea, who obviously only want military-basing rights to peddle their own brand of hatred and destruction. Those are the messages we have to impart to members of Congress who have the power and influence to change the military strategy of the United States and cause countries to respect and fear us again. We need measures to tell the world we are reliable, predictable, and also decisive when it's necessary."

Rosemary added, "This is not entirely your message to convey. Most of that falls to Denny and me and our committees. The president has our backs on these items, so some political salesmanship is required. But I think we can handle that. Your message needs to reiterate that our military is strong, responsive, and thorough. Once given a task, the military can efficiently take it from there to see a mission through to success. Let's just hope we don't have to call upon you often for such missions. But we know you practice continuously in order to be ready when the call does come."

"Gentlemen," Denny then said, "let's adjourn for now and remain in contact. My committee staff and Rosemary's will be in touch with you soon for near-term testimony dates and times. Meanwhile, if there is a mole somewhere in our organizations, we want to help you find him or her. Count on us to help. But for now, since you have your sources mobilized for the search, just keep us in the loop."

Andrews Air Force Base, Suitland, Maryland

As the C-38A USAF executive jet was taxiing out to the active runway for its takeoff and return flight to MacDill AFB, Bud turned to Ray Andrews and said, "If De La Plane pops up with another tinhorn tyrant, we're going to get him. It would be great to take him alive. But if he wants to die, I'll be glad to help him out. He has planned too many genocide operations."

"I agree," replied Andrews. "It's sad, but some countries just get too much enjoyment and profit from getting the hopes up of a small, belligerent nation. They get their leaders whipped up into a fever pitch, only to be taken down in a destructive raid."

"I worry, Bud, that some covert action someday will result in a serious setback for us. As you know only too well, each time we undertake one of these operations, we give away secrets about our tactics, personnel performance, weapons, and modes of transport. We can't keep our secrets forever. If there's a mole who is tipping off De La Plane, he or she only needs to be observant in the MacDill area, or with our staff and the Phantoms. He or she can then make educated guesses about our actions and their timing. The only way we can be totally secretive is to move our operations to the South Pole—and that's not going to happen. The president was right: Someday soon we'll have to come partway out from behind the black curtain. But where and when we are to strike will always have to remain a secret."

"As soon as we get back, Ray, I'm going to try to plug that leak—if there is one," Bud remarked with a tinge of anger in his voice.

50

New Information

JCS, J-3 SOD, the Pentagon, March 2019

Colonel Keith Powers was seated at his desk in the basement of the Pentagon in the special operations division at his usual spot next to three different computer terminals. One was for open-source, unclassified e-mail and routine Google searches. A second was connected to the SIPRNET, classified and secure servers for access to Top Secret intelligence data and reports. The third system gave him access to the Central Command, CENTCOM, network, which provided detailed reports on foreign military activity, U.S. tactical operations, and status reports on threatening actions by a variety of counterinsurgency forces and amateur international bandits who simply liked to steal personal treasure and kill people.

Powers was just finishing reading the Top Secret RAMPART final report on the military actions in Al Hudaydah, Yemen. Four pages of narrative were included at the end of the report covering the testimony of Admiral Andrews and Colonel Patrick before classified committee hearings on the RAMPART military operations in Yemen, including tactics and weapons that were used, reactions of the radical Islamic terrorists, and support believed to be rendered by foreign governments that anonymously backed the Al Yamani terrorist and Sal Khandar piracy regimes. One of the last paragraphs contained their comments on and recommendations for military force structure for the United States' reaction to future similar events. The SASC, the SSCI, the HASC, and the HIPSC committees all received the same reports. All committee proceedings were closed because of the classified nature of the military operations. In spite of that, some more liberal members of the Senate and the House of Representatives issued vague statements of disapproval for the use of certain strategies and tactics employed by U.S. military forces when called upon to intervene in international situations. These members were identified and quoted in the report, much to their chagrin. By having their personal opinions leaked, the members knew they risked complaints from their constituents that could ultimately affect their chances of reelection. But the people would decide that in the 2020 elections. For now, however, Powers sat quietly staring at the last paragraph of the report.

Operations were completed at 0230 hours on 29 January 2019, and all tactical U.S. and Coalition forces were extracted without incident. The Phantom force was able to retrieve sufficient evidence that the Yemeni Islamic terrorist leader was being supported with weapons, munitions, and intermediate- and short-range missile assets with nuclear and toxic agent canister warheads. There is incontrovertible evidence that this materiel was provided by the governments of Russia, the People's Republic of China, and the Democratic People's Republic of Korea. There is also positive evidence that this military materiel and large amounts of money and gold bullion were provided in exchange for land, sea, and air base agreements in an effort to provide forward-servicing bases for military deployments from those nations.

Two days earlier Vice President Smith, Dr. Hollen, the DNI, Jane O'Donnell, the Secretary of State, and Admiral Chet Nagle had been called to the White House for an undisclosed and unannounced closed-door meeting. Only the principals were aware of its purpose. President Chenoa needed their input on the wording of individual back-channel messages to be transmitted through the American embassies in Moscow, Beijing, and through the Diplomatic Exchange Office in Panmunjom. The draft of these messages, to each of the leaders of those nations, informed them that it had come to the attention of the president of the United States, from an unimpeachable Middle-Eastern source, that their countries, individually and collectively, had been parties to the disruption of and meddling in the normal domestic activities of the countries of French Guiana and Yemen. As a result of this activity, a chaotic ripple effect had been created in the governing practices in the countries of Surinam and Brazil in South America and in the countries of Oman, Qatar, the United Arab Emirates, and Djibouti. This foreign meddling by groups within the three cited nations had resulted in economic failure, devaluation of currencies, serious increases in financial interest rates, inflated prices for commodities, and a near-total disruption of functioning infrastructures in the affected countries.

The draft message went on to say, in several strongly worded and irrefutable accusations, supported with evidence now in the possession of the United States, that their illegal and catastrophic activities had resulted in hemispheric chaos that could not be tolerated by the global community of nations. Further and continued activities of this nature by their countries, or the use of the same disruptive tactics in other countries, would result in serious punitive actions by the United Nations, regional signatories of mutual security agreements, or even violent reactions by individual nations that believed their national security was threatened.

Neither President Chenoa nor any of the closed-door-session attendees believed that these notes to the individual leaders would evoke a change in behavior. They all agreed, however, that they would do at least two things. First, they would put all three nations on notice that their surreptitious actions were no longer private and that widespread knowledge of their disruptive actions would identify them as untrustworthy international partners in any future economic, diplomatic, military, or technical exchange plans or programs.

Second, it put them on notice from the United States that they were not to be considered believable partners who could be trusted to stand by their allies in times of crisis. The final thing that did not need to be said, but was emphasized nonverbally, was that the United States and its closest allies would sift through the forensics of the actions occurring in any nation of the world to lift out the unique signatures of Russian, Chinese, or North Korean meddling in the affairs of any nation in turmoil.

The attendees agreed to send the messages to each of the three violators. They recognized that the three were collaborating and would likely continue to do so. That meant the next recourse would be a personal phone call from President Chenoa. That would be embarrassing for the guilty parties, but it still might not result in a modification of their behavior.

Powers wondered quietly, *Why are these nations working so hard to marginalize and displace the United States as a stabilizing influence in the region, or for that matter, anywhere in the world where we are trying to help create peace, especially where we have been invited to be present? They are working so hard to retaliate against America using multiple proxies. They have to know we are on to them, and that we know they are doing nothing but creating massive global catastrophe.*

With that final observation, Powers knew there was no one from whom he could get a clear answer or with whom he could carry on a free-for-all intellectual conversation, so he exited the report. He then moved to his SIPERNET terminal to check the alphabetically itemized list of nations on the "Watch List" to see if local forces anywhere on the globe were up to more mischief with the backing of any number of Al Quada, Sunni, Shiia, Hezbollah, Hamas, Boko Haram, or Al Shibabab Islamic terrorist groups or any other radical rebel zealots. ISIS was distributing "hit lists" of human targets in the Western world they wanted their lone-wolf radicals to kill at an early date. The targets included national elected leaders, Christian pastors, military generals and admirals, and first responders on fire department and police forces. Keith concluded that so far, the bloodletting had not abated. There were still troubles in Chad, the Central African Republic, Kenya, Libya, Lebanon, Malaysia, Mali, Mozambique, Nigeria, Pakistan, Somalia, Syria, and Ukraine. He scrolled down to a section entitled "New Alerts" to see if anything unexpected had popped up in the last forty-eight hours.

"Well, what's this?" he said out loud. "We haven't heard anything out of the ordinary in a long time from Cameroon." He read on, digesting all the reports from the American ambassador, the station chief, and the army, navy, and air force attachés in and around the capital at Yaoundé.

Keith looked up Cameroon in his classified world atlas, but he found very little of an intelligence nature about the nation. It was mostly tutorial. The short article noted that the Republic of Cameroon had begun as a German colony in 1884 and became a territory in 1919, before later becoming a territory of France then Britain. It declared its independence from France in 1960 and annexed the British Cameroons a year later. The nation had a population of over twenty-two and a half million people who occupied nearly 183,000 square miles. It was bordered by Nigeria to the west, Chad to the northeast, the Central African Republic to the east, and Equatorial Guinea, Gabon, and the Republic of the Congo to the south. Cameroon's coastline opened to the shores of the Gulf of Guinea and the Atlantic Ocean. French and English were the official languages, and the majority of the people there were Christians. More than 20 percent were Islamic, however.

Keith was familiar with some of this data about Cameroon, just as he was with other more or less obscure nations around the world. With Cameroon, however, its access to the South Atlantic, its geographic location, its Christian population, its familiarity with anything French or English, and its Islamic population provided, he thought, the potentially explosive ingredients for disagreement and conflict.

Cameroon's government had become a federal system before changing to a United Republic. It enjoyed years of agrarian bounty and income from timber and petroleum reserves. But in 2008, splinter political groups became disenchanted with a variety of government and private investment arrangements. They created disarray and violent labor protests against everything from the presence of Christian churches, to the speaking of French and English languages, from poor health care, to substandard educational institutions, to unemployment, to food and money shortages. By 2018 the country was ripe for the invasion of radical Islamic jihadists who resented everything about the country and saw it as a place for eventual domination by Islamic State military forces and the remnants of the Unified Islamic Yamani Empire.

Now, in the first half of 2019, Al Yamani and Sal Khandar were being regarded as martyrs for the few radical Islamic soldiers who remained and were searching for a figurehead to lead them in their quest for radical Islamic freedom. These radical Islamic groups had made connections with the principals and practices of Boko Haram, which had aligned itself with ISIS and was trying to integrate with UIYE—until all contact with anyone in the Al Yamani Islamic caliphate had suddenly stopped.

As Powers read through the attaché reports about the dissension in the meager armed forces of the small western African country, he saw the UIYE acronym, which piqued his interest. As he read further, he saw the two-day-old intelligence report that a freighter transport vessel registered in Madagascar had docked in the coastal port of Duala with a load of rice. The report curiously noted that the freighter exactly matched a description of a North Korean vessel rumored to be in the same region.

"Now, why would a North Korean transport, disguised in a neutral nation's identity, travel all that way with a load of rice from a country that has barely enough rice to feed its own people? And why would it go to a country that grows most of the rice it needs, along with much of the other agricultural products it needs to live on?"

With that, he quickly sent out three e-mails before moving on to another small crisis in the Philippines, half a world away. The first e-mail was to his boss, Jim Mullaney, to advise him that a new country had been added to the "watch list" and that there were some curious details about its sudden emergence as a country to watch.

The second e-mail was sent to the three attachés in Cameroon, asking for added detail on the vessel in the port at Duala, with the five thousand tons of rice, as well as more detail about the crisis in leadership in the nation's capital. An obscure and little-publicized political figure named Benjo Ahmadou Adama had suddenly come on the scene as a popular hero of the people. The report mentioned an unidentified individual who seemed to be doing some politico-military planning for Adama. More data was needed on this person and any other individuals who might be guiding the leader's decisions. The attachés were in the best position to gather this type of data.

The third e-mail was sent to Admiral Ray Andrews and Colonel Bud Patrick at MacDill AFB, to inform them to check their SIPERNET intel reports on Cameroon. It almost sounded like a déjà vu all over again" situation. He apprised them he would continue to watch events in that area of the world, and he would report any interesting activities he noticed in the future.

51

Unhappy Trails

Portland, Oregon, March 2019

It was 5:00 p.m. Pacific Standard Time, and Denny was on the phone in his apartment, Number 1212, at the top of the hill on Southwest First Street. The Senate of the United States was in a seven-day recess.

Denny really liked his apartment here. It was private and serene, and it had a terrific view of the skyline of Portland. On more than one occasion, he had considered retiring from the Senate, secluding himself in the apartment that he loved so much, and writing spy novels just for the hell of it. After all, he had been everywhere, done everything, and spun a lot of stories about angels as well as assholes. Then he decided, *No, I'm too young to stop doing what I'm doing right now.*

Life, he decided, was still exciting to him: *I still have not yet achieved some of my goals.* Moving the forces of the United States toward a predominately covert first-response force had not moved fast enough to make it a foregone conclusion. The president's goal of creating a counterbalance to offset the need for an army of occupation to respond to tyrants around the world was still a distant "brass ring," but it was getting closer to becoming a reality.

Denny, Rosemary, Ray Andrews, Bud Patrick, and God knows how many other close-hold, need-to-know individuals had all been energized to see whether there were any nefarious ties to foreign governments or their agents that might have expressed a more-than-passing interest in the activities of the Phantoms. There could still be a mole out there somewhere.

He called Jason Foster in the D.C. office, knowing he would still be there even though it was nearly 9:00 p.m. in Washington. Denny nonchalantly asked Jason about the status of actions on routine office tasks, correspondence to or from dignitaries and constituents. This nonchalance was not demonstrated by happenstance; it was deliberate. He didn't want to immediately ask about contact with people who might have suspicious intentions. That would imply mistrust, and Denny couldn't do that. After all, he had known and trusted Jason for more than three years. Jason had a Top Secret clearance and was aware of the penalties for revealing classified information, and there had never been an occasion when Denny was suspicious of Jason's actions. So Denny was being circuitous with his questions and comments. He was surreptitiously grilling Jason about people contacting the office, just to be certain Jason didn't misread some query that had come his way under the guise of a legitimate request for information. When Denny decided he had exhausted all of his routine questions, he needed to ask one final question on a subject he didn't really want to broach, but he needed to ask it anyway.

"Jason, I'm curious about one of the issues we are working on from the office. I want to be careful about my choice of words for reasons that will be obvious in a moment. As you know, I am working closely with some members of the military on some defense-related topics. Do you recall anyone from the public, or others within the Congress or the White House, inquiring about anything at all having to do with that subject?"

"Senator, I don't know why you are asking, but no, there have been no specific questions that I can recall about your involvement in defense issues. But after all, you are a key member on the Armed Services Committee, and any question that could have come up might have been handled by me without suspicion. I do know it's public knowledge that you are on both the SASC and the SSCI. So when private sector, industry, or media representatives call, I am usually able to redirect their inquiries to the staff aide who is handling the background on the issue in question. I don't want to sound flippant about your question, so I would hasten to add that if the caller or their sponsor were totally unfamiliar to me, I believe I would have been alert to a query from an unfamiliar source, and would quickly become evasive."

"Thanks, Jason. I'm sure you would, and that you would also bring it to my attention. I'm just trying to ensure that our office security is intact and no one is inquiring about or knows anything about the details of my meeting agendas."

"Senator, only one thing has happened that I have not shared with you—because I thought it was innocent: a meeting I had with a headhunter for a school of foreign relations from Venezuela. The lady whom I'm currently dating has been recruited from her current employer to attend this school at some future date, and they are looking for other persons currently in U.S. government service who also might be interested."

Denny thought, *Hmm, this is news. Is he looking to move on?*

"Well, Jason, if you are considering accepting any offers from this school and leaving my office, please let me know if you need any references. You know I will support whatever goals you may pursue that will improve your position."

"Sir, I'm currently undecided. I do know that if I accept his offer beginning late in the year 2019, I'll miss not being here. And I mean that sincerely. When I told him that, he asked me what kinds of activities I would miss. And I said…uh-oh! Holy shit!" There was a moment of silence.

"Jason? Jason? What is it? What did you tell him?"

"Uh, uh, uh, Senator, he asked me to meet with his university registrar and a professor of foreign policy on a certain date. I told him we had important visitors from MacDill Air Force Base coming and they were working on some special Middle-Eastern issues."

"I see. Well, that seems harmless enough. Unless he had other corroborating dates and details, he couldn't possibly have connected any dots, could he?" Denny asked while actually seething under the surface of his casual tone. "Did you mention the visit to anyone else?"

"Well, yes, sir. I mentioned it in passing to my girlfriend, Consuela."

"I don't think I recall you mentioning her role with this Venezuelan university. Has anyone in the office met her?" Denny asked in a calm, reassuring tone. He thought this might calm any misgivings Jason might have about wrongdoing. His ploy worked, but he knew it was only temporary because this whole episode would need to be investigated.

"No, Senator. She and I have only been together for about six months, and she, too, is going to enroll in the university foreign relations program soon. She has dreams of someday returning to government service in Venezuela to—" It suddenly occurred to Jason, and certainly to Denny Smith, that there were indications of coincidental, unintentional, or deliberate collusion in this incident. At that moment, Denny knew he needed to advise Jason to say nothing more to anyone on this subject.

"Jason, let's not discuss this anymore on this call. We can talk about it later tomorrow. Meanwhile, think deeply about all your recent conversations with any of these individuals, and try to remember exactly what you said to all of them. Make notes on your thoughts if you need to, but try to be specific. Now, I think you should go back to your apartment, not talk to your new girlfriend for a day or so, and certainly say nothing or no accept phone calls from this person from the university. Jason, you and I have a very good working relationship. I want to be clear: Go home, make no phone calls to anyone, and if anyone other than me calls, do not answer. Do you understand?"

Jason had never heard the senator talk this directly in the past, and certainly to no one else in the office. He sensed this was a serious situation for some reason, but his limited experience in intelligence or matters related to espionage, if that was what this was, didn't permit him to objectively process what had just happened. It did, however, resonate with him that the senator had said to go home and not talk to anyone. He would do what the senator told him to do.

"Jason, do as I say tonight, and I'll talk to you in the office in the morning as usual. Do you understand?"

After hanging up, Denny then made two more phone calls. The first was to an unlisted number in Washington used exclusively by members of the Senate of the United States. It was to a central emergency number for the Secret Service. As he had been instructed months ago, it was to be used only in circumstances of crisis. To Denny, and certainly to Jason, this was a crisis. The Secret Service caller ID option identified Denny, and the person on the other end said, "Yes, sir, Senator Smith, may we be of service to you?"

After twenty minutes of explanation, the voice on the other end said, "Thank you, Senator Smith. I am aware of the possible problem and now will take it from here. I have the address of Mr. Foster from your office roster and will get back to you within a day to give you a status update on our inquiry. Meanwhile, Senator, be cautious with whom you talk to on the phone and be wary of any visitors to your residence who say they are there to take a poll, to check your Internet connectivity, or to look for a gas leak. Thank you for your call."

Denny felt both relieved and more nervous than before. *Could this be the leak? Is Jason unwittingly involved? Is there espionage going on here?* he thought as he tried to decide what to do next. He sat for a moment. He knew he needed to be careful in what he said and whom he called.

Then he thought, *I'm letting this issue get the best of me. I need to maintain control and recognize the difference between fact and fiction. Sometimes I get too wrapped up in all the secrets that come through my office.*

He took in a deep breath and sat back in his chair. *I need to maintain my focus. Who was it who said that in a crisis it's important to keep your head about you when everyone else around you is losing theirs?*

He made a brief call to Rosemary, to advise her that he was experiencing some irregularities in his office and had asked the Secret Service to look into it. He suggested she be overly cautious about her unsecure phone calls. She understood completely his meaning, even on this unclassified phone, and said she would be back in touch in a day or so.

Denny then called Admiral Andrews and gave him the same message. He was informed that Ray would pass this on to Bud Patrick, but that Bud had found a loose thread on his end, too. They agreed to collaborate in the next day or so, to compare information on a secure line.

After hanging up the phone, Denny sat for a minute looking out the patio doors at the Portland skyline in the dusk. He stared at the city lights that were beginning to come on, heard the muffled city traffic noises from the streets below, and mentally shifted into neutral, which didn't happen very often. He looked down at his wristwatch. It was now 6:30 p.m., and he suddenly realized he was hungry. Just then his phone rang, and he answered.

"Hello?"

"Senator, this is Joanie from the SAE Corporation. Can you talk for a moment?"

"Why, yes, Joanie. How are things?"

"Things are good, and business is continuing to be productive. I just happen to be in Portland visiting with one of our Pacific Rim subsidiaries, and I find myself free for the next few hours. Have you had dinner yet? If not, we should talk."

Denny thought for a moment or two and found himself feeling a bit defensive after the phone calls he had just completed. But he decided that to be forewarned was to be forearmed. Besides, Joanie had never asked anything from him, and she had actually passed some valuable open-source information on to him that turned out to be extremely relevant.

He said, "No, I haven't had dinner yet and was just thinking of doing so. Can you join me as my guest?"

"Yes, I'd like that. Where?"

Denny decided to stay on firm ground and in territory he knew. "Do you know the VQ on Southwest First Street?"

"Yes, I do, and I can be there in thirty minutes if that's alright?"

Denny quickly thought, *She is certainly a take-charge kind of person, and she may have some information that is highly perishable that she needs to pass on. Or it could be just social. In either case, let's see where this goes. It certainly can't be romantic. Julie told me that Joanie is engaged to the CEO of a rival company.*

"That would be perfect. I'll see you in thirty minutes."

52

A Startling Revelation

Portland, Oregon, March 2019

Denny informed Fred at the VQ Restaurant that he was expecting a business associate and there would be two for dinner. Somehow Denny sensed that Fred knew that he was in town and, even more peculiarly, that there would be two for dinner. As it turned out, Fred had seen that Denny was in town in the Portland *Oregonian* newspaper. Usually Denny ate alone. But Fred was always prepared for Denny to arrive with a congressional colleague, a local businessperson, or a staff member. That was what Fred was supposed to do. He was required to always be ready for a change in the dining habits of his best patrons.

Fred showed Denny to his favorite table, and Denny said, "Ms. De Arc will be joining me shortly, so I'll wait till she arrives before we decide on cocktails."

"Very good, Senator. I'll show her to your table as soon as she arrives."

Six minutes later Joanie arrived in an unceremonious manner and was shown to Denny's table. Denny politely stood, shook her hand, and she was seated by Fred, who stood to one side, awaiting the gesture from Denny that a cocktail was in order. Denny ordered two Chopin vodka martinis, stirred, not shaken, and with two olives in each.

"Perfect!" Joanie said.

Their conversation was businesslike and mostly benign. They talked briefly about tax bills in Congress, countries that were trying to attract American businesses to move overseas, American and foreign-nation relations that had been working in favor of the United States, and how the international consulting business was becoming increasingly successful for companies like the SAE Corporation.

They ordered dinner, and the conversation remained friendly and casual. They talked about politics, the economy, foreign business opportunities, and vacation travel plans. As dinner was completed, they moved into the coffee phase. Denny could sense something interesting was coming. He was not to be denied.

"Senator, I have always been accurate and truthful in my discussions with you. I am a loyal American citizen, and I realize that if my country is successful, my company and I will be successful, as well. The mission statement of SAE is to be truthful and honorable, to never cringe before power, and to always speak with frankness and sincerity. I have always honored that creed and have never faltered from it. I hope you know and understand that?"

"Yes, Joanie, I do. I also know you have never asked me for an exchange of information, which I find refreshing and honorable."

"That's right, Senator, and I don't intend to break that unspoken vow of honesty between us now. First I want to tell you something that you may already know. But if not, maybe this will be a data point that you can use. A very large shipment of gold bullion has arrived in the Port of Duala, Cameroon, aboard a freighter registered in Madagascar. The Cameroonians, the Nigerians, and others know about it. It's a charade. It is supposedly filled with rice. Many people know about the rice, if it is indeed rice, but only a very few know about the gold. It is possible there could be something else of a nefarious nature aboard the ship, but that's only a vague suspicion. The freighter is actually owned and operated by the Democratic People's Republic of Korea. With some deep digging through many open-source archives, this information could easily be uncovered. But banks and insurance companies don't make such information easy to find. At this time I have no idea to what use Cameroon would put the gold. It is rumored to be worth close to one billion American dollars. I can't confirm that.

I can confirm, however, that the gold is there and that it's very valuable."

"Hmm. I must tell you I had been informed about the ship, but no other information has been provided. And because of other pressing issues and topics, I frankly have not focused on it. But it occurs to me that that kind of wealth could serve as a formidable leverage to persuade individuals or nations to be willing to negotiate. It could buy a lot of weapons for a small country, or it could make many poor people in Cameroon suddenly wealthy. But for someone with aspirations of grandiosity, it could buy a lot of influential friends."

"Denny, you are right on all counts. A nation with the subtle means to find out things might be able to ferret that out. Another bit of information that will not be easy to verify at this early date is that there may soon be a governmental transition in Cameroon because of the age and ill health of the current leader, President Modibo Ruben Um Adamo. Please don't repeat this as the unequivocal truth, but it is rumored that his grandson is favored by the family, and the people, to succeed him. The grandson is Benjo Ahmadou Adamo. I am sure you are aware of Adamo's now-deceased friends from Yemen. You needn't confirm or acknowledge any of this information. I give it to you freely to do with as you see fit. As always, I expect nothing in return."

"I understand, Joanie, and I'm sure you know I have sources that can validate anything you tell me. Once done, I am unsure, at this time, what we would do with that information, however."

"Yes, of course, and I expect you will consider the advice of those sources. But an interesting added bit of information is that Adamo has a new advisor, who is quietly and privately advising him on how to grow his assets and resources, how he should relate to his various international neighbors, and how he might encourage the people of Cameroon to be loyal and faithful to him. I don't have any information on what that advice is, or whether it is political, economic, or military—or some of each. No one at this juncture even knows who this advisor is, or in what political direction that advice is nudging Adamo. The informal word is that Adamo is his own man, that he likes input from all quarters but he makes up his own mind. One of my sources informed me Adamo seems to be for the people of Cameroon and knows he he is where he is because of their loyalty to his family. He is reported to be a loyal worshiper of Allah, a devout Islamist. Beyond that, I have no further information. None of my sources will speculate on which direction he might take the country. One report, however, says that he has been repulsed by the actions of Boko Haram. Another report says that he is becoming impatient to assume the reins of power, so he can bring structure and regimentation to the country. It is, after all, easier to control people when they respect the power of their leader.

"There is one other bit of information I believe you should know. This information could change things between us, or maybe not. It comes down to a matter of trust and honesty. My sources tell me there is a quiet but urgent search ongoing by American authorities in cooperation with coalition forces and INTERPOL. They are scouring the planet for a fellow by the name of Francois Ricardo De La Plane. Again, you needn't acknowledge one way or the other. I will admit I don't know where he is or what he has done to deserve such attention. I simply know that people are trying to find him.

"I know, however, that he is smart, well-educated, elusive, well-connected to the radical Islamist community, and that his goals in life appear to be disconnected, almost schizophrenic. He seems unsure of who he is or who he wants to be. I honestly cannot shed any light on this, and neither can any of my colleagues."

Denny knew he needed to tread carefully on this subject. He knew about the search for De La Plane, but he could not confirm or deny any information without jeopardizing national security. So he answered obtusely.

"I will be honest with you, Joanie. I have heard of this individual and have read somewhere that he is a bad person who is brilliant but badly needs counseling assistance." Denny wanted to be honest, but he did not want to, nor could he, reveal how much he really knew about De La Plane.

Joanie continued, correctly sensing Denny was being guarded. She cautiously selected her next words. "You're absolutely right. From everything I've read about him, he is unbalanced and is either running from something or toward it. Almost everything I know about this man's activities in the last two years is because I have read it in my private corporate business documents, or it is simply rumor and innuendo from various foreign sources. Since he has been such a pivotal person in all the recent activities in the Middle East, you would think that I, my company, or our international contacts would know more about him. But we don't. I will also tell you in confidence that many, many years ago, I knew this man as a boy. You see, my full name is Joan De Arc De La Plane. He is my brother."

53

Closing in on the Targets

The Oval Office, the White House, Washington, D.C., March 2019

"General Mossman," the president said with tones of both confidence and uncertainty, "we have had a modicum of success in decapitating the efforts of at least two, and maybe four tyrants in parts of the world where American national security was at risk."

"Yes, Madame President, our activities in French Guiana and Yemen have reaped military victories and some unintended positive consequences in Somalia and other neighboring nations. In South America, our Venezuelan friends have toned down their rhetoric, and have, either by coincidence or by deliberate action, backed away from their belligerence against French Guiana, Surinam, and Colombia. The nations around Yemen, and on all sides of the Red Sea, have moved military action forces away from their borders with neighbors they previously were about to confront. Things could still become chaotic there, because the Houthis, the Shiites, and all the radical Islamists in that country cannot agree on anything. There are just too many diverse tribal and political interests. At worst, we could someday be facing a divided Yemen based on clearly defined province borders. At best, a popular leader might emerge whom a majority of the people could get behind. The problem becomes more complex as surrounding nations persist in probing into Yemeni affairs and attempt to woo factions to their own ways of thinking. Secretary Vargas definitely has her work identified for her. The future is not easy to predict or to prepare for.

"The Houthis tribes are firmly entrenched in Sana'a and in the northern part of Yemen. Forces loyal to the former president of Yemen that were displaced by Yamani are gathering some support from those in the south of Yemen. Even though Al Yamani was a tyrant, he did manage to keep the warring factions at bay and he got all of them to swear allegiance to him, as long as the money held out. Our State Department first-responders are in most large cities in Yemen, and I'm hoping that under the leadership of our American ambassador, who was escorted out of Yemen three years ago but is now back, we can forge a reasonable treaty of peace for the country. Afghanistan, Pakistan, and Syria are not helpful."

President Chenoa sat behind the Resolute Desk with the fingers of her hands interlaced, her chin resting on the backs of them. "I would like to believe some degree of quiet has been achieved because of the actions of our Phantoms. I think there is evidence that a lot of belligerence has been taken out of the population and the tribal leaders. Unfortunately, I am told that emotions are still running high. But not as high as when Al Yamani had everyone whipped up into a feverish frenzy. No nation has yet asked the United States for an explanation or has requested a diplomatic discussion about our or anyone else's activities. They are either still uncertain about what happened and who did it, or they are reluctant to broach the subject because we are liable to ask them to explain their own nefarious activities with foreign nations."

She then said optimistically, "Tom, I want to think the latter is the case. They know that if they asked us for a full accounting of our involvement, we would ask the same of them in the conduct of their foreign policy. In addition, I want to think that they believe the same disruption that has befallen the Guineans and Yemenis could happen in their countries. None of the other nations who know about the reversal of fortunes in those target nations want to have the same unmasking happen in their countries."

"Madame President, I believe, for now, that any of the countries we are familiar with know we are the only nation that could mount such an assault. Since they are uncertain about how they are regarded by the United States, they are backing off for a short while. Most of them still believe we are infidels. And the strength of their beliefs say we should line up and have our heads removed. Progress will be at glacial speed to begin with.

"The larger nations involved here, such as China and Russia, know we have evidence of their involvement and don't want to ruffle our feathers until they know when the political winds will be more favorable toward them in the international forum. Your communications to them via back-channel means and in roundabout language in the UN, as well as through our ambassadors, that we have incontrovertible evidence of their involvement in the political unrest, in not only those nations but more than a half-dozen others, as well, has not fallen on deaf ears. They are not anxious for another disgrace. But neither are they hesitant to restrain some of their bolder international maneuvers that they have been planning for many months. Our intelligence community believes they will simply move with caution rather than drama or surprise."

"And the North Koreans? What are you hearing about their intentions?"

"The North Koreans don't know when to quit. Their 'bull in a china shop' diplomacy tactics have gotten them some gains with smaller countries. They have made no headway with the United States. Their foreign policy continues to be conducted like that of a grade-school bully. They keep blustering, pushing, posturing, and occasionally punching out somebody. They are begging for a full, face-on confrontation. They have been doing this for years. We have shown them nearly eighteen years of restraint, and they have misinterpreted that as weakness, indecision, and uncertainty. Sooner or later, we are going to have to confront the playground bully and knock him down.

"But the downside of their habits and patterns has not been encouraging. They are emboldened by technology. They have tested the Road-Mobile KN-08 ICBM. They have also continued testing the components of a miniaturized version of a nuclear warhead. They profess the missile and the warhead can reach the continental United States. Our intelligence community reports that the nuclear reactor complex at Yongbyon is active. That means the North Koreans are producing fissile materiel for nuclear warheads. They will continue to do so as long as we do nothing to discourage them and as long as there is a worldwide market for nuclear munitions in a variety of destructive sizes. Manufacture and export of these explosives can't possibly be connected to a happy ending.

"We have deployed terminal high-altitude air-defense batteries to South Korea and Japan. They are trained to control and fire the system. If the North Koreans were to fire on either of them or on the United States, I think we could successfully intercept whatever missiles are launched at us.

"We are not, however, prepared just yet for the export of North Korean nuclear warheads to other belligerent countries in central Africa or the Middle East. If the North Koreans were to relocate such a system to the control of an irresponsible tyrant in Africa or around the Red Sea, the results could be widespread and disastrous.

"Their strategic plan seems to be to find a surrogate nation who will take their missile and launch it against an adversary to destroy that nation's will to resist. They seem to believe that no one would ever suspect it all happened because of North Korean insistence. Their tactics are to profess ignorance, and they will lie and say they had nothing to do with it. They are untrustworthy, disingenuous, and barbarous, and they must be confronted and exposed with each lie they tell.

"For now, Madame President, there is consensus among your advisors that we should keep our heads down, be extraordinarily alert, quietly build the readiness of our forces, and integrate the latest technological changes into our military capabilities. General wisdom and common sense says we should follow our plan to leverage state-of-the-art intelligence-gathering and build our covert-operations capabilities. Continued support for Senator Smith and Congresswoman Doolin is essential. The House and the Senate traditionally follow leaders who are in the know, have insider information, and are cleared for information that has limited channels of distribution. We absolutely must keep them in our loop of closest confidantes and advisors."

"Thank you, Tom. My concept of a counterbalance is proving to be the right move, at the right time. I want to do whatever is necessary to reinforce it and keep moving toward a smaller, more lethal, more mobile force, and away from a large army-of-occupation strategy. We and the American taxpayers simply can't afford the loss of treasure and blood that comes through the use of those tactics.

"Tom, let me change the subject to a separate but related topic. I hope we are exploiting all of our sources to find the mole who is leaking information to our adversaries."

"Yes, of course, Madame President. My latest update on that subject is that a number of individuals have been questioned in bipartisan and impartial ways. The Secret Service has followed all the leads they have been given. I won't characterize their reaction to this task as relentless, but they have been thorough. They have thus far reported they have not identified any leaks. I have an update report scheduled for me in less than two weeks."

"Good, thank you. Please keep me apprised of any breakthroughs or progress in sealing that leak. If you think there is a role for me to perform similar to the Blackthorn mission, you know I will gladly stand up for this country, against any adversary."

54

Sealing the Mole Hole

Phantom Headquarters, MacDill Air Force Base, Tampa, Florida, March 2019

Colonel Bud Patrick and LuAnn Hernandez were seated across a table from one another in a secure vault conference room. They were sharing coffee in a congenial, conversational atmosphere. Bud was casual and informal, but Luann was a bit on edge and fearful that she was guilty of a misstep in protocol or had even violated security in some way. They had spoken earlier in the day, and once LuAnn revealed certain innocent discussions she had held with several individuals, the dominoes began to fall.

"LuAnn, I sincerely appreciate the way you came forward and volunteered information after our classified briefing this morning, which noted we were seeking a possible mole. I have to tell you, I never believed the leakage of information came from here. And I still believe that."

"Thank you, Colonel. As I look back on my telephone conversations and casual contacts with people on the base and friends on the phone, I can't see how anyone could conclude I had any information about operations."

"LuAnn, as we piece this all together, I have to tell you that someone with an elaborate network of connections and people in public government offices could pick up enough critical unclassified, open-source data that, when put all together, could make a very clear picture of government plans and operations. It's clear to me someone was watching you and listening to your conversations, and has taken your innocent comments and treated them as puzzle pieces that were parts of a possible larger plan. Rest assured, however, someone is looking into the activities of the people you have been in contact with over the last several months. Even as we speak, someone is talking with Consuela and her university contact, Bill Loh.

Johnny's Half Shell Restaurant, Washington, D.C., March 2019

Secret Service agents Phil Masterson, Beverly Bernard, and Kurt Belsten walked into the busy bar area of the restaurant and separated five to six feet apart in a Flee, Capture, and Arrest—an FCA—phalanx formation. They positioned their right hands on the pistols under their jackets in case of unexpected trouble. They focused on an Asian-looking gentleman standing at the bar talking to an attractive, professional-looking woman. The man was known by the public name of Bill Loh. He was commonly thought to be a recruiter for a foreign university that was looking for candidates for a lucrative program that promised an eventual foreign government position. The supposed program was advertised such that after graduation, an appointment to a government position could be expected and that it would be influential in the international marketplace for the country of Venezuela. The problem was that, even though the nation of Venezuela knew of Mr. Loh's activities and were postured to validate any inquiries that would come their way about his recruiting activities, there were actually no such positions or educational opportunities available to back up his claims of legitimacy. In fact, the government of Venezuela was actually being paid a handsome sum of money by the People's Republic of China to validate Loh's claims.

Agent Masterson walked up to Loh and stepped between him and the woman, turning his back to her. "Mr. Loh? Or should I say, Colonel Bong Wang Guanzhong? I'm Agent Masterson; this is Agent Bernard. And this is Agent Beltson of the United States Secret Service.

Would you come quietly with us now? This can be easy or difficult. We are prepared to escort you out of here either way." The three agents and Loh casually walked out of the bar onto First and North Capital Streets to a waiting black Chevrolet Suburban SUV, got in, and drove away.

The Level 8 Lounge, Tallahassee, Florida, March 2019

The Lounge was located at the intersection of North Monroe and East Virginia Streets. It was on the eighth floor of the Duval Hotel overlooking the city, and was known for its little black dresses and its free champagne. Consuela Vera Cruz was meeting with a potential candidate for the University in Venezuela at the behest of Bill Loh. Consuela didn't know this potential candidate personally, but she had reviewed a short dossier on him that had been forwarded to her earlier in the day. Curiously, she was talking to a young Cuban-American man who didn't need the books she was selling. She was asked to surreptitiously inquire about his technical qualifications for a potential defense-related government position in the university—or so she said. The young man worked for Northrop Grumman Aviation in Pensacola, Florida. In the middle of her discussion with him, three Secret Service agents interrupted her in midsentence—in much the same way that Bill Loh was interrupted. Consuela claimed she was conducting business for her publisher to sell textbooks. Earlier in the day, she'd tried to contact LuAnn to no avail, but she did connect with Jason Foster in Senator Smith's office and with Dahlia Morgan, a Senate Armed Services Committee legislative assistant in Senator Fred Shoemaker's office. Jason and Dahlia had given her only minor tidbits of information that indicated there was little or no interesting military activity in the areas with which those offices were involved. The agents were polite but insistent and they approached her using the same FCA tactic used on Bill Loh. The four of them left the eighth floor lounge in the Duval Hotel to a waiting black Chevrolet Suburban SUV at the street-level front door of the hotel.

The Russell Senate Office Building, Washington, D.C., March 2019

Two agents walked into Denny Smith's office and politely asked for Jason Foster. He was waiting in the reception area of the offices. He knew they were coming to question him and had already consented to go with them to talk about Consuela and their relationship. He didn't want to create a scene or embarrass anyone in the office, especially Denny Smith, whom he admired. This was an easy, low-key apprehension by the Secret Service agents, requiring no special tactics or added conversation. Jason went voluntarily and quietly, expecting he would be back in his office by 2:30 p.m. at the latest. He was never seen in his office again.

The West Wing, the White House, Washington, D.C., April 2019

A week later, Senior Agent in Charge Randy Billings was meeting with General Mossman to provide an interim report on the search for the mole.

"Sir," Billings said to General Mossman, "we have conducted a sweep of all the parties who may have been involved, voluntarily or unwittingly, with gathering information about a U.S. covert operations military group and its activities. So far we have the testimonies of more than twenty-six individuals who either work on Capitol Hill for members of Congress, or are civil service employees who are assigned to a variety of areas between Florida and Virginia military installations, bases in Italy and Egypt, and embassies in various U.S. offices in foreign nations around the Gulf of Mexico, the Mediterranean, and the Red Sea. The U.S. citizens we contacted overseas were of little help. For the most part, they all said they had heard that some military maneuver was being conducted but there was very little known about who, where, what, when, or how it was going to be conducted. The stateside contacts, however, had a little more detail, and when all data was taken together a vague scenario was pieced together that cited numbers of military personnel, locations they originated from, and what aircraft or vessels on which they were to be transported. Names of commanders and operations leaders were also identified.

"I have to tell you, General, the network was very amateurish and rudimentary, but it was very effective. It appears as though a cell of expert analysts in a foreign facility in Washington took all of the input and pieced it together into a story of a military attack. I can't tell you it was very detailed or conclusive, but the story did tell a listener somewhere that there was irrefutable evidence that something was happening, or was about to happen. I think, based on the clues, no one knew what the objective was or exactly where it was to be conducted."

"Thank you, Agent Billings. That's useful information in order to beef up our operational security practices, but I'm not sure how we can plug every OPSEC hole. It occurs to me there is some critical information we are lacking, but I'm not certain I know what it is. For example, the individual who has eluded our capture is somehow alerted to flee each time. How does he know to do that? Someone is warning him. How do they know where he is? How does he know how to escape and evade our forces? We are missing some crucial details."

"General, you're right. There's more to this scenario that I couldn't uncover in the short time I was given. Now that I have at least another thirty days, maybe I can unearth more detail.

"Please tell the President General that we are still pursuing a number of leads. We haven't given up on this yet, and we are being assisted by the Defense Investigative Service from the Pentagon. So we are now able to search more broadly with the added manpower."

"Thank you, Agent Billings. I will pass your report on to her this afternoon."

The Aftermath, Worldwide

As the Secret Service and the FBI conducted further meetings and discussions with larger numbers of individuals, a pattern emerged. By the time the meetings were concluded with persons known to have been contacted about the movements of U.S. military personnel and transport vehicles, persons suspected of subversive activities, possible suspects, persons of interest, potential witnesses, and observers who had some connection with all of the 113 persons on the list, very little information was revealed that could positively be identified as a violation of U.S. national security laws.

The trails to senior intelligence operatives of the PRC, or any other nations, and the ties between the observers or supposed informants, were tenuous at best. The ties between these observers and national intelligence collection agencies of any foreign nations were obscure, and all trails eventually led to dead ends. It demonstrated a brilliant pattern of covering tracks and leads between people collecting data and people reporting data to outside countries. It seemed too organized to have been managed by a group or a small nation of minimally trained intelligence workers. Once completed forty-five days later in May 2019, the results of the investigation were reported to Admiral Andrews; Denny Smith; Rosemary Doolin; selected members of the SASC, the SSCI, the HASC, and the HIPSCI; and of course, Tom Mossman and the president.

While the reactions of all those closest to the Phantom force operations were that of both disappointment and astonishment since no villains were uncovered, certain small achievements were fortunately achieved in the aftermath. Colonel Bong Wang Guaunzhong, alias Bill Loh, of the People's Liberation Army of the PRC, was deported from the United States. As was expected, the PRC retaliated, and an air attaché in the United States Air Force was deported from the U.S. embassy in Beijing on a trumped-up charge of conducting some irregular travel activities.

Jason Foster was offered a job at the Health and Human Services Department in Washington. He said he would take it, for a while. He claimed he really cared for Consuela a great deal, but he hadn't heard from her in a week.

LuAnn Hernandez underwent additional security and counterterrorism tactics training, and she was returned to the front office of Phantom Headquarters. She still didn't know what the Phantoms did. She was working harder to stay away from operational activities, and she still was in love with Darrin.

Consuela underwent brutal interrogation by the FBI, but the Bureau could not pinpoint any espionage activities in which she may have been involved. She was very cool under the pressure of intense questioning. Bureau agents took that to mean, after four days of interrogation, that either she didn't know, or hadn't done, anything they could charge her with. Or she was so well-trained and disciplined as an undercover agent for some country that she had been rigidly programmed to be stoic and able to feign innocence and ignorance.

An analysis of the networking arrangements set up by the PRC, and executed by Colonel Bong, revealed many interesting connections, reporting routines, code word alerts, and unusually sophisticated, rerouted, and roundabout communications-reporting procedures. This investigation did not, however, uncover how connections were made to Francois Ricardo De La Plane or who had contacted him. That would continue to be examined and investigated.

All the others who might or might not have had contact with activities of the First Special Operations Regiment, Special Forces Division, assigned to the Department of Defense, claimed no specific knowledge of these troops. They also claimed they were never aware of what the troops were charged to do. They did, however, say the forces were always hungry, always needed to clean their weapons, were always sleepy, always were noncommittal about keeping dental appointments, were always evasive about every subject including the weather, and were always horny—not necessarily in that order.

There were no e-mail trails, or cell phone connections, or face-to-face discussions that could verify someone had nefarious intentions regarding special overseas operations related to the United States military or to the Phantoms.

The fact remained that Francois De La Plane had escaped tight combat security constraints twice, and there were no obvious reasons or explanations about how he had managed that, unless he was clairvoyant, and that was not likely. One Secret Service investigator observed, "You know what? There were no complex technical reasons we can verify that a special tipoff process was used to send separate alerts to any one individual, no secret codes were transmitted to anyone's receiver device, and there was no high-tech bug in someone's lampshade that sent intelligence alerts to anyone. This could be something as simple as a note left on someone's pillow by the maid, or it could have been a simple fifteen-second phone call from a burner phone from a guard or friend outside."

Someone did indeed alert De La Plane that a counterforce was about to disrupt his life—on two separate occasions. He took this information either knowing the caller or believing the call was anonymous but credible, or he did not know the caller and simply accepted on faith that the warning was real. Even though this phase of the investigation was over for now, it was clear that there would be another clue that would trigger a deeper review later.

55

Cameroonian Unrest

The Minister's Villa, Yaoundé, Cameroon, March 2019

In early December 2018, Benjo Adamo's grandfather, President Modibo Ruben Um Adamo, died a quiet death from a series of age-related maladies. He was ninety-six years of age. His presidency had been generally peaceful, and the people had been prosperous. There had been some conflicts in recent years with radical Islamists, but the antagonists had mainly been small splinter groups of low-profile dissidents who thought they were making more of an impact on the population than they actually did. For those reasons, the people, the members of the National Assembly, and the Senate all believed the reins of power should remain in the hands of the Adamo dynasty. There was, however, an undercurrent of discontent tied to support of the Boko Haram jihadists. They confined their barbaric activities primarily to the northern part of Cameroon. Most of their attacks were "hit and run "strikes. But they were becoming more emboldened as the president and the current administration of Cameroon showed little interest in retaliating against them.

Um Adamo recruited a retired Nigerian army general to be his national defense minister. Major General Charles Quintana Damboa had kept a modicum of order in the country. However, many times he had been accused of overreacting with the Cameroon citizenry in response to public demonstrations. He was, of course, more comfortable in disciplining nonviolent and unarmed Cameroonians. Results and security progress had been easier to report with them than with more belligerent lawbreakers. However, he appeared to be effective in his control of law and order, and bonuses for appearing effective and efficient were welcome incentives for him to keep doing what he was doing.

General Damboa was less formidable with the hit-and-run strikes by Boko Haram in the northern part of Cameroon. Some in Cameroon believed the general was actually on the payroll of the jihadists, and in some cases they thought he allowed Boko Haram, Al Shabaab, and other offshoot radical Islamic groups to attack small villages and towns in order to rape, pillage, steal, kidnap, and/or kill the village leaders, women, and children at will. In any case, the defense minister showed little ability to stem the flow of terrorism.

When politically high-level individuals were threatened, injured, or even worse, and when entire villages in Cameroon suffered surprise attacks from the jihadists and both people and treasure were taken, Benjo took notice. He knew something had to be done to protect Cameroon, but Defense Minister General Damboa only showed a low level of concern, a high level of incompetence, and little forward thinking. So, one month earlier, Benjo confidentially requested that Francois quietly observe the terrorist activities and prepare a solution to strengthen Cameroonian forces to deal with the Boko Haram threat—with or without the defense minister. Something had to be done soon, or disaffection with the Adamo government would inspire a change in popular support.

An appropriate presidential funeral ceremony was held for President Um Adamo, with no viewing. Several family receptions were held for all of the people to participate in the mourning. The reception held at the presidential palace included all members of the Adamo family and was considered the most significant of all the events, because all of the political and tribal elite from around the nation were in attendance. Francois De La Plane was present, but he kept his visibility low and unobtrusive. He watched the governmental and tribal leaders and he listened to their public and whispered comments. He was developing a plan to present to Benjo Adamo after he was inaugurated.

The parliament of Cameroon was made up of the 180-seat National Assembly and the 100-seat Senate. The Senate was overseen by Ferdinand Bon Dibango, a longtime friend and confidante of the late president. In his capacity as the Senate president, under the Cameroonian constitution, Dibango was next in line for the national presidency should the president resign or passed away. However, Dibango himself was eighty-nine years old and in ill health, and he had privately declared he would step aside if President Um Adamo should ever pass away. It was no secret that President Um Adamo and Senate Leader Dibongo wished the country's presidency to pass to Benjo Ahmadou Adamo, who had proven his ability to lead and govern by serving eight years as interior minister for five of those years, and then as minister of foreign affairs in the Um Adamo administration. Benjo himself kept a low profile at the behest and advice of a close circle of peers and advisors. When speaking in public, he professed a moderate and centrist political posture, much like that of his grandfather and the Senate leader. But under this moderate veneer, he was seething with an anger that made him wish the inauguration would be sooner rather than later so that he could take positive actions against those within and outside Cameroon who threatened the nation's very existence.

At the funeral reception in the presidential palace, most, if not all, political and tribal leaders sought out Benjo Adamo in order to express their heartfelt sadness at the passing of his grandfather. They also quietly pledged their loyalty to him as he moved through the parliamentary process to become the only candidate to succeed Mobido Ruben Um Adamo as the president of Cameroon. Francois had privately advised Benjo to assume such a posture, and he had himself become part of Benjo Adamo's "kitchen cabinet of invisible advisors."

Sambisa Forest, Northern Nigeria, February, 2019

In the far northeastern corner of Nigeria, in the Sambisa Forest, a meeting of one hundred Boko Haram terrorist soldiers was in session. They were the strategic planning force whose purpose was to lay out tactical plans for the 2,300-strong members of the Kanuri ethnic group army. Their plan was to employ tactics and logistic support capabilities to take over the government of Cameroon, capture its capital, and begin conversion of the entire population to a pure Islamic state ruled by Sharia law. The leader of the group was Zingo Abubakir Kambar, a longtime student and understudy of the now-deceased Boko Haram leaders Mohammed Yusuf and Abubakar Shekau.

Kambar was tall, very muscular, and had threatening-looking tattoos on his arms and chest that resembled the frightening mythical creatures the Watusi tribes of two decades ago had feared. He wore aviator sunglasses, a French Foreign Legion tunic with a general's insignia on it and the sleeves cut off, and a military-style garrison cap with braid embroidered on the bill. He thought, and others in his army believed, too, that he looked both official and authoritarian. He would, indeed, have appeared resplendent even in an American Goodwill thrift store. But since his soldiers were dressed in rags and tattered clothing, he was satisfied he looked far better than they did.

His instructions from Yusuf and Shekau had been to work in concert with, but independent of, a second 2,800-strong army of Boko Haram fighters that would simultaneously take over the government of Nigeria. Together, the leadership of Boko Haram believed Nigeria and Cameroon would solidify the Central African caliphate. This new caliphate had already sworn its allegiance to Al Qaida and the Islamic State of Iraq and the Levant. Its plan was to swallow Nigeria, Cameroon, Niger, and Chad. Kambar then would see himself as, if not a caliph, then at least a continental governor.

Kambar stood on a platform at the front of a large room that had served as a cafeteria for a now-vacant hospital building in the village of Marte Town. The town was now mostly deserted buildings since it had been attacked repeated times by Nigerian soldiers, then re-attacked by Boko Haram fighters. This seesaw activity had left the region a vast wasteland of grounds and dilapidated buildings where Boko Haram fighters had set up their temporary offices, living accommodations for family persons, and storage space for ammunition, weapons, stolen booty, and canned food items. The families were meant to be human shields for the terrorist supplies while the fighters were off pillaging other towns and villages.

The fighters attending this all-day session in the now-defunct hospital were only somewhat attentive and easily distracted by whispered discussion items about women, food, new training tactics that were more bloody than the last, and what they were going to do to the Cameroonians they were about to vanquish.

Behind Kambar, a large map hung on the wall, perhaps twelve feet by twelve feet in size, showing the entire eastern frontier of Nigeria and the border of Cameroon down to the Gulf of Guinea. East of the Nigerian border lay all the lands of Cameroon divided by political groupings, starting with the political segments unimaginatively identified as "Far North," then moving southward to the North province, then southward to the Adamawa province, named after a revolutionary fighter, the Center province in the middle of the Cameroon map, and the four smaller states to the west called Littoral, West, Northwest, and Southwest. That left only the East and South provinces remaining to be identified as targets for selected groups of jihadist soldiers. The province areas and the major cities that served as the provincial capitals, or seats of local area administration, were identified in large letters so that the uneducated but observant fighters might recognize the names of the cities that were to be their targets if they appeared on road signs.

Kambar announced, "Ten of you have been assigned to brigade staffs who will lead up to eight hundred fighters. Each brigade is assigned a province target, and the attacks will all commence simultaneously. We are all to be pre-positioned along the eastern Nigerian border with our weapons and transport vehicles fueled and poised to attack when the command is ordered."

One of Kambar's trademarks was his very loud, excited, and threatening rhetoric. It was his habit to speak this way in large as well as small groups. He had come to believe he needed to energize his fighters to be as brutal, as bloodthirsty, and as violent as possible in order for those being vanquished to give up the four most valued treasures for Boko Haram: gold, silver, weapons, and women.

"You are the leaders of our conquest of all of the African states. Your fighters are to look to you for leadership and strength. You must show more ferocity than anyone in your command. You are to bring back more of the four treasures than anyone else among your fighters.

You must show less mercy to Christians, politicians, Americans, and European citizens than anyone else under your command. The world must come to know that Boko Haram is here to stay. We are now in charge of the world. Sharia law is the law of the land. You must never forget that Boko Haram means 'Western education is forbidden.' If those you conquer refuse to hand over the four treasures, kill them immediately. If they are Westerners, don't ask them for anything; just kill them immediately. If women and children refuse to join you, kill them immediately, too. Our rules are few but they are simple.

This message is in keeping with the very philosophy that Boko Haram supports. History records that they have been more barbaric, more blood thirsty and more devastating to innocent victims than ISIL or any other radical Islamist organization. They have become so, by attacking, killing and maiming innocent victims who were unable to defend themselves or fight back. Their most prominent victims, who can be terrorized to send a message of fear to others, are old men, old women and children. ISIL on the other hand, slays their victims in battle situations, which in and of itself does not dignify what they are doing; but their conquests are deemed somewhat more militaristic and slightly less barbaric.

Kambar's tactic now, in keeping with a Boko Haram theme of fear, theft, and carnage, is to move in the next few days to take all of Cameroon and change it into a functioning part of the caliphate.

"We will not take *no* for an answer. If laws are needed, we will announce those laws when we take over leadership in those provinces. If the people want laws, we will pass the laws and they will find out what those laws are once they are passed. Regardless of what is asked of us, they will conform to Sharia law."

56

Something Is Up

Phantom Headquarters, Mac Dill Air Force Base, Tampa, Florida, March 2019

"Keith, thanks for keeping us in the loop on the things going on around the world. But I know that you know we're interested in activities that might involve De La Plane." Bud Patrick looked down at his encrypted telephone to be sure the small green light on the top of the instrument was still illuminated, which meant the circuit was still secure.

Since the last mission to Yemen, when plans didn't work out as expected, there had been security control changes implemented that were intended to tighten up the exchange of telephonic and face-to-face exchange of classified data. Bud was now in a secure telephone booth inside a secure vault in a secure building. As usual, the military had overreacted to plans to alter how they did classified operations, right down to playing white noise in the restrooms of all of the facilities in the complex. In addition, all personnel, both civilian and military, were briefed on an eight-hour course in espionage practiced by all known terrorist groups and governments.

When the Department of Defense thought it needed to change directions and tactics, it leaped into action—in which everyone who was involved must sign statements saying they had received training and indoctrination. This effort had become an activity in which phone calls were monitored, mail was censored, individuals had to sign into and out of secure phone booths, visitors to the administrative offices were being photographed, and special visitor's badges were being issued to generals and admirals who visited—and even to the pizza delivery guy. And it was necessary.

"Bud, there's very little new news from anywhere around the world. I have to tell you, that, in and of itself, makes me nervous. There is always some horrific event happening somewhere. But there's nothing going on in the Middle East or in Central Africa right now, other than general discontent, which has piqued my interest. That makes the hairs on the back of my neck tingle. Something is going on somewhere, and intuition says it's in Nigeria and Cameroon."

"I know what you are saying, Keith. I, too, have been following all the intel traffic from that area for weeks now, and I haven't detected any signature patterns or actions that would make me think that chaos is about to erupt. But, like you, my gut says something is up in Central Africa and that they're trying to come this way."

"Bud, you're right. Something's up, but I can't give you an unequivocal threat alert because I don't have anything specific. The best I can do is to say 'be ready; something is happening.'"

"Okay. Thanks, Keith. We've got three different scenarios we are practicing for three different areas of Central Africa, Libya, and the Gulf of Aden. You know we'll always be prepared for whatever the mission is."

"Roger that, Bud. You know I'll get back to you as soon as anything appears on the radar. That's all from here. Thanks for the talk. Please give my best to Barb. She'll probably know what's going to happen, and where, before you and I ever do."

"Thanks, Keith. Best to Serita, too. We need to have you two here for a few beers and some tarpon fishing and eating sometime soon."

Military people had a special bond between themselves and the members of the other services with whom they served. A friendly spirit of competition had always existed between the services and members of each branch. But when they served together on the same or related missions, the bond became even stronger and formed an invisible tie that bound the leaders of units, the enlisted operators of units, and the support personnel who provided the tools to battle a common enemy. Their uniforms might look different, but their attitudes, values, beliefs, and loyalties were all the same. Skin color, religion, hometowns, and education made no difference. In battle the mantra was "all for one and one for all."

In this case, Colonel Keith and his wife, Serita Powers, USAF, would one day soon travel from Washington, D.C., to Tampa, Florida, to spend some well-earned time with Colonel "Bud" and wife, Barbara, Patrick, U.S. Army, to fish and to share dinners and sunsets.

57

Corruption and War

The Presidential Palace, Yaoundé, Cameroon, March 2019

The presidential inauguration of Benjo Ahmadou Adamo was a resplendent affair. There were the usual ceremonial trappings of a change in administration. In this case, it was a bit more subdued in deference to the death of a much revered president who had met his demise while still in office. Nevertheless, there were military units from each of the services, two marching bands—one military and one civilian. There were hundreds of schoolchildren marching and carrying flowers and an entourage of duly elected senators, one from each state representing the people of that state. They were attired in colorful ceremonial robes indicating their legal authority and rank.

There was the usual modest but respectable number of six armored personnel carriers and four Jeeps with fifty-caliber machine guns mounted on the back. A small flight of eight aircraft flew low over the ceremonial reviewing stand. The flyover consisted of three transport aircraft: one U.S.-made C-130; one Canadian-made DHC-5 Buffalo; and one German-made Dornier DO-128. They were followed by two Russian-made Mi-8/17 helicopters; one Italian-made MB-326 fighter aircraft, and their only American-made presidential Grumman Gulfstream lll executive jet. The Gulfstream De La Plane had flown into Yaoundé and its two pilots were not included in the number, but they were being held as backups for possible later, unspecified use. The two pilots were very happy to have found a home and a new mission.

All of these aircraft made up nearly 30 percent of the nation's air force. The army, navy, air force, and naval infantry each were represented by stone-faced, ferocious-looking marching units with unloaded rifles shouldered and unloaded pistols appropriately holstered. While the military representation at the parade appeared formidable, the 38,000 men and women in the armed forces, their equipment, and tactics have had little effect in deterring the fast-moving thugs of Boko Haram and their unorthodox attack maneuvers.

The entire celebration was deliberately subdued at the request of Adamo because of the death of the previous president, his grandfather. It had only been a few months since President Um Adama had passed away, and his memory was still held in high esteem by the populace.

The people were becoming increasingly concerned about the threats of Boko Haram and the speed and ferocity with which they hit targets in Cameroon, Chad, the Central African Republic, and Nigeria without warning. The economy of Cameroon had also taken a turn for the worse, and there was inflation in the Central African franc, the CFA. Money was becoming scarce to loan or to borrow, and the interest rates for borrowers had risen to more than 18 percent and threatened to go even higher. This made it imprudent and unpopular for Adamo to start new projects, to slow down ongoing national construction efforts for roads and buildings, and it all affected jobs; unemployment was beginning to rise significantly and noticeably. It was now the end of March 2019, and time to focus on saving the country.

Most of Adamo's cabinet had been retained because of their corporate knowledge and intimate familiarity with certain key governmental initiatives, which had been only marginally effective. As he began to look more deeply into the structure of the government staff, he found a great deal of cronyism among the ministers and their family members, who had been hired to fill out the staff rosters. Some were only minimally qualified to perform the tasks for which they had been hired. Most were poorly educated, had low experience levels, and had no creative abilities to manage the matters overseen by their respective offices. Still others were listed as full-time employees receiving full-time salaries, but they were only working twenty or fewer hours each week. Adamo discovered all of this the hard way—through action meetings intended to report on program progress. Francois also discovered these shortcomings through his own quiet and low-key inquiries, as well as through the interception of letters and e-mails among and between offices.

Francois was given a small office and a computer in the rear offices of the presidential palace, and he was granted carte blanche access to all economic and military administrative information. He was responsible only to Adamo, the president. He also had access to the national planning staff meeting minutes and the reports for economic initiatives and defense-related activities sponsored and overseen by the Defense Minister General Damboa; Francois could also access the general's daily and weekly calendar without being detected.

The phone on Francois's desk rang. "Yes?" he answered.

It was Elizabeth, the president's appointments and personal secretary. President Adamo had requested that François meet with him in twenty minutes. He was also requested to bring his recently completed draft report on national defense matters for Cameroon.

"I'll be right there," he answered.

The secretary quietly knocked on the door to the president's office and then opened it, stepping aside to allow Francois to enter. De La Plane walked in and the door was closed quietly behind him.

"Ah, Francois. I'm glad you could come so quickly. I guess I didn't know the affairs of state of a small country like Cameroon could be so demanding. These last few days have been busy, and in some cases chaotic. But it's a worthwhile kind of busy—rewarding, too. I have some questions and a request, but first the questions."

"Of course, Mr. President."

"Francois, we are alone for a few minutes, and I want to be assured you know I have not been tainted by all the pomp and circumstance. I am still the Benjo you knew ten years ago, and the Benjo in search of truth I asked you about when you arrived six months ago. I want your honesty and candor right now."

"Of course, Mr. President…Benjo." Francois knew his time with Benjo was limited, so he decided he would present the firehose version of his findings.

"In short, the economic status of Cameroon is spiraling downward.

Its treasury is being drained of money faster than you are earning it back. Projects within the country are over budget and the money is being siphoned off into nondescript black holes. Your transportation, social services, mining and exploration and agriculture ministries are riddled with corruption and theft, and your military services have been promised pay raises that have never materialized. The military equipment your services are using is wrong for the threat you are currently facing; your troops are not only poorly trained, but are tilting at windmills that don't pose a threat to the country. You do remember the lessons of Don Quixote from World Literature in Switzerland, do you not?"

Francois continued, "On top of it all, your suspicions about your Nigerian-born defense minister are correct. I have evidence to suggest he is collaborating with Boko Haram, and he is being paid handsomely for it.

"I will be honest with you. When I arrived here a few months ago, the small canvas bag I carried off the airplane contained two point five million Euros. That is all I have to show for my advice and friendship to Al Yamani. That money is now in a Swiss bank account. Yamani's reward to me was an invitation to attend an international meeting in Riyadh with a suicide vest on my body meant to blow up twenty of the most influential foreign ministers in the world." Benjo's eyes widened and his eyebrows rose in surprise. But he said nothing.

"Your defense minister, General Damboa, has thirteen point nine million Euros in his Swiss account. It has not all come from the three thousand CFAs you pay him each month. He is somehow tied to a fellow by the name of Zingo Kambar of Boko Haram. Now, do you want me to kill General Damboa?"

This last series of statements, and certainly the final question, frankly took Benjo by surprise. He took a deep breath and sat down in a chair facing Francois.

"As long as we are being honest, you are telling me some things I already either had evidence of, suspicions about, or had been advised of by three other longtime government friends who would never lie to me. I will share one other thing with you. This government is teetering on financial collapse and economic ruin. We are being robbed by many of our own people. There are certain Asian political and military persons who are trying to extort land use and petroleum products, and they want selected government-to-government agreements from us. Cameroon is in trouble. I have some courses of action I am considering, but I would also like your opinion."

"Mr. President…Benjo. You should invoke certain dictatorial actions, and begin quietly purging your government of those who are overtly robbing you. Tell them you need certain government cutbacks to meet debts to the underprivileged, to widows and orphans programs. Who could argue with your initiative of charity? They will not suspect you have an ulterior motive until it is too late for them to refuse. Next, offer the most corrupt of your government employees buyouts and early retirements. I have a list of those who have stolen from you and your grandfather, and some should be offered smaller buyouts than others. In a sense, make them an offer they can't refuse.

"You must fix your military loyalty program and undertake a threat review immediately, and you should buy and use only military equipment you need to counter the current threats. The primary threat is the Boko Haram ground army. In my view, Benjo, you have two choices regarding this barbaric band of cutthroats and pirates: You can fight them or you can join them. If you fight them, you will need better weaponry and tactics than you presently have. You need helicopter gunships more than jet fighter aircraft or a new naval destroyer. If you join them, your army and theirs will become a formidable force that could take over all of central Africa. But once that is done, Boko Haram will want to take over you and all of Cameroon."

"Francois, both your mind and mine have been operating along the same lines of reasoning and on the same frequency. I have something to share with you and a request to make." Benjo rose from his chair and went to his desk to retrieve a letter. He found it and returned to his chair in front of Francois.

"The contents of this note are classified as Most Secret, and only one other person and myself know what's in it. You will now be number three. Please read it."

Francois read through the note.

Mr. President,

Plans are now complete by Boko Haram to take over all of Cameroon and neighboring countries within the next four months. Yaoundé is to be the capital of the new Central African caliphate and the center of Sharia law for the continent. I invite you or your emissary to meet with me in Calabar, Nigeria, just across the Cameroon-Nigerian border on the coast in the Niger Delta on April 1, 2019. You or your emissary will meet with only me and my closest advisor. It will be a peaceful meeting and a closely held secret.

I want you to join with me to conquer all of Central Africa and remain as the most important and powerful force in all of Cameroon. I request your answer as soon as possible.

Respectfully,
Commander Zingo Abubakir Kambar

    Francois finished reading the letter and slowly looked into the eyes of Benjo. "You personally should not go. But you should send someone you trust to attend for you."
    "I agree completely. Francois, if you agree, I request that you go to the meeting for me, tell no one of your mission, and report to no one but me when you return. If I choose to fight him, I need to reinforce my military forces to do so, and I need a better defense advisor than has been provided to me. If I chose to join him, I need irrevocable safeguards to ensure the national security of Cameroon, not for just a year or two, but for an indefinite period of time.
    "If you agree to go to this meeting as my emissary, I will send my strongest, most trusted, and smartest commando commander with you. He is Franco Kamumbe Otuba. You will be flown by helicopter to Calabar for the meeting, with the expectation that you will return in less than eight hours. This gives Kambar sufficient time to fully brief you on attack plans, logistics, force levels, tactics, and any guarantees that he will not rape, pillage, steal, or destroy Cameroonian people or resources. I will tell him my expectations in a response to him and inform him of whom I am sending, without revealing who

you are—or were. Is that satisfactory?"

"Mr. President...Benjo. Of course I will go. I'm sure he will be forewarned and armed, but so will I. If he is intent on eliminating me and the commander, we will do irreparable damage before it is over. But I suspect that he is sincere in knowing your mind before he acts. It would be easier for him to decide a course of action after knowing what you believe. Boko Haram is not equipped to meet organized armies head-on. They are more comfortable when the risks they face are minimal. We already know they like nighttime, surprise attacks on unguarded towns and resources. They like targets of pregnant women, old men, and children. That does not sound like a force to which you would like to be subordinate. But I will ferret out their strengths, capabilities, and plans as best I can in the short time I will have there."

"One other thing, Francois. It is customary in the Middle East and Central Africa to offer a tribute to a man who is believed to be strong and principled. I have access to a small chest of uncut diamonds that was confiscated from an illegal drug seller. I have been told they could represent up to six hundred thousand American dollars. A better estimate of their value is probably less than one hundred thousand U.S. dollars. But they make an attractive and apparently valuable gift. Most importantly, they will be a distraction and may delude him into thinking I respect him and think him formidable."

"From what I know of the man," Francois responded, "he will accept the gift as adulation and will not care what its actual value is. He will use it in some later negotiation, for something else that he wants."

"Good! Then it is settled. We will talk again in two days and I will fill you in on last-minute details. Two more things, though, before you go. First, I knew you arrived with two point five million Euros in your bag. I had it checked when you were distracted. I wanted to ensure you were not sent here on an assassin's task. I don't care about money. I am glad, however, that you put it in your bank account. Possessing that amount of cash on one's person makes one a ready target.

"Second: Yes! Kill him. I know you can take care of it discreetly."

Francois looked Benjo in the eyes, extended his hand to shake with the president, and said, "You have been good to me. Consider all tasks completed. I will offer you my best judgment of the circumstances when I return."

58

The Unveiled Threat

Ediba Beach Village, the Kwa River, Nigeria, April 2019

The MI-8/17 Russian-made helicopter was never intended to be a luxury passenger aircraft. It had six canvas and metal-frame passenger seats facing each other: three facing forward and three facing aft. There were no other passengers on the aircraft, so there was abundant room. The sliding door openings on each side of the helicopter were outfitted with support frames for automatic machine guns and holsters for weapons munitions. None were included on this flight so as not to provoke suspicion.

The lone helicopter skimmed the tops of the trees ten kilometers east of the Kwa River just inside the Nigerian side of the border with Cameroon. The time was 0825. The pilot was flying the 099 radial of the omni directional navigation signal from Margaret Ekpo International Airport. The airport was six kilometers east of the city limits of Calabar. The distance measuring readout on the navigation instrument panel of the helicopter said twenty-seven kilometers to the airport. But the chopper was not going to the airport. The Cameroonian Air Force pilot and the copilot were on course and on time, and they were looking for a green smoke flare that would be fired when the ground party had a visual on the helicopter approximately six kilometers east and short of the airport. The flare was anticipated to be visible when the DME readout reached six kilometers.

Francois and his companion, who was serving as a second pair of eyes and ears/bodyguard/counselor/assistant/confidante was Army Lieutenant Colonel Franco Kamumbe Otuba. He was the commander of, as the French would say, the Battalion Special Amphibie, or BSA. It was patterned after the French Special Forces battalion that covertly and invisibly neutralized adversaries. They were a counterpart to the U.S. Phantom force. He was a Cameroonian version of a U.S. Army Special Forces soldier, a Green Beret or a Delta Force warrior all rolled into one. He spoke fluent French, English, Spanish, and three other Central African tongues. He was a graduate of the University of Yaoundé holding both bachelor's and master's degrees in political science. He attended the U.S. Army Command and General Staff College at Fort Leavenworth, Kansas, and the U.S. Army War College in Carlyle, Pennsylvania. He had attended one six-month post-graduate military training course in France and a similar course in Shanghai, China. He was no fool. He could snap a man's neck with the twist of his right arm. He could hit a target at one thousand yards with a sniper rifle. He was fiercely loyal to President Adamo and Cameroon. He would protect Francois with his life because he had been asked to do so by Benjo Adamo. And he would give his honest advice and opinion when requested and candor when needed. Maybe just as importantly, he knew when to keep his mouth shut. This was just such an occasion when all of those skills and abilities were needed.

The forward speed of the helicopter began to slow when the aircrew saw the DME readout approach seven kilometers, then six kilometers, and then ahead from a stand of trees, a green smoke flare appeared above the treetops. The chopper's forward motion slowed, and a clearing appeared one hundred fifty meters below. The pilot skillfully stopped the forward motion of the chopper and began to slowly descend into the large clearing below—then touchdown, and then shut down.

Zingo Kambar walked out into the clearing and up to the sliding hatch door on the side of the helicopter. Inside the chopper, De La Plane rose and looked at his escort.

"I have no reason to trust this man Kambar. I will try to be continuously observant and know that you will do the same. I am expecting the unexpected."

"I agree with you, Mr. Ambassador."

Francois was mildly surprised at the mention of this title. He didn't expect it, but he was hopeful that if it was not permanent, it at least was temporary enough to give his mission, his escort, the flight crew, and himself immunity from suspicion and possible harm.

"I think you should be careful, and we need to be curious of what we *don't* see. I will do my best to alert you if the situation changes from congenial to something else. I also believe, Mr. Ambassador, that we should not become separated."

"Agreed, Colonel. We'll stay close."

Francois gathered up the small ornate box of diamonds and stepped off the helicopter with Otuba close on his heels, his head moving as if on a swivel. Both he and Colonel Otuba were dressed in simple beige robes with subtle fringe of the national colors of Cameroon. Otherwise, there was nothing to identify which of the men was the ambassador and which was not. There was no insignia of military or political rank, and there was no expectation of any ceremonial recognition.

Nonetheless, Kambar strode up to Francois with his hand outstretched and said, "Mr. Ambassador, welcome to my humble home and country. You honor us with your visit. We are all hopeful we will find much common ground upon which to agree."

Francois was mildly surprised that he had been recognized as the president's emissary. But he remained polite and expressionless.

"Colonel Otuba, I welcome you here, as well. Your reputation as a warrior has preceded you, and I assure you, we have much to discuss about forces, tactics, and strategies." The two men shook hands, and Otuba simply said, "Thank you, Mister Governor." Francois's and Otuba's eyes briefly met in response to being so quickly identified. Both knew their descriptions had been passed on by some Cameroonian bureaucrat of questionable loyalty to his country, who also mysteriously had access to a phone number in Nigeria for Zingo Kambar.

De La Plane and Otuba were not disarmed by the congeniality of this barbarian and butcher. In fact, they had just the opposite reaction. Their senses were heightened by the friendliness, and they subtly scanned the perimeter of their surroundings expecting to have to defend themselves. And they could do just that, if required. Each man had nine-millimeter Berretta pistols strapped to the insides of their thighs with another twenty-five-round cartridge attached to the thigh holster. They had been briefed that if they needed more armaments, they would have to take it away from their captors, which was a bit disconcerting to Francois.

It was possible they would be searched and would have to relinquish their weapons. But Francois was prepared to request that his "friends" surrender theirs, as well. There was already an air of mistrust in the atmosphere. So surrendering their weapons was thought by Francois and Otuba as not a prudent action.

There were no other persons visible other than a driver for the shiny black Chevrolet Suburban seven-passenger van at the edge of the lush green clearing. All three men walked over to it and got inside. Kambar was effusive in his gratitude that President Adamo had sent them there in good faith for a "summit," as Kambar called it.

Even before the helicopter had left Yaoundé, Francois recognized and appreciated the seriousness of this meeting and felt certain that once they were on the ground, time for the exchange of pleasantries and courtesies would be sorely limited. In fact, he was anticipating anger and animosity before accord. This was, after all, a negotiation on how to surrender one's country to an all-encompassing, theocratic governing body.

"Governor Kambar," Francois began. Kambar's brows rose at the mention of the exalted title to which he aspired but had no right to use. He was nonetheless pleased at the recognition. "My president has requested you accept this small gift from him and the people of Cameroon for hosting this important meeting. We hope it pleases you."

Kambar untied the velvet ribbon tied around the box and opened it. He was surprised and obviously pleased with the sight of the dazzling diamonds, as the morning sun's reflection off the bezel cuts illuminated the inside of the vehicle.

"Please express my profound thanks to your president for his thoughtfulness. I, of course, will not keep these for myself but will distribute them to the underprivileged people of Nigeria who support my cause to liberate them. I thank you, Mr. Ambassador, and your president."

Based on the research he had done on the actions of Kambar in the last two years, Francois knew that any value derived from these gems would probably wind up in Kambar's own pockets.

Otuba thought to himself, *Just wait till the son of a bitch finds out the minimal value of these stones. He'll curse every pleasant word he said about President Adamo and Cameroon.*

The Suburban drove slowly, for a distance of less than a kilometer, under the cover of the trees to a Mediterranean-style house tucked into the forest. It appeared more like a small two-story hotel, but it was large enough to accommodate fifteen or twenty guests and their privacy. The vehicle stopped at the front door, and all three men exited the vehicle and started walking slowly up the front walkway to the ornate front doors etched with glass figures of Nigerian animals in the full-length glass windows.

Otuba then offered a friendly observation, but it was worded so that Francois would know the comment was actually a surveillance report. "What a lovely getaway location. There appear to be no crowds, no children, just serenity and peace everywhere. Even the river over there appears content to not be disturbed by small boats or swimmers."

Kambar responded, seemingly taking pleasure that his choice for a meeting place had been approved by his guests. "Yes, it is an off-season locale for tourists and visitors. But even if it wasn't, this location is very secluded and is seldom used for anything except private conferences such as this. You can be assured that security is nearly invisible and seamless."

Francois and the colonel's eyes met for a split second in affirmation that so far, all was satisfactory.

Kambar led them to a room where coffee carafes, water pitchers, and small plates of fruit were arrayed on a table in the center of the room. Restrooms to freshen up after the hour and a half flight from Yaoundé were provided. Francois availed himself of the facilities to quickly urinate and wash his hands. He took a moment to adjust the nine-millimeter Berretta holster inside of his thigh and quickly felt to ensure the twenty-five-round magazine was in place and the spare was attached. He was careful in doing so because he felt he was being watched and listened to. He quickly emerged from the restroom and found Otuba just outside the door talking with Kambar about the agriculture and fruit productivity in the surrounding areas. He approached the two men and Otuba excused himself to do what Francois had just done.

"So, my new friend," Francois began, "you have embarked on a grand adventure and there seems no place more appropriate than right here to clear one's head of daily tribulations and challenges."

"Yes, Mr. Ambassador. I was born not far from here, and I have many fond memories of friends, good times, useful lectures from my father and mother, and swimming without clothes in the River Kwa."

Just then, Otuba emerged from the restroom and joined the other two men.

"Let's convene in the next room to have discussions and an exchange of views about the future," Kambar said.

He opened the door and gestured for both men to enter. They did and when inside they found a long, brightly lit room from an open-to-the-air latticework in the ceiling with a conference table large enough to seat fourteen or fifteen persons. But there were only six chairs around the table. Two robed men were standing across the table beside their chairs.

Francois and Otuba both thought the same thing at the same time: *Have we been ambushed, or are there to be new rules to the meeting? There were not supposed to be any other attendees here.*

Kambar showed Francois to one chair at the side, Otuba to the chair next to him, and the two chairs across the table were occupied by the two gentlemen neither De La Plane nor Otuba immediately recognized. But they seemed somehow familiar to Francois.

"Mr. De La Plane and Colonel Otuba, let me introduce Sheik Widari Al Shemani from Yemen, representing DAIISH, and Chieftain Muhammad Bin Gormandin from Afghanistan, representing Al Quaida and other unspecified Islamic sects."

Francois nodded politely while quickly scanning the perimeter of the room for more people, but he saw none. He also was a bit surprised that Kambar had now addressed him as "Mr." De La Plane, which showed François that Zingo Kambar was shrewder than he appeared. Otuba picked up on the facial twitches, scanning eyes, glances, and bows shown by all the attendees. Francois and Otuba thought at the same time, *I wonder what the next surprise will be?*

"Governor Kambar, I was not aware that other guests were invited to our meeting, but I am pleased to see that you appreciate the depth, breadth, and importance of this meeting. I am pleased to hear the wisdom of DAIISH and Al Qaida, and I know that Allah looks upon this meeting with favor."

Sheik Al Shemani spoke, seemingly for both men. "We thank you for the wise decision of your president and yourself to agree to these discussions. We are hopeful you find favor in our proposals and that your president will agree to join with us in saving all of Central Africa and the caliphate that extends from the Gulf of Oman to the South Atlantic Ocean. We are familiar with your service to our brother Al Yamani, and we are aware that you barely escaped with your life when the unknown infidels attacked his villa at Al Hudaydah last January. Your loyalty to your friend was admirable."

Francois knew the sheik was lying through his teeth because, as Francois began to recall, the sheik and his loyalists were the lone holdouts who kept Al Yamani's perimeter of solidarity from being completed. Al Shemani was much like Zingo Kambar in his manner of rule over people. They both conquered tribes and villages by taking almost a psychopathic delight in slitting the throats of pregnant women and disemboweling living old men to demonstrate their own ferocity. Francois knew he needed to tread lightly and cautiously agree to very little. He also recognized Bin Gormandin as a ruthless and strident tyrant who possessed wealth beyond all expectations. Most of it was probably already locked safely in a Swiss bank account for some future use when escape and anonymity would seem to be propitious. Francois also assumed both men were allied to Asian connections that provided money, influence, and weapons. He knew beyond any shadow of doubt that none of these three men were to be trusted.

Kambar then quickly and a bit nervously said, "Gentlemen, let's be seated so we can discuss our plans and objectives." It was apparent that Kambar wanted certain concessions and was trying to take charge of the pace and direction of the meeting.

As they all began to be seated, François chose to add additional comments to ensure that his position in the discussions was established.

"Seeing you gentlemen involved in these discussions means you see this as a success-oriented venture. My president has sent us here to ensure that Cameroon will share in any and all successes envisioned by Governor Kambar."

Francois gratuitously again threw out the title of "Governor," assuming a royal title might be needed to inflate this barbarian's deflated ego. He had always been a criminal and he would always be one. But for now, he was playing diplomat. Kambar recognized that De La Plane had done his research as well.

"So for now, let's follow Governor Kambar's lead and discuss the plans, the capabilities, and the goals for the future. I, of course, will also need to better understand the roles of DAIISH, Al Qaida, the Taliban, and Al Shebaab, as well as what role any outsiders may be expected to play in the plans."

Francois had stolen the thunder of Kambar by announcing in advance what Kambar had intended to say. Zingo Kambar now felt he was the one being interrogated rather than the interrogator. But he quickly decided that progress and agreement in the meetings was more important than his own personal feelings and status.

The discussions began. Explanations, identification of roles by outside elements, division of property and resources, governing responsibilities, and most importantly, the range of authority of all participants in this conquest were addressed. The theocratic leadership was to be assumed by Boko Haram in this region, for now. A small disagreement came at the end of the meeting as to where the caliphate would reside and who would be the caliph. Sharia law was to prevail in the final organization, and treasure and wealth would be centrally controlled and doled out as justification was provided. Kambar, the sheik, and the chieftain continued opposition to the intervention of Western nations. They asserted and nearly demanded that introduction of Western parties or weapons was to be rejected, fought, and defeated by all participants. Military leadership of battle plans and tactics, and the dividing up property and booty were discussed in general percentages, and finally, the role and needs of the Asian benefactors who were providing wealth and weapons to this global reorganization of influential people were addressed. The Asians had insisted that there were to be no boundaries in the use of lethal force capabilities to achieve success. Francois took that to mean the possible introduction of nuclear capabilities, which opened a new perilous path to the future. None of the attendees except François and Colonel Otuba cringed at this, but they offered only mild objections here and again.

Fifteen hundred hours was fast approaching, and the list of discussion items was quickly disappearing. The end of the agenda was at hand. Francois and Otuba knew they needed to depart well before dark to carry back the message of conquest and submission to Adamo. Neither De La Plane nor Otuba felt good about what seemed inevitable. But they voiced positive tones of good relations between all parties and an intention to protect the national monetary, agricultural, and mineral treasures of the nations in Western Africa.

Zingo Kambar had already decided he was going to destroy Cameroon in this conquest, and that he himself would rule both Nigeria and Cameroon. He casually mentioned he might just change the country names to Nigeroon to make his point. He received no vibrations of enthusiasm or approval from De La Plane on that account.

Francoise knew Kambar would have to make a face-to-face case in front of Adamo while surrounded with well-armed Boko Haram fighters ready to slaughter Cameroonian citizens to drive his decision home, just as he had done everywhere else. Kambar also knew he had one formidable threat in his favor. He had two or three weapons that no nation would want unleashed on them. He thought to himself that this conversation was to be continued, but he firmly believed it would be finally decided in his favor.

59

Summit Results

The Presidential Palace, Yaoundé, Cameroon, April 2019

Upon the landing of the helicopter on the palace grounds, Francois and Otuba were met, with no pomp and circumstance, by Elizabeth, the president's personal secretary. As the helicopter shut down and the rotors were winding down, she approached the access hatch on the side of the aircraft. De La Plane quickly emerged first, followed briskly by Otuba.

"Welcome back, gentlemen. The president wishes to see you immediately. Come with me please."

De La Plane and Otuba were expressionless and silent. They had quietly and privately on the return flight discussed and compared their reactions. They were in agreement on all observations and disagreed on only one positive action.

Elizabeth walked ahead of the two returning emissaries and quietly knocked on the door to the president's office. She heard the command, "Come!" from inside and quietly opened the door and stood aside as the two men walked in. Adamo extended his hand to first De La Plane and then Otuba. The colonel smartly saluted his president and then firmly grasped his hand.

"Before you begin your reports to me, let me share two brief messages I have received in just the last hour while you were airborne.

The first is from Sheik Al Shemani, representing DAIISH and all their ISIL allies. I won't bore you with the platitudes, assertions that we have only a local role in maintaining order within certain cities in Cameroon, and making certain funds available within thirty days, but I will get to his main point. He has asked me to come as soon as is practical to Saana, Yemen, to consummate our territorial and local enforcement role.

"The second message is from Zingo 'the Butcher' Kambar, expressing his disappointment that my emissaries were not empowered to agree to all his terms, but he believes we can meet again in a week to identify cities in Cameroon that would be open to Boko Haram forces to begin indoctrinating and recruiting men of all ages into the army of the Boko Haram caliphate."

"What is your assessment?"

Francois spoke first. "Mr. President, Colonel Otuba and I spoke freely on the return flight and are in agreement on all our observations about their statements, gestures, ideas, and plans for future actions. Between Boko Haram, DAIISH, and Al Qaida, we are seriously outnumbered and could even be overpowered if we are not reinforced. They believe that whatever resources our country possesses, if not freely volunteered to their forces, will be confiscated and taken by force with destructive results. They are supported by certain Eurasian and Asian countries, and while not explicitly identified, the soldiers of Boko Haram, DAIISH, and Al Qaida will be working their way to Cameroon through Chad, Niger, Kenya, Somalia, Mali, and other less well-protected nations. Cameroon is to be the gateway to the Atlantic and the Americas beyond. Their intention of conquest is insatiable, and they will stop at nothing to get what they want, when they want it. It is simply a matter of time before they plan to sweep into Cameroon from the north and the east. They ended the meeting by saying that as time goes forward, we will be glad to join them versus the alternative of isolation.

"Immediately after this meeting, Mr. President, I intend to begin discussions of my own to ascertain the basis of their certitude and confidence. I will need a day or so to ferret out the source of their aggressive tone. Meanwhile, the news is not all damning for Cameroon. Colonel Otuba has suggestions that can improve our tactical posture."

Francois then looked at Otuba with a glance that seemed to say, *It is now your turn to speak and share your views.*

"Mr. President," Otuba began. He was tempted to use an expression he had learned at the U.S. Army War College that was all-inclusive and final. It went something like, if he recalled correctly, "We are fucked." But that expression was not only inappropriate in this meeting, it also implied in the American vernacular that resistance was futile.

Instead he chose to be more pragmatic and analytical. "They implied their forces would be formidable if they were able to mount unified armies of conquest and were able to sweep across Central Africa unopposed and forcefully relentless. It is easy to say they could do it, but to make it happen is another more difficult task. All their fighters are from different tribes and sects, with different motives and loyalties for fighting, and for the most part, they are undisciplined and have trouble following tactical and strategic orders. Losing sources of privileged information of intelligence within the government of Cameroon and within our neighboring countries and losing senior fighters and field generals could set them back for serious amounts of time.

"We cannot ask for Western assistance without drawing undue notice to ourselves. Our ability to resist them with our indigenous forces is limited. But our ability to act as small quick-strike teams should not be underestimated. There are persons in our military forces who have been trained in the best covert operational insurgency tactics in the world. They have been to France, the United States, China, and some have even been trained in Russia."

"My forces, Mr. President, can be counted upon to take the fight to Boko Haram, Al Qaida, and DAIISH. We can significantly slow them down by carefully and quietly eliminating their leadership. I hasten to add, Mr. President, that we can significantly slow them down, but we cannot stop them because of their sheer numbers.

"At the same time, Mr. President, we must begin preparing our citizens to protect our country by quietly calling up reserves and arming ourselves for serious battle. Border control is essential, and transportation center inspections and control of seaport dockings must be tighter. The alternative is capitulation."

At this point, Francois interjected, "Mr. President, there is a North

Korean vessel in the Port of Douala. It has a bogus registry in Madagascar, where no such vessel exists. It has been in Duala for two weeks and is guarded twenty-four hours a day. The guards have prevented detailed inspection of the ship's cargo by our customs officials. It is reported to only carry a cargo of rice. But Cameroon grows its own rice, and the ship has been here so long now that the rice would probably be starting to rot. I and my sources believe there is something else aboard the vessel that its sponsors don't want us to see or know about. My sources tell me only a few persons have been allowed to board the vessel. My sources also tell me the visitors are closely affiliated with Boko Haram.

"Zingo Kambar is self-assured about his ability to convince Cameroon, and you specifically, that we should capitulate to his whims and orders. Why is that? I suspect he has a secret that he thinks gives him an edge. I need to find out what that secret is. So, Mr. President, in one day I will report back to you what my progress is on several different but related issues."

Adamo knew that De La Plane had not had time to gather more intelligence, and moreover, he had not had time to take care of the Nigerian defense minister in his own cabinet. He also knew that Francois had the uncanny ability to find out information when no one else could. He had sources and methods to garner important facts when it was necessary. Adamo did not want to probe deeply into Francois's practices. Instead, he wanted these two key individuals to help him save his country from crazed zealots and political maniacs.

"Gentlemen," Adamo stated matter-of-factly, "our tasks are daunting. I must reach a decision within forty-eight hours about my course of action. Your observations are exactly what I need. I will confer with three other trusted confidantes to obtain their guidance and recommendations. Meanwhile, only the three of us and my other three confidantes know of our discussions.

"Mr. Ambassador, please report back to me within twenty-four hours of the progress on your tasks.

"Colonel Otuba, as of this moment, you are promoted to the rank of brigadier-general with the responsibility and blanket authority to organize, train, and equip the forces of Cameroon you choose, to carry out the missions you have described. Elizabeth will be sending the appropriate secret orders and requests for cooperation to all other military organizations in our armed forces. You are not to be denied any request you make for support."

"Yes, Mr. President," replied Francois.

"Yes, Mr. President," replied Otuba. "And thank you for this opportunity."

60

Comply or Resist

Presidential Palace Grounds, Yaoundé, Cameroon, April 2019

Francois returned to his quarters and quietly sat in the hand-carved African leather wingback chair that he found so comfortable. It had been a long and trying day, and it was now 6 p.m. He sat looking for a long moment at the panoramic view of the western hills of Cameroon. He thought of where he had been the last few years, what he had accomplished, and where this was all leading. He drew a blank on this last point. He decided that all he had was the here and now. He gave brief thought to returning to French Guiana, facing the charges leveled against him there, and letting come what may. But first he had some unfinished business to complete.

At 7 p.m., the private phone of Defense Minister Major General Charles Quintana Damboa rang. The caller ID readout in the window of the phone read simply *De La Plane*. If it wasn't for the fact that he knew De La Plane was a close confidante of the president's, he wouldn't have answered the call. He thought for a few brief seconds and then pressed the Answer button.

"Yes, Mr. De La Plane, this is General Damboa."

"General, I have just returned from an unpublicized mission for the president and would like a few minutes of your time to brief you on some of the details of my meetings."

Damboa had already received a secure call from Zingo Kambar, and he knew what had transpired at the meeting. But what he did not know was what the president's reaction was to the meeting and what he intended to do. He thought, *This could be valuable information to Boko Haram and also might be worth an added bonus to my bank account.*

"Why, yes, De La Plane," he said in his most official, superior military voice. "Let's meet tomorrow morning at eight o'clock and discuss this issue."

"General, there is a high degree of urgency to get your input, and time is of the essence. I urge that you and I meet at your residence in forty-five minutes. I don't want to appear overly brusque, but the president needs to know how you feel about certain issues."

"Hmm, oh, very well," he said with a slightly irritated edge to his expression of consent. "I will inform my aide to expect you in forty-five minutes, De La Plane. Please don't be late." He spoke in an officious tone usually reserved for those whom he was indifferent toward. His comment about punctuality had two purposes. One was to subtly inform De La Plane that Damboa was of a rank and status in the ministerial group that usually commands special respect. The second reason was that the general's wife was to go to bed at 8 p.m., and a very attractive and curvaceous brunette woman was expected at the general's house at eight thirty to give the general his biweekly private massage.

Promptly at 7:45 p.m., Francois was shown into the general's home office. The two men exchanged brief greetings, and then they sat facing one another across a small table.

The general took the initiative to get the talks started and over in thirty minutes or less. It would not be appropriate for De La Plane to be departing while the masseuse was entering.

"So, De La Plane, what is so urgent?"

"Mr. Minister General, there have been discussions with individuals outside the government of Cameroon concerning the activities of Boko Haram."

"I would have to say that I am one of the president's closest confidantes on the subject of Boko Haram, and I am aware that the president is deciding certain courses of action with Boko Haram activities in Nigeria. Why, we spoke just three days ago on the role of Boko Haram in Central Africa."

Francois knew then the general knew nothing of the president's thoughts on what had transpired earlier in the day.

"I must be brief, Mr. Minister General," Francois said before the general could say anything more. "What many of us in the nation are really concerned about is your collusion with Zingo Kambar and the hierarchy of Boko Haram. We are also concerned about the thirteen point nine million Euros in your Swiss bank account, number 755482 dash CRN dash 9821."

"What?" The general's face turned beet red, and he remarked with indignant surprise and anger. He feigned innocence to the accusation. "Where did you get that number? You have no right or authority to make such assertions, and I will have you arrested for treason, disloyalty, and insubordination, right here and now." With that he began to arise from his chair and reach for his telephone.

"Sit down, General!" De La Plane said with quiet authority and force. "You have taken the last bribe and made the last treasonous release of secret government information to Boko Haram, or anyone else. You see, I also know about your ties to DAIISH and the information you passed to them just today concerning the operational readiness of the Cameroon air force and navy."

"That is preposterous. I have done no such thing. Where did you get such outrageous information? You will get out of my house, and I will have you arrested before you can reach your quarters."

"For your information, we have discovered your collusion with the vice chief of staff of the army, the minister of finance, the deputy minister of foreign affairs, and a whole host of mid-level bureaucrats who have recently admitted their roles in this conspiracy."

"That's impossible, De La Plane! They are all lying to save their own reputations and government pensions. They are all well-rewarded and would never betray me for…er, rather they are consummately loyal to this country."

"General, I said that time was of the essence earlier, and the president wanted to know how you feel about certain issues. I want to tell the president you don't feel anything. By this time tomorrow evening all those individuals will have departed government service and the security of Cameroon will be preserved."

While quietly and calmly talking to Damboa, Francois visibly removed a forty-five-caliber pistol from beneath his robe and calmly screwed a silencer onto the barrel. It was exactly like the pistol that was owned and used by the general for a variety of purposes, not the least of which was to persuade unwilling persons to do things they needed physical encouragement to complete. It had been verified that he owned five or six such weapons.

"What are you doing? You will not get away with this. Benjo Adamo is a neophyte when it comes to managing a country. He needs me. There are powers in the world much greater than him, and I intend to advise him of that later this week. Why, he doesn't even realize that he and his grandfather before him have already lost Cameroon to the forces of Boko Haram and others."

Francois slowly rose with the pistol in his gloved hand and walked around to the other side of the table. Damboa nervously began capitulating and said, "No, wait! I will resign. I will see Adamo in the morning and confess to all that has occurred. I will."

"No, General, you will not. The time for you to advise the president on anything has passed." Francois grabbed the general by the front of his shirt and placed the forty-five-millimeter silencer under his chin, then pulled the trigger. There was a muffled *thunk*, and the back of the general's head flew across the room.

Francois took out a cloth from his pocket and wiped the pistol clean of fingerprints. He had already wiped off the ammunition magazine and the bullets. He placed the pistol in the general's hand and let it fall into his lap. Using both gloved hands, he then removed a carefully written note from his pocket with a forgery of the general's signature at the bottom, admitting to his treason and acceptance of bribes from Zingo Kambar and the high council of Boko Haram, along with his meetings with DAIISH and Al Qaida representatives.

Francois looked around the room to be sure he had not left evidence of his actions, and then he walked to the door. He removed the gloves from his hands, took out a clean white cloth, and wiped it across his face to make sure any specks of flesh or blood were wiped away. He then placed the gloves and cloth in a sealed plastic bag, and put it in an inside pocket for later incineration.

As he passed through the door, he turned back toward the room and announced in a calm voice, "Thank you for seeing me, Mr. Minister, before your other appointments. I will pass your regards on to President Adamo." He closed the door and walked to the front entrance, where he was met by the general's aide. Francois was quite certain the aide had overheard his departing comment and believed the general shared with De La Plane that others were expected here soon. This would lead him to conclude that Francois was not the last one to see the general that night.

He then said to the aide, "The general said he needed an hour or so of privacy to examine his next courses of action. He said to tell you he didn't want to be disturbed for at least an hour and a half."

The aide thought this was entirely consistent with Damboa's actions, since he always made that request before each visit of the young curvaceous masseuse. The aide responded, "Thank you, sir. I know the general will call me when he needs something." The aide then retired to his quarters to prepare for the next day's activities.

De La Plane confidently strode out onto the street and back to his room in the presidential palace.

The Office of the President, Yaoundé, Cameroon, April 2019

At 6 a.m. the next morning, President Benjo Adamo had just awakened and was sipping coffee. His phone rang. It was a call from the defense minister's office informing him that General Damboa was found very early that morning and had evidently committed suicide. He left a note that had been sealed and was being hand-delivered to the president's office.

At 8 a.m., the vice chief of staff of the Cameroonian Army was killed in a parachute drop training accident. His chute failed to open. At 10 a.m., the minister of finance, Madame Charlene Ibn Farniba, submitted her immediate resignation, saying she had been told she might have cancer and she wished to spend the next months and years with her family in Botswana.

Just after noon, the deputy minister for foreign affairs fell off of a remote cliff while sightseeing with an unrelated female friend overlooking Lake Lagdo in the north of Cameroon. The female friend had disappeared and could not be located for a statement. Curiously, the deputy minister had no pants or undershorts on when the body was recovered. It was suspected he might have fallen from the cliff in a moment of orgasmic ecstasy, or he might have soiled himself and was trying to get to the lake waters to rinse his clothing. No one reported an equally scantily clad female in the area.

As the day wore on, more than an additional half-dozen mid-level government supervisors failed to arrive at work. Excuses were received from their offices that they were either in need of a vacation, their relatives had suddenly taken ill and needed immediate attention, or they simply resigned, saying the stress of work was becoming unbearable.

At the end of the day, by 6 p.m., President Adamo gazed at nearly twenty notes regarding absences, personal tragedies, and accidents that had befallen members of his government. Each person was known by him, and he had been furnished with confidential proof that they were guilty of treason, theft, embezzlement, corruption, and other unspeakable crimes against the people of Cameroon. He felt sympathy and remorse only for their families, who would never know of their guilt. Statements on the loss of each were carefully arrayed before him on his desk, placed there by Elizabeth. He surveyed all the notes, then muttered out loud, "Allah indeed works in mysterious ways."

61

A New Terrorist Threat

JCS, J-3 SOD, The Pentagon, Washington, D.C., April 2019

Colonel Keith Powers was monitoring his e-mails, Facebook announcements, chatter sources, Twitter blivits, voice mails, Post-it Notes, and all other forms of social media that had been made available to him. After all, in the classified notepads that were passed around in this section of the Pentagon basement, it was common knowledge that any sources of information, or RUMINT, were acceptable. He even accepted KOTFD, Knocks on the Front Door, alerts to capture his attention. It was no secret in this suite of offices that he was involved in something big, related to national security and highly classified. But most thought, *So, what's the big deal? That's what we all do down here next to the purple water fountain.*

He logged on to the SIPRNET terminal and looked for anything out of the ordinary. Most of the time, the information he saw had already appeared on FOX News or CNN. About half the time, though, the information was so classified it couldn't be discussed or displayed. His job was to highlight extraordinary activities that could have the potential of spilling over into the civilized world and create total chaos. None of those instances had occurred in the past few months. Project TEMPEST in French Guiana and Project RAMPART in Yemen were just those sorts of events. In the last eight weeks, he had had hours and hours of boredom interspersed with moments of sheer terror.

Powers scrolled through events in the Middle East, and the South China Sea region that had turned out to be potential real threats. Each had to be reviewed and assessed for the international danger it represented. These events included the India-Pakistan fistfights in which neither party really wanted to pull the trigger; Middle-Eastern atrocities that continued from day to day; Syrian, Turkish, and Greek refugees streaming across European national borders seeking asylum; hundreds of ISIS infiltrators masquerading as refugees crossing into neighboring countries; Russian pushes and shoves against Lithuania, Estonia, Ukraine, and the other Baltic and North Atlantic states in an attempt to coerce them to rejoin a dying empire; and then there was Africa.

Keith scrolled through the daily political and military events starting alphabetically with Algeria with the intention of finishing with Zambia. When he got to Cameroon, he had to stop. Reports from the United States and international military attachés were both objective and ominous. Repeated threatening conversations between Cameroonian and radical Islamic jihadists started to appear more frequently in the NSA communications intercepts. Something tumultuous was happening. A report from the NSA described the calls as nationally destabilizing. The country was fraught with treasonous activity, tumult, upheaval, and hand-to-hand warfare. The NSA Assessment Report asserted that a shooting confrontation was close. But maybe there was still a reasonable amount of time to allow saner minds to prevail. But Keith knew that when dealing with radical Islamic terrorism, there was no room to expect sanity or reason from such groups. Keith also knew about attaché anxiety and he chose to dig further.

As he somewhat calmly, but with heightened analytic attention, continued to sift through the data, he discovered several key Cameroonian governmental officials had capitulated to Boko Haram threats, and they had been bought out to surrender key national security information, agreeing to help overthrow the existing government. So what was new about that in Africa? Keith dug further and found that the newly elected president of Cameroon was a people person and not a tyrant at all. He wanted to follow in the footsteps of his late grandfather and French, German, and American mentors, and save the country for his people.

Reports and corroborative NSA telephonic intercepts confirmed that President Adamo was purging his government of treasons and Boko Haram, DAIISH, and Al Qaida activists, and he was trying to run his country the way a democracy and an independent nation handles its affairs. Reports indicated he was being supported and advised by only a half-dozen trusted supporters and advisors. One was identified as a longtime ally and newly promoted brigadier general, Franco Kamumbe Otuba. He had longtime ties to American military education institutions and was well known in senior U.S. military circles as being objective and loyal. A second advisor was less known among diplomatic circles, but he seemed to have the ear of the president on foreign policy initiatives and some certain useful military tactics. He was Ambassador Francois R. De La Plane, who seemingly had many ties to Middle-Eastern governments and regional policies.

"Holy shit!" Keith shouted out loud. "I know this guy! So, what's he up to now?"

Keith dialed the secure number of Admiral Ray Andrews and Colonel Bud Patrick at Mac Dill Air Force Base for a conference call. It was 10:30 p.m., Eastern Daylight Time.

Admiral Andrews was the first to answer. "Keith, what the hell is it this time? Are we going to Ukraine? If so, you know we are ready."

"Stand by, Admiral, let's wait for Bud Patrick to pick up."

Then on the line after a short delay, "Patrick here."

"Bud, this is Keith. I have the admiral on the line and I have some good, or maybe, not so good, news for you both on a topic of interest. Guess who I just found?"

The White House, Washington, D.C., April 2019

Tom Mossman knocked on the door to the Oval Office. President Chenoa replied, "Come in, Tom."

"Madame President, I have the sec def, the chairman of the JCS, and four others on your secure video teleconferencing line, regarding an item of national security interest. I've blocked out forty minutes on your calendar to listen to what we have discovered and to decide on a course of action."

"Good, Tom. Let's put them on the video and speakerphone circuit."

The large video-teleconferencing screen in the Oval Office came up as a split-screen display. The president could see Arnold Stafford, Admiral Chet Nagle, Assistant Secretary Jim Mullaney, and Colonel Keith Powers. They were all in the sec def's secure office in the Pentagon. The other half of the screen showed Ray Andrews and Bud Patrick in their secure conference room at MacDill. They, in turn, could see President Chenoa and Mossman.

Mossman opened the discussion first. "Gentlemen, thank you for taking the time for this important matter. Arnold, why don't you take the lead and get the briefing started? We have thirty-eight minutes on the president's calendar."

"Thank you, General Mossman. Madame President, there has been an incident in Cameroon that Colonel Powers will brief you on, and it has many facets that could cause events in Central Africa to spiral out of control if positive restraint is not soon imposed. He has a brief assessment of the situation, and then the chairman and Admiral Andrews are prepared to give you a recommended course of action. Colonel Powers, go ahead."

"Madame President, General Mossman, we have verifiable communications interceptions of conversations between the new president of Cameroon, Benjo Ahmadou Adamo, and two of his closest governmental advisors. One is his minister of foreign affairs and the other is his minister of domestic economy. We also have intercepted a call between the president and the commander of Boko Haram in Nigeria, Zingo Abubakir Kambar. This later call threatened Cameroon with near-term invasion and complete takeover of the country by a combination of forces representing Boko Haram, Al Qaida, and ISIL or DAIISH, as it is referred to in central Africa.

"The army of Cameroon is apolitical and loyal to the presidency. Its leaders are Western-trained and the soldiers are not afraid to fight. The army is supported by naval and air forces, but these latter two elements are small and poorly equipped for large, sustained military offensive operations. The army also has a skilled and efficient covert operations commando element entitled Battalion Special Amphibie, led by a newly promoted brigadier general, Franco Kamumbe Otuba. He is primarily U.S. and French trained and educated, and he is completely trusted by President Adamo. Unfortunately, General Otuba can adequately defend the presidential residence and conduct limited covert operations, but he is not organized or equipped to defend the entire country.

"President Adamo has secretly directed his administration and the armed forces to prepare for an invasion and border incursions, but the radical Islamic forces are too numerous for the country to resist for very long. In addition, there is strong evidence that the jihadist forces are being supported by North Korean and Chinese weapons and military advisors, and some yet-to-be-identified weapons support from Russia. President Adamo has not requested assistance from any other nation yet for fear of accelerated and widespread barbaric radical Islamic retaliation. For some reason, he is delaying full mobilization and is trying to buy time. We are assuming he is attempting to implement a diversionary tactic or strategy of some sort—"

"Colonel Powers, let me interrupt to ask a couple of questions," the president said.

"What is the evidence you have that the North Koreans, Russians, and the Chinese are supporting the radical Islamists?"

"Good question, Madame President. Islamic terrorist soldiers are being paid in gold coins emblazoned with either the trademark of China or the Wan mark of North Korea. Weapons and ammunition being used by radical Islamists in Nigeria, Chad, Niger, and the Republic of the Congo are Chinese. Some equipment is American in manufacture, but inventory disposition shows that those resources were left behind or stolen in Afghanistan and Iraq in 2015. They were transported to Nigeria via Russian airlift and cargo vessels. Also, communications intercepts confirm calls made between radical Islamist leaders, the authorities in Beijing, and the nuclear reactor facility in Yongbyon north of Panmunjom, where requests for weaponry have been satisfied by Chinese and North Korean shipment cargo vessels.

"Finally, there is a cargo ship in the Cameroon harbor of Douala. She is overtly a small Greek tramp ship called the *Aegean Sunrise*, ostensibly registered in Madagascar. No such registry exists. A registry does, however, exist for a vessel exactly like the *Aegean Sunrise*, right down to the ship builders' hull identification numbers shown on the current captain's master's papers.

"This ship, possibly with the same cargo, was first reported as it transited the Suez Canal in October 2017. It was again seen in Somalia in July of 2018, and it is now in Douala, Cameroon. That ship is the *Kwang Ju Maru*, registered in North Korea. She has been in Douala since March 15 or 16, and she has been continuously guarded by a six- or seven-man team to prevent police, customs, or any unauthorized boarding. Radioactive scans and an infrared interrogation by collaborative intelligence operatives show a nuclear signature buried beneath one hundred tons of what is described as rice in the cargo hold. It almost appears as though this is a ghost ship with both treasure and doom on board, in search of a tyrant or a dictator who would take the bait and steal the treasure as he lights the fuse on the weapon to announce, 'I was here and now I am rich and you are a cinder.' The threat is real."

"Okay, thank you," the president responded.

Admiral Nagle then interjected, "Madame President. Our assessment is that we have, at the outside, thirty days before hostilities erupt and Cameroon is lost. If that happens, the radical Islamists will have an Atlantic seaport capable of launching insurgency forces to any number of African, European, and even U.S. ports. The presence of a nuclear device, even if it's low-yield, will cause untold and long-term nuclear damage to Western Africa. The tactical and strategic planners of these radical groups will move ahead with their devastation of Cameroon, Equatorial Guinea, and Gabon, and they will suffer the radiation sickness and destruction of their own resources and those of the invaded nations. The international community has not accepted that the threat needs to be dealt with soon. This is a very sick situation."

President Chenoa, fully aware of the individuals on the line and the capabilities they represented, said, "Admiral Andrews, what is your view?"

Admiral Andrews replied, "Madame President, the counterbalance strategy very aptly applies here. If the United States does not take the lead and stop this madness, there will be an international holocaust. Boko Haram is a rabble of renegades and criminals. They will shrink before the presence of a better disciplined and organized armed force. Their leadership is egocentric and believes they are immortal. They are not. There is a core of competent and loyal special operations forces existent in Cameroon. They need encouragement and reinforcement. A quick, lethal, decisive counterstrike attack will cause the barbaric soldiers of Boko Haram and ISIL to give second thought to taking on the nations between Kenya and the Atlantic. We may not be able to stop them over the long term, but we can set them back by five years by destroying their supply lines, their communications connections, and their supply depots. Knowledge and training is decisive, and we have it all."

"Admiral Nagle, what do you recommend?" Chenoa asked, already knowing the answer to this threat.

"Madame President, the USS *Truman* is in the South Atlantic now. Our Phantoms have been continuing to sharpen their skills. We need a week to practice neutralization scenarios for replicas of the Cameroonian target areas and thirty-six hours to transit to the *Truman*. We have already opened the channels of communication with several agents, countries, and military contacts. We have made no promises or commitments and have only asked questions. They all know the United States is concerned."

President Chenoa continued, "Arnold, Admiral Nagle, gentlemen, let's move forward with the Phantoms to neutralize this situation before it gets out of hand. Boko Haram in Nigeria must be deterred, Al Qaida in Chad must be routed, and the government of Cameroon must be quietly advised that they are not alone. Is there anything else?"

"Madame President," Bud Patrick then interjected, "there is one other unfinished task. We are informed by very reliable sources that Francois Ricardo De La Plane is advising President Adamo on strategy and certain political maneuvers. You will recall that we missed him in French Guiana, he got away in Yemen, and we now know where he is in Cameroon. If possible, we would like to attempt to capture him and return him to the United States for intelligence interrogation and extradition to France."

There was what seemed to be a long silence by the president on her end of the line. She sat with her chin resting on her interlocked fingers and her elbows on the table in front of her. The silence from her was so pronounced, all the parties thought the line had gone dead, as if she hadn't heard the request. Finally she said, "Hmm. Yes, okay. Let's bring him back. But I want him alive and unharmed. He could be a treasure trove of intelligence. Is that clear? Alive and unharmed, do you hear me?"

"Yes, ma'am, understood." Bud gritted his teeth and consented. Bud wanted to simply put a bullet in De La Plane's head and bring the body back. But the president's comment about intelligence had merit.

Then President Chenoa made one last request before signing off. "Admiral Nagle, will you see to it that Senator Smith and Congresswoman Doolin are thoroughly briefed on this meeting, its details, and the timeline? I would like that done as quickly as possible. I have requests of them, as well, and this information will be key to their actions. Thank you, gentlemen."

Mossman turned off the secure video teleconferencing communications receiver and said, "Will there be anything else, Madame President?"

"Yes, Tom, two things. First, let me know when there is a draft of the Phantom force attack plan put together. I want to approve it before it's executed. Second, get me President Benjo Adamo on a secure phone."

"Yes, Madame President, right away."

62

Congressional Support

*The Russell Senate Office Building,
Washington, D.C., April 2019*

Admiral Chet Nagle sat in the backseat of the plain black government sedan en route to his meeting with Senator Smith and Congresswoman Doolin in Denny Smith's Russell Building secure vaulted office. The time was 6:52 a.m., and he would be exactly on time for the 7:00 a.m. meeting. This would not take long, but it was a lynchpin to the new strategic counterbalance plan of the president's. He had called each of them the night before and asked for a single place for a meeting. They agreed to coordinate a place and a time, and this was it.

At this time of the morning, very few members or aides were in the building. The chairman had been cleared in and was escorted to Smith's office by two capital police officers. Denny uncharacteristically met him at the door to the main corridor. He escorted the chairman to his private vaulted office and closed and locked the outer doors. The chairman, his personal army colonel aide, carrying a large, thick, and apparently heavy briefcase, and Denny walked into the secure office and closed the door.

The chairman saw that Congresswoman Doolin was already there, and he politely greeted her. There were four chairs arranged around a table large enough to accommodate twice as many seats. Denny had anticipated there would be handouts, papers, pictures, or multi-page study documents, and he believed a little elbow and display room was going to be needed. He was right.

Coffee was poured by Denny, and the admiral began. "The president has specifically requested you both be briefed on this military operation, just as she has for the past two operations." Admiral Chet Nagle looked at both members of Congress directly and said, "This operation is classified Top Secret Code Word ENDEAVOR, and it is named Project LIBERTY." Chet Nagle took forty minutes to cover all of the details that had been discussed by Keith Powers the afternoon before with the president. Denny and Rosemary nodded their heads knowingly at all the facts as they were laid out. They each asked brief tactical and foreign nations questions, money and cost queries, and timeline milestones and personnel questions about who was in charge and what the exit plan was. At the end, Chet Nagle asked if there were any other questions.

Rosemary was the first to speak. "Did the president comment on or suggest what she thought our actions should now be?"

"No, Congresswoman, she did not. She simply said she had made requests of the two of you, and she implied she would be in touch for your follow-on activities."

Denny then asked, "When will we be informed of the detailed strike plans with locations and times, and are we allowed to be in the Situation Room when the launch code is directed?"

"Senator, I will assure that you are notified before the mission is launched, and you both will be present in the Sit Room at the Launch Hour," said the admiral.

"Mr. Chairman," Rosemary said, "I for one am especially appreciative of you taking this time to fill us in. We each have Armed Services Committee and Intelligence Committee meetings in the next three weeks, in which we can support the president's counterbalance initiative.

"Admiral Nagle, I, too, thank you for taking this time to brief us. Know that if we have later questions, we can count on you to ensure we get answers. This is the third time we have sent American forces into harm's way, and the previous mission objectives have all been achieved. I want to be assured that we are three-for-three using this new strategy. We are both positive this will change the way we employ our military forces in the future. Secrecy, superior equipment, maximum training, and exceptional leadership will usher in a new era of the way we protect the national security of the United States and that of our allies. Be assured you can call on us for any future support you may need."

The admiral and his military aide packed up all the material they intended to take back to the Pentagon, exchanged the pleasantries this special relationship enjoyed, and left. It was exactly 0800 hours.

When the door was closed after the chairman, Denny turned to Rosemary and said, "I'd like to go on this one. How about you?"

Rosemary simply beamed an approving smile.

63

Get Ready

Mac Dill Air Force Base, Tampa, Florida, April 2019

At 0730, all Phantoms of Admiral Andrews's and Colonel Patrick's regiment were mustered together in the secure briefing theater—all 196 of the combat elements of the regiment. It included logisticians, transportation specialists, parachute riggers, weapons maintenance personnel, munitions keepers, medical personnel, civil service officers, coalition military exchange personnel, and many others. Only the civilian administrative staff was excluded.

Master Chief Petty Officer Barrett entered the theater from the back and ordered in a loud, commanding voice, "Attench-hut!" Andrews, Patrick, and Barrett marched in crisp steps to the front of the room. Patrick and Barrett stood in front of the seats in the front row. Admiral Andrews walked to the center of the floor in front of the first row of seats. Andrews commanded, "Seats!" As if by practiced drill, all 196 Phantoms were seated at the same time.

"Gentlemen," the admiral began, "we have been assigned a new task, not unlike the previous ones we've completed in the last two years. It seems that each time we do this, the mission has a slightly different twist than the last one. This time we are going to the West Coast of Africa to a country called Cameroon. As usual, the mission will be conducted at night. Not as usual, however, there are no hostages at this time to rescue. As usual, we will neutralize as many of the bad guys as possible in the time we have on the ground. Keep in mind these bad guys are habitual killers, murderers, and criminals masquerading as radical Islamic jihadist fighters. Just like the usual radical Islamic soldiers, they believe they are fighting and dying for Allah. But they are also being paid handsomely to do so.

"The radical sect is called Boko Haram. They are being supported and augmented by Al Qaida, Taliban, Al Shabab, and ISIS. Don't underestimate them. They are willing to fight to the death in a skirmish, and they believe you should be the one to die rather than them. They think you are considered the worst kind of infidel.

"Another variation to this task is that we will be augmenting a Cameroonian commando unit under the very capable command of a U.S.- and French-trained covert ops brigadier general who knows what he's doing. We don't know yet whether we will back him up, cover his flanks with suppressive fire, or be integrated with his small force of clandestine operators. This general's goal is to neutralize the leader of the terrorists and up to five of his henchmen. They all think they are immortal and cannot be killed. They are quite comfortable in killing women, children, and old people at night while they sleep. They are not professional fighters, but they are experienced.

"In summary, that's the mission task. I'll now defer to Colonel Patrick for details about the mission."

Bud Patrick stood and looked out over the regiment. He began by saying, as he always did, "All of us going on this mission are coming back from this mission. Many of the details are still being worked out, and we should have the plan completed in its final form in two days. Meanwhile, we will practice what we know. Since airports, seaports, and parachute assaults are too visible and sometimes less precise, we will be flown in to the target areas by *Truman*-based Ghosthawk choppers and placed on the enemy's doorstep. I assure you he will be surprised. The Cameroon general will tell us where, when, and how. We will have a link with him in twenty-four hours.

"There is another, more delicate task that also needs to be completed. There is a North Korean cargo vessel in port in Douala, Cameroon, that has been there for over three weeks. We believe it has a dirty nuclear device onboard that is intended for the Boko Haram forces leader. He knows how to pull the trigger on it, but we have the experts who can disable it. There may be other weaponry aboard the vessel to include bugs, gas, booby traps, C-4, or SimTex explosives. We can handle those, too. An option is to tow the ship out to sea and scuttle it. That's TBD right now.

"Our mission is to neutralize as many radical Islamist jihadists who want to collect their seventy-two virgins. We need to quickly and decisively accommodate them. Disposing of the nuclear threat, if that's what it is, will be a high priority. The next highest priority is to defend yourselves and our teammates. When all that is done, we get back on our Ghosthawks and return to the *Truman*.

"I'll now turn it over to the master chief for some clarifications."

"Thank you, colonel. Gentlemen, the classification of this mission is Top Secret Code Word ENDEAVOR, Project LIBERTY. Your families, just like mine, already know we're going someplace without you ever having to say you are preparing to leave again. I haven't figured out how they know; they just do. Nonetheless, you may not reveal any details you have just learned or will learn in the next two weeks. You are to leave here and go to your personal lockers to inventory your weapons, ammunition, offensive and defensive disabling devices, your Kevlar vests, and your protective clothing and make sure you have no personal identification tags or labels on anything you will wear. Other than that, stay healthy, stay fit, and be ready. The shore party strike team rosters are now pinned to the back wall of this theater, and those members of Teams one, two, three, and four will fall in at oh-six-thirty tomorrow morning, at Training Facility Four on this base. Are there questions?"

There were none, and the master chief looked around the room. He then said, "Attench-hut! Dismissed!" They all filed out and moved toward the rosters at the back of the room.

The President's Office, Yaoundé, Cameroon, April 2019

President Adamo rose from his desk and strode to the door as General Otuba entered. "General, thank you for coming on such short notice. I have some good news for you, but first I want to ask how the planning is coming along to find and manage Zingo Kambar and any DAIISH, Al Qaida, Taliban, or Shabaab officers he might be working with."

"The planning goes well, Mr. President. My intelligence gathering has been fruitful, and we have continuous and verifiable information on Kambar's movements and whereabouts every two hours. As time draws near to confront him, I will have that reduced to fifteen-minute intervals. The actions by my seven-man team will be swift, quiet, final, and secret. I and six others have been practicing and training for five days, and we are planning to move out in ten to fourteen days for the mission."

"That is good; very good. Do you have any updates on the whereabouts and plans of the DAIISH and Al Qaida operatives and leaders?"

"Yes, my president. My reports verify Sheik Al Shemani and the second-in-command to Chieftain Bin Gormandin will be meeting with Kambar and three of his lieutenants on April 29. I am watching their movements and communications closely."

"Excellent. You will, of course, let me know if you need anything you don't yet have, and you will inform me when it is time to move," Adamo responded favorably. "Now the good news, General. A good friend of yours and mine will be providing a nine-man team of clandestine operation warriors for you to use where needed. They will follow your commands and plans and have the same covert skills as you and your men. They are prepared to attack the site, to neutralize Kambar and his cohorts as you direct. They will be equipped with a level of lethality that will match a one-hundred-man army, and they will use it as you allow or need it. They are not interested in prisoners, but then, neither am I. Their mission is to support you to ensure your mission is a success and to assist you in making a rapid and safe withdrawal."

"That is excellent news, Mr. President. I am indeed a little short of skilled and experienced manpower, but I am planning to do the best we can with what we have. Added experienced soldiers will exponentially increase our chances of complete and total success, and, more importantly, it will significantly reduce chances for combat losses. How will I meet these persons, and when?"

"They can be here as soon as two days from now or as late as eight days. The decision will be yours to make. All I know of the contact is that the leader goes by a strange code name; he is to be called 'Duke.' You will know him by that name. All of his men simply have numbers. They are called Number 2 through Number 8. When you are ready for them, just call Elizabeth and she will obtain a secret time and place of arrival that will be of your choosing. You see, we, too, have a trick or two up our sleeves."

"Thank you, Mr. President. I am confident we will protect the Republic. I know you have longer-term plans to give our people assured security. If I can assist in those plans, just ask and I will respond."

"Thank you, General. I will, indeed, call upon you."

64

Lobbying Pressures

*Russell and Rayburn Office Buildings,
Washington, D.C., April 2019*

Four well-dressed gentlemen in finely tailored suits, carrying briefcases, strode toward Denny Smith's private office door with outstretched hands of greetings. Pleasantries were exchanged. Denny knew why they were there. They all were seated around Denny's conference table, and they each provided business cards with their names, company positions, and contact information printed at the bottom of each card.

Two of the men were corporate chief executive officers, or CEOs, of different corporations that provided defense hardware and machinery. The older of the two, David Deerborne, represented Deerborne Armored Vehicle Manufacturing. Charles Sanfield, the other CEO, represented the Sanfield Diesel Engine Corporation. Deerborne spoke first and indicated he would defer to his colleague, Sanfield, in a few moments.

"Senator Smith, we are here to reaffirm our loyalty to the United States military and the missions they are charged to complete. We have a special capabilities briefing we want you to have that explains our capabilities, our products, our research and development programs, and the all-American workforce that keeps our production lines open and thousands of Americans employed."

Denny sat quietly and intently listened to what David and Charles had to say. They spoke glowingly and eloquently about the power and versatility of their armored personnel carriers, their MA-2C high-speed, multi-weapon tanks, and the lightweight titanium trucks that could carry more weapons, personnel, and logistics farther and faster than those vehicles used in the Afghan and Iraqi theaters. The capabilities of their armories were, indeed, amazing and had protected innumerable American lives because of superior American ingenuity.

Sanfield finally interjected, "Senator, we have major interest in continuing to supply the armed forces of the United States with top-quality manufactured armored vehicles powered with the most capable, fuel-efficient engines and auxiliary equipment that has ever been produced by the United States. The Russians and the Chinese can't hold a candle to our products.

"We want to assure you that we will continue to provide the highest performance and explosive-resistant vehicles with the lowest Mean-Time-Between-Failure rolling stock the military services of this country have ever seen. We plan to install heavy-duty shock-resistant electronics in the current generation of our vehicles that will provide interservice connectivity to fighter aircraft, JSTARS Command and Control aircraft, to satellite C2 systems from the theater to the States in microseconds."

Charles and David went on to speak in glowing terms of how much more improved and cost-effective the new production line innovations had become. They both were indeed eloquent and said all the right things—if the United States was going to buy increased and larger quantities of their products and services. But the United States was *not* going to do that if the SASC had anything to say about it.

When it came time for Denny to speak, he knew what needed to be said. "Gentlemen, we are in a secure room, and you all have the highest security clearances. What I am about to say is confidential and is not to be publicly disclosed. In years gone by, I have been the strongest advocate of your skill, your technology, and especially your field support to fix little things that went wrong. Your companies are, indeed, national treasures, and I assure you that I completely understand the impact on industry when the government reduces its need for quantity, while trying to maintain higher quality.

"In short, however, the president's priority for a lightning-strike, covert-operations force will replace past concepts for armies of occupation, nation-building resources, and continuing operations to deter insurgency attacks. The president, the armed services, and the intelligence committees in the Senate support the vision of this counterbalance. The military forces of the United States simply do not need the quantity of armor your corporations currently provide. They certainly do continue to need the quality of your American-manufactured equipment and always will. But the law enforcement agencies of the country also need your equipment and service support. Our foreign military sales export program desperately needs your equipment, and our allies are always clamoring for new capabilities to support their own foreign military exchange programs. Also, recent events have identified a need for more efficient amphibious vehicle to get covert ops personnel from ship to shore, within the battle space, and back to the ship. If you have concepts related to that role, we would be very interested to see and hear about them.

"In the meantime, the United States is committed to transitioning to a smaller, more lethal, more agile, more technologically advanced mobile force, using disposable resources that can be easily transported across the country, or across the globe.

"Gentlemen, the United States, the president, and the Congress will no longer be the nine-one-one call recipient in the middle of the night. We don't have the national treasury to support it, and we can't keep sending our military forces into harm's way for years at a time. It's not fair to them, and it's not fair to the American taxpayers."

Denny's guests left after his points were expressed, and he sensed they were at the same time both disappointed and better informed. They didn't get assurances that the United States would be increasing its orders for more equipment, but that the government would continue to buy the best and the newest capabilities they could make, but in smaller quantities. He also had assured them that the path to national law enforcement entities and foreign sales would be easier.

He looked at the calendar of appointments on his desk and saw that two aircraft manufacturing corporations were next to talk with him, presumably about the same message. After them, ship building

CEOs would be making the rounds to discuss advanced surface and sub-surface mission capabilities. And after them, the handheld weapons and munitions CEOs would be there. He knew he would share the message he gave to the armaments CEOs with these gentlemen, as well. He noted the handwritten comments Julie had placed underneath their appointment lines.

They each will be coming from Congresswoman Doolin's office. She will be receiving the ground hardware representatives at the time when the aircraft manufacturers are here. While the aircraft executives are here, she will be meeting with the shipbuilding executives. You both are invited to cocktails and heavy hors d'oeuvres at five thirty in the Indian Treaty Room of the Old Executive Office Building next to the White House. It is sponsored by the munitions industry. All of today's visitors will be there, too, one hour after you and the Congresswoman arrive.

Denny thought, *I guess industry has broken the code and know we are working the Congress for the Executive Branch. I guess also they have to try to sell more equipment and ferret out where we are going so that they, and we, are prepared for the future. I wish I could get out of town for a week or so, to let the other members receive these briefings.*

Denny then sat in the hard-backed rocker at the side of his executive desk to reflect on the visits and what he thought about them. He sat for about three minutes. The rocker had always helped him to sit quietly for a few minutes while he sorted out salient details of some very natty subjects. That mental sorting process had always allowed him to see a pathway ahead more clearly. He was sipping on cold coffee. He set his cup down, arose, and went to his desk and reached for his phone.

Denny pushed the intercommunications line button to Julie. She responded, "Yes, Senator?"

"Julie, could you please get me Admiral Nagle on the secure line for a short call?"

"Yes, Senator, right away."

When Denny had hung up the secure line with Chet Nagle, his intercommunications line from Julie rang. "Senator, Mr. Osbane from Bellingham Airplane Company and Mr. Crickmore from Lansing Aircraft Corporation are here to see you."

"Thank you, Julie. Please send them in."

65

Moving to Be in Place

Lajes Field, the Azores, May 2019

Nine hundred ninety miles west of Lisbon, in the North Atlantic, off the coast of Portugal, lay the islands of the Azores. They were made up of nine separate islands, divided into three groups unimaginatively named the Eastern, Central, and Western groups. In the Central group lay the key island of Terceira among the grouping comprised of Sao Jorge, Faial, and Graciosa. Terciera was different in that it hosted a large military air base called Lajes Field, which was operated by the Portuguese Air Force. The base dated back to its activation in 1928 and it lay approximately halfway between North America and Europe in the Atlantic Ocean.

The runway was 10,873 feet long and accommodated a whole host of friendly nations' military and civilian aircraft on a daily basis. The base provided support to fifteen thousand aircraft each year. In 2012 the U.S. Administration announced it was going to reduce the U.S. presence at the field, and since that time only about nine hundred U.S. military personnel and their families had resided there. After that announcement, the People's Republic of China opened a continuing dialogue with the Portuguese government to negotiate a base rights agreement for Chinese military and civilian air traffic. The agreement was now in place. This action, along with the increased emphasis and presence of the PRC and the DPRK, had enhanced the relationship between the PRC, the DPRK, and radical Islamist activities in Central Africa, and especially the subversive forces in Nigeria and Cameroon. This agreement and newfound common ground in the western hemisphere did not bode well for the American influence in the area.

On this date in 2019, U.S. Air Force and U.S. Naval aircraft still regularly employed the services of the base on a consistent basis as personnel and materiel were airlifted to various locations in Europe and Africa. Today, however, the base would be a transfer point from one location to another for three people. The mission was not classified, but deliberate efforts had been made to keep the activities unpublicized and unheralded. These three people had just boarded one of two U.S. Navy E-2D Advanced Hawkeye airborne early warning and control aircraft. The flight leader of the two Hawkeyes was Lieutenant Commander Terry Dale, USN. His call sign was Salem 01. The two call signs were in honor of the USNS *Salem* that had been lost with all hands in the North Pacific in mid-2017. Commander Dale explained to one of the guests on board with the comment, "We hope that meets with your approval?"

"Yes, it does—very much so," was the answer.

He was helping his three guests get settled in their seats and strapped into their safety harnesses. He adjusted the floatation vests over their shoulders and under the arms of each passenger and loosely placed the shoulder harnesses and seat belts over the float vests. He had already pre-briefed them on the overwater mission and explained ditching procedures if it became absolutely necessary. There were several other items he also needed to explain since this mission was confidential.

"Folks, once we're at our cruising altitude of twenty-six thousand feet, which will take about twelve minutes, you may get up and walk around. You know where the Honey Bucket is located, so feel free to use it at any time. We are normally a crew of five with all positions manned. But today we are a crew of three to accommodate the three of you. Please be assured that you are not inconveniencing any of us or our other two crew members. I, the copilot, and the radar officer are sincerely pleased to have you aboard. There is coffee and water in the small galley in the aft of the aircraft, and we each have a box lunch on board. It contains a freshly made sandwich, chips, a Three Musketeers candy bar, a Power Bar, and a small container of milk. Since you three are VIPs, you also get a fresh Washington State apple. We each also get a small packet of pretzels." Everyone chuckled at that.

"We have secure voice comms onboard in case anyone wants to talk to you or you want to talk to someone. Our cruising speed is about 260 knots per hour. Our flight plan will take us directly to the Cape Verde Islands and will take about two hours and thirty-eight minutes. We won't be on the ground long there, but it will be long enough for you to stretch your legs. We'll refuel; recheck our flight plans and the weather; and then leap off for the USS *Truman*. She is another one hour and fifty minutes downrange and they are expecting you.

"My wingman is Lieutenant Senior Grade Patt Gibson. Her call sign is Salem 02. She and her full crew complement will stay off of our starboard wing and will double-check our navigation, weather conditions, and all changing events, and will stay in constant sight and communications. Both she and I will have regular contact with the *Truman* to give them our position reports. I'm told Zero-two has yesterday's bologna and cheese sandwiches for snacks. So it's fortuitous you're with us. Are there any questions?" All three passengers shook their heads. Commander Dale then said, "Okay, we'll be wheels-up in fifteen minutes or less."

Dale turned and sealed the entrance hatch, walked forward to the cockpit, and strapped in. The copilot had already checked and double-checked the takeoff checklist, and Dale began the engine startup checks and actions. Once the engines were running at peak ground taxi efficiency, the tower gave Salem 01 and Salem 02 clearance to proceed to takeoff positions at the end of Runway 33. Salem 01 was cleared for takeoff and Salem 02 was cleared for ten seconds later.

Commander Dale pushed the two throttles forward to full military takeoff power, and the two Allison T-56 turbo-prop engines spun the eight-blade propellers through the humid Azorean air with all their 5100 horsepower might to hurl the awkward-looking but efficient and technically sophisticated aircraft into the air. The aircraft lurched down the runway as if to eager feel the wind across its wings and be airborne where it belonged. The sleek triple tails and aerodynamic rotor dome gave additional direction and lift to the shark-nosed aircraft. Twelve minutes later, both aircraft were at 26,000 feet on a heading of 175 degrees.

Congresswoman Doolin turned to Father Norm Desrosiers and said, "Father, I think many people would think having a chaplain aboard an aircraft or a ship was an ominous gesture. But I don't. I think having you here and aboard the *Truman* with the Phantoms is comforting and reduces the stress we are all feeling about this mission and all those like it."

"Thank you for that, Congresswoman. I know that comes from your strong Episcopalian background and that your faith will sustain you in the things you are about to experience. At one time or another, we each should take a coin from our pocket to read the words *In God We Trust* on it as a reminder. And you, Senator Smith, your strong Methodist upbringing has likely seen you through some dark times, too. Now the two of you are heading into harm's way when you don't have to. You both will be an inspiration to all of the service members you are about to meet."

"That's considerate of you to say, Chaplain," Denny responded. "Our military forces have been operating at a disadvantage for many years. Our adversaries have grown to view our forces, and the purposes for which the United States stands, with disdain. They don't fear our power any longer, and they don't respect us as a nation, either. If they did, we wouldn't be here right now."

"I would have to agree with you, Senator. Our forces have been significantly outnumbered in most of our past confrontations. Our loyalty to one another and our faith in God has held us together."

"That's true, Chaplain," Rosemary interjected. "Fortunately we have had technology and the lethality of our weapons on our side. It's too bad we have just not had the political will to fight and win our battles. And, I might add, I have seen too much apathy on the part of the Congress and the American public. It frightens me. President Chenoa is a refreshing change."

For the next hour, the conversations ranged from politics; to activities in the Middle East; to European and Mexican vacations; to good French restaurants versus good Italian restaurants in Washington, D.C.; to the differences in fishing between Florida, Tennessee, and Oregon. No one won that last discussion.

Commander Dale announced over the intercom system that he

would be descending to the airport at Praia on the Island of Sao Tiago, the Cape Verde Islands. One hour later the two Advanced Hawkeyes were airborne again, heading for the *Truman*.

66

On Board

The USS Truman, May 2019

The *Truman* was sailing southeasterly into the wind in the South Atlantic. She was on a heading of 120 degrees awaiting the approach of the two E2D Advanced Hawkeyes. The guided missile destroyer USS *McKinley*, the Aegis Cruiser USS *Alamo*, the fast-attack submarine USS *Montana*, and the oiler USS *Puget Sound* were all arrayed around the fantail of the *Truman*, in appropriate surveillance and protective formation. Surveillance radars and sonars were not pinging on any unknown targets. The *Truman* battle group was alone in this part of the globe—so far.

The arrival of the Hawkeyes was important for two reasons. First, it was imperative to get the aircrews and the high-level guests aboard. Second, these two Hawkeyes were an integral part of the carrier battle group battle space command and control. They belonged to the *Truman*. Their continuing mission was to provide long-range airborne early warning and control coverage for the entire battle group.

Salem 02 was first to land aboard the deck of the *Truman*. The deck crews would get Salem 02 towed and stowed quickly so that Salem 01 could land and the small recognition and welcome ceremonies could be quickly and appropriately conducted. The time was now 1530 hours and the *Truman* battle group needed to make plans for moving toward the Cameroonian coastline and prepare for dark and low-profile running operations.

Salem 01 came to a sudden but uneventful stop on the deck, and the arresting cable was disengaged so the aircraft could taxi forward to the disembarkation stops on the deck. The aircraft hatch was popped open, and the doorway was opened and steps extended. Congresswoman Doolin was the first to emerge according to protocol, since she was the most senior member of Congress aboard and also because she was a Navy mom. Denny followed and Chaplain Desrosiers then waited a few appropriate seconds so he could disembark without ceremonial flourishes that allowed him to get to the Phantoms, his reason for being there in the first place.

Captain Bill Chandler, USN, captain of the USS *Truman*, was the first in line to welcome Rosemary and Denny. They were dressed in tan navy flight suits, which made each of them only slightly uncomfortable for small but different reasons: Rosemary, because she didn't feel very feminine, and Denny because the suit was navy tan and not standard air force dark green. Nonetheless, they both reveled in the fact that they were there as a part of the team and the mission.

Captain Chandler was followed by Admiral Ray Andrews, and then by Colonel Bud Patrick, both representing the Phantom Force Regiment. Rosemary and Denny were very happy to see the familiar faces and knew that precision plans had been finalized for this tactical action.

Moreover, everyone knew that Rosemary and Denny were there at the behest of the president of the United States. As elected representatives of the American people, they were advocates, and charged to return to Washington to present unequivocal justification for the president's new strategic strategy for the military forces of the United States. Everyone present had something to gain or lose. This mission was of crucial importance not only for the United States but also for the Republic of Cameroon.

The congresswoman and the senator were shown to their private quarters to freshen up and were informed there would be a pre-brief overview at 1915 hours in the pilot's ready room following the light dinner in the Officers Ward Room at 1745 hours.

The distance to the Cameroonian coast was a little over 1,900 miles from the *Truman*'s present position. The plan called for the four Ghosthawk helicopters with the twenty-eight Phantom Strike Force members, to be launched from one hundred miles offshore. But since Russian and Chinese imagery satellites transited this area periodically, the battle group feigned a turn to the starboard and headed south rather than east at a speed of all-ahead-slow. In four hours, under the cover of darkness and electronic wizardry, the battle group would appear to be continuing a heading of south, but it would be cloaked in an invisible cover and would turn east toward Cameroon.

It was now 1914 hours and all the principals chatted as they filed into the Pilots Briefing Room for the pre-brief. They all extolled the virtues of the excellent dinner menu made exclusively for the two honored guests. The broiled almond-encrusted South Atlantic grouper was done to perfection. It was served with mango-coconut key lime chutney and accompanied by grilled green and yellow squash with red peppers and herbs. The dessert was key lime pie with a small dollop of fresh Oregon raspberry sauce on top. Rosemary was informed that the chef was Petty Officer First Class Herman Rodriguez from Tampa, Florida, her home congressional district.

She said, "Please give my personal compliments to Petty Officer Rodriguez, and I'd like very much to express my thanks to him personally and get a photo of the two of us. That would be very special to me."

Captain Chandler replied, "I'll take care of it."

They all took their seats. A single word appeared on the screen at the front of the room: *WEATHER*. Lieutenant Commander Ballard stood at the podium, at the right corner of the platform. "Ladies and gentlemen, the classification of all the information you are about to see and hear is classified Top Secret Code Word ENDEAVOR, Project LIBERTY.

"There is very little of remarkable meteorological significance to report for the next seven days in the target area. The prevailing light winds from Central Africa will cover Cameroon and Nigeria. Temperatures will be in the low eighty degrees Fahrenheit; no rain expected; no dust or sandstorms known to exist; clear days and nights. Questions?" There were none.

The screen word then changed. *INTELLIGENCE* appeared, and

Lieutenant Commander Alvarez walked to the podium. "Ladies and gentlemen, if I were to give intelligence advice to our adversaries, I would suggest that if they don't see or hear anything, they are probably in trouble. We are stealthy, determined, and effective. We have HUMINT and ELINT reports that the twenty-five-hundred-man armed force of the Sambisa Forest arm of the Boko Haram army is equipped with some dangerous materiel that they know little about. They think only of effects and results, not handling. They have the usual weaponry carried by radical Islamist forces in this part of the world. They have an abundance of Kalishnikov automatic rifles, 7.62 mm Russian PKM light machine guns, many remotely controlled propelled grenades, RPGs, satchel charge devices, IEDs, and a variety of C4 and SemTex plastic explosives. They also have some American-made Striker vehicles and armored personnel carriers that were left behind or surrendered by defecting or fleeing Iraqi and Afghani forces. They have been trans-shipped to Nigeria via Russian and North Korean cargo vessels.

"The terrorists also possess Sarin, VX, and mustard gas canisters that can be fired up to four miles away by long-rifle missile firing, ground-mounted cannons. They also have a small low-yield nuclear device aboard the cargo vessel currently moored at the port in Douala, Cameroon. The name on the bow of the ship reads *Aegean Sunrise* and the stern shows Madagascar as the nation of origin. The ship is, in fact, the *Kwang Ju Maru* from North Korea. She has been in port since mid-March and is still guarded twenty-four/seven. For two weeks the six or seven guards appeared to be East Asian, but they are now apparently six Boko Haram soldiers from Nigeria. They seem to be awaiting some kind of a Go Code.

"Two days before our Phantoms go ashore, there will be repeated over flights of U.S. Air Force X-37B low orbiting intel collectors. That data will be down-linked to the *Truman* CIC. The day of our move inland, there will be continual surveillance of our target area, plus up- and down-linked communications by an air force Phantom Eye Drone orbiting at sixty-five thousand feet altitude, also continuously down-linking data and comms. We will also be launching from and recovering back to the *Truman*, several long-duration X-47B U.S. Navy stealth drones, to collect imagery, communications, and weather data from the targets."

"This is what we have finalized so far. This is the first of three briefings for this mission over the next three days. Are there any questions?" There were none. Both Denny and Rosemary had several questions, but they chose to not belabor the briefing now.

The word on the display screen changed a third time. It now said, *OPERATIONS*, and Bud Patrick took the podium.

"Ladies and gentlemen, I will give you a brief overview of our operations plans, but will skip some of the details for now. Those details are still being finalized. We will have three separate operations underway simultaneously. First, a team of nine Phantoms will leave here tonight aboard a Ghost Hawk chopper and go to the deck of the USS *McKinley* of our flotilla. Their code name is Trigger Two. The squad will be under the command of Lieutenant Colonel Duke Westcott and the *McKinley* will take them to within fifty miles of the Cameroon coast. The Ghost Hawk will then deliver them the rest of the way to a rendezvous point, to link up with Cameroonian General Franco Otuba, who, at the request of President Adamo, is to neutralize the leader of the Boko Haram army and three of his henchmen. If the intel reports are correct, General Otuba's six men and our ten men under the direction of General Otuba will also take out senior Al Qaida and senior ISIS leaders who are meeting with the Boko Haram leader.

"Second, a squad of nine Phantoms will go ashore at the same time that General Otuba and our Phantoms are engaged, to neutralize the guards aboard the *Aegean Sunrise*. Their code name is Trigger Three. These Phantom members and our nuclear munitions technical advisor will clear the ship of booby traps and disconnect any remote triggering mechanisms, if there are any, and detach any placards or identifying tags that link the weapon to its nation of origin. They'll then cast off the mooring lines. A small but powerful tug from the *Truman* will be in place to tow the *Sunrise* out to sea, beyond the sixty-mile line from shore, and scuttle the vessel in five hundred fathoms of water. Trigger Team Three Phantoms will then be taken off the *Sunrise* and returned to the *Truman* aboard the tug.

"Third, a squad of six Phantoms under my command, Trigger Team Lead, will rendezvous at the Cameroonian presidential palace in Yaoundé to meet briefly with President Adamo and take custody of one Francois Ricardo De La Plane, and return him to the *Truman* for incarceration and transport to the United States. All these activities will take place between 0130 and 0400, May 23, three days from now. Are there any questions?" There were none.

Three hours later, Duke Westcott and his eight Phantoms, weighted down with double the usual ration of weapons and ammunition, left the deck of the *Truman* aboard a Ghost Hawk stealth helicopter for the chopper pad at the stern of the *McKinley*. Once aboard, the *McKinley* took a hard port turn to a heading of 090 degrees toward the Gulf of Guinea, to rendezvous with General Otuba ten kilometers from Calabar, Nigeria.

67

Boko Haram Surprise

Near Calabar, Nigeria, May 2019

General Otuba had one of his men place a beeping beacon in the center of a two-kilometer-by-two-kilometer field located ten kilometers from the old Mediterranean home where Otuba and De La Plane met Zingo Kambar in early April. The beeper was transmitting a discreet, scrambled homing signal that only the two Ghost Hawks could receive. The chopper with Duke Westcott and four of his eight Phantoms and extra ammunition aboard were ready for a fight. One of the Phantoms was his best sniper, Sergeant Darrin Hall. Thirty minutes before departing the *Truman*, it was decided a second Ghost Hawk was necessary because of the extra weaponry and the final decision that General Otuba and his commandos would also be airlifted out at the end of the mission. Both Ghost Hawks would then take the ten Phantoms, the seven Cameroonian commandos, and the added hardware that was to stay with General Otuba, and head straight for the presidential palace grounds in Yaoundé. This would allow General Otuba to both report on the mission results directly to President Adamo and to back up Trigger Lead in his extraction of the prisoner.

Duke looked at his Phantoms in the cabin. He looked them over, seeking a loose strap, or an open pouch, or a weapon safety that was off. He saw nothing out of the ordinary. They were all ready. He knew they all were hoping this one would be quick and easy. But it never was.

Over the intercom, the pilot said, "Locked on to beacon. Slowing to prepare to land. All scans appear quiet. Two flicker lights spotted. Friendlies know we are here. Descending now. Be ready, Colonel. Good luck."

The stealthy chopper slowed to land and touched down without incident. But the pilots kept the RPMs up in case an emergency departure was needed. None was. Duke and his Phantoms made a quick exit and set up a perimeter barrier five yards around the chopper. Their Ghost Hawk rotor blades were still spinning, making a soft *whup-whup-whup* sound, ready for acceleration if required. All were down on one knee and weapons safeties were definitely off. Several of the Phantoms were wired with cameras and voice communications packets, as were the teams to take over the ship and Bud Patrick's team to arrest De La Plane. Duke quietly ordered, "Comm packets On." Transmissions back to the *Truman* and then on to the White House Situation Room began immediately.

The second Ghost Hawk landed twenty-five yards behind Duke. The Phantoms in that chopper quickly dismounted and established their perimeter also. There was no light. All were wearing night vision goggles and they could see as if it was evening dusk. They were waiting for orders from Duke to secure the landing site. Before departure from the *Truman*, it was also agreed that Duke and Otuba would attach a small low-intensity flashing firefly light to their left shoulder epaulets. Duke reached up and turned on his, then waited ten seconds. Several yards ahead, Duke saw a small very subtle flashing green light. Duke crouched lower and took aim with his M-14 at the light just in case it was not Otuba who wore it. The light slowly came toward Duke, and he began slowly moving to the light. He tightened his grip on his weapon in case the light turned out to be an unwelcome surprise. Within five yards, he recognized a large, well-built man with both hands raised to be visible. It was indeed General Otuba.

Earlier it had been agreed that sign and countersign would be used. All agreed to keep it simple and quick. Sign was: OTUBA. Countersign was: DUKE. It worked. Both men shook hands and chuckled a little at the simple game. Duke said over his intercom, "Secure the site and muster on me." Duke turned to the chopper cockpit and gave the slicing hand motion across his throat to the aircraft commander to cut the throttles and shut down. The same word went to the second Ghost Hawk aircraft commander.

Duke, the eight Phantoms, Otuba, and two of his commandos moved the entire group to a sheltered and secluded spot in the shrubbery beside the clearing. The other four Cameroonian commandos were around the perimeter, acting as spotters and guards. They were in open-mic radio contact with their general. Otuba informed the group he was on Channel 4 on his discreet, scrambled ops transmitter. Everyone reached to switch to Channel 4. Otuba then briefed the group on the whereabouts of the seven targets, the ten perimeter guards who were drunk by now, and the layout of the house where the targets were meeting.

Otuba finished the plan, then accepted a couple of small suggestions from Duke. He said to the general, "I have two snipers with me. Suggest we position them seventy-five yards from the residence and dispatch as many sentries as possible from a distance to ease our penetration."

"Excellent suggestion," Otuba said and pointed to his schematic of the grounds. "Put them here and here." Westcott looked at Hall and Willoughby and nodded. They nodded back in the affirmative. "Is there anything else?" There was not.

Otuba then said, "Good. I have two horse-drawn wagons there to your left. They are equipped with soft rubber tires. Wagons are much quieter than motorized vehicles. We can mount up and move out when ready after my four spotters get here. We will quietly go the ten kilometers, surround the building, and eliminate sentries as we move in. All agreed? When all is complete, we will rendezvous at the wagons and swiftly return to the choppers. It all should not take more than forty minutes. All agreed?" Everyone nodded their heads and gave the thumbs-up signal.

Duke then suggested, "All check to see that silencers and muzzle flash suppressors are in place."

Otuba then said, "Good, let's move out. When we get to the house, I will command GO! GO! GO! And we enter. Watch for tripwires and pressure plates." They all quietly moved to the horse-drawn wagons and climbed aboard for the ten-minute ride. "I personally will check the bodies of Kambar, Bin Gormandi, Al Shemani, or whomever they send to represent them. We will need the confirmation that they have been dispatched." Again, everyone nodded in the affirmative to General Otuba.

Aboard the *Truman*, in the CIC, Admiral Andrews, Denny Smith, Rosemary Doolin, Chaplain Desrosiers, and several *Truman* staff officers watched intently. They and the White House Sit Room were watching the actions of all teams on split-screen video displays. Video feeds were streaming from the helmet cameras, from the Phantom Eye drone at over sixty thousand feet altitude, the X37B air force and the X-47B navy drones. No one was second-guessing the comments, the plans, the tactics, and the proposed actions of the Phantoms on the ground. This was decidedly the most sensitive part of the mission. Secrecy, stealth, invisibility, and precision for both the Phantoms and the Cameroonian commandos were imperative. There were one or two light moments during the mission, but it was serious from beginning to end. Denny and Rosemary took detailed mental notes of this classified and clandestine operation and intended to put those details to good use back in Congress.

The mission start time was 0140 hours. The mission end time would be 0317 hours.

68

North Korean Surprise

*The Douala Wharf, The Aegean Sunrise,
Douala, Cameroon, May 2019*

The USS *Truman* and the other ships in the small battle group had moved to within twenty-five miles of the Cameroon coast and the harbor at Douala. It was pitch-black dark. They were now sailing a large, all-ahead-slow, lazy figure-eight pattern in the South Atlantic awaiting mission completion. All surveillance and detection equipment aboard the ships and a single airborne E2D Hawkeye were at maximum alert.

Trigger Team Three had left the deck of the *Truman* at 0100 hours, aboard a Ghost Hawk stealth chopper, and were deposited at a darkened soccer stadium field, one-eighth mile from the dock where the *Aegean Sunrise* was tied up. Navy SEAL Special Operations squad leader, Lieutenant Senior Grade Taylor Austin, USN, leading Trigger Team Three, had his six other Phantoms and two nuclear weapons ordnance disposal technicians arrayed around the ship. Two Phantoms had inflated a black rubber two-man raft and stood by on the seaward side of the ship. The forty-foot, four-man crew aboard the seagoing tug that did triple duty as a tug, an assault transport for SEAL teams, and a boarding and inspection patrol boat, sat at anchor twenty-five yards away in the harbor. Both deck-mounted fifty-caliber machine guns were armed and silently manned by two crew members. All was quiet, but Trigger Team Three was taking no chances. Their silencers and muzzle flash suppressors were in place. On Austin's command, they all were to silently board the ship via mooring lines, gangways, and climbing ropes attached to any hooks or rings affixed to the ship.

Lieutenant Austin looked around the wharf and the ship for any movement to ensure none of his men had been seen. All weapons were armed, NVGs were in place, and all Phantoms were ready to engage. Their all-black battle dress uniforms, helmets, and bulletproof armor reflected no light or emitted any kind of signals. Several of the Phantoms and *Truman* crew members had helmet-mounted cameras and comm. transmission packets on their uniforms.

Austin whispered into his intercom mic to all Phantom Trigger Team Three members, saying, "Comm packages On. On my mark of GO, GO, GO, we board the ship and neutralize targets. If anyone sees the Korean man who is rumored to be aboard, take him alive, if possible. I have confirmed one sentry on the bow; one on the stern; and at least one on the bridge. Be prepared for at least three more. Watch for booby traps, tripwires, and pressure plates."

Onboard the USS *Truman* in the CIC, the battle staff plus Admiral Andrews, Denny Smith, and Rosemary Doolin were still watching and listening to all activities on a large split-screen video display. The White House Sit Room split-screen displays were identical. They were all mesmerized with what they saw transpiring. Video came from all the prepositioned overhead sources, but the most declarative were from the helmet-mounted cameras. U.S. forces were in this battle to win; not to seek a split decision and not to lose.

Thirty seconds passed. Austin said into his mic, "Mark: five, four, three, two, one, GO! GO! GO!"

Simultaneously nine silent shadows, all clad in black, began rapidly and silently to board the ship. They confronted three sentries on the deck who were instantly dispatched. Lieutenant Austin and Sergeant Sammie Lee, USMC, of South Korean descent and fluent in the Korean language, proceeded to the bridge, and three Phantoms went below decks in search of other guards. Three guards were found sleeping and when awakened reached for weapons but never made the connection. The nuclear disposal technicians waited on deck, at the hatch leading to below decks. They waited for the signal to proceed in search of the suspected nuclear device.

All Phantoms reported over the comm line, one after the other, "All secure and all clear!" This was the cue for the nuclear technicians.

On the bridge of the cargo vessel, an officious-looking North Korean man, assumed to be the captain, was surprised and arose from a bunk in the rear of the wheelhouse. He had been rarely seen but must have been the custodian of the ship and the suspected weapon believed to be aboard. He reached for a radio-transmitting device, and Lieutenant Austin said, "NO, NO, NO." The captain sat back down on the bunk, looking defensive. Austin suspected a weapon was hidden under the pillow. He was right. The captain reached for it, and Austin fired his silenced M-14. The captain's right forearm was shattered. The man began wailing and angrily muttering, then alternately waving his one good arm and holding his injured arm with his still-working left hand.

According to a plan devised before coming aboard, if they came across a belligerent whom they wanted alive, one of the Phantoms would wound him while the other searched or administered first aid. Lieutenant Austin held the muzzle of his rifle to the face of the Korean while Sergeant Lee bandaged the man's right arm.

"Sir, the man says that Premiere Kim Teong Unong, the Dear Leader, will file a formal complaint with the French government about this egregious violation. You and all of us will be arrested and executed for piracy and international crimes against the state."

Austin looked at the man for a few seconds, and then back to Lee, and said, "Tell him okay." In his usual matter-of-fact manner, Austin didn't want to debate with this SOB. The Korean was surprised at the answer, but he was in too much pain to discuss it with the intruders.

After bandaging the man's arm, Lee gave him an injection of morphine to ease the pain and force him into a state of euphoria that would last for four hours or so. Lee and one of the other Phantoms helped the groggy man off the ship and into a small warehouse on the pier, where he would be found in four or five hours. After discovery he would surely contact someone in North Korea to report that things were not going so well in Cameroon, and that his ship had been stolen. This was exactly what President Chenoa and President Adamo wanted.

The nuclear explosive disposal technicians found what looked like an explosive device encased in a large metal box about the size of a Volkswagen in the center hold. It had Cyrillic symbols painted on it, indicating it had originated in Russia before being handed over to the North Korean government. They advised Austin of what they found, and said, "Lieutenant, there is no rice down here. The cargo hold is filled with Styrofoam chips that look like rice."

They reported they would inspect further and report back in a few minutes. They quickly began opening panels and circuit boxes to see what was inside that required disconnection, and also to expose as much of the weapon's innermost electronic workings to the deteriorating effects of saltwater corrosion and decomposition that was soon to occur. They reported to Lieutenant Austin and to the observers onboard the *Truman* and in the Sit Room, they had indeed found a nuclear weapon ostensibly from a now-destroyed Russian medium-range ballistic missile. Its size was about three megatons and it could create blast and radiation damage out to a radius of three miles if detonated. After closer inspection, they found a remote transceiver that had not yet been activated that would allow the device to be detonated via satellite signal from as far away as the other side of the globe. The implications of such an action occurring were too horrible to be contemplated right now. But, in saner moments, this evidence would be useful. Their helmet cameras were recording all their discoveries and disconnection actions. They found and removed two identity plates that had Russian warhead nomenclature on them and a third plate with North Korean identity codes and contents inventory on it. Those, too, would be valuable evidence.

The technicians continued to sever communications circuits, connections to the fusion rods, and electronic interfaces to all key components needed to activate the weapon. While they were engaged in this activity, the other Phantoms cast off the mooring lines. The tug then quietly began to tow the ship away from the dock and out of the harbor on a westerly heading that would take it to its watery and corrosive grave, sixty miles out to sea and below five hundred fathoms of south Atlantic sea water that would make everything aboard the ship inert. The technicians and the Phantoms had at least two hours to complete all scuttling actions.

The mission start time was 0142. The mission end time at the dock was 0239.

69

De La Plane Surprise

The President's Office, Yaoundé, Cameroon, May 2019

The phone next to the bed of Francois quietly buzzed. It buzzed again, finally stirring Francois from a deep sleep. He answered it in a sleepy voice. "Yes, this is Francois."

"Francois, my friend, this is Benjo. I am sorry to have awakened you. I know it's nearly two a.m. I am in my office and I would like you to join me for a private meeting."

"Yes, Mr. President, I can be there in ten minutes."

"That would be perfect. Thank you, and I will apologize again when you get here for awakening you so early. I will see you in a few minutes."

In ten minutes Francois was softly knocking on the president's office door. "Come in, Francois," was the reply. He opened the door, and Benjo was walking toward the door to greet him.

"Francois, please pardon me for the abrupt phone call and the suddenness of my request. But General Otuba is due here shortly to give me a report on the actions in Calabar regarding Zingo Kambar and his Middle-Eastern allies, and I wanted you to be here to also receive his report. I will need your counsel on the next moves we should make. I fear Boko Haram may know we are responsible and could either retaliate or retreat away for some time. I'm hoping it is the latter.

Would you like some coffee or tea? Come, sit."

"Thank you, Mr. Pres— Benjo. I would like some coffee, thank you."

"I must tell you, Francois, I'm a bit hyper about all this. Military actions and the use of force are new to me, and I want to confide in you that I don't want this sort of thing to be a regular occurrence."

"I understand, Benjo. But we must assess the after-action events and try to determine what exactly occurred, who was terminated, whether there were any escapees who could report our actions, and other facts. Then we can look at our options. Certainly the national security of Cameroon has to be paramount."

Francois was seated, sipping his coffee, while at the same time mentally sorting through what he knew and what could be the range of results of this action. Benjo was pacing the floor back and forth in a measured way, not a frantic one. He was listening to Francois, but only on a superficial level. His mind was racing between all the limited points of information he had so far. "Yes, yes, options. You're right. We don't have enough information to arrive at any conclusions and make decisions, let alone plans for our next actions. You're right, of course. I'm glad you're here to assist me in going through the events. Otuba will be here soon, and he will also have thoughts for us to consider."

"Benjo, regardless of the outcome, you may be faced with making a statement to the Parliament. There may be press requests for appointments. There may be repercussions from government heads of state from Nigeria, from Chad, from Guinea, from Central African Republic, and from other neighboring countries. We'll need a little time to go through the inquiries. But I believe we have time on our side. We certainly don't want to make any public, or even private, pronouncements prematurely. My advice is to make your statements measured for now. The less said publicly, the better for now."

"Yes, Francois, of course you are right." Benjo seemed calmer now that he had a sounding board that he thought was not as close to the problem, although Francois had been one of the planners of the military action.

"Francois, having you here is very helpful. I am glad you have chosen to stay, and I hope you will think of Cameroon as your home.

Tell me, what are you thinking about in the near- and far-term with regards to your future?"

Francois took another sip of coffee and looked at Benjo, then to the wall hangings and then the window as if trying to gather his thoughts. He hesitated a moment, then said, "I have been very relaxed here and enjoy my advisory role. I am learning a lot and have concluded I am better able to function in a peaceful environment than in the constant crises I left in Yemen."

The two men talked in a calm and unemotional manner for more than an hour about the future, the impact of the present on both of their lives, and about past events in which the two men had been at the same time both proud and regretful. They mostly discussed those events that gave them the most satisfaction.

It was nearly 0400 hours when a soft knock was heard at the door. "Ah, that must be Otuba. Come in, come in." It was Otuba and a captain of his commando unit. The captain remained outside and quietly closed the door as General Otuba entered.

"Mr. President," Otuba began. "I have good news. Our mission was a complete success. Mr. Ambassador, good morning. I am pleased you are here, too, to hear my report."

"General, I am pleased you came through it all unscathed and it was a success," Francois said.

Benjo then said, "General, please forgive my manners. Please be seated here at the conference table and give me a brief sketch of what happened. Please have coffee with us."

Benjo poured cups for himself, Francois, and the general. Then Otuba began to talk, beginning with the horse-drawn wagons. He deliberately made no mention of the Americans. Before the mission Adamo had talked privately with Otuba and discussed this exact mission debrief with either the good or bad news. They agreed that only the two of them would know of the American intentions for support and involvement unless a tactical catastrophe occurred in the attack. They would then deal with it as required. Fortunately, a good plan with good people worked to their advantage.

General Otuba finished his report, down to rearranging all the Boko Haram, Al Qaida, and DAIISH bodies with their weapons to appear as though the three groups had experienced a major disagreement and fought with each other. All presence of Cameroonian forces and activities had been erased.

"I believe we were efficient enough to have been invisible and blameless for this fight. Your plan, Mr. Ambassador, worked perfectly. Whoever discovers the site will easily conclude the combatants annihilated each other over some tactical, military, or monetary dispute. Again, your plan was brilliant. We'll now wait to see what the repercussions, if any, will be. Your input to future actions by my forces will be much appreciated."

Francois was appreciative and humble. He knew his presence was beneficial and welcome.

The time was 0450, and there was another soft knock at the door. Adamo said, "Yes, come in." It was Otuba's captain, who simply said, "Mr. President, General Otuba, you have visitors."

The captain opened the door fully, and Colonel Bud Patrick, Lieutenant Colonel Duke Westcott, and Master Chief Reed Barrett walked in. They were still dressed in their black battle dress uniforms, body armor, and side arms. Bud and Duke turned on their helmet-mounted cameras and comm packages just before entering President Adamo's office. This activity, though less dramatic than the two battle actions, was nonetheless highly important. They carried their helmets under their arms, saluted the president of Cameroon, and moved to the back of the chair in which Francois was sitting.

Adamo and Otuba stood, and President Adamo said, "Gentlemen, thank you for coming. I've been expecting you. I want to give you my profound thanks for assisting me and my general of the commando forces in this hour of need by my country. Your services have been invaluable."

Francois felt nervous and somewhat intimidated after receiving words of praise and now suddenly being ignored. He looked from man to man thinking he would be addressed, or introduced, or dismissed, or something. He looked over the three warriors more critically and began to recollect he had seen these unmarked uniforms before—once in French Guiana and once in Yemen. He thought it best to remain silent as a sense of foreboding came over him.

Otuba then spoke, "Mr. President, I have not been acquainted with these gentlemen for long, and I know them only as Trigger Lead,

Duke, and Chief. They saved me and two of my men from certain death at the hands of Boko Haram and DAIISH by their battle-tested tactics and armaments. I am indebted to them for saving Cameroonian lives and actions that could have resulted in the destruction of most of our country. I have not yet reported to you about the vessel in the harbor at Duaolo that Ambassador De La Plane identified to you. It did, in fact, have a nuclear device aboard, and it was wired to have been triggered from a location in Asia. The men these officers command disabled the device and have disposed of the remnants of the weapon far from here."

"Gentlemen, it seems I am indebted to you more than I can ever repay. Please pass my regards to your leadership and inform her I will soon be in contact." To this point, neither Bud, nor Duke, nor the master chief said anything. The president's and Otuba's comments had been carefully scripted to ensure they mentioned no personal titles, nationalities, or official government representatives. Both Adamo and Otuba were aware of the need for anonymity of this group.

President Adamo then turned to Francois and said, "Ambassador De La Plane, my friend, Francois, I want you to go with these gentlemen. They have some topics to discuss with you in the hope you can assist them in deterring future destructive international events. I have their assurances you will be treated with respect and care. Both General Otuba and I hope to see you here in Cameroon in the future. You will always be welcome."

Bud Patrick then said, "Thank you for your courtesy and understanding, Mr. President. It has been our honor to serve you and General Otuba. Now, Mr. Ambassador, will you please stand and place your wrists together in front of you?"

At the moment Bud spoke, Francois knew they were Americans. He thought to himself, *I guess it could be worse. They could have been Russian or German. At least I won't be found in an alleyway somewhere with a bullet in my head.*

Francois did as Patrick asked while Duke Westcott placed a plastic wrist restraint around his wrists and cinched it snugly. The master chief frisked Francois for any items that could be used as a weapon or suicide device. Duke then grasped Francois's right arm and the master chief grasped his left arm.

Bud Patrick smartly saluted President Adamo and handed the president and General Otuba each a small round cloth patch. The perimeter of the patch was surrounded by stars and it had a large American eagle emblazoned in the center. At the bottom it said, "*Second to None*" and "*PHANTOM FORCE.*" Both the president and the general said, "Thank you." They both knew it might be years before they could talk about the last hours and the mission.

On the simple grass field, fifty yards behind the presidential palace, sat a Ghost Hawk helicopter starting its engines. Two Phantoms stood guard with weapons at the ready on either side of the entry hatch as Bud, Duke, and the master chief escorted their prisoner aboard the chopper. Once in their seats and strapped in, Bud turned to De La Plane and read him his rights as a combatant prisoner of war. When completed, Bud said, "Do you understand what I have just said to you?"

Francois answered, "Yes, I understand."

As the observers aboard the *Truman* and in the White House Sit Room sat in stunned awe from having been in the midst of a clandestine, multi-phased battle, they recognized they were witnessing the end-to-end scenario of an American military, success-oriented operation, in which nothing was acceptable except victory.

The Ghost Hawk lifted off and headed for the USS *Truman*, which was located sixty miles to the west, where it was already on a heading of 260 degrees toward Norfolk Naval Base, Virginia. It was a fifteen-minute flight to the deck of the *Truman*.

This part of the mission end time was 0530 hours.

70

The Wrap-Up

The President's Office, Yaoundé, Cameroon, May 2019

President Adamo was in his office early to catch up on some affairs of state that had been on hold for a few days. General Otuba knocked and entered with Elizabeth, who then quietly closed the door behind her as she exited for the privacy of the two men. It had been a little more than twenty-four hours since these two men had met in this same office with their anonymous guests.

"General Otuba, thank you for coming on such short notice. I want to discuss briefly a couple of courses of action, and get your opinion on how to proceed. Boko Haram is not defeated; they are just delayed. Last night Nigerian and Chadian aircraft conducted a massive air strike against Boko Haram strongholds in and around the Sambisa Forest. There are reports of very large numbers of casualties. Weapons and fuel storage facilities have been destroyed. It may take them a year or more to build up to the numbers of men they had yesterday, and then they need training time. What should we do to bolster our country in the meantime?

"The United States has also offered a team of five or six consultants to give us advice on making plans for the future. They have an assistant secretary of state for foreign affairs whom they say is very congenial, not officious, and extremely competent. She is prepared to suggest how we can function more efficiently internally and with the rest of the international community. She is prepared to travel here on very short notice to offer her assistance. What do you think?"

The Virginia Coast of the United States, May 2019

Three Ghost Hawk stealth helicopters lifted off the deck of the *Truman* headed for Patuxant Naval Air Station, Virginia. They were to rendezvous with a US Air Force MC-130J Super Herc aircraft belonging to the Phantom force. It would take them directly back to Mac Dill AFB in Florida.

A fourth Ghost Hawk took off with four security personnel and Francois Ricardo De La Plane, headed for a secure helipad at the extreme south end of Reagan National Airport in Washington, D.C. There, a joint security team of naval criminal investigative service, or NCIS, CIA and FBI representatives waited in three standard black Chevrolet Suburban SUVs and would whisk De La Plane to the Federal District Courthouse in Alexandria, Virginia. Francois was to be held there for a short period of time. In a matter of hours, he was then to be relocated to an undisclosed secure location outside the Washington, D.C., area for an undetermined period of time until appropriate political and legal authorities decided on a course of action.

The *Truman* battle group moved slowly into Norfolk Naval Base, Virginia, for rearming and for taking on food and essential supplies. The plan was for the battle group to be there for twenty-five days before returning to sea duty. Nations such as Russia, China, and North Korea had now surmised that the presence of the USS *Truman* battle group in the area of major foreign political and military setbacks in certain countries had been more than a coincidence.

Information that the *Truman* battle group had been ordered to the Pacific was carefully leaked to the American public and military press services. Since the North Koreans, Chinese, and others closely monitored military news in open source American news media, they might begin to think the arrival of the *Truman* battle group in the Pacific could only mean that they were next. It was also possible, but maybe too much to hope for, that the information would elicit behavioral changes and the relaxation of the use of military forces by those countries.

Truman crew members were given two weeks of shore leave and were instructed to behave themselves. Sailors do, you know. Phantom operations in the Atlantic would now be provided by the USS *Ronald Reagan* carrier battle group.

The Oval Office, the White House, Washington, D.C., May 2019

Tom Mossman and Bill Frederickson both concurred on the current view. Bill said, "Madame President, this series of covert operations in the last year and a half has been a real tribute to the concept of covert strikes using a smaller force of U. S. military personnel. Just like the ISIS plan is to use individuals instead of armies to attack their neighbors and instill fear in everyone, we can more easily strike tyrant strongholds instead of entire nations. We have turned the sense of national fear around and reoriented it toward them. You have proven it works. There will be some international outcry that our actions were tantamount to an invasion, but privately, countries will applaud our efforts to avoid a major international confrontation."

Then Tom interjected, "Both Senator Smith and Congresswoman Doolin are energized to take these series of activities, citing nonspecific events of course, to their respective committees and to the full Senate and House when the time is right. There are many in Congress in both houses and in both parties, who are now convinced that your concept is efficient, affordable, and beneficial to the foreign policy and national security of the United States. The senator and the congresswoman think the time to seek committee approvals is at hand. The Department of Defense, the intelligence community, and all the military services are onboard with the concept and will be ready to implement the plan at your direction. Nearly everyone involved is thinking we should move sooner rather than later."

Fredrickson said, "For now, both Tom and I agree that the fewer specifics revealed, the better off we are. There is quiet back-channel mop-up work to be done with the Russians, the Chinese, and the

North Koreans. We have a solid foundation on which to complain about their practices of international cooperation, and I say that with some degree of sarcasm. We have the evidence. They obviously didn't heed our warning of exposure of their actions, after the Yemen attack.

"If they were to believe we might take this evidence to the security council of the United Nations, they would be more motivated to be conciliatory. I must add, however, I'm not so sure about North Korea. They thrive on bad press and love the attention notoriety gives them."

"You're both right," said President Chenoa. "I'll work the back-channel route first. A threat of international public exposure and embarrassment could work wonders for a lengthier period of time. These countries haven't accepted that our reticence to act in the past was not out of fear of them, but out of respect for their achievements in this decade. I need to inform them we don't fear them. I would also tell them, by international standards, I think they have an abysmal record of success in foreign relations. I want to tell them we will no longer only do what is politically correct in our foreign relations and foreign policy. We will do what is right."

Mac Dill Air Force Base, Tampa, Florida, May 2019

The time was 1730 hours. The MC-130J Super Herc was given a straight-in approach to Runway 22 and touched down with no other traffic in the pattern. The Herc was cleared to its usual hangar for night and day cover. They adhered to standard protocols, to avoid bringing attention to a change in routines that could be picked up by unwelcome observers. The engines were shut down just short of the hangar doors and an aircraft tug attached itself to the nose gear of the aircraft and towed it into the large hangar facility. Once inside, the giant doors began closing, and the low-level inside hangar lights were illuminated.

Three dozen wives and children were gathered to greet their warrior dads and husbands as they deplaned in the hangar area. Before deplaning, Bud Patrick announced to the Phantoms that there would be a mission debrief at 0900 tomorrow morning in the Phantom briefing room. He announced they would be standing by for new orders the day after tomorrow.

Admiral Andrews then walked over to Bud and said, "I've got a back-channel message from Keith Powers that the Air Attaché in Peru has reported there is a small radical Islamo-Patriot disagreement brewing there. We'll talk in the morning." Bud looked over at the master chief and nodded. The master chief nodded back recognizing that the two men had just communicated that something else was up. The nods meant that *We are one and I am at your side. We will stand together, no matter what is next.*

LuAnn was there waiting for Darrin to disembark. When he did, she almost ran to the aircraft to grab him, but she waited. When he saw her, he thought, *Holy shit. I'm in uniform, I can't do something unmilitary! Bullshit! I want to hold her!* He picked up his pace, dropped his backpack, and grabbed her as hard as she grabbed him. She said in his ear, "I want to marry you and have children with you. I don't care how difficult this career is. We will always have each other."

Darrin said in her ear, "You've got it, babe!"

Barb Patrick was there, too. She walked up to Bud and gave him a respectful kiss and a squeeze and said, "I'm really glad you're back. I was worried. But somehow I knew things, whatever they were, would work out." Then, like a good military wife who didn't want to say exactly how good it was to have him back from another deployment, she disguised her pleasure by simply saying, "By the way, the faucet in our master bathroom sink is dripping."

Andrews Air Force Base, Maryland. May 2019

A fifth Ghost Hawk helicopter flew Denny and Rosemary from the deck of the *Truman* to the VIP passenger terminal on the ramp of Andrews. The president's office sent a car to deliver them to their respective quarters in the downtown Washington area. While driving down the Suitland Parkway into the District, they continued to talk about the exhilarating feeling of success they were feeling from the mission operations. They both agreed that their back-channel report to the president from the *Truman* was upbeat and positive and that President Chenoa's Phantom force concept was a rousing success.

Rosemary said, "I saw the operations in Yemen from the Sit Room. But this was different. Being just a few miles away and seeing how American ingenuity, planning ability, and mission execution as it is carried out by professional military people, was a rewarding thrill. You know something, Denny? American military people are really good at what they do."

"I felt the same way, Rosemary. I felt like I was part of the mission, just as I did when I was on active duty in Bosnia, Iraq, and Afghanistan. I have come to believe that when you are as close to the problem as we were, you can see more clearly the difference between right and wrong," Denny replied.

They continued to discuss ways to address tactics and equipment subjects in their respective committees, and on the floor of both Houses. They agreed to coordinate meetings, topics, and times for presentation, so as not to conflict with one another, but instead to complement the other's agendas.

Pyongyang, North Korea, June 2019

"Comrade Defense Minister General Yang Dong Phun," said the premier of the Democratic People's Republic of Korea, Kim Teong Unong, in a one-on-one, face-to-face meeting in the premier's office.

"You have embarrassed me, our government, and the people of the Republic. I have received a call from the president of the United States. She claims to have more than one hundred twenty-three billion Wan of our gold, a nuclear warhead that we procured from Russia that was to have been a retaliatory bargaining chip, and other incontrovertible evidence that confirms we have been involved in plans to undermine the governments of three nations."

"But, Dear Leader, I—" said the defense ninister.

"Shut up, you fool," continued the premier. "Your task was to advise me of your plans and apprise me of the distribution of all resources. You were to have covered all evidence of our involvement in these activities. I expected you to succeed in all the tasks I gave you, and now you have failed, and I am embarrassed in front of the entire world."

"But, Dear Leader, I—" pleaded the defense minister.

"Be quiet, you bumbling idiot! By now we should have had seaports, military bases, and a space launch facility under our control, and you instead have bungled all your assigned operations. In addition, you failed to advise me that the president of the United States was going to call and threaten me with exposure of all our plans," screamed the premier.

"But, but, Dear Leader—" begged the defense minister.

"Be quiet, you buffoon, and get out of my office. You have two hours to take your pistol and shoot yourself, or I will have someone do it for you. Do you understand me? Now, get out of here and the next time I see you it will be in your coffin. Now, get out of my sight! Get out! GET OUT," bellowed the premier.

Beijing, China, June 2019

"Ah, Comrade Minister General Quan Ming Yang, come in. I'm glad you could come so quickly after my short-notice request, "said President Xi Jangpon, president of the People's Republic of China.

"Of course, Mr. President. I serve at your pleasure and am always available at your request," said the defense minister.

"Yes, you did serve at my pleasure, Minister Quan. I have just received an embarrassing phone call from the president of the United States. She claims to possess a large sum of money from the People's Republic that was turned over to her from sources in French Guiana, Yemen, and from a North Korean vessel that had been moored in Cameroon. She also claims to have unequivocal evidence of our involvement in attempts to undermine and destabilize the governments of three nations. She has documents from three People's Republic nuclear engineers who were sent to French Guiana to activate nuclear short-range missiles, and she is in possession of parts and schematics from at least six intermediate-range ballistic missiles, in Yemen," said the president.

"But, Mr. President, how is that possible? I have assurances from our colleagues that our involvement was to be invisible," the defense minister said meekly.

"Mr. Minister, who gave you that assurance? Was it the North Koreans? The Russians? The simple truth is that they failed, and so did you! Our country is now embarrassed once again over an international incident. Our China Dream Strategic Plan was to have included initiatives in Cuba, Iran, Ukraine, Syria, the South China Sea, and Venezuela. By your action, or should I say, inaction, you have shown light on schemes we had intended to make us stronger and the rest of the world weaker," explained the president.

"But, but, Mr. President—" begged the defense minister.

"Mr. Minister General, or should I say Captain, you are to be reassigned immediately to the North of China, as a team of one, to oversee the deportation of the Chinese Uighur radical Islamists and stop their attempts to overthrow the government of the People's Republic. The alternative is for you to simply disappear. You choose which avenue to follow. And do it in two hours. Now, get out," said the president sternly.

Moscow, Russia, June 2019

"General Vokovich, thank you for coming at my order. I want to say good-bye to you," said the president of Russia, Vladimir Pushkin.

"But, Mr. President, I have no appointments or plans to go anywhere," replied Defense Minister Colonel General Alexandrovich Vukovich.

"Ah, but you do, General Vukovich. I know Foreign Minister Lavorinski has briefed you on my phone call from President Chenoa. Your dachau in Siberia is in need of repair and winterizing. So, as of this hour your services to Mother Russia are no longer required. You are dismissed," stated the president briskly.

"But, but, Mr. President—" said the defense minister, in shock.

"Vukovich, *good-bye!*" said the president.

Epilogue

A New Beginning—II

The State of the Union Address, Joint Session of Congress, United States Capitol Building, Washington, D.C., January 20, 2020, 9:00 p.m.

President Sally Marie Chenoa's statement began, "The State of the Union is stronger now than it has been in eleven years." She received a long standing ovation for that one single sentence. Everyone knew, or had received hints as to why. She then worked her way through the status of economic, immigration, tax, medical care, veterans, judicial, and states issues. She suggested very few new initiatives in order to help bring spending under control. Instead she offered to revise existing policies, regulations, and laws to make them more streamlined and efficient for the people of America. She saved foreign policy and national security issues for last.

"For over two years our national security team has been operating globally with smaller, more mobile and lethal, well-trained forces from each of our military services. Without divulging classified information, I can tell you we have altered the destructive actions certain tyrants have wanted to impose on their own, and neighboring nations that would have had a direct deleterious effect on the national security of the United States. At my direction, the United States has taken certain actions to prevent the unleashing of nuclear destruction on many nations and have prevented a holocaust of immense proportions," she continued.

"Let all nations who do not belong to the small circle of governments who responsibly manage their nuclear assets be on notice that if they undertake to build, or acquire, a nuclear weapon or any forms of chemical, biological, or nuclear WMD, we will see to it that they will never use them.

"If tyrants and dictators choose to vanquish their neighbors, the United States will have an opinion. But we will not dispatch armies and navies to become permanently entrenched in their foreign lands. We are not planning to employ military occupation, but by the same token, the United States will not be the nine-one-one call recipient for countries when they can't or don't want to take actions to defend themselves.

"My administration has discussed with the Congress, and we have agreed, that effective immediately, we will reduce the total end strength of all our armed services to protect this nation. We will do so with the most technically advanced, most lethal weaponry, using smaller multi-service teams to stop aggression before it turns into unmanageable international calamities. Our responses will be swift and final. At the same time we will continue to embrace the concept of the Triad to defend the national security of the United States.

"Our State Department has created a rapid response team to help nations in crisis where we have provided restoration assistance. Our military forces will no longer have missions of nation building or fighting climate change. The State Department, under the leadership of a senior assistant secretary, will provide advice and limited resources to countries who request it for areas of infrastructure improvement, recruitment and training of competent civilian manpower, access to equipment, tools, processes, procedures, and education. This will allow their governments to get back on their feet and begin functioning as they should. Those nations will not be required to do it our way, and they may avail themselves of our services, or not.

"I have suspended cash payments of foreign aid to countries who hate us, who give our money to terrorist groups, or who use our funds to support initiatives that are inimical to internal American goals, visions, and the objectives of our country. Those countries or groups include Russia, Libya, Nigeria, Pakistan, Kazakhstan, Syria, Iran, and groups like Hamas, the Muslim Brotherhood, and Al Qaida. These actions will initially cut the flow of money out of this country by more than six-point-two billion dollars per year. More cuts will follow. If they want food, medical care, or advice, they will get it, but they will receive no more of the American tax payer's cash."

When her address had ended, she had received a total of fifty-eight rounds of applause, thirty-one of them standing ovations. Since the year 2020 was a presidential election year, the hue and cries for her reelection were increasing from both sides of the aisle.

Mac Dill AFB, Tampa, Florida, February 2020

Colonel Bud Patrick knocked on the office door of Admiral Ray Andrews at 0900. The reply came back, "Come."

"Bud, you and I have been requested to meet with the director of central intelligence at Langley tomorrow morning, at 1000 hours. I have no idea the reason or purpose. I'm guessing it could be in response to the unrest in Malaysia, Zimbabwe, Peru, or Colombia. I don't know. In any case, we have an Air Force C-38A flight leaving base ops at 1600 today for Andrews. They'll wait for us and bring us back here when the meeting adjourns. Let's go find out what's next."

"Yes, sir. I'll see you on the flight line," replied Bud.

CIA Headquarters, Langley, Virginia,
Office of the Director, The Next Day

On the seventh floor of the CIA building, the director's assistant buzzed Director Geist's inter-communications line and announced, "Admiral Andrews and Colonel Patrick are here."

He replied, "Please send them right in."

Ray and Bud entered the director's office and took a quick scan of the persons already gathered. They saw the director, General Tom Mossman, Senator Denny Smith, and Congresswoman Rosemary Doolin. There was a young woman whom they did not know, and a man whom they did, but he sported a cleaned-up, more Americanized appearance.

As Ray and Bud became transfixed on the man, they both almost said out loud but instead consciously thought, *Holy shit! It's Francois Ricardo De La Plane!*

Director Geist said, "Ray, Bud, I think you know everyone here, except for Ms. Joanie D'Arc De La Plane, Francois's sister."

Both Ray and Bud were suffering from cognitive dissonance; what they were seeing and hearing didn't coincide with what they knew—or thought they knew. They each said simply, "hello," to her. She nodded in acknowledgement.

"Please be seated. I know you two gentlemen must be terribly confused with all of this," Director Geist said.

"That's an understatement, Mr. Director," Bud said. "We've spent hundreds and hundreds of hours seeking the whereabouts of Mr. De La Plane with the intent of arresting or shooting him, whichever was to be the most expedient thing; that is, until President Chenoa directed us to bring him in unharmed."

"Yes, I know what you have been through over the last three years. But the truth of the matter is that he has been and is still working for us in deep black cover since he left graduate school in Switzerland more than twenty years ago. To do the things he has done and to establish the relationships he has made, and to telegraph activities that are about to happen or were being planned, is a precarious position for anyone. To protect his cover, and for him to be able to go where he was needed, meant he would have to have a criminal profile. He had to be sought by international intelligence services in order to remain credible. Cleverly, he personally broke very few laws and committed no serious international crimes that would warrant his arrest and incarceration. Others killed people and destroyed international property in place of him. In those few cases where he actually pulled a trigger or wielded a blade, both we, and the French government, concluded they were events where self-defense was required.

"In those few cases where one could make a circumstantial case that he might have been implicated in some nefarious crime, we and the French government have agreed to take a cautious approach. Mr. De La Plane has been sentenced by the French government to six years of public service in French Guiana. He will teach Public Policy, International Affairs, and Inter-Government Relations in the National University in Cayenne, French Guiana, and he may not leave the country for six years. After that period he will be on probation for another two years and must consult with the governments of France and the United States on issues relating to Middle-Eastern and South American government activities.

"In these last six months we have completely debriefed him, and he has provided incredible data and identified many, many persons throughout the Middle East and Central Africa whom we now know are probable extensions of North Korean and Chinese operatives and the destructive, strategic intelligence plans of those nations. As a result of his experiences and activities, we know how to deal with clandestine Russian, Chinese, North Korean, Venezuelan, and Pakistani intentions. We have shared his knowledge with our counterparts: MI-5 in London, Canada, the DGSE in Paris, and those allies whom we believe have been targeted for disruptive or exploitive activities by the Eurasian triumvirate we have confronted.

"Ms. De La Plane has been working with us for several years and did, in fact, lose contact with her brother until recently. We also lost track of him for nearly a year, but he fortuitously popped up on our intercepts, asking where we had been. We asked him the same. Once contact was reestablished, we were able to tip him off when the U.S. Phantom force was en route. That's how he got away. Under certain circumstances, we even were able to provide him with bottles of very old, very rare sixty-year-old Remy Martin Napoleon cognac—two of which I understand are in your possession, Colonel Patrick. If you look closely, Colonel, you will even be able to see coded messages to him in the fine print of the label."

For the first time De La Plane spoke. "Colonel, you and the admiral should take an occasional drink from one of them. I know it will give you insight and clarity into the events of each day and into your future missions. It worked that magic on me as a boy and still is a useful elixir for vision into what is next for me. I will be returning to French Guiana in the hope that my people have forgiven me. I hope and pray for your forgiveness and would look forward to a future meeting with you both to offer my observations about the world. I sincerely thank you for not ending my life. There were times when I would have welcomed it."

Joanie then spoke, "I will be remaining here in Washington with my company, the SAE Corporation, and will continue to serve the Agency, the United States, and France if called upon."

Then the director said, implying the meeting was nearly over, "Are there any unanswered questions that any of you have of Mr. De La Plane?" Everyone looked at one another and shook their heads in the negative.

"Mr. De La Plane, and Ms. De La Plane, are there any questions or comments you have of any of us?" Francois and Joanie shook their heads.

"Then I will remind everyone that the proceedings, comments, and persons here are classified Top Secret, and they will be for an indefinite period of time. If future contacts are needed with, or between persons present, please contact this office and we'll be glad to facilitate. Thank you all for coming."

Denny and Rosemary rose and shook the hands of Joanie and Francois and wished them well. Ray and Bud did the same, but kept their comments short and succinct. They needed more time to internalize what had just happened. But whom could they talk to about it and what more did they need to know?

As Ray and Bud left the DCI's office and got into the government car that would take them back to Andrews AFB, Ray turned to Bud and said, "You know what, Bud? When we get back to Mac Dill, I think we should open one of those bottles, have a snort of that cognac, and find out if we can see into the future."

"Ray, I may just have two snorts of it to find out what's going to happen and to see if it will also tell me what would have happened if I had taken that job with Home Depot that was offered to me when I graduated from college thirty-five years ago."

JCS, J-3 SOD, The Pentagon,
Washington, D.C., February 2020

Colonel Keith Powers was back at his usual desk monitoring his e-mails, Facebook announcements, chatter sources, Twitter blivits, voice mails, Post-it Notes, and all the other forms of data available to him. He had seen many notes on many incidents on all these sources before. Once in a while, a relevant fact or observation stood out that everyone else had overlooked. That was what he was looking for now.

Most of Keith's colleagues would think the work was monotonous and repetitive, but Keith didn't think so. He thought of his work as the first alert of trouble in the world. His boss agreed.

It was 0645, and he logged on to the SIPRNET terminal just as he usually did and began looking for anything out of the ordinary. Also as usual, some of the information he had already seen on FOX News or CNN. However, this network contained reports from all sources and specifically, those from Secret and Top Secret observations, so this version was more comprehensive.

Since the completion of covert operations from Project TEMPEST, Project RAMPART and Project LIBERTY, things around the globe had been relatively quiet. Yes, there were still the usual labor parades demanding higher wages, student demonstrations demanding more freedom, breakouts of diseases that needed international attention, and random radical Islamic gunfights and looting. But reports of multiple deaths and massive waves of destruction caused by megalomaniacal tyrants were not apparent—yet.

Powers scrolled through events in the Middle East, Europe, Asia, Southeast Asia, Africa, and South America. All incidents in each global region were reviewed and had an assessment attached about the international danger they represented and their threat to U.S. national security interests. Nothing of major import was identified.

Keith scrolled through the daily political and military events in South America, starting alphabetically with Argentina. He got to Peru and had to stop. A report, only thirty minutes old, from the U.S. Air Force and the U.S. Navy attachés there was startling and especially ominous.

A group of about sixty rebels, called the *Sendero Luminoso*, or Shining Path, led by a leftist dissident named Luisa Peralta, had conducted a nighttime raid on the president's personal residence. The president, his entire family, plus ten guests who were attending a dinner party, had been brutally killed. Two of the guests were the American ambassador and his wife. There were no survivors. The rebels were overheard by witnesses as shouting "*Allah Akbar*" as they killed the president and his guests. The terrorists then destroyed the residence and set fire to it.

The dissidents took credit for the attack on Peruvian national television only ten minutes after it had begun. They wanted all U.S. and other foreign military service members out of all countries in South America. They claimed they had three nuclear warheads they would detonate in the capital in Lima, in Quito, Ecuador, and in La Paz, Bolivia, if the United States did not deliver one hundred million dollars to the National Bank of Colombia in Cartagena within four days. Later intelligence reports would verify that a North Korean tramp steamer registered under a bogus Malaysian certificate had put into port in three Peruvian Pacific ports; once in Mancara in the north, once in Callao outside Lima, and once in Mollando in the south.

"Holy shit!" Keith shouted out loud. "Here we go again." He reached for his Red Phone to Phantom force headquarters at Mac Dill.

CPSIA information can be obtained at www.ICGtesting.com
Printed in the USA
LVOW11s1321100316

478588LV00001B/1/P